An

ABRIDGED HISTORY

of the Construction of the RAILWAY LINE Between Garve,

Ullapool and Lochinver; And other pertinent matters;

Being the Professional JOURNAL and Regular Chronicle

of *ALEXANDER AUCHMUTY SETH KININMONTH*

Edited by

ANDREW DRUMMOND

With a Foreword by

ALFRED MARJORIBANKS

EDINBURGH:

PUBLISHED BY POLYGON,

WEST NEWINGTON HOUSE.

———

MMIV.

First published in Great Britain in 2004 by
Polygon, an imprint of Birlinn Ltd
West Newington House
10 Newington Road
Edinburgh EH9 1QS

www.birlinn.co.uk

An extract from this novel first appeared in *Writing Wrongs*, the
Canongate Prize Anthology 2002, published by Canongate

ISBN 1 904598 09 9

British Library Cataloguing-in-Publication Data
A catalogue record for this book is available
on request from the British Library

The publishers acknowledge subsidy from the
Scottish Arts Council

towards the publication of this volume

Typeset by Antony Gray, Oakfield Road, London
Printed and bound by Creative Print and Design,
Ebbw Vale Wales

Contents.

Foreword.

Students of this fascinating history may be interested to learn something of its provenance.

I received at my office one day in June, 1901 a large brown-paper parcel which, on initial inspection, revealed large numbers of cheaply-printed hand-bills; I was confused by these bills, some of which proclaimed the virtues of "Aikman's Lentil Food" while an equal number called my attention to "Clarke's Blood Mixture", available in bottles at 2*s.* 9*d.* each, since my blood needed neither purified nor restored; far more to my taste were the stacks of hand-bills advertising "The Talisker Blend" at 42*s.* per dozen, or "The Glenlivet" at 36*s.* per dozen, from George Ballantyne & Son, and I wondered if I might be able to use them to decorate my rather plain rooms in Preston-street South. Thinking that the parcel was perhaps intended for Mr. Mackintosh who presides over an efficient shop nearby, I placed the parcel to one side, for removal by Bell the office-boy, and continued with the more pressing business of the day.

It was not until later in the morning, when I was enjoying a round of golf upon the Links at Bruntsfield, that I was struck forcibly by the idea that if I turned the bills over I might discover some manner of secret message on the reverse. Hastening back to my office from the eleventh green, therefore, without even completing the game in which I was leading my friend Mr. Young Johnston Pentland by two strokes, I retrieved the parcel from the slovenly Bell, and thereby saved for the Scottish reading-public a most extraordinary biography: for what I discovered on the verso of each sheet was a neatly-written account of the building of the railway from Garve to Lochinver.

Of "Mr. Kininmonth", who wrote this History, very little is known to myself or my respected fellow-editors. Mr. Kininmonth forgot to enclose his address, or that of the nearest post-office at which I might contact him. I would encourage the purchaser of this book always to pay attention to this small detail of a return-address. I myself have over-looked this matter on occasion, as my fellow-editors here at Dobie & McIntosh can confirm, most famously in the matter of the sole copy of a manuscript by a young man named Buchan, which I sent without explanation or return-address to my father in Gifford for his amusement, he being much taken with adventure yarns. My father, all unsuspecting, read it and then threw it into the fireplace in his study. And although Mr. Buchan will probably never rise to fame and we have by my error lost nothing, I have determined never to repeat this oversight.

During an evening of entertainment in the Assembly Rooms, in the first-rate company of Messrs. Blundell and Howard, my fellow-editors, I have frequently pondered with them the fate of the author – would he be alive and flourishing, or perhaps living in some squalid slum somewhere in Fife? We cannot tell, for all we have is the author's name. At Blundell's suggestion, we placed small notices in the pages of *The Scotsman*, but heard from no one, save a "retired school-mistress" in Lochgelly who had known Mr. Kininmonth in Ullapool; I arranged to meet this lady under the Walter Scott Monument opposite Jenner's; but she failed to appear at the agreed hour.

I make no claim to be either Geographer or Historian, and so I cannot comment on the accuracy or otherwise of Mr. Kininmonth's History. I must believe it to be true, but would ask the public to make some investigations for themselves and determine whether the facts set out hereinafter are verifiable. I myself was still at school when these events took place, and can make no comment on them; and having been a rather inattentive school-boy, I can scarcely be expected to comment upon the world-historical events to which Mr. Kininmonth alludes!

I now present Mr. Kininmonth's work, and all the startling facts contained therein, to the discerning reading-public. In strict adherence to the requirements of editorial practice, I do recollect having retained somewhere in my own archive the original hand-bills sent by Mr. Kininmonth, as well as some other papers and newspaper-cuttings; and these may be examined by readers, on application to myself at the offices of Dobie & McIntosh. As an introduction to what now follows, I will quote one such cutting from *The Ross-shire Journal* of the second of December, 1898, describing Sir John Fowler's funeral at Brompton Cemetery; a post-script to which contained the following:

> Major Houston . . . writes to Sir Arthur: "We cannot forget the pleasant intercourse of a few years ago, when your late father and yourself were so kind and good to my aunt, Lady Matheson, in the great project she had so much at heart (the Garve and Ullapool Railway)." The immense mass of correspondence now in the hands of the late Lady Matheson's solicitors, with regard to the Garve and Ullapool Railway contain sufficient evidence of the great interest Sir John took in the promotion of this undertaking, which he always felt only needed time and prudent patience to become an accomplished fact.

I hope you will enjoy, as I did, this illuminating account of recent events in distant Ross and Cromarty. I understand from a fellow-alumnus of mine, Mr. Alfred Morrison, that good shooting and fishing are to be had in that part of the world, a fact to which Mr. Kininmonth himself alludes. Mr. Morrison is a sound fellow in his own way, but he was not able, when pressed, to pass comment specifically on the excellence or otherwise of the railway to Ullapool, nor on the visit paid by Mr. Rinck to that small town; however, he does think he heard some of these events being discussed by some gillies near Lochinver last August.

ALURED MARJORIBANKS,
Dobie & McIntosh, Publishers.
December, 1901.

Volume I:

From Garve to Braemore
or,
The Age of the Plutocrats.

Monday, August 28, 1893.

My name is Alexander Auchmuty Seth Kininmonth: this is my Journal of the construction of the Railway-Line between Garve, Ullapool and Lochinver, according to the Act agreed at Westminster in the month of August, 1890.

I witnessed to-day one of the most important events yet seen in this part of the kingdom. On this day, Monday, the twenty-eighth of August in the year 1893, the first turf was cut for the first section of railway, which will run simply from Garve to Ullapool. Sir John Fowler, in his capacity as the celebrated Engineer of the Forth Bridge, was the most apparent choice to undertake the opening ceremony, for he is also a major share-holder of the Great North-West of Scotland Railway Company. But the great man had an unforeseen engagement and so it was his son, Arthur Fowler, who did the honours.

What a splendid spectacle it was to-day at Garve! The Directors of the Company were all assembled: Lady Matheson; Major Matheson; Major Houston; Mr. Arthur Fowler. Many other local dignitaries also took advantage of the occasion to mingle with the assemblage. They all posed before the famed photographer, Mr. Louis Wilson of Aberdeen, and then, in the presence of almost five hundred souls, and under the keen eyes of a number of imposing police constables, the first sod was lifted from the damp earth by Lady Matheson. It was perhaps unfortunate that a stray dog bounded out from the crowd at that point and began to dig for its bone in the sweet-smelling earth thus revealed, and that no one had understood that Major Houston had a terror of dogs, which manifested itself in his rather precipitate retreat to the back of the assembled crowd. But the incident and the hilarity it occasioned were quickly covered over by and forgotten in the arrival of some local men, bearing trestles of food and drink. In short, the whole event was very properly got up. Nor indeed was the day upset by the ungentlemanly conduct of Mr. Pirie of Leckmelm who, after partaking over-zealously of the liquid refreshment, became over-familiar with Lady Tamara Coffin. That man assuredly is one who will receive full punishment on the Day of Judgement!

Thus, after several years engaged in persuading both the land-owners in this part of Great Britain, and the Government of the country, of the justness of our plan to build this pioneering railway, the Great North-West of Scotland Railway is finally begun. And when persuasion was complete, what a struggle it was to restrain those grasping hands of the Great North of Scotland Railway Board, who wished to run it entirely to increase their own power over the movement of people and goods in the north and west of Great Britain. But to-day, the harvest of our tilling and sowing has been reaped!

The railway-line will be magnificent in the landscape through which it passes and in the feats of engineering by which it will reach its destination. It will start from five furlongs past the station at Garve on the Highland Railway between Dingwall and Strome-ferry. From there it will be laid due north and then north-west along the right bank of the Black Water to its first halt at Black Bridge. Thence it will run in a north-westerly direction past Aultguish and alongside the Glascarnoch River to halt at Braemore. At Braemore it will descend precipitously into the glen of the River Broom, halting at Inverlael, where the waters of Loch-broom are met. Then the line will follow the shores of that sheltered loch, halting for the Very Honourable Mr. Pirie at Leckmelm, before running into the centre of the little community of Ullapool.

In these short thirty-three miles and seven hundred and forty-two yards – as it has been surveyed – the line will offer to the travelling public of the nineteenth and twentieth centuries one of the most magnificent and extraordinary journeys to the Atlantic Coast. The scale of the adventure and the perfection we now witness in the engineering designs for both the railway and its locomotives will, I am convinced, act as a mainspring for the revival of the wasted parts of the West Highlands, and perhaps bring some peace and prosperity at length to both the landless and the landed poor. And I fully expect that the success of the line will bring even more challenges to our nineteenth-century engineers, and opportunities for myself.

Therefore I, Alexander Kininmonth, Engineer appointed by the Board of the Company to oversee the construction of the Great North-West of Scotland Railway, will keep a daily Journal of the construction of this line. In this Journal I will record all the events which befall us, the greater and the lesser, closely minuted at the end of each working day, so that my descendants and the world at large in years to come will understand the task we have set ourselves, and the extent of our achievement when our contracted workmen lay the last length of steel rail in the station at Ullapool.

To some degree, also, this will be a race against the works now in progress to extend the rival Railway from Strome-ferry to Kyle. It is our best intention to break through to the coast before our rivals and so to secure a railhead for ships and fishing-fleets. To this end, the Board of the Great North-West of Scotland Railway has expressly instructed me to ensure that all speed is made towards Ullapool.

It is late now in the evening, and to-morrow we start in earnest on the construction of the railway. There are careful measurements and instructions to be given, difficulties of Nature to be overcome, coarse and wayward contractors to keep on the path of righteousness. I will therefore not excite myself or my future readers with the prospect of the expected extension of the Garve to Ullapool Line as far as Lochinver in Wester-ross. That inspired plan will be laid out in the Journal which I commence to-morrow.

I have lodgings with Mrs. Campbell in her cottage in Garve. She is a kind woman and is greatly impressed with the work we are about to undertake. "It is a long road to Ullapool," she tells me, "and I fear you may have trouble with your railway." I have re-assured the woman that her fears are groundless.

Memorandum for Mr. Kininmonth: In this Journal, it is my intention to set down a Memorandum to myself each day, with some uplifting thought arising from my experiences, or some insight into the scientific categories of Man which an honest day's work has afforded me.

Sunday, September 3, 1893.

A day of rest at last after so many long, long days! I am thankful just to be able to lie on my narrow bed and consider the events of the past week. Alas! My intention of writing daily in my Journal has suffered greatly. The days are just not long enough!

Since last Tuesday, we have made but little progress up the glen of the Black Water – Allt-na-Dubh-Choille as the local men call it. I had personal reservations about the fitness of the contractor's foreman, Mr. Albert Gollan, a native of Kilmarnock. But now that I have seen what material he has to work with, I pity him, rather than lament his incompetence. His first travail on Tuesday last was to awaken all the navvies, who had spent a considerable part of the Monday night and all of their bounty from the Company, issued as part of the opening celebrations, on spirits and beer. It was a wet day too, as only a wet day can be in Ross and Cromarty, on Tuesday. So that, once we had raised the men from their barrack, there was little work to be done until the late afternoon. And so Mr. Gollan had to ensure that the men worked late into the evening, they by that time having slept out their exhaustion and their sore heads and being willing to make up their lost wages.

Our greatest bane this week has been the army of midges which has been in exemplary attendance each day. If there is one creature calculated to turn the gentlest human being into a reckless destroyer of natural life, I surmise it must be the Ross-shire Midge. There he floats, with thousands of his comrades in the evening air, above the bracken and in the damp places which abound along the Black Water. The shade cast by the trees, in particular, proves a fruitful hunting ground for this tiny monster. When a man feels the almost imperceptible touch of its bite, it is already too late: the Midge has struck home and injected its poison under the skin, where it festers maddeningly for hours, sometimes days. And for every one a man contrives to crush under his finger, a dozen, a hundred of its relatives crowd around the man's head, looking for exposed flesh. Once one has landed, a man imagines thousands more, feeling them on every exposed part of his face, on his scalp, under his very trousers! But such a trial makes this railway undertaking so much the more admirable in its achievement!

I have made friends with none of the contractor's foremen or labourers: they are a surly lot, disrespectful when I pass, slow to rise, quick to sit at their ease and smoke into their long beards. Mr. Gollan seems more concerned at keeping his men moving earth with their shovels than in the precise direction the earth-digging should take. However, he makes no comment when I correct his instructions, as I must do a dozen times a day. Among the navvies themselves there is one, MacIvor is his name, who has a frame like one of Hawthorn of Leith's steam-locomotives, and can remove barrow-loads of earth as a man like myself can carry a bundle of firewood. But he is also the worst of them in his attitude both to Mr. Gollan and to me.

Memorandum for Mr. Kininmonth: To-morrow I must talk to Gollan and warn him that the conduct of his men should improve. I find it unworthy that I, the sole representative of the visionary Railway Company which is providing them with employment in these straitened times, should not be given due respect. There are, the Lord knows, many unreasonable and cruel men among the employing classes of this nation, and perhaps crueller here in this island than in the hotter countries of the Empire. I do not aspire to be one such; nor, I believe, does Mr. Gollan. But it is surely reasonable to expect men receiving wages to be outwardly civil, even if inwardly rebellious, to those on whom they and their families immediately depend. How Mr. Gollan can tolerate the general and manifest lack of respect, I cannot understand!

Sunday, September 17, 1893.

A fortnight has passed since I last wrote in this Journal. My best intentions of recording a minuted account of this great Labour of Improvement have been thwarted by the weak constitution which has been mine since youth. The days we work are long. I rise from my bed at five o'clock in the morning – it is possible on some mornings to hear the bell in the clock-tower at Strathpeffer – and splash my face with a jug of cold water. Then I descend to Mrs. Campbell's kitchen, take myself a few slices of bread and butter and set out for the end of the line. With a short break at ten o'clock, and again at two in the afternoon, I labour hard at bringing the railway-line away from Garve. It is back-breaking work: sometimes I am directing a man to chip away at the solid rock to determine the best way through on a level, or assess the easiest way up an incline; sometimes I will take a pick or a shovel to clear the earth myself, for I have decided that I might only win the respect of the labourers by showing them that I am not shy of physical labour. And then I must inspect every yard and every chain of land that is cleared, make sure that the ballast has been set down correctly, that the sleepers are not rotten and are laid straight, that the rails are level and well bolted to the sleepers. I do not stop my labours until seven o'clock at night.

The Board of the Company are very eager that the work should continue rapidly, and that we are out of direct line of sight of Garve Station by the end of September. This is a strange and disturbing wish of the Board, but I suppose that if the earth-works are out of sight of the main line from Dingwall and a fine new steel line extends into the mouth of the glen, then passing travellers might suppose, and similarly report, that the work is proceeding apace and may safely be invested in. However, it would be pleasing if a member of the Board were to come and inspect the work at first hand, and perceive the Herculean task we have of bringing the line safely past the gorge at Torr Breac.

Perhaps I ought to describe in this Journal the exact line taken by the Railway from Garve. At a point just ten yards past where the Black Water bends sharply to the south-east beside the Dingwall and Skye Railway, a low-lying bridge is being constructed by the men across the small river coming from Gortin. The line then proceeds across boggy ground into the Black Water Glen, crossing the road which takes the traveller to Ullapool. This crossing of the road will be on the level, with gates, thus avoiding the costly construction of a bridge. The line then drives hard alongside the road until a point just short of the Torr Breac gorge is reached. About three chains short of the splendid stone bridge used by the road, the railway-line cuts due north and follows the western bank of the river through rough and trackless territory. Just at this point, then, my masters on the Board will be satisfied, for here the railway-line disappears from the sight of villagers and those bound for Strome; even out of sight of the weary traveller on the road to Ullapool, thinking no doubt of the time, not so far distant, when he will be able to sit back in the comfort of a railway carriage and be drawn at an enviable speed to his destination.

The line is laid up as far as the bridge, and from the north end of the bridge as far as the road-crossing. The bridge itself, although of simple construction, gives me many worries. Because it is exposed to many weathers and to a flooding river, it will require skilful engineering and skilled stone-masonry. My plans will assure the former, but I doubt whether Mr. Gollan can supply the latter.

Memorandum for Mr. Kininmonth: I incline more and more to the use of a pipe during the day and the consumption of a small dram of spirits in the evening. They may be habits frowned upon by my mother, but they give passing comfort and help to lift the weight of despair that frequently afflicts me as I consider our slow progress.

Sunday, September 24, 1893.

We have now extended the work two miles away from Garve Station, but we are still labouring to cross the river outside Garve. While the work on the bridge continues, gangs of navvies have crossed the river and are driving the earth-works northwards alongside the Black Water. Once away from the gorge cut by the torrent at Torr Breac, the land yields relatively easily to the spade and the mattock. But I am almost at my wits' end to supervise the work on the bridge and to re-assure myself that the line forwards is cut according to my plans. My feet are weary with running between the forwardest extent of the line and then backwards to where the arching masonry of the bridge takes us from Garve junction. Worse still, the upturned earth seems to have raised even larger numbers of midges from their resting places among the bracken and birch. To enter some of the more secluded groves to answer the call of nature is to enter a veritable fog of biting jaws and irritating wings.

Having once entered, one must simply be about one's business in the quickest possible time, and then out again, sometimes in a state of undress. There are times when parts of a man's anatomy which are best left unbitten have been subjected to a cruel and unprovoked attack, leading to several nights of discomfort.

No one seems to share my concern about the bridge; they all feel that it is finished. They have not seen what the weight of a powerful locomotive and carriages can do to stonework, even if inforced by steel framework.

Mr. MacAulay from the Company was here on Friday and took me to one side to explain that the Company would turn a blind eye to a thinner layer of ballast, or the use of one bolt less in each of the sleepers, or the use of iron rather than steel on the upper works of the bridge. I was startled by what he had to say, and remonstrated strongly with him. I reminded him of the disaster on the Tay and vowed that the name of Kininmonth would not come to be reviled like that of Bouch!

He then advised me that some of the share-holders had not yet fulfilled their obligation to provide the capital to purchase certain necessary materials, and that the Company expected me to cut the line according to the cloth I had. Mr. MacAulay assured me that the Board of the Company would not be favourable to any excessive expenditure during the construction of the line, and that any progression I wished to make within the Company, such as to Superintendent Engineer, might depend upon my strenuous efforts this year.

I confess that I find Mr. McGeorge MacAdam MacAulay as indigestible as his name. He is a small dark man, with a habit of keeping his hands tucked into his armpits, even on the hottest September day; he wears a shiny black coat that has seen a deal of ink applied to the threadbare patches. His voice grates on me. I know not whether he is telling me the truth about the financial situation of the Company. I must ask someone in higher authority than this book-keeper. In the meantime, I must tread a cautious path between what is good for the Company and what is safe for the trains. Is this the end of my dream of the greatness of this railway?

Memorandum for Mr. Kininmonth: Mrs. Campbell does not like her gentlemen lodgers to smoke. I must be mindful to walk up and down the road outside to rid my clothes of the fumes before I return in the evening. Perhaps also I should seek some solace one day in a visit to the fine town of Strathpeffer, whose facilities, residences and airs are ones we should copy at Ullapool. It is a dream of mine, which I confess only to my Journal, that perhaps I may one day own such a house in Ullapool as those which line the leafy roads of Strathpeffer, and be able to look from my drawing-room over the railway-line which I created in my younger years.

Sunday, October 1, 1893.

This is now the fifth Sunday I have had in which to rest since the first turf was cut at Garve. It seems to me that a lifetime has passed. My patience is exhausted, my clothes smell abominably of the cheap tobacco I have been obliged to burn to avoid the nuisance of the midges, my back aches from a continual life of bending down to inspect the earth. There is not time at night, and scarcely even on the Sabbath, to write my innermost thoughts in the Journal. When I return to my room in the late evening, I am content merely to eat my rations and to fall upon my mattress and sleep dreamless until the dawn.

It is a relief to be able to record that the Great North-West of Scotland Railway-line is finally linked across the river at Garve, the rails supported by the new bridge being laid last night in the gloom at eight o'clock by myself, Gollan and the man MacIvor. Most of the other men had already disappeared into the twilight, back to their encampment near Torr Breac, despite my exhortations to stay and lay the final rail. I thought to raise the last rail myself from the wagon, and slipped in the mere attempt. I had not thought just how heavy these rails are! I have seen a man like MacIvor strain over the lifting of one, and was impudent enough to imagine that I could even lift one end. MacIvor saw my plight and laughed; he called up two stragglers from his gang and together they took the last rail from the wagon and laid it in position. Without so much as a glance at myself as I mumbled my thanks, they disappeared into the gloom, leaving only the stink of their pipe-smoke, and Mr. Gollan, who had appeared. "Mr. Kininmonth," said he, "you maun be careful. I have seen a man's back snap like a twig under such a rail." I could not think of words to continue such a conversation. Mr. Gollan stayed leaning on the wooden parapet of the bridge, smoking his own mixture and saying nothing. It was not a moment of great triumph that I felt in my soul, rather one of the fiercest solitude.

We have arrived at and driven through a small wood on the bank opposite the croft at Ach-na-Clerach. Since the line is now continuous for two miles and three furlongs out of Garve, far beyond the sight of its good citizens, even the most curious of them, the Company has sent an old carriage up the line, formerly used to transport sheep, in which I may sleep at night and from which I may work during the day. I was at first inclined to treat as an insult from the Board this inelegant and stinking vehicle. Nevertheless, for convenience I have moved out of the comfort of Mrs. Campbell's lodgings and into this carriage which now stands amidst the unsavoury and sprawling transient village of the contractor's foremen and navvies.

It was a great comfort to me to read the Laws of the Lord in the book of Leviticus this morning. I had intended to walk back down to Garve to attend the church service to-day, but I slept late and did not awaken until I could already hear the church bell being tolled. None of the men emerged from their huts until well past noon, most of them the worse for beer and whisky taken the previous night: I heard them carousing until the small hours. At around two o'clock in the morning there was the sound of a brawl, which terminated rather abruptly in a shout and a splash, as of some heavy drugged body falling into the river. I did not venture out, as I felt it unfitting to my station to intercede. In the morning, as I took a constitutional and reflective stroll, I found a small dark fellow named Angus McGhee lying soaked and oblivious on the river-bank, his breeches apparently filled with reeds and a broken branch tied to his beard. It was not apparent how he had arrived in this state, but there was no one to ask: I left him to sleep off his stupor and to determine for himself his memories of the previous night.

To-morrow I expect a visit from Sir Cosmo Coffin and his wife, who will be interested to see our progress before they return to Edinburgh for the winter.

Memorandum for Mr. Kininmonth: I find some small comfort in ascertaining that the season for the Midge has now passed. Where they go in winter, I cannot tell. I feel that other Men of Science should investigate this disappearance and find a means of annihilating the Midge in his winter lair.

Sunday, November 19, 1893.

It has been a long cold and wet autumn, and the rain has come down almost unceasingly since I last wrote in my Journal. I laugh now with bitterness in my heart as I think that the word 'Journal' implies a day-ly record of events. The mundane tasks of keeping comfortable and level-headed are too much to bear. In my cabin on wheels, I find it difficult to keep warm and dry. My clothes are damp, cold when I awake. I find myself coughing incessantly. The words of the Scripture give me but little comfort; the righteous men of the Holy Bible did not have to contend with perpetual water, overhead, underfoot, in the clothes, in the bed. Perhaps Noah and his family suffered, but they had a well-made boat. I have nothing but a cabin on rusty wheels, sunk into the sodden earth, surrounded by the mist-laden hills and, as far as the eye can see, pools of water and the rain on the surface of the lochans.

I have not seen anyone from the Company since we arrived opposite Ach-na-Clerach. When Sir Cosmo Coffin came to inspect the works, McGeorge MacAdam MacAulay turned up on a cart in the company of Major Houston, and together they kept Sir Cosmo away from me as much as possible. Beyond a brief handshake and a distant smile, Coffin had no time for me, nor for the men who had performed all the hard labour to bring the railway out of Garve and in the future to bring returns on his Capital. We had had to construct a rough wooden pontoon in order that the dignitaries could cross the river from the road; her Ladyship was handed over the bridge by MacAulay with simpering looks. The man MacAulay was like a honey-bee, buzzing around Sir Cosmo and his wife with great business, while Houston speechified on the virtues of hard work and good financial sense.

We received last Thursday a brief visit from an itinerant preacher. I looked up from some work I was puzzling over and was startled to encounter, almost at my very shoulder, a most memorable figure. In appearance, he was tall, dressed as any common man in a cheap suit and stout boots. Over his right shoulder hung a voluminous black leather satchel. He wore no hat and his hair was extraordinarily white and bulky; and he had a long white beard. The whiteness was not due to senility or decrepitude, for he was about the same age as myself and gave every appearance of being muscular and strong.

He introduced himself in a voice that betrayed both American and German influences. Of Americans I am suspicious, for their habit of driving easy rail-roads across vast plains with no apparent trouble: such ease is not natural and can scarcely lead to permanence. As for Germans, I know little of them, notwithstanding the fact that my maternal uncle spent more than a year in the town of Nuremberg, studying the manufacture of biscuits. (Uncle Robert had returned from Nuremberg with all the secrets of German biscuit-making locked up in his notebooks, an optimistic slant to his hat, and dozens of lengthy and completely unintelligible words at his lips; with which latter he was used to amaze, amuse and overwhelm myself and my sister, at that time small children. Alas, our Uncle Robert had not carefully considered that the common biscuit-eating public had no inclination for his new spicy creations, despite the fashionable taste for all things German; and, after a promising first week of trading, his emporium in Dalry-road lasted no more than a few months, after which my uncle retreated in impecunious bafflement to his previous employer, Mr. McVitie of Robertson-avenue. Thereafter, only my sister and I were the grateful consumers of his German biscuits, at Christmas-time.)

The man introduced himself as "Melchior Rinck", spelling his name carefully for me lest I get it wrong. (I would add that he persisted in calling me "Kinnimunt", despite my polite protests.) He asked if he might sit and share bread with us. It being then noon, and my stomach being empty, I acquiesced. Within minutes I found myself engrossed in Rinck's words: he argued that if someone has never heard or seen the Bible in his whole life, then he could still have an honest Christian belief for himself, by means of the correct reception of the Spirit, just like all those who wrote the Bible without any books at all. There was no need for reverend churchmen, nor for any lawyers or politicians, for the common people could be guided by their inner torment and the Spirit alone. From such fertile ground as this, a wrathful God would be able to root out all Evil from the Earth. Some of the navvies stood around us, at a respectful distance, and were enthralled by what Rinck had to say. In truth, I too found his words oddly agitating.

At length, Rinck packed up his bag and continued on his way to Ullapool, where, as he told me, he hoped to find good ground for his message. The men drifted back to work, leaving me to muse on what Rinck had told me.

Memorandum for Mr. Kininmonth: I fear I may have become too reliant on the malt whisky. Gollan acquired for me (I did not ask too keenly whence) a bottle which originated in Skye, and it was in truth a very fine drop of spirit. But I have found that I take a nip out of habit, and not just when I feel low in my soul. I must put the bottle away, and cease the tippling. Perhaps it is only to be consulted on a Saturday night, when the noise of the men carousing fills me with a nameless dread and an insuperable loneliness which even the Scriptures cannot extirpate. There is much that a man can find in the Scriptures of comfort, but even more that is discomposing.

Sunday, November 26, 1893.

The navvies, the cook, the contractor's foremen are wet and sullen; Gollan is of little help in my efforts to keep the line moving onwards. I am inclined to accept this as a sign that no more work is to take place before the spring. On some days, I could not get any work done at all, even after talking to them. The navvies stand in groups, with their eyes concealed below their dripping brims. On other days they would start work, but after a few hours disappear in silent groups to the Inn further up the glen. A low place that inn: I followed them there one day, thinking perhaps to persuade them to come back after buying them a drink. In the dark and stinking gloom, they simply eyed me in utter silence, then turned their backs when I spoke to them. I found little consolation in a pipe and a dram of adulterated spirits, the like of which I never wish to taste again. It must have been the stuff with which experienced engine-men clean their locomotives. I left the place dejected.

Memorandum for Mr. Kininmonth: It is late. I look back on the visit of Rinck which so excited me, and consider just how far removed from me was such a man. I – a Man of Science – believe only in the power of righteous men to build righteousness on Earth, employing whatever wisdom the Good Lord has given to me; he – a Man of Religion – believes only that a Wrathful God will stride out among His people, as a reaper with His scythe in the corn, to root out evil and establish Paradise. But it cannot be done that way. The man Rinck is a phantast: I confess I had been fired up by him, for he had a fine way of talking; many of the things he said struck deep within me. But on sober reflection I think that only the deeds of skilled men such as myself will relieve the burden of the poor and root out injustice.

Sunday, December 10, 1893.

I am now back at Garve. The work on the line to Ullapool has been halted by a great blizzard which, on the night of the twenty-eighth of November, swept down the glen from the north-west and buried us as if under a frozen ocean in a few short hours. The cold was tremendous, the wind terrifying. I huddled together with the cook, Mrs. Macbeth, and a number of the men in the good woman's wagon, for there at least was a fire which never went out, try as the elements might. Mrs. Macbeth seems to lead a charmed existence where the cold and the damp are concerned; I believe, but can never adduce evidence, that, over and above the allowance made by the Company for her cooking, she is provisioned with additional coal and wood from the Company stores and from Sir Cosmo's estate, thanks to the men whose stomachs she warms with her broths and stews and porridge. Certainly, we were all glad of the warmth that night as the wind howled and the wagon shook.

We stayed there all night. Outside, in their hovels, the rest of the men and their families sought warmth together in blankets, unable to move. When morning came, the storm did not abate, but raged around us until, at noon, there came a deathly hush. We stepped outside and found the land transformed into a uniform dazzling field of whiteness. Work on the railway had clearly finished for the year. Gollan sent MacIvor with another man back down to Garve to request that a locomotive be dispatched to withdraw the wagons and ourselves back to the main line.

It was only yesterday, after a long wait of ten days, that we welcomed a tired engine, hooked up the wagons, and were pulled back to Garve. No more work was done in the interval, except to secure some of the earth-works at the head of the line, and to ensure that all tools were cleaned and loaded on to the equipment wagon. A small number of men tired of waiting and set off back to Garve, or towards Ullapool, to their families. Many of the men came from the wild islands of Harris or Lewis or Skye, and returned there as a group via the railway to Strome-ferry. Whither the others went, those far from some Irish hovel, those without families, I do not know; they seemed somehow to retire into the wilderness like the Midge, neither asking attention nor receiving it.

It should be added that, after the blizzard had ended, three labourers of foolhardy spirit decided to set out to climb Sron Ghorm, which over-looks our position. Certainly, it was a tempting sight, the mountain gleaming white and bridal in the sudden sunshine. I saw the three men make their way across the snowfields and up the southern slope of the mountain. On the following day, only one came back. James MacDonald, a man from Uist, had lost his two companions in the snow high on the mountain and had searched into the night for them; then he managed to come back down to the lights of the Aultguish Inn, where he had to be revived almost from the point of death. Of the other two, there was no further news.

I must spend the next two months with Mrs. Campbell, writing my reports for the Company, recovering some community with civilised men, mending both my clothes and my body. I have to appear before the Board of the Company in a week, to make my report on progress, defend without doubt my profligacy in the matter of materials used, request more men and better materials for the next stage, and try to make a good appearance. If the position falls vacant, I intend that I shall be the next Superintendent of the Great North-West of Scotland Railway. This will be a great step upwards from my recent misfortunes. I can scarcely believe that it was hardly a year ago that I was living in that squalid and dark tenement building in the Burgh of Dunfermline, deserted apparently by all hope and with scarcely a penny to my name! But a chance encounter has set me on my path to promotion and success. So despair is now all put behind me, and I intend to let nothing turn me back.

Memorandum for Mr. Kininmonth: When I have become the next Superintendent, I will ensure that my descendants will be masters of the Company. Although in my forty-second year, I am still confident that I will marry and have children and build a future for a family bearing my father's name of Kininmonth.

I was struck by the germination of an idea as I waited out the blizzard: to write a fictional account of how I envisage the Earth to be after the Lord has despatched the wicked and the evil-doers. Although I had few books with me in the Black Water Glen, and little enough time to read them, among them I had two works by that French master of prose, Jules Verne. In the manner of these works, I intend to write my account. I hope to use some of this enforced idleness at Mrs. Campbell's lodgings in putting words on paper.

Monday, December 18, 1893.

My appearance to-day before the Board of the Great North-West of Scotland Railway Company was without any great mishap or any great success. I had hoped to see Sir John Fowler there, but once again he was represented by his son. Lady Matheson was there, a forbidding presence; Sir Cosmo Coffin also and Mr. Pirie; Major Houston, who had once come to inspect our labours, was also present. They accepted my reports without close questioning; I suspected that they had been debating some weighty matter before my arrival and wished to return to it afterwards. Arthur Fowler listened to the account of my work on the bridge at Garve, and proclaimed himself interested enough to examine it on his next journey to his house at Braemore. I confess I felt annoyed at his words for he is no engineer, merely the son of one; he basks in the reflected glory of his father's renown.

Before I left, Mr. MacAulay furnished me with a notice to be displayed on a board next to the line when the works re-commence. It is an appeal by the Board of the Company for more capital to be raised to further the construction of the Garve & Ullapool Railway extension, and asking anyone with an interest in this matter to submit money to the Board of the Company. Many copies have been printed by Messrs. Groat & MacNab of Inverness, to be distributed throughout the realm.

MacAulay informed me that already the Company had received a total of two hundred and thirty-six pounds sixteen shillings and fourpence three farthings in donations from individuals. He cited moneys received from Ross men and Cromarty men far in the south – from coal-miners at Dalkeith in Mid-lothian, from servants in large houses in Perth, from several inmates of the Crichton Institution for the Insane in Dumfries, even from men working on the South-East Railway Company in Kent. I do not know whether he expected my gang of navvies to donate some of their hard-earned wages – in this he would have been bitterly disappointed – or whether I was to accost the few travellers who pass on the road to Ullapool and beg for Capital. I will not lower myself thus far for the Company, not while there are men like Coffin and Pirie within a few miles. It is entirely possible that MacAulay's notice will go astray in the next fortnight, and that I will be unable to find it again.

Monday, December 25, 1893.

Whereas Mrs. Campbell has been very kind to me on this Christmas Day, and has fed me well, and her husband has kept me entertained with his playing on the pipes, an activity where the oiling of the good man's windpipe beforehand with spirits may have improved the tunes beyond human recognition; as I say, whereas the Campbells have made me feel at home to-day, I could not prevent myself from bursting out of their home in the late afternoon, to feel fresh air in my lungs again.

I walked from the Campbells' residence to my bridge. It was already about half-past the hour of three, very dark and gloomy. Huge clouds were stretched above the hills and there was little light to see by. I disdained to smoke my pipe on my walk, for the air smelled so fresh and sweet it seemed almost sinful to taint it.

Below the bridge I encountered a most magical sight. The river had for several days been frozen hard and thick ice had formed from bank to bank, such as a man could walk over with ease. But this afternoon there had been a thaw in the air, and the centre part of the river was slowly flowing, carrying with it the ice across its surface. There was majesty in its flow, unhurried, untroubled by the onset of night. The large pieces of ice which it bore rode up against one another or against the still solid edges of the current and broke off in huge square tablets, riding up to resemble the ice-mountains seen by explorers in Spitsbergen. I stood there for about ten or fifteen minutes. Then, within the space of two breaths, the noise of cracking and creaking suddenly subsided, and the flow of ice below my bridge perceptibly diminished and then stopped. The river was frozen again, in absolute stillness. I stood there for some more minutes, unable to tear myself away from such a miracle. And as I stood, then the ice began to move again, slowly, gathering pace and force. And just as suddenly after several minutes, it stopped once more.

I felt myself to be in the presence of some great power which will finally hold sway against the seemingly immutable. The silence of Garve and the hills was profound. The only sound came from the occasional creaking of the ice as it moved forward and then halted again.

All this time, my bridge stood strong against the river.

I returned from my walk at five o'clock, refreshed, elated and with eyes glowing for the simple wonders of the Earth. Mrs. Campbell was at her door, looking out for me, worried lest some nameless misfortune had befallen me on this Christmas Day.

It is my intention to take advantage of the enforced idleness of the season to reflect on the greatness of the project to bring the railway to Ullapool and of the likely mantle of fame which will fall upon my shoulders as a result. On my shoulders and on those of my descendants, who shall most certainly profit from this. I will use these long winter days and nights to compose a Journal, for amusement and inspiration, of how my Railway and my Family will progress. I will begin this composition to-morrow with an entry dated "December 26, 1943"!

Sunday, March 25, 1894.

I discovered this Easter Day, as I sat down to write up my Journal, that several pages have gone missing. It must have been last Tuesday, when a violent gust of wind tore open the door of my wagon and scattered papers to the four corners of Glen Glascarnoch. I thought that I had managed to gather them all up again – some vital papers, such as the plans for the next stretch of line and my first drawings of the descent at Braemore, were retrieved from further back along the line – but it is now apparent that all of my Journal from January to the present has been cast to the icy winds of Glascarnoch. I must therefore write down a synopsis of these missing entries.

We returned to the work on the line in the third week of January, when the snows had begun to disappear. Gollan suddenly turned up on Thursday morning at Garve to announce that work would be re-commencing the following Monday. In some haste, I made arrangements for a locomotive to draw our wagons from Garve to the head of the line, to un-earth Mrs. Macbeth from her winter quarters in Dingwall, and to bundle up my possessions, bid farewell to Mrs. Campbell and depart for Glen Glascarnoch.

Work commenced and almost uncannily all the old familiar faces emerged from the hills and glens and from distant island communities: I confess that I felt genuine pleasure at seeing them all again and, despite my best intentions, could not conceal a welcoming smile; but received none in return. Many of the men had aged considerably in the passage of winter. Thin, they were, emaciated, their clothes a hundred times worse than before. God knows what miseries they must have suffered in these few weeks, while I was warm and well-fed in Mrs. Campbell's guest-house. How did they survive at all, if not with the charity of the towns? With such thoughts weighing heavily, I began my year's work.

The storms of December and January had taken some toll, and there was urgent repair work required at a number of places. I am proud to say that my bridge at Garve had withstood unscathed the worst of the storms, even though the river itself was growling and worrying at the raised earth like a maddened dog at a bone. Up the Black Water Glen, the icy waters had torn away some of the foundations; in other places, small slips of earth had entirely concealed the line so that excavations were urgently required. But when we reached the head of the line, at Black Bridge, a scene of devastation met our eyes: the advance earth-works on the right bank of the river had been entirely obliterated by the depredations of winter. Even as we arrived, the waters were rushing out of their bed, ignoring utterly the requirements of civil engineers and the future travelling public. Considerable reparations must be made before we continue. I have asked Mr. Gollan to initiate these works with a gang of his best men.

While the repair-works proceeded, during February, we made slow progress along the southern slopes of Glen Glascarnoch, several days being lost to severe snowstorms and torrential rains. There were some nights when it was impossible to sleep, so violently did the winds shake the wooden wagons. On all mornings, it was necessary for Mr. Gollan's extra-ordinary gang, led by MacIvor, to retreat back up the line to re-establish some piece of embankment that had slipped away in the night. Only last week did the weather begin to moderate itself and the air grow warmer. To-day, for example, the sky was clear and the breeze warm and scented, almost as if spring had arrived.

We now find ourselves adjacent to the Aultguish Inn. This is fortuitous only in the sense that the workmen have less far to go to spend their weekly wage, and there is less danger of some mis-adventure befalling them during their return-journey to their beds. But it has taken seven weeks to advance the line the past two miles.

The scene ahead of us to the west inspires with awe, but also with dread for the work which must be undertaken. A broad bleak valley opens up, swept cruelly by strong winds and towering squalls of rain. At the head of the glen, great Alpine fields of snow still lie over the northern slopes of Beinn Liath Mhor, and the top of Tomban Mor is still capped in white splendour, to remind us of the remoteness of our situation. Apart from the Inn, we are alone with the river, the hill and Heaven, pushing forward the railway-line.

The next habitation is Aultguish House, a lonely lodge a mile further on, owned by Emeritus Professor Cardew-Smith from Aberdeen. I am advised by the Board that the Professor values his solitude and privacy. As good fortune would have it, he is not in residence, having departed on a scholarly trip to Persia and Egypt last September, and is not expected back until the Easter of next year. But an obligation is embodied in the Garve & Ullapool Railway Act of 1890 that we must shield the railway-line from the Professor's gaze where it passes by his residence. We are to use trees and a cutting in the earth. There are still recalcitrants on this Earth who would deny the railway its rightful place!

Memorandum for Mr. Kininmonth: I had begun my fictional account of the future clan of Kininmonth during the days of winter idleness in Garve. Alas, the papers which I lost to the predatory winds of Glascarnoch included the first chapter of my Novel; I had retained in my engineer's notebook only the opening paragraph, on which I had been working for some weeks, and so I must re-commence. I confess that it gives me great pleasure, which I cannot deny myself, to dream of fame and fortune for myself and my descendants. The spring of the year fills me with emotions of success for this project and I hope to take up again my account in the style of Jules Verne. Perhaps I will write a little of it each night, after work has finished, and when I can rest up with Mrs. Macbeth's soup in my belly, a pipe between my lips and a dram of malt at my side.

Sunday, April 8, 1894.

Aultguish Inn is now behind us, and Aultguish House up on our left. I have now established that to excavate a cutting past the academic's house is quite beyond the ingenuity of Man. The soil here is desperately thin over rock where it is not sheer bog, and a cutting of a furlong's length, which is laid down in the Act, would delay us here for six months and cost the Company most of the capital raised for the entire line. I have consulted with members of the Board, and we have agreed, in the Professor's absence, to raise an embankment behind which the line shall run, rather than a cutting. The Board decreed that the embankment shall be liberally emplanted with trees, an undertaking already in hand: however, it does not take much foresight to realise that these small saplings will be swept to oblivion by the first storms. In some trepidation, I approached the House one afternoon to detect whether the Professor's view would be spoiled by a raising of the level of the land below. In two respects, I need not have worried: the house was entirely empty, windows shuttered, gates padlocked; and the view from the Professor's front lawn was already blocked by his collection of Rhododendron-bushes, which appear to grow like weeds in this damp atmosphere.

Last week, there was a deputation from members of the Board, led by Lady Matheson and by Sir Cosmo Coffin. They were accompanied by Archibald, Lord Inverpolly, who conducted them in his carriage. It is said that Lord Archibald owns an automobile, but I note in this Journal that he does not dare risk that contraption on these wild roads. Perhaps due to his interest in the motor-car as a means of conveyance, he is not on the Board of the Company, although it is said that he put up some of the capital for the line. His Lordship was also accompanied by McGeorge MacAdam MacAulay — what a loathsome name to write down! Lord Inverpolly condescended to converse briefly with me, despite MacAulay's obnoxious attempts to conceal me; he quizzed me on the difficulties in traversing the river at Garve, and whether I thought that the descent past Braemore would cause great engineering problems. It was pleasant to talk briefly of my hopes and plans with such a man as this. Would that his neighbour, Sir John Fowler, could visit our labours and give me the benefit of his experience, engineer to engineer!

When the visiting party left in Inverpolly's carriage, we watched it for half an hour, almost all the way to Loch-droma at the head of the glen, some five miles away; then my men relapsed suddenly into a fit of torpor, and I could neither encourage nor shame them to work again that day. I resigned myself to this and spent the afternoon idly taking measurements and inspecting the most recent earth-works.

Memorandum for Mr. Kininmonth: It is scarcely to be marvelled at, but I have failed completely to advance my fictional chronicle of the Kininmonth Family in the Twentieth Century. This results largely from physical exhaustion at the end of each day, when my nerves are worn out by the continual need to encourage the labourers, and the doubts and uncertainties I have about the stability of my earth-works. A pipe and a dram are good companions, but are not conducive to cerebral powers such as a historian must exploit.

I must confess to this Journal that there is another reason for my inability to retire in solitude and compose, and that is my attraction to the woman of one of the labourers. There are few enough women in the navvies' encampment, as I have stated. The man's name is McCallum, and I have no idea what his woman's name is. She is young and, like the rest of her people, ragged and dark. I believe that she is happy with her lot. She has a glow in her eyes which is like fire, a slow-burning power of life. Her face, although dirty, is perfectly formed and as yet unlined by cares. She goes about the business of trying to manage her affairs in her hovel with a grace and easiness which is to be imagined in some carefree dark-haired countess of Portugal. I have followed her with my eyes these past three weeks, and take every opportunity to be seated where I can observe her, or to divert my steps so that our paths cross as it were accidentally. She barely looks at me, but I am smitten. I sit dreaming in the evenings, contemplating the breaking down of the barriers between this girl and myself, marital and social. Wicked thoughts cross my mind, which I can attribute only to the increasing temperature and the scents on the breezes of April. I must make every endeavour not to make a fool of myself, nor to be observed in my fixation by any of the labourers. I am, after all, the sole representative of the Great North-West of Scotland Railway Company in these parts.

Sunday, April 15, 1894.

Incredible though it may seem, I was to-day bitten by an early plague of midges! I was not expecting them for another two months. Mrs. Macbeth, who had earlier assured me that the cold winter and cool spring would delay their re-appearance, was unmoved by my complaints. It was her considered view that the Lord knew what He was doing in Nature. I am sure that a theologian from St Andrews or Old Aberdeen might not disagree with her on this, but that is small comfort. She relented somewhat at my tone and proposed some potion extracted from her witch's cauldron, which she claimed would cure the poisonous bites and also prevent further attacks. With considerable caution, I agreed to experiment with whatever she concocted. After some hours, she summoned me to her inner sanctum, and with all her dignity and pride, presented me with a bowl of some thick green broth which gave off the pungent odour of a foul cess-pit and had the consistency of phlegm. I recoiled, but felt I had to honour my earlier contract with her. She advised me to apply it to the area of the bites already received, and then to smear it upon my person without regard to expense.

Having retired to my own wagon to do so, I was almost immediately overwhelmed by feelings of nausea and disgust. It was certain that no midge would wish to sacrifice itself upon my flesh; but equally it was clear that no human being furnished with the most rudimentary olfactory sense would willingly come within yards of me. I despaired. In a fit of strict fairness, I walked out into the moor to confirm that the first effect of the two was true. Like Daniel into the Den of Lions, I walked deliberately into a dancing cloud of midges and stood, braced for the fearful tickling sensation. None came. Mrs. Macbeth's mixture appeared to work. As I stood there, I felt the cruel irritation of the previous bites subside also. But it was on walking back in elation to my wagon that I received absolute and devastating evidence confirming the second effect. I came across a crowd of women down near a burn, collecting water and gossiping. My eye leaped to McCallum's wife among them, and my heart pounded with secret anticipation. Imagine then my anguish when all the women stood up, some visibly recoiling, and burst out in angry or mocking tones, holding their noses and screeching! The female McCallum, to my eternal shame, revealed herself for a low-born and unworthy woman, out-doing all her companions in deriding me as I passed by.

It was clear to me, when I regained the safety of my wagon, that I would have to choose between the company of midges or the company of humankind. Outside the wagon, I could hear residual cries of hilarity. I resolved to await the close of day and, under cover of the twilight, partake of a bath in the freezing waters with some coal-tar soap.

So ended my first experiment with the contents of Mrs. Macbeth's herbal pharmacy. I think that she herself was surprised to see me without her ointment smeared upon the exposed parts of my body, and perhaps a little hurt, for she was very short-tempered with me thereafter. I am determined to face up to the depredations of the midges. I can now see in them a trial by God of the weakness of the flesh. I am also determined to overcome with cold baths, increased labour and bracing walks the lunacies arising from the warm spring weather. There is serious work to be done in this part of the land and I cannot allow myself the idleness which leads to an unhealthy coveting of the wives of other men.

Memorandum for Mr. Kininmonth: I will return next week to the true purpose of the Journal, which is to record the advancing of the railway from Garve to Ullapool. Future generations will learn from my scientific observations how severe engineering difficulties were overcome, what measurements were taken and how rails were fixed in place. Professor Cardew-Smith will learn to regret how we concealed from him the resolute lines of the railway. Sir John Fowler himself will learn new techniques from our descent from Glen Droma into Inverbroom, down the inhospitable slopes of the hills at Braemore.

Thursday, April 19, 1894.

I make this unexpected entry in my Journal to record a terrifying and tragic discovery. To-day, several men were down at Black Bridge, effecting some repairs to the embankment. The edges of the river were still covered by a number of large banks of snow or blocks of ice. One of the labourers, taking his ease with a short stroll, noticed a black boot sticking out from one of these huge pieces of ice which was grounded on the west bank in the shadow of the hill. Why the man was permitted to wander about in this way, I have not yet asked. Notwithstanding this, when he pulled at the boot, more out of acquisitiveness than concern, he discovered that it was attached to a foot and, furthermore, that the foot appeared to be attached to a leg which was locked into the ice. Peering into the blue ice, he could dimly see a black shape which he supposed to be the corpse of a man.

The navvy, whose name was O'Byrne, called on his companions and they dug into the ice with their picks and shovels and soon excavated the perfectly preserved body of a man, whose skin was almost blue in tone. There was no sign of injury or expression of pain on the body or face of the man. The cut of his clothes and the little axe stuck in his belt indicated that the man was a sportsman, a climber of the hills around.

Gollan was summoned to Black Bridge by the men, and he in turn sent a messenger back down the line to Garve to inform the authorities.

We are astounded and lost for an explanation. What is the identity of the corpse? How came he to be encased in ice at Black Bridge? Truly, the northern mountains are regions of great enigma! The body has been carried to Aultguish Inn and there laid out in one of the outbuildings, so that it might not decompose before the authorities arrive.

Sunday, April 29, 1894.

The matter of the corpse at Black Bridge is now behind us. Inspector Campbell and two constables arrived from Inverness on the day following the discovery. He asked several questions of the men who had made the gruesome find, of Gollan and of myself, made entries in a notebook, took some measurements, then disappeared back east with the corpse on a wagon. With the despatch of the body, the unpleasant affair was closed and we once more returned to our railway.

Monday, April 30, 1894.

When the train with materials arrived this morning, Inspector Campbell and Sergeant Campbell were on board. They had more questions they wished to have answered. Also on this train was a Mr. Gibson, a journalist from *The Inverness Press and Journal*, anxious to ferret out a good penny-dreadful story for his readers.

Inspector Campbell informed me that his investigation had determined that the corpse excavated from the ice was that of a well-known Alpinist, the Reverend Alfred Smith of Perth. The Reverend Smith had set out from Lochluichart Lodge, to the south, on the first day of December last year, intending to make a circular tour of the mountains. His route, as he had advised his hosts at the Lodge, was over the Kinlochluichart Forest to Glascarnoch, then up Tomban Mor and towards Beinn Dearg, before proceeding back to Lochluichart. The wrath of the weather had subsided after the blizzard, and although there was deep snow on the hills, the clerical gentleman was an experienced and strong walker and had a stout stick with him. Notwithstanding this, he had not returned.

Inspector Campbell had previously established that three others had been on the hills that day – the three navvies from our undertaking who had suffered some mishap, and of whom only the man MacDonald had survived. The policeman therefore wanted to know if there was any connection between the disappearance of the navvies and the death of the Reverend Smith.

MacDonald, it appeared, could not enlighten Inspector Campbell. After repeated questions and the application of a number of artful devices to trick the man, MacDonald could advance no other story than the one he had told us on his return from Sron Ghorm after losing his companions. He did not recall having seen anyone else on the mountain.

The Inspector then sat with myself and Gollan to expound his theory that the unfortunate climber had simply lost his footing in the treacherous conditions, plunged into the river and drowned, and that his body had been entombed by the winter. It was possible, surmised Inspector Campbell, that the same fate had befallen our two navvies, and he strongly advised us to despatch a party to investigate other pieces of ice lodged along the bank of the river. I could detect a certain morbid enthusiasm in his face as he made this recommendation. Nothing, it seemed, could make him more satisfied with the eccentricities of life than the discovery of three bodies encased separately in ice.

Mr. Gibson, the newspaper correspondent, accompanied Campbell in his interrogations and seemed disappointed to find that there was no evidence of "foul play". As he waited for the train to take him and the policemen back to Garve, I offered to describe to him the present situation of the line. He sat politely and took notes. I described the triumph of the bridge at Garve, and asked him to pay good attention to its construction on his journey back. I confess that my description of the trials and tribulations of the construction tended to increase somewhat my stature and importance. But I am sure Mr. Gibson will write a fair report. I am sure, also, that his mind was not much directed to what I said, but rather to the story he would write of the unfortunate Reverend Smith and our two navvies. However, he promised to pass his report on the Line to his editor.

I spent the remainder of the day-lit hours in speculative examination of the snow-banks and ice around the river bank. To my great relief, I made no other tragic discovery there.

Monday, May 14, 1894.

To-day I received a copy of the latest edition of *The Inverness Press and Journal,* the newspaper for which Mr. Gibson corresponds. I read it with little interest, until I came across two articles side by side on an inner page.

One of the articles noted the sad accident suffered by the Reverend Alfred Smith; the fate of the two navvies was banished to a short footnote. The other article bore the caption "An Excellent Example of Civil Engineering" and described quite faithfully the progress we had made up the glen with our Railway. My own words were cited in several places, and on the whole it was a very fine piece of journalism. One phrase stood out: my insistence "that the engineering works at Braemore will far exceed anything which Sir John Fowler has accomplished until now". I cannot recall saying this to Mr. Gibson, but I may be mistaken.

Memorandum to Mr. Kininmonth: I showed Mr. Gibson's article to Gollan when we had work to do together this afternoon. He read it carefully, but returned it to me without much comment. I was disappointed, but reflected that perhaps he was right not to attribute too much to the words of a journalist – Gollan may be an anchor to hold me back from the excesses of my own imagination and enthusiasms.

Sunday, May 27, 1894.

It is the Sabbath Day again. We are at the croft at Glascarnoch. The land is very harsh here – long endless slopes of the hills coming down into the damp and boggy valley floor. In the distance towers the great mass of An Teallach, truly a brooding mountain. On a hot day, the air shifts as I have heard the air shimmers magically in Arabia. But this is not Arabia: the nights here are not full of scented women and strange tales, but of peat smoke, harridans and midges. I thought perhaps we would be rooted for ever in Glen Glascarnoch, so long have we laboured through it. The days went past with the arrival of the engine and its wagons from Garve, the further construction of the line, an occasional passing traveller on the road, and the evening when it was time to rest. The midges have been a torment. I have, on several occasions, now, allowed myself to submit to Mrs. Macbeth's repulsing ointment. It has never failed in its efficacy, and has driven off the beasts without mercy. Neither has it ever failed to drive off my human companions. When the ointment becomes too great even for myself to bear, I surround myself with smoke from my pipe. I am truly anathema!

The building of the railway in this part of the glen is dull and uninspired, but solid enough. From dawn until dusk the navvies labour away at carving a straight and dried track from the featureless bog, following the markers laid down by myself. Yard by yard, the oily pools and dank reeds, useless for animal or man, are replaced by crushed rock, wooden sleeper and steel rail. Embankments are built over the many gullies which appear in the bog, shored up by large rocks or stonework. The ascent is steady and slow. In the evening it is possible to stand upon the very last sleeper laid and survey the achievements of the day. The men are working well, and I no longer question their attitude towards me, nor their propensity for drink. I am not one to judge those who labour in my behalf.

On Wednesday last, we were again visited by Mr. Rinck, whom we had seen last November. He did not on this occasion preach to us, but he strolled among the labourers, both Godly and Godless. It must be said that he found more of the latter than of the former.

He then spent a some time with me, discussing spiritual matters. I asked him particularly for his interpretation of the plague of midges which we are forced to endure year after year. His answer was to read to me from the Book of Exodus, where the plagues upon Egypt are described. And the Lord sent a swarm of flies upon the land of the obdurate Egyptians, until Moses prevailed upon the Lord for a westerly gale. Truly, this is very like unto the conditions here in Glen Glascarnoch, where the midges are black upon the land until a westerly gale comes and blows them all away. But after the swarm had gone, the Egyptians hardened their hearts and would not set the Israelites free.

He then referred me to the Hundred and Fifth Psalm, where the plague of flies and of lice is described, and the orchards are laid waste, until "the people asked". Mr. Rinck brought these words to my attention: "The people asked, Mr. Kinnimunt," he repeated, "and God satisfied them with the bread of Heaven." He looked into my face, seeking a reaction to what he had said; and, reluctant as I am to say so, it seemed all of a sudden as if I had been exposed to some profound truth; but what that truth was, I cannot clearly state.

At the end of this discussion, Mr. Rinck told me of his brief residence in Ullapool, where he had suffered the insults of oppressors ("obdurate Ullapudlians" as he was pleased to call them). It seemed that the significant people of the town had finally risen up against him for his preaching and had driven him from town that very day.

Thus we passed an elevating hour until the man had to take his leave and pass on towards the east; he had, he told me in his strongly-accented voice, "received a call to preach the Word of God in the south". As he left, he pressed into my hands a dog-eared pamphlet, directing me to read it and to understand. The title it bore was "The Fear of God is the Beginning of Wisdom: Brief Notes for Common Men from One Who Has Been Purged by the Torrents and Scarred by the Plough".

Memorandum to Mr. Kininmonth: After some hours of cool reflection, I think that Mr. Rinck's enthusiasms are ill-founded and his abuse of my name impolite. But I am agitated, for his words strike echoes within me. I have chosen not to read his "brief" pamphlet, which runs to a hundred and thirty pages. I will spend the rest of this quiet evening in continuing the fictional account of my descendants.

May 27, 1954.

It is sixty years now since my ancestor worked to build the Great Railway between Garve and Lochinver. The line to Ullapool was completed with much travail by the labourers in the summer of 1895. The engineering work was entirely supervised by Alexander Kininmonth, and it was this line which made the name of Kininmonth as famous in Railway and Engineering circles as that of Fowler and

Stevenson. The hydraulic lift which my ancestor constructed to bring the line to sea-level at Braemore ranks now as one of the marvels of railway engineering; in daring and grandeur it dwarfs even that of the great red Leviathan over the Firth of Forth, and is celebrated in the many histories and photographic records which have astonished the peoples of the planet.

My ancestor's Chronicle, which I keep in a chest in the great bay window of the Kininmonth House here above Braemore, records how he survived the Second Deluge which was sent by the Lord to afflict the wicked and the evil, to sweep away the exploiting classes and trample down those with no virtues. It was on the tenth day of the second month of the year 1900 that Alexander Kininmonth was visited by a preacher of the Word of the Lord, who advised him to conceal himself with trusted friends and his family in a cabin which he was to build high up on Ben Wyvis. This cabin was to be sealed tightly and a fire was to be caused inside to burn the finest cedarwood.

This my grandfather did, taking with him to the cabin only his wife and children, for he trusted none of his friends. And on the eleventh day of the second month of 1900, the Lord sent down an unseasonable Plague of Midges and a Plague of Clegs, which sorely afflicted the people of the Highlands and of the Lowlands. For forty days and forty nights the insects swarmed in the kingdom, with no regard for wealth or high position, and they finished off in agony the great and the glorious, and left unscathed most of the poor and the virtuous, including my grandfather and grandmother in their cabin high on Ben Wyvis. Rich landowners from Aberdeen perished in this plague, also fawning railway functionaries. And there were numbers of the poor whom He also struck down, loose mocking women and brawling navvies.

And then the Plague of Midges and Clegs was lifted from the land, by a great gale which blew out of the west from over the Atlantic for one hundred and fifty days, and scoured the land of the midges which never again returned in great — or indeed in small — numbers. And when the storm had abated and the wicked and the powerful and the base had been cast down, the righteous people emerged from their places of safety, and there was peace and equity among men.

My grandfather stepped forth in the congregations of equal men and agreed to construct railways which would allow the wealth of nations to be spread equally among their citizens and to be shared equally with brothers and sisters overseas. This he was pleased to do. And so in 1901 was founded the Great Benefactory Railway Society, of which I, William Morris Kininmonth, am the present Chairman.

During the first two decades of the century, the Great Benefactory Railway continued to flourish. In 1911, the line was transformed into a dual-track line, permitting much faster journeying times between Dingwall and Ullapool – in 1912, a locomotive completed the journey of thirty-three miles in the astonishing time of twenty-six minutes – an average speed of some seventy-six miles per hour.

In 1912, the Company purchased four of the most modern and powerful steamboats from the yards on the Clyde; these Juggernauts of the Minch carried freight and passengers from Harris and Lewis and the Uists into Ullapool, and brought much prosperity to Lochbroom.

Since 1913, the route between Dingwall and Ullapool has been used by wagons specially designed for the portage of fishing-boats from the counties of Moray-shire, Aberdeen-shire, Banff-shire, Nairn-shire and the eastern coast; having fished in the North Sea, the fleet could then sail to Dingwall. Strengthened cranes, capable of lifting fifteen Imperial tons and each one originally costing £247 17s. 8d., lift each boat from its temporary berth on to the wagons, and a full train then traverses the breadth of Ross and Cromarty-shire, twenty boats at a time, in the space of two hours. It became possible for nets to be cast from the same boat in the morning to the Moray Firth and in the evening to the Little Minch; above all, the fishermen avoided the known perils of the Pentland Firth.

In 1918, the Great Benefactory Railway Company acquired the Dingwall & Skye Railway from the failing Highland Railway Company, and likewise improved its facilities. The Skye Railway was always a poor cousin to the Ullapool Railway, and its construction from Strome-ferry to Kyle was beset by under-investment and many engineering problems. Nevertheless, after 1918, a strong capital investment by my grandfather, coupled with his solid know-ledge of construction, made this line as efficient and beneficial to Skye as its neighbour to the north.

When the founder of the Railway retired in 1922, at the age of sixty-nine, it was his eldest son Daniel who continued the running of the business. Under his guidance, the Railway flourished. By 1932, the Dingwall to Skye Railway had been extended by means of a steel bridge into the Isle of Skye itself; by 1939, a 'light railway' brought it as far as Uig on the island's north-west coast. In 1933, the Ullapool Railway itself was again expanded, this time to four tracks, and is much used by the travelling public, and is traversed by huge clean locomotives driven by humming dynamos.

Sunday, June 3, 1894.

It is now the glorious height of a Scottish summer. The sky is so high and the air so warm that I can almost believe that I live in a Paradise upon Earth. It is no hardship to arise early from my bed at five or even four in the morning, when I hear the rest of the encampment stirring. This, even though the night has been so short and the sun seems scarcely to have descended behind Beinn Dearg. On Friday, the first day of the month, I awoke at four: all was still and peaceful. I dressed quickly and looked out upon the most inspiring panorama of hills, water and moor that has ever stirred my heart. The sight back down the glen was less attractive, it must be admitted, since the scar of the railway workings has been cut across the landscape. But, it may be accepted, the moor now grows back. I quickly put on my boots and stepped out into the cool air, filled my lungs to their capacity and set off towards Loch-droma, which now lies barely a mile from where we are encamped. By half-past the hour, I was dipping my body in the cold waters of the loch and floating on my back to study the profound eternity of the heavens. High above me, an eagle was out early, king of the upper airs and all the land.

To-day, the early morning was again overflowing with possibility, and I struck out early, this time back along the line we have carved through the landscape. Low shreds of mist were vanishing above the hills, leaving a sky so still and clear that I felt transported to another life altogether. I walked back along the steel rails, over the virgin gravel ballast, adjusting, after more than half a mile of concentration, the length of my stride to the gaps between the heavy wooden sleepers. The only sound I could hear was from the sheep on the far hill, the larks which burst up into the heavens, and the step of my own boots.

I found myself approaching the Professor's house at Aultguish. A careful study of the house, from the safety of the new embankment which we had raised, re-assured me that there was no one at home. The windows were entirely shuttered, the garden thoroughly overgrown: there was no sign of life. The tall iron gates, galvanised against the hostile attacks of winter, were firmly padlocked with a lock and chain which would likely never again turn to any key. Feeling adventurous as I have not done for perhaps three decades, I clambered over the railings which stretched out to either side of the gates and furtively crept through the vegetation towards the house. I expected yet the challenge of the owner, and so kept to the shadows. The bushes led round to a side door. The silence felt at my throat and tickled the back of my scalp.

I stood like a statue for a full five minutes, then stepped forward to try the door. To my very great surprise and horror, it opened. It did not open silently, for the wood at the base rasped over the stone floor. I stood again, listening. There was no sound, either inside or out. I took one pace forward and crossed the threshold. I was in a scullery. I stepped hurriedly inside and pushed open a door leading into the kitchen. It was cold and damp. Dishes were stacked neatly in a dresser, pots and pans were piled in rows next to the great cold black range.

Taking my fear with both hands, I called out, at first quietly and then more forcefully. There was no answer.

For the next hour I wandered at liberty through the rooms of the Professor's house. Each room was more extraordinary than the last. The Professor's study, which was situated on the first floor and which occupied most of the front of the house, facing north to the huge slopes of Sron Ghorm, was more rewarding than the great Museums of Edinburgh, more fascinating than any picture encyclopaediae which I have ever consulted. There were glass jars full of dried plants and flowers, masks from some ancient mausoleum, wall-hangings from China or Nippon, simple pottery and priceless ceramics probably worth more than I will ever earn, painted with dragons and other fearful devices, their glaze cracked with age. The high walls were covered with shelves and the shelves with books of all shapes and sizes.

The man's bathroom was as a temple to rituals of purification. In the centre stood a huge bath, large enough to accommodate a giant, standing on four golden claws. A mighty pair of taps would fill the bath with torrents of water in minutes. The cold tap was dripping and there was a long green stain running down the white surface. The hand-basin would have served a whole College of Professors washing simultaneously. The high window was glazed with coloured glass, forming the picture of a scene from some Asian wash-house for men. I blushed to remark some of the detail, and forbear to write down in my Journal any description of the scene.

There were a number of bedrooms, but only one was obviously used. The drawing-room, facing the long slope of the hills to the south, was lavishly furnished, and a huge fireplace, with its mantel carved from a solid piece of oak, occupied most of the western wall. From a framed sketch done in charcoal which hung on the wall, I have discovered that the hill which can be seen to the left from the window is named Meall Mhic Iomhair – I later advised MacIvor in jest that I had found his hill! In this room again, there were enough books to satisfy the most demanding of students. Hung above the fireplace and on other walls were the heads of a horned deer and of some kind of buffalo, their eyes looking out upon the world with surprise rather than anger at their demise.

I must have been in the house, as an uninvited but respectful guest, for more than an hour. Every two minutes I would cross rapidly to a window to peer out, half-expecting a figure of authority to stride across the garden and demand to know what I was doing. So would come to an abrupt end my dazzling career as engineer! But at last I left the house the same way as I came in, pulling the door firmly behind me and climbing through the bushes and over the embankment.

When I finally returned to the encampment near the croft at Glascarnoch, the world was beginning to stir, and there was a confused smell of cooking and the cries of children playing.

Memorandum to Mr. Kininmonth: I found my entry into the world of Professor Cardew-Smith so invigorating, that I know I must return. But be careful, Mr. Kininmonth, of leaving any traces of your visit, or of being caught *in flagrante delicto!* Your position within the Company and your responsibility both to yourself and your contracted labour must keep you from indulging any foolish whims.

Sunday, June 10, 1894.

I returned to Aultguish House again this morning. The weather was less calm than heretofore, and there was a cold wind blowing from the east. Without the sunlight, the interior of the house had lost some of its charm. There was a smell of mustiness in all the rooms. However, I fell to reading in some of the books which the Professor kept in his study. One of them was quite remarkable, being a compendium of ancient alphabets and scripts from Arabian lands and the Orient. Some of the scripts were labelled as being very ancient, possibly the most ancient known to modern students, contemporaneous with the Pyramids of Egypt. Staring at the rows of letters, which meant absolutely nothing to me, I was swept into another world, where only a privileged few men guarded the secret of writing and wrote down whatever necromancy or secrets of religion they had to pass on. Among an ignorant people, men with a knowledge of writing were men with power.

Wiping the accumulated dust from a small display cabinet, I happened upon some broken pieces of clay with the most curious marks upon them, like those made by small garden-birds in the snow, tiny scratches and lines and little triangles. Each one was labelled, in the Professor's grand handwriting, with a name and a date. As a thief in the night, I raised the glass lid of the cabinet and picked out one of the pieces; the label described it as being almost five thousand years old. I almost dropped it to the floor in awe: here, in my modern engineer's hand, was a piece of writing created by a man who lived in the earliest days of the Old Testament! With the utmost caution, I replaced the clay and closed the cabinet. What did the marks mean? Did they describe the visions of a priest who had been visited by a Jealous God? Or the plans for a grand palace for a King, with a thousand rooms for his warriors and wise-men and – though I swiftly suppressed the thought, unworthy to the Sabbath – his concubines?

But perhaps, I reflected, when once again out on my breezy railway-line, the pictures and unfamiliar script simply represented an order for stones and mortar for some half-hearted Hittite building work, or a lament by an ancient engineer on the laxity of his labourers! I will never know, for I can hardly ask the Professor!

We make considerable progress on the line now. The men are working with something approaching vigour, and even Gollan is walking around without those engraved lines of care upon his brow. I am pleased to report that the line is now turning more to the west, in towards the Dirrie More, the glen in which Loch-droma lies. Both the road and the railway curve to the left just where the river shallows and the track heads off to the tiny croft at Airicheirie. I expect that we shall come upon Loch-droma by the end of September or earlier. The only engineering difficulty of any significance is the crossing of the river coming down from Beinn Liath Mhor to the south. My Ordnance Survey map gives it a name – Abhuinn a'Ghiubhais Li. MacIvor advises me that this means the Stream of the Colourful Pine and that the 'Beinn' directly to the south of us is the Big Grey Hill of the Colourful Pine. In the absence of any pine-trees at all, Gollan exercises his right as Lowlander to call the river the Grey Water; I, contrariwise, call it the Colourful Water.

Memorandum to Mr. Kininmonth: In an uncommon and pleasant episode this evening, Mr. Gollan sat with me for a few minutes and we smoked a pipe and drank a glass of spirits together. The midges clouded around us, but the combined efforts of our pipe-bowls kept them at bay. It was one of those rare times when I felt I was not utterly alone on this Earth. Mr. Gollan gave me a report of an episode on the railways which I had not heard before, and I set it down here as a colourful interlude in this rather dry Journal:

It seemed that Gollan had learned some aspects of his trade on the railway-line which runs between Dalkeith in Mid-lothian and Penicuik in that same county. It was a small but busy line which passed through a number of small villages and descended with some rapidity into the valley of the River Esk. In 1888, a circus owned by an Italian family by the name of Crolla was touring the south of Scotland, and a train with a number of carriages and wagons was hired to transport them more easily between towns. On the eighteenth of December, the circus left Dalkeith to pass on to Penicuik. An engine with three carriages for the numerous Artistes and seven wagons for the paraphernalia and beasts was loaded up at ten in the morning, and departed for the neighbouring town. Gollan himself was supervising a gang of navvies who were repairing some damage caused to the line by snow and frost. As the train came down the hill from a place named Rosslyn-castle, it was observed that the brakes had failed. There was nothing that Gollan and his gang could do except stand by powerless as the train sped past them, onwards across the river and into the tunnel near Auchendinny.

Some moments after the last wagon disappeared from sight, there was heard a roar and a crash, which struck terror into their hearts. Gollan and his men raced to the entrance of the tunnel to find a scene of devastation: the wagons of the train had jumped from the rails and crashed against the walls or the roof of the tunnel. It was only later discovered that the carriages carrying the circus people, and the engine itself, had by some miracle remained on the line, their precipitous career halted abruptly by the crash in the rear.

However, no sooner had Gollan sent his men into the tunnel to see what could be salvaged than the men raced out again as if in fear of their lives. And no wonder, for, as Gollan explained to me, from the broken wagons now spilled a variety of wild and injured beasts – lions, seals, horses, dogs, even an elephant – rampaging, shrieking and roaring, fighting each other in their attempts to escape the wreckage and gain the natural light of day. Of their trainers and masters there was no sight, and Gollan could only retreat to the safety of some nearby trees to watch as the animals ran in circles, headed back up the line or, scaling the embankments, disappeared towards Auchendinny. Alas, one of the lions pounced upon a navvy from North-humberland, a giant of a man with more muscle than sense, who had tried to corner it, and had torn such a chunk from him that he died on the spot.

Gollan confessed to me that this was the worst moment he had ever experienced in his life on the line, and I was able to sympathise with him. I have witnessed some minor de-railments of trains on lines I have worked, but no crash which resulted in the loss of life, and certainly none which unleashed the wildness of untamed beasts upon the world.

As a post-script, Gollan told me that the elephant which escaped was never found, although several countrymen reported seeing it browsing in the wild vastnesses of the Pentland Hills for weeks thereafter. The tiger could not be re-captured alive: it was shot while devouring hens in the vicinity of Rosewell and buried in the garden of a retired potato-merchant, who retained its head for mounting in his drawing-room. The other animals were, after some hours, re-captured by the circus folk.

Sunday, July 1, 1894.

We have all been working without a break during June. The weather has been calm and mild, and the hours available for work are long. The earth underfoot is relatively dry. The moor is boggy in many places to be sure, but the Good Lord seems to smile upon us, and there have been few places where additional earth-works were required to underpin the track. Indeed, a fortnight ago, everyone was so keen to advance the line that there was a debate between myself, Gollan and MacIvor on whether we would allow the men to work on the Sabbath. Gollan was a fierce advocate of this.

In the end, the decision was mine. It was enough that the navvies laboured from early morning to late evening for six days in the week. The sanctity of the Sabbath was inviolate. In case another argument was required, I asked MacIvor to enquire among the more spiritual members of the labouring mass. I was startled, and Gollan more so, by MacIvor's news that any such breach would be answered by a gathering of a veritable militia of defenders of the Godly way. Such an uprising would inevitably require the mobilisation of the constabulary – of which there are precious few members in this part of the County – or even of the regiments in Fort George. There were hints even of sabotage. MacIvor reminded us of the events at Strome-ferry ten or eleven years ago, when there was a threatened civil disruption over the working of the fish-trains on the Sabbath. All this was enough to persuade Gollan to back down from his untenable position.

So we work six days a week, bringing the line forward towards Loch-droma, which has now become a landmark for all those who labour here. From Loch-droma, Braemore will be visible, and that will be one third, and the most unfriendly and bleak third, of our journey done.

A fortnight ago, I went again with Gollan and MacIvor towards Braemore. We stopped at Loch-droma, for there was a tinker there, with his cart, his three children and his dogs. He hailed us heartily enough as we approached, and MacIvor struck up an intimate conversation with him and shared a pipe. We sat down in the lee of his two-wheeled cart, forbearing to enter the tiny smoky tent in which the entire family lived. Thomas Stewart was the man's name, a native of the land north of Lochinver. More than five years ago he had lost his home when a gentleman from Middlesbrough came and bought up the estate. As a cottar, a crofter without any rights or titles to the land he worked, he and his family were turned out from their community, to make shift as they could.

Stewart was yet a man at his ease and he had made the best of their fate. High summer was when they went out on the road, selling and mending and passing on news. It seemed a healthy enough life for the three children, I suppose, who were about six, eight and twelve years of age. In winter, they must seek out some friendly crofter or landowner and live through the cold months on their meagre savings and some handiwork.

As we left the tinker and his family, I passed the eldest child a coin in secret and advised her to buy some clothes for the family. There was nothing else a man could do, out here in the wilderness.

Memorandum to Mr. Kininmonth: It only occurred to me later in the day that I had, in a short space of time, encountered on the one hand an empty but inhabitable house and on the other a worthy but homeless family. Would that it had been in my power to put these two unfulfilled items together! Would that a society could be born which would reconcile the estates and grand houses of the wilderness with the dispossessed and the paupers of the land! Would that a fabric of railways could be built which would open up the vast emptiness of Ross and Cromarty and link isolated communities!

Sunday, July 15, 1894.

I have assailed the reader with my complaints upon the humble, yet voracious Midge, Tick and Cleg. It is my firm belief that all three must be rooted out and extirpated from the face of the Earth!

I found a man to agree wholeheartedly with me on this matter in the shape of Sergeant Warren Righteous, officer with the Ordnance Survey Corps, who passed by with a small troop on Tuesday. Mr. Righteous – who did not, alas, live up to his name – was surveying the land here for a new edition of the maps which Colonel Farquharson, the Director-General of the Ordnance Survey, is preparing for publication. The sergeant has more than a thousand square miles to verify and has a pack full of maps on which minor corrections are being made. He showed me some of them. Of most interest were, of course, the maps which now show a barred line drawn inexorably from Garve up the glen of the Black Water as far as Glascarnoch and representing the Garve & Ullapool Railway, as built by Mr. Alexander Auchmuty Seth Kininmonth. What pride I had in seeing the fruits of my labour now being etched for posterity! Why, even should the track be torn up in two hundred years, the maps which future generations will study will still show my Railway leading across the wilderness!

Sergeant Righteous had seven men with him, and a number of horses, of the slow solid kind, carrying their tents, baggage and survey equipment. All eight men were weather-beaten and smelled almost as bad as we did ourselves; but their smell was of peaty moors and honest sweat. They had begun their journey at Garve, and had followed the course of the railway, pausing to investigate any changes at Strath Rannoch and Strath Vaich, taking in the distant Glen Beg and Glen Mor in Glencalvie to the north, and then returning over the Strath Vaich Forest to come down again into Glascarnoch. In truth, very little of the existing maps, surveyed twenty years ago, had changed. No new houses had been built, although some crofts had disappeared. Such is the sad state of our nation! The most significant change, which Righteous had faithfully recorded, was the railway-line.

I tried to persuade the surveyor to mark out the remaining part of the line on his maps, so that the barred line would stretch all the way from Garve to Ullapool by the time the map was engraved and published. It would save much time and cost, I argued. But the man would have none of this: his duty, he informed me, was to record what was on the ground, and only what was on the ground, and he was not permitted to record the plans and intentions of men or the Devil. How blinkered are the eyes of officials!

Wednesday, July 25, 1894.

The Board of the Company came upon us to-day, in a visitation which happily went without major incident. I had not seen any of them, except for the younger Fowler (who now also sits on the Board), since April. They all came: the loathsome MacAulay, Sir Cosmo Coffin and his lady, Houston, Pirie of Leckmelm, and, once again, although still not a member of the Board, Lord Inverpolly. As before, Sir John Fowler was absent on some other enterprise. It seems I am fated not to display my work to him! They came aboard a train, whose labouring engine was especially scrubbed and polished for the occasion. The sky was overcast and there was a weight of thunder in the air.

The short train arrived at about eleven o'clock, having left Garve Station at nine sharp. Although there was only fourteen miles of track, the engine had been halted at several places to permit the members of the Board to descend and make inspections. I was advised by Major Houston that the Board had been pleased with the work at Torr Breac and at Black Bridge, where Coffin's men have now arranged a wooden platform on the south side of the bridge. Provided for in the Act was a halt for the exclusive use of Sir Cosmo Coffin. It

was at this halt that the Lady Tamara Coffin joined the party, whom –
because of the Cleg – we never saw outside the carriage.

McGeorge MacAdam MacAulay advised me with much rubbing
of his greasy hands that a long inspection of the embankment at
Aultguish House had been undertaken, and that the Board might
have to order some more embellishment and strengthening. It
would seem that a letter has been received from lawyers in Old
Aberdeen representing the Professor, requesting detailed drawings
and photographs of the front, side and rear elevations of the earth-
works, so that these can be forwarded to the Professor. The Board
has commissioned a draughtsman to undertake this, on the understanding that the drawings will be examined and changed as
necessary before forwarding to the advocates. The matter of the
photographs is of more concern, but MacAulay believes that Mr.
Wilson of Aberdeen can alter photographic images in his studio.
Nothing will surprise me any more about the dishonesty of certain
people: it is of less monetary expense to falsify a photograph in
some distant studio than to excavate earth-works on the ground. A
saving in money is made by the sacrifice of the facts. Such is the
brutal fate of truth in these un-Godly times! What unpleasantness
will occur when the Professor returns and finds that he had been
mis-led, I dare not even imagine. But that is not my concern.

It fell upon me to conduct the group along the road as far as Loch-
droma, from where they could see the projected descent of the line
towards Braemore. I offered to take them further to show them how
the line would wind down the Braemore Descent, which offer was
greeted with a stony smile from the younger Fowler, and a hurried
refusal from the other members of the party, acutely conscious no
doubt of the luncheon which awaited them in their railway carriage.

As we made our way back along the road to the head of the line,
Sir Cosmo advised his friends that the line would be used in earnest
on the tenth of August next, to bring a party of house-guests from
Inverness to Strath Vaich, where he, Coffin, would disembark them
at his private halt and initiate them into the pleasures of shooting
the grouse. A special train had been hired with engine and three
carriages – two for the guests, one for the servants and dogs and
baggage – to convey the party from the London train when it

arrived in Inverness to the very doorstep of Strath Vaich. Sir Cosmo was not shy to advise all assembled that he expected the cost of the hire of the train to exceed one hundred pounds Sterling. MacAulay was the only one of the party to utter some polite exclamation of surprise. The others, obviously accustomed to Coffin's shameless publication of his affairs, considered the weather.

Friday, August 10, 1894.

To-day was the day that Sir Cosmo Coffin's house-party was due to make the journey from Inverness to the new station at Black Bridge. For station staff, Sir Cosmo has had to make do with a pair of surly estate-workers drafted in for the great occasion with the promise of a silver shilling apiece.

I had decided that I should attend the arrival of the first passengers on the line. I therefore borrowed the only bicycle which is present at the rail-head, belonging to a navvy named John Dunlop – rather inappropriately, given the unyielding nature of the machine's tubeless tyres. Dunlop jealously guards this rather rusty and singularly agonising conveyance as his own, rarely to my knowledge using it as anything more than a symbol of relative wealth. However, I prised it from his grasp in exchange for a sixpence, and set off down the road to Black Bridge in order to arrive in good time for the expected midday train. It was a comfortless journey and a thick mist came down as I was jolted down the road.

I gained the halt at the head of Strath Vaich at half-past eleven o'clock. I found there two carriages and a cart belonging to the Coffin estate, attended by members of his house, and, on the wooden stage which acted as platform, the two local men dressed up as Station-Masters, in fashions dictated by Lady Coffin's summer tours. The two unfortunate men were paying hard for their shilling, for their Tirolean costumes were the object of excited ridicule of the drivers lounging on the carriages in the roadway. The stage had been decorated with, first, a large wooden board newly-painted with neat lettering proclaiming this, despite its enacted private nature, to be the BLACK BRIDGE STATION (FOR STRATH VAICH AND LUBFEARN) and, secondly, some red-and-blue bunting, which was suspended from the board to a post erected for just this purpose, lending a barely festive appearance to this halt lost in the mists of the Wyvis mountains. The gloomy shape of the School-house could just be seen along the track, as silent as a tomb.

None of those present paid much attention to me as we all settled down to our vigil.

Twelve o'clock came and went. As did one o'clock. At half-past one, a servant appeared on a bicycle from the Lodge to enquire after the reason for the delay, and at two o'clock, another servant arrived to enquire after the reason for the absence of the first servant. Just then, one of the men on the platform called out, and we listened. Sure enough, there was the distant and broken sound of an engine labouring somewhere in the fog. The two house-servants hastened away up to the Lodge.

The engine emerged from the mist and screamed to a halt in billowing clouds of steam. The two Station-Masters sprang to life: each seized a door, wrenched it open as if to drag the passengers from their carriages, and obliged them to descend. This was a noisy crowd, and I felt an instant and deep-rooted dislike for the people they were and the society they represented. They had eyes and ears only for themselves, and assumed by right that their trunks and hand-baggage would be taken care of. Not one of them paid any attention to me. The driver and his engineer stood in their cabin, arms folded, enjoyed a pipe and ignored the disembarkation of their charges.

After a great deal of confusion, all the passengers were seated within the two carriages, and their more senior servants within the cart. The carriages and cart then vanished into the mist past the School-house and up towards the Lodge. The guns, luggage and dogs were left on the platform, under the care of the lesser servants, who huddled quietly by themselves, awaiting the return of the conveyances.

With the departure of the main party, the engineer descended to oil and to polish. I enquired of him what had been the reason for the delay. He advised me that there was a problem at Inverness with payment for the hire of the engine and its carriages from the Caledonian Railway; some officials of the latter Company had refused to let anyone board the train until Sir Cosmo Coffin had handed over the full payment agreed. There had been a good deal of haggling, until Coffin and the representative of the Caledonian had retired to Sir Cosmo's bank in Castle-street to raise a draft upon his account for half the amount, the balance to be paid within a week of the party's safe arrival at Black Bridge. There was apparently some argument even at this arrangement, the Caledonian man being unwilling to admit of the existence of a station at Black Bridge, which lay well beyond the horizon of his travels.

I reflected on the use so far made of my Railway-Line. It is my intention that it should be used for the greater good of the poor people of this land, and that the opening up of the glens and the coast should contribute greatly to the establishment of a prosperous land. And yet I observe as travellers only the wastrels, the un-Godly and the idle, spilling out from their boudoirs and clubs. How easily can an instrument of Good be turned to one of Evil!

At length, the brakes were released and the engine pushed the carriages back down the line towards Garve. I set off back up the stony road towards Loch-droma, just as the cart returned from the Lodge for the remaining party. What a terrible road it is! Mud overwhelms it in the hollows, boulders litter every yard and streams flow freely in its rutted passage across the moor. At the slightest declivity, the surface of the road will tilt the traveller downwards into a ditch or a bed of reeds from which he struggles to regain the crown. Compared with travel upon roads such as this, travel by rail is like a ride on a magical carpet! When my Line is finished, the road to Ullapool can only fall into total disuse and be swallowed up for ever by the rivers and barren moors around us.

Memorandum to Mr. Kininmonth: I must ask Mrs. Macbeth – in the strictest confidence, for if any word got out among the men, or worse, among the women, I should make myself another laughing-stock – if she has any of her famous ointments which might relieve the raw rash around the top of my legs, caused solely by the rubbing of Dunlop's saddle as the bicycle rattled over the most uneven ground.

Sunday, August 19, 1894.

Grouse-shooting began in earnest last Sunday, the twelfth of the month. Since then, the hills have been noisy with the sound of shotguns and the echoes of shotguns. Parties of hunters and beaters have criss-crossed the hills around us, but none has come near. The road which runs alongside the railway is traversed by carriages, horses and the occasional powered vehicle with a cargo of rich idlers from London.

Amidst the sounds of the surrounding carnage, we have now brought the line as far as the bridge over the river with its colourful name. There was a brief pause for celebration on Friday, as at last the river was bridged by rail. And then we continued.

This morning, however, the usual Sunday peace was shattered by a hunt of a different kind. The shooting-parties who have been out on the hills this past week at least paid some measure of respect to the Sabbath. Some navvies, on the other hand, decided that to-day, being their resting-day, would serve as good as any to indulge in some wild escapades of their own. As a result, I was alarmed to be visited at about noon by the keeper from the Strath Vaich estate, in a fit of temper inconsistent with my own mood, who announced that a group of navvies had invaded his master's grouse-moor and were intent on pursuing the grouse from top to top; he demanded that I should call them down from the hills and discipline them before summary justice should be meted out.

At first, I suspected the man was in the grip of some private fantasy, but then realised that his wrath was real and that, if I did not act, the man might well turn his guns against innocent men. So I summoned both Gollan and MacIvor and outlined the situation to them. As I did so the keeper, whose name was MacFadzean, persistently interrupted me to elaborate on each detail with incongruous warmth, and repeated his threats to have the men shot on sight.

At last, MacIvor stared MacFadzean down and cautioned him that any injury to his men would be regarded as an injury to MacIvor himself. MacFadzean was about to issue a challenge in return, but then re-considered and fell silent. With this agreement, we mustered a party of men of the more sober kind, and set off from the navvies' town into the grouse-moor. The walking was very hard, particularly in the ascent of the hill behind the house at Airicheirie, where we followed the burn straight upwards to a plateau at more than two thousand feet above the level of the sea. I felt myself to be the least fit of the party: at times, my heart would pound fit to burst, my breath would fail me and my legs felt like water. I could barely stumble up some of the slopes. Continually, I had to stop, clutching my sides or my back, catching my breath. But I feared most being left behind, and so I battled upwards.

On the plateau, and with no break for a rest, we split into two parties, the one led by MacFadzean the gamekeeper, the other by MacIvor. Gollan went with the keeper in the general direction of Strath Vaich Lodge, from where the errant party had last been sighted, while I went with MacIvor, striking north.

After an hour's hard walking, we came upon the hunting-party sheltering from the wind at the shore of a high loch. On my return to my cabin later that day, I learned that this loch was Gorm-loch, situated high on the hill over-looking Loch-toll a'mhuic. There were five men in the party, and all bar one were asleep under the sun. To no one's surprise, they had had no luck with their hunting, being armed not with shotguns, but with crude wooden spears and catapults. Quite how they expected to entice a grouse within a distance suitable for slaying, I cannot explain. I surmise that they did it for play, for exercise and the thrill of the chase, rather than from any serious expectation of dining upon tender meat. For men whose lives are enclosed by the squalor of life in a hovel, and the daily back-breaking work with pick and shovel, and scarcely a look heavenwards, such a day as to-day would be spiritual nourishment for many a week. MacIvor soon dealt with them, and the entire group started back to our agreed meeting-place with the other search-party on the shore of Loch-a'gharbh raoin, a stretch of water far less splendid than its name.

It was then that a nightmare was repeated. In the course of finding a suitable path back, we came unexpectedly upon the remains of two men, side by side in a dip in the land, almost entirely concealed by the rampant bracken which had grown up around them. Not this time encased in ice, our discovery, but rather half-eaten by scavengers. We stopped and stared in horror. Each one of us immediately came to the same conclusion – that we were gazing upon the relics of Hamish Macrae and William Dyer, who had been lost upon the mountain last November. Our supposition was confirmed by MacDonald, the men's companion on that snowy day, who recognised Dyer by a gold ear-ring he wore and MacRae by a cheap metal ring. It is presumed that they must have found shelter in this small basin at the height of a snowstorm and then frozen to death in the night. And lain here, rotting and undiscovered on the lonely hill for nigh on nine months.

We have returned now to our encampment, leaving behind MacIvor, who volunteered to watch over the last resting-place of the unfortunate men. We then posted one of the men at Loch-a'gharbh raoin to await Gollan's party and to tell them of the tragic circumstance upon which we had stumbled. Another, the most respectable-looking and with the most comprehensible accent, has been sent down to the Lodge to advise Sir Cosmo of the gruesome find. For my part, I have been into the navvies' encampment to break the news. When the supply train arrives to-morrow morning, I will send back a note to the authorities in Dingwall, and no doubt we shall receive another visit from Inspector Campbell and the journalist Mr. Gibson. The bodies will have to be left *in situ* until the police have arrived. I am growing accustomed to the necessary procedures to be followed in such cases.

What a tragic end to a day which must have begun in such high spirits for this navigators' hunting party!

Tuesday, August 28, 1894.

Although I have rarely had the time to continue my occasional Journal on the Sabbath days as I had intended, I find myself with sufficient time this famous Tuesday to sit at ease in my cabin and record the events of the past few days.

First and foremost, it is exactly one year since the first turves were cut at Garve, to commence the engineering works for the Railway to Ullapool. And we have to-day, at two o'clock, laid the last rails which have brought the line to the head of Loch-droma. There was a great shout from the men as the last bolt was tightened in place, and, perhaps carried away by the circumstances more than I should have been, I stood upon the wagon with the remaining rails and thanked the men for their strenuous efforts and declared the rest of the day to be paid. Many, I fear, immediately set off for Aultguish Inn, to rekindle an old acquaintance with the whisky-bottles. No sooner had I beheld this migration than I regretted my kindness and humanity. However, there was nothing to be done for it.

We had projected a year to reach Braemore. We had not included in our reckonings the severity of the past winter. I suppose I should feel satisfied that we are now at Loch-droma, barely four miles short of Braemore. But I expect that the Board of the Company will see things differently. If only we can reach Braemore by the time the winter snows set in! But that is a forlorn hope – four miles of boggy ground ahead, against the winds off the Atlantic. At best, we progress at about a mile for each month on the calendar, and, while we might expect by that calculation to reach Braemore on Christmas Day, this would only come to pass if we were favoured with a mild autumn and winter.

With the overwhelming sense of achievement at the working day's conclusion, I had almost forgot that we were visited last Tuesday by Inspector Campbell and his co-onymous sergeant, to conclude the sad affair of MacRae and Dyer, the two navvies who had perished upon the Strath Vaich Forest. Mr. Gibson of the Inverness newspaper did not this time join them – I presume because either he or his editor did not consider the death of two navvies worth the expense of the day's travel. After a journey into the hills to examine the bodies *in situ*, the policemen returned with a judgement on the tragic outcome which concorded with my own supposition. Four men who accompanied them, one of whom was MacIvor, brought back the gruesome remains on stretchers. It was unclear what should be done with the bodies: it was known that MacRae was married, but his wife had disappeared after the tragedy; Dyer came, it was generally believed, from Clackmannan-shire; but no one could provide any further details. In the end, Gollan agreed that the men should be buried in the municipal cemetery in Dingwall, in paupers' graves, with the men's gang paying the expenses. I immediately offered to contribute to such a fund. The train which had brought Campbell then departed with two additional passengers, now comfortably encased in plain coffins, which our carpenter had hurriedly constructed. The affair was closed.

Memorandum to Mr. Kininmonth: Truly, the life of Man is short and painful! If I, like our poor friends, had died this day, in my forty-second year, what would I have left behind? A Railway which I had not completed. Alexander Kininmonth: that is a name which will not live long in the memory. He has no children. He leaves no widow. No recognition from Sir John Fowler. No great work by which he would be remembered. All that I grant myself to-day as great achievements would be forgotten in a week or a month by those who might recall my name. Even in a hundred years, who can tell whether the Railway itself might not be torn up, or covered up by a deluge? Would I be remembered any more than Macrae or Dyer? Only those could remember me whom I might have fathered – and have not, alas!; and even those might not – I cannot remember much of my own grandfather, and certainly nothing of my great-grandfather. Do great works left to posterity have any value? Are those lives led without great works simply worthless?

Every man who was labouring to bring the Railway to Ullapool laboured to a purpose: to free himself. Many of those among us would never rise above the very hardship they tried to escape and would die, like our late friends, ignorant and crushed. Some, like myself and Mr. Gollan, even Mr. MacIvor, might briefly soar above our daily toil and find solace or freedom in our dreams, only to crash on a new morning to the ground. To few people in this world will it be given to climb to greatness through their own bold deeds.

Sunday, September 16, 1894.

On Tuesday last, in part in an effort to escape the ministrations of the insects, I went with MacIvor on towards the descent at Braemore, armed with Gunter's chain, a theodolite and a map. We made a careful survey of the proposed descent down the western edge of Strath Broom, as far as the house at Achindrean.

So the morning and early afternoon passed well, and we arrived at the gate of Achindrean a little after three o'clock. The weather had held fine all day, although it was overcast. I had a mind, as we reached the house, to call in on the owner and pay my respects. As it chanced, the owner himself was not at home, but his mother, a bright-eyed lady of some seventy years, invited us both in, paying as much respect to MacIvor as to myself, although he was obviously only of the labouring class.

This was Mrs. Beatrice MacMahon. The younger Mr. MacMahon was a sea-captain and much away on his voyages. This month, it seems, he was sailing back from Canada. The elder Mr. MacMahon, also a sea-faring man, had died some years previously. During our visit the old lady talked of many things, almost incessantly; enquired with the greatest intelligence and perspicacity after the progress of the railway; asked to be shown how to peer through the theodolite and mastered the instrument in measurements of her policies. I state with confidence that, had this widow been thirty or forty years younger, she would have found in me an ardent suitor! She talked also of the iniquities of our times, the rapaciousness of her near-neighbours at Inverbroom, at Inverlael and Leckmelm.

She asked MacIvor for more details of the lives and relicts of the two men who had died on the shores of Gorm Loch. MacIvor told her details of their lives of which I had been unaware, and told her also of his vigil after the discovery of the bodies. To my very great astonishment, I beheld the spectacle of Mrs. MacMahon softly touching MacIvor upon the wrist as he spoke, and only then realised that this hard-bitten giant of a man had been profoundly affected by the hours he had spent in the company of two rotting corpses in the lonely darkness at Gorm Loch. I was filled with guilt that I had never considered this man's natural feelings in the affair.

Memorandum to Mr. Kininmonth: Mrs. MacMahon gave me a book to read, which her son had sent to her from America. It is written by Ignatius Donnelly and entitled *Caesar's Column*. I have already read much of it and am greatly inspired by Mr. Donnelly's account of the Populist crusade against the rich and powerful men (or plutocrats) of America, which would last for a hundred years. In my own

Journal, I will now extend my fictional account of my descendants far into the next century.

2 Vendémiaire, 1994.

Almost a full hundred years after the completion of the Garve to Ullapool Railway-Line, I – Seth Proudhon Kininmonth – will now share with my Journal the plans of the North Atlantic Bridge Common Stock Railway Company for the future expansion of its locomotive power and its network. These are plans which are to be put to the Board next Monday, and which I fully expect will be approved. It has been made known to me by our local Honourable Deputy that the Government in London will set aside funds for such a socially useful undertaking!

It is forty years since my late father, William Morris Kininmonth, chronicled the early history of the Great Benefactory Railway Society, which arose from the smoking ashes of the sinful society of earlier times. Since that time, great advances have been made by labouring engineers and academic navvies in our egalitarian society, advances that could never have been imagined in earlier times.

In 1958, all the stock-holders in the Benefactory Society voted to adopt a plan for the expansion of the Society. At that time, the Society set up the North Atlantic Bridge Common Stock Railway Company, in which it kept a full share-holding, so that the new Company would always act in the interests of the common people, and never be a vehicle for Godless accumulation and personal self-interest.

Between 1970 and 1975, one of the greatest engineering feats of all time was undertaken, the construction of a bridge some twenty miles in length – the world-famous North Atlantic Bridge itself! – across the Little Minch between Trotternish on Skye north to the Shiant Islands and thence westwards to Harris, thus linking the Hebridean Railway with the mainland. In 1976, a train carried the most daring souls from Stornoway on Lewis to London, the old Kings Cross Station now renamed the North and Atlantic Terminus, in the astonishing time of twelve hours and fourteen minutes. To the men of my great-grandfather's generation, such an undertaking would have been utterly beyond their wildest fantasy. But such was the

conviction and inspiration of the Railway Company, under my father's direction, that the wildest storms of the Minch and the
strongest tempests cast up by the North Atlantic could not bring
down the steel bridge which was constructed between islands and
skerries on sturdy pontoons and pillars.

There is now, thanks to the planning of my forefathers, a sturdy
network of railway-lines: leading north and west from Inverness to
Ullapool, and thence to the thriving centre of Lochinver and southwards to bustling Gairloch; leading south and west to Kyle, and
thence to Kyleakin, Uig on Skye, Harris and Lewis. This network
has justifiably cast its shadow over the lines further to the south –
those to Mallaig and to Oban, both simple fishing villages and
holiday resorts served by a twice-weekly passenger-service (each
week-day except Tuesday at the height of summer). The throbbing
heart of commercial and industrial development now beats in the
north, fed by the arterial web of the North Atlantic Bridge Railway
Company lines.

It is now our plan to establish:

primus, at Lochinver, a sky-ship terminus capable of receiving the
gargantuan air-filled ships which ply the skies over the North
Atlantic, from New York, from Newfoundland, from South
America, and from the plains of Russia;

secundus, on all express-train routes from the Outer Isles to
Dingwall and to London, fully-provisioned sleeping-car facilities,
so that passengers may set their heads down on departure, and
awaken refreshed and ready for commercial success in London;

tertius, from the main railway-lines into those smaller glens
which branch off to north and south, both on the mainland and
on the islands, a finer web of light-load railways, carrying small
numbers of passengers and items of freight.

Without exposing our plans prematurely, I would paint this
picture of the positive results of these three undertakings:

At Lochinver, there will be established, on land which the Company
will purchase, a field protected from the squalls of the ocean by
surrounding hills. On this land will be built 'sky-termini', buildings
for the reception and comfort of passengers, and storage of freight

which is intended for, or originates in, other lands. To this field will be drawn, as by magnets, huge sky-ships, bearing hundreds of passengers and many tons of cargo. The trains of the sky are like our iron ships, but made of lighter material, filled with light gases and driven by propellors. They come from the Americas, from Norway and Sweden via Orkney and Shetland, from Germany and France, from Spain and Russia. The sky-terminus at Lochinver will become a central junction for all of this sky-traffic, and the railway-line established there will carry the people and goods south and east to more local destinations, or indeed to London.

On all the long-distance trains which now traverse the lines from Stornoway, from Portree, from Lochinver and Ullapool, newly-built carriages will be hauled. These will be designed on the model of the carriages introduced in my great-grandfather's day by Mr. Pullman from North America, but will be fitted with all modern conveniences. In these carriages, commercial gentlemen, engineers, families, ladies, students, ordinary men and women, may take their ease, dine in comfort and without disturbance of noise, enjoy each other's company or the company of entertainers, and at last retire for a full night's sleep before breaking their fast as the train at last draws into its far-away destination.

Finally, to serve those smaller communities in the glens and hills adjacent to our existing lines, smaller "light" railways will be set up at junction points. They are termed "light" from the size of the rolling stock and the relative lightness of the lines and ballast. The first such line, built by my great-grandfather, is an example of what could be done. It runs from Inverewe to Dundonnell, then crosses the two Loch-brooms by suspended bridges which are generally agreed to be of breathtaking boldness. And we have projected a line running into Strath Vaich from Black Bridge on the Ullapool Line, serving the modest community re-established there. Picture the effect of a regular, clean, dry train, hauled by an efficient economical engine on a small-gauge track! The doctor could despatch his sick patients to the modern hospital in Ullapool without concern for the effects of the journey. The school-master could receive new books from Edinburgh almost as soon as they are published. The grocer could ask for citrus fruits to be delivered by the next train. The student could advance his knowledge by daily visits to a higher school in the town. As the lines are extended, so the task not yet completed, of eradicating the Cleg from every glen, will be accomplished. Soon, it is to be hoped, the muddy pot-holed roads and tracks of the Highlands, traversed by horse, carriage and horse-less carriage alike, and fallen into disrepair, will grow again with weeds, bracken and heather!

It is fully expected that these plans will finally remove the blight of social discontent and inequality from at least this part of the land. It is historically proven that, wherever the railway-lines have run, commerce and industry have either improved or even arisen from what was seemingly a wasteland. Barren moors have been clad again with strong-growing trees; swift-running rivers have been harnessed for power; fields and crofts previously turned over to sheep have been cultivated once more. Harbours flourish and factories are established to provide for the needs of the local populace. Barely a hundred years ago, crofters and cotters were living in abject misery and had to break unjust laws to feed their families. To-day, the descendants of those crofters and cotters make the laws and live in peace and harmony with their neighbours.

Further south, where the penetration of the railways has not been so great, discord and strife still stalk the towns and the muddy roads. Here, the hand of the Plutocrat still oppresses the people. Inequities continue to make miserable the vast majority. These are places suffering from a lack of investment in the capacity of the railways to bring social improvement. As recently as 1989, a slum-dwellers revolt in Hawick, where the railway-line was allowed to die out through lack of investment, cost the lives of dozens of innocents. Further, the impoverished masses of Fraserburgh have great cause on their side after the closure of their branch-line. And who will forget the tragic scenes in Dunoon, where diphtheria was rampant and the militia were called in to deal with the railway-less hordes of sufferers!?

In contrast to those miserable scenes, the plans of the North Atlantic Bridge Common Stock Railway Company will set a beacon for the twenty-first century and establish a new order in the civilised world.

Sunday, November 4, 1894.

It is some time since I had the leisure and energy which allow me to sit down on the afternoon of the Sabbath and write in my Journal. It is not that events worthy of record have been absent. Indeed, quite the opposite has been the case.

To-day it is bitterly cold, and there is a continuous dusting of flakes of snow in the air outside. The air is hard and cruel. I have sat for several hours with Mrs. Macbeth and a favoured circle of her acquaintance around the old woman's stove, supping at the strongest hottest broth imaginable, and listening to the muttered stories and comments of the assembly. Outside, the inhabitants of the encampment must shift for themselves. The hovels have been reinforced with peat and heather, the fires have been lit so that the air inside each residence is poisonous, the men sit shivering and pale in thin clothes. A number of the navvies – those with wives or families – have moved on since the start of October, hoping to find work further south, or simply retreating to a more sheltered encampment nearer to their homelands. I noted this morning that Stewart the Tinker and his family are still with us: but one small child has died of illness. The Reaper stalks unseen, taking away the weakest with scarcely a whimper. I only discover that the Reaper has visited on the rare occasions when Mrs. Macbeth tells me of it.

Memorandum to Mr. Kininmonth: The talk among the men to-day turned to earlier railways which they had worked. It seemed that we have gathered on our Railway-Line representatives from almost all of Scotland's web of railways: men who worked the lines into Edinburgh from Mid-lothian and East-lothian, the lines through Hawick and through Newcastleton, the labyrinth of lines in and around Glasgow, from Crieff to Callander to Stirling, the Great Glen; there was even an old man here who remembered the Portsoy & Strathisla Railway.

This talk reminded me of my father's brother, James Kininmonth, an honest and plain-speaking fireman who had spent many years working the railways in Strathmore. I remember when I was still a young boy that he would visit us on a holiday and tell us exciting tales of his work. I truly believe that it was he who instilled in me my ambition to be a Railway Engineer.

On one occasion, he visited with a truly wondrous tale. It seemed that a pair of rich young gentlemen had hired a train to take them from Perth to Edzell, where, it became clear, they proposed to play a practical joke upon some ancient relative. The train had been hired with the stipulation that two carriages should be attached and should be painted in colours resembling those of our Monarch's Royal Train, and that the engine should be bedecked with Union Jacks and other flags which they would bring on the day of the trip.

The train was duly assembled and the two gentlemen arrived, an hour late and a little the worse for drink. They were accompanied by several noisy companions of the same age and social background. They heartily approved of the appearance of the train, boarded, and my uncle James guided the train from Perth Station along the line towards Luncarty. At Stanley Junction, where the Highland Railway-Line branches off for Inverness, the train headed in an easterly direction to Coupar Angus and Alyth. It was at this point that one of the young gentlemen, to my uncle's horror, clambered from the carriage, over the tender and into the cab beside him. There he instructed my uncle that the party intended to make themselves out to be Moldovan Royalty, and that the whole charade was to provide much amusement. My uncle was given a guinea and instructed to act his part. As long as this charade did not imperil the passengers and the safe working of the Caledonian Railway generally, my uncle agreed.

Thus it was that, on entering the station at Coupar Angus, the entire party, now dressed in outrageous wigs, knee-breeches and coloured kerchiefs, descended briefly, jabbering in some language which was not Moldovan, although the surprised citizens of Coupar Angus could not have known this. As soon as the crowds began to gather, the party leaped back on board the train and course was set for Alyth Junction and thence to Glamis.

Evidently, word of the train was telegraphed forward from Coupar Angus, as no doubt the young gentlemen had planned; so that when the train pulled into Forfar Station, a hurriedly assembled welcoming party stood waiting, flags at the ready. There were loud huzzahs as the train stopped and the Moldovans descended to shake hands and to embrace the daughters of the town's leading citizens full on the lips, much to the outrage of those assembled.

From Forfar, the journey continued past Guthrie Castle, where a brief halt was made to admire the bridge, before the train branched off short of Friockheim towards Farnell and the junction at Bridge of Dun. At this point, the party demanded that my uncle take them into Montrose, which, after a brief consultation with the timetable of the Brechin to Montrose Line, was duly done. At Montrose, another crowd had already gathered, in hope of seeing the Royal party. After a short reception with tea and cakes, hurriedly arranged by the Provost, the train backed up the line towards Dun and Brechin. Some care was taken by the 'interpreter' for the party to announce that the train would be calling in at Brechin for luncheon.

It is easy to envisage the consternation which the telegraphed message from Montrose to Brechin must have caused. The Royal House of Moldova arriving for luncheon, and no one at the Town Hall had been told! With the able assistance of the local butcher and grocer shops, and the "Ladies of the Empire", a splendid buffet lunch was prepared and carried to the Station, at which, in due course, my uncle's gleaming and decorated train arrived.

The manners of the Moldovans towards the ladies caused some surprise in Brechin, and, later that day, a meeting of the Town Council agreed to write formally to the Moldovan Ambassador in London, expressing polite concern at certain behaviour. A diplomatic incident was narrowly averted by my uncle, who, seeing the way matters were leaning, decided to blow the whistle and get up steam. The Moldovans were obviously accustomed to running for trains, for, without thinking, they abandoned their hosts and leaped into their carriages, shouting gibberish. And the train left on its final leg via Stracathro to Edzell, where, despite the short notice, a welcoming party was waiting. No sooner had the party disembarked to bamboozle the farmers of the area, than my uncle considered his hire to be completed and took the train back through Tannadice, Forfar and Kirkbuddo to Dundee, and thence by the most rapid route to Perth.

I forbore to tell this tale to my companions in Mrs. Macbeth's temple, for I feared it reflected badly upon my uncle and his employers. Mr. Gollan might have considered it to be a fiction, although invention was as foreign to my uncle as the Greek Epics. In any case, once I had fully recalled all the details, the conversation had moved on to other matters, and the opportunity was lost.

Sunday, November 18, 1894.

Any hopes I might have harboured for an early completion of the line to Braemore have been dashed by the weather in the past three days. Snow has been falling almost without any interruption since Thursday afternoon. We have just passed the location where the stream known as Allt Leacachain comes tumbling down from the peaks above in a waterfall – more than well-fed in the autumn rains! – and rushes into Droma River. Ahead of us is the continuous slope down to the entrance to Braemore, so near at hand! But there is no likelihood that we shall reach it this year.

In order that the local populace should not be disadvantaged by our inability to reach the road-junction at Braemore, I have received authority from the Board to establish a temporary halt for passengers, to be named 'Braemore Halt', until such time as Braemore itself can be attained. Thus, passengers for Ullapool and Dundonnell will be able to travel from Garve in comfort through-out the winter; but they will have to walk the additional mile and one-half to and from the road junction; however, I am convinced that most travellers will be prepared to accept this lesser hardship than face the prospect of walking or riding across the wind-swept glen of Glascarnoch in December and January.

Next week, therefore, we shall construct a small platform, at a position about two furlongs past the crossing of the stream, and a hut in which prospective passengers might wait. Fares will be taken from the passengers at Garve, as they disembark or as the train waits to move off to Dingwall. Stewart the Tinker has been contracted to make us a tin-sign with the bold words braemore halt written upon it, which we intend to nail securely to a post on the platform. The whole edifice will sit at the edge of the line, perhaps a bit incongruously, as a monument to our success. But this will be the first station owned and operated by the Great North-West of Scotland Railway Company on the line out of Garve, and its establishment signifies greatly. The order I received from MacAulay in Dingwall was most particular about the erection of a Platform and Waiting-Room which would be a credit to the Company; and equally particular that the wood to be used in its construction should not be of the best, but "of the sort which will see out the storms of winter, but not endure the spring, so that the materials used will not be missed when the permanent Station is established". I believe that I need add no other commentary to this instruction.

In preparation for the coming winter, I moved my lodgings last week to Ullapool, to the house of a Miss Kilroy of Argyle-street. She is a bitter, pinched woman of uncertain age, with a grudge against all of humanity, but especially those who dare to lodge with her. From some words she let slip at the breakfast table, it seems that she had also given shelter to the preacher Mr. Rinck during his brief residence by Loch-broom. Miss Kilroy seems greatly to regret Mr. Rinck's departure; I notice that she has one of his tracts displayed beside the coat-stand: "Whoever Truly Loves the Truth: A True Message of Brotherly Truth for the True Common Man". Truly, I did not read it.

Tuesday, December 25, 1894.

Work has again stopped for the winter. The last two weeks of November were cold; the first weeks of December were colder still, for the snow fell down from the sky with no abatement. We managed only to construct our platform at a half-distance between Braemore and Loch-droma, and to strengthen some of the cuts and embankments so that they would not suffer the fate of our earth-works last year at Black Bridge. The first train from Garve to Braemore ran to a make-shift timetable on Monday, the third of December, 1894. The timetable was hastily put together, after a brief inspection by the Board of Trade which permitted trains to be run on the Line. It allowed for just three trains a week – on Mondays, Wednesdays and Fridays, leaving Garve at 11.30 a.m., and arriving at Braemore sixty minutes later; leaving Braemore Halt at 1.45 p.m., and returning to Garve at 2.35 p.m.

Last Wednesday I travelled into Dingwall. The Board of the Company had summoned me to attend their final meeting of the year and to make a formal report on the progress on the Line. It was an honest pleasure to sit on the hard seats of the carriage alongside three surly bodies from Ullapool and to be bowling along over the lines which I and my men had laid out over the inhospitable countryside. I knew that, in the adjacent First-Class carriage, Mr. Arthur Fowler travelled, to the same destination. He greeted me in an off-hand manner as we waited for the train to arrive. There was another gentleman with him, who I was given to understand was a Mr. Campbell Ross of Ullapool, a great advocate of the Line. We were in Dingwall only one hour and thirty minutes after leaving Braemore Halt.

As had been the case the previous year, my report was accepted almost without comment by the Board. At the urging of Lady Matheson, the Board congratulated itself – not me, nor the workmen who had spent so long in the wilderness, but itself! – on the establishment of the make-shift halt at Braemore, and then dismissed me with a vague promise of a visitation in early March.

I had to spend two nights in Garve, with Mrs. Campbell, awaiting the next departure of the train to Braemore. On the journey back, which took place in a freezing fog, the three carriages were quite occupied, with people arriving from the south and from Inverness to take advantage of the rapid journey-time to Ullapool. One gentleman struck up conversation with me and complimented me loudly on the excellent work undertaken. The pleasure I took from this public recognition was slightly tempered by delays in rising from Aultguish Inn, where the cold and damp weather had made the rails very slippery. The tiny engine, already old and due for retirement, could make but slow progress up the incline. However, we arrived safely, if an hour late, at Braemore Halt and disembarked into a variety of carts and conveyances, or simply vanished by foot into the gathering gloom of a late December evening.

Wednesday, January 2, 1895.

I have found it impossible to settle down to any rest in Miss Kilroy's establishment in Argyle-street. During the day, I can wander out in the few cold streets of Ullapool, down to the Pier or along Quay-street to see where the Line will terminate. If it is not snowing or raining, as it has been for several days, I can retrace my steps in the direction of Braemore; but the road is poor and muddy, and it is not a pleasant walk.

I share my winter exile with William Wallace Forbes, traveller in women's under-garments. Like any rational enquirer, I was desirous of knowing more details about the nature of his business, and I engaged him frequently in conversation, until we became good friends. He was a young man of great ambition, from Marchmont in Edinburgh. Once, he slapped his trunk full of samples and exclaimed: "With these, I shall make my fortune in America!" He designed to emigrate, as soon as he had made sufficient sales in Ross and Cromarty, and to become the "Carnegie of Crinoline". I was intrigued to view his samples, but he did not open the trunk at any time.

On Monday past, Forbes had to go on business to Lochinver and I took the opportunity of seating myself beside him on the cart which he had hired. The wind was biting and it was no day for an idle jaunt into the countryside. But a day alone with Miss Kill-Joy (as Mr. Forbes had wittily christened her) was more than I could face, so I buttoned up well, donned muffler and gloves, and wrapped myself in my great-coat. We set off at seven o'clock in the morning. It was almost pitch-black, and I could not make out the features of the carter, who grunted a greeting as we emerged from the house.

The road to Lochinver is long. The road to Lochinver is cold and wet. The mud on the road to Lochinver defies any polite description. The road to Lochinver is one which I shall never willingly travel again. We slipped and slid, bumped and jolted our way up from Ullapool. After about an hour of this torment, the wind suddenly increased and rain like needles cut into our faces as we came over the crest of the hill which looks upon Isle Martin. On a fine day, I expect that there is a splendid view of the Isle and the mountains behind.

On that day, we glimpsed the clouds and bent our heads again. The cart lurched down the hill to Ardmair, and then a long weary way up until we came to the junction at Drumrunie, where an even more dismal road leads off to the left, towards Coigach and Lochinver. It was the bleakest landscape I have ever seen. The rain eased off as we penetrated the glen below Cul Beag and An Stac, permitting us some glimpses of the latter's extraordinary sheer slopes, on which only eagles or Alpinists might stand. The mountain towered over us for many miles, then passed behind as we came to the God-forsaken cross-roads at the end of Loch-bad a'ghaill, where the waters of the loch crashed down in torrents into the lower Loch-owskeich, as if the very Earth had slipped at an angle to shed the upper Loch.

It was past midday by then; Forbes and I shared our pieces and a flask of rum which we had brought to warm us up. Although there was a weak sun behind the clouds, I was no nearer to seeing the visage of our carter than I had been in the early morning. Had I at that point been attacked by the man, and robbed of all my possessions, I could no more have given a description of him to the constable than I could of the King of Chaldea. Luckily, the man seemed not concerned with his passengers one whit, neither for conversation, nor for larceny.

Until then, I had felt that we were passing over the lands of the Moon, our barren circling planet. But on crossing the Polly River, we entered a landscape that was so lost to the outside world that I firmly believed we would come across neither house nor living soul again. The road so dipped, curved, crept up and down, that I barely knew how far we had come. When I consider that we plan to bring a railway-line through here, I can only laugh, for the idea is so absurd, so beyond reason that there is only laughter remaining. The railway will stop at Ullapool. Beyond the western edge of Ullapool is the End of the Earth, and those who wish to make this journey can do so by cart, boat or balloon – but not by train.

We came back to the shoreline after night had again fallen, and finally into Lochinver after about twelve hours of travel. Twenty-five miles lie between Ullapool and Lochinver; but there might as well have been two thousand and five hundred leagues, for the pain of the journey.

We slept poorly in Lochinver, in a cold and damp inn. On the following day, Forbes completed his business and we returned to Ullapool. The weather for the return-journey at least was pleasant, the sky clear, and the sight we had of the strange mountains of the region was impressive. Suilven we watched, trapping the clouds from a blue sky and casting them over her shoulder, for what seemed hours.

I must submit a report to the Board, containing my thoughts on the proposed extension from Ullapool to Lochinver, and suggest to the Board that the idea is impractical in the extreme, certainly for a heavy railway. There may be a way of reaching that remote village, but I cannot see that it will pass by An Stac and the River Polly!

Sunday, February 3, 1895.

The winter, although hard, has now abated so much that Fairley of Inverness has decided to risk a re-commencement of the work. We began to collect our gangs of navvies and our materials last week, and already there is a small encampment of smoking tents and grubby huts upon the land above Braemore. The snows on the north-facing slopes of the Braemore Forest, on Creag Dhubh, are still white and deep: last week I walked over to the closest snow-field and found, to my utter astonishment, that it attained a depth of eight feet and seven inches in one place, and in most places it was more than four feet thick. However, it is not so bad by far upon the south-facing slopes on which we shall now continue our construction-work. The earth underfoot is still frozen hard, and may cause us some difficulties, but perhaps not so many as boggy ground has given us in the past. In any case, we hope to have established the permanent Station at Braemore by the end of this second month of 1895. The Board of the Company advised me that they will employ a trustworthy man to act as Station-Master just as soon as the platform is built, and a lodging for himself.

Memorandum to Mr. Kininmonth: So we re-engage with the Braemore Descent to-morrow! I am filled with a sense of foreboding, for it is a work which I have anticipated for many months; but the length of anticipation has created room in my imagination for all manner of failure, catastrophe and ruination. I can foresee disaster coming upon my schemes, although I have been exceedingly careful in checking and checking again my plans and measurements; I believe that I could recite the angles of descent, and the curvature of the line at any given point in the descent, even in the midst of my dreams; I have every reason to feel confident. But I know from past experience that there is always some detail, great or small, which I will forget, some problem best considered slowly, but needing to be overcome in haste when surrounded by navvies awaiting orders, or by an audience of the Railway Board.

Thursday, February 14, 1895.

Yesterday a terrible accident occurred, which resulted in the endangerment of human life and the destruction of property belonging to the Company. It happened as follows.

We awaited the arrival of the supply train. The weather was particularly unpleasant: the rain came down from the sky in vast sheets which soaked you through to the skin almost as soon as you had stepped out from shelter. There was a cruel wind from the south-west, which cut through sodden clothes as if they were not there. Iron froze in your hands. Wood became greasy and slipped from the grasp. The mud, which was being churned up underfoot, adhered thickly to our boots, so that there was a considerable effort even in walking. The mood of the navvies was not agreeable. The train was late. At about one o'clock, the sound of the engine was discerned through the wind. In expectation and out of sheer weariness, everyone stood back from their work, leaning on shovels and pick-axes, backs to the wind, pipes fiercely clenched. Several minutes passed and then the train came slowly down past the edge of Loch-droma. There was the customary screeching sound as brakes were applied. Less customary, however, was the rate at which the momentum of the train decreased – in short, the train did not slow down sufficiently to come to rest before the head of the line.

There were cries of warning from all by-standers, a look of panic on the faces of the driver and his stoker, a rush away from the site of the impending catastrophe. As if holding its breath, the wind itself appeared to cease and leave our ears open only to the sound of the brakes, the wail of iron upon iron, then the rustle of iron upon stone; then an almost majestic silence, during which the engine sank gracelessly into the bog beyond the end of the line.

By good fortune, neither of the men aboard the engine were in the least bit injured; it was the pride of the driver, a trustworthy man of twenty years' experience, which was so badly hurt. He stepped down from the tilted cab and surveyed the damage, almost in tears. The engine and its tender, and the first of the wagons, were beyond the reach of the iron rails, the engine now hissing sadly and sunk as if to its left knee in the bog, the wagon perched precariously upon a pile of ballast.

In the immediate aftermath, there was little that could be done. All hands worked to unload the wagons and to back them one by one up the line to a secure position in the passing-place at the bridge where, wedged and braked, they awaited their further fate. With the assistance of Gollan's skills and the navvies' musculature, the leading wagon was placed upon a short make-shift track and dragged back, as it were, from the precipice. This endeavour took the rest of that bitter and wet day. No further work can be done until the engine is removed from its ignominious bed.

I am obliged to sit down and write a report for the Board. But I know that the driver is held responsible for the maintenance of his engine, and so have to steer a course between blaming him, the atrocious weather conditions, and an Act of God, for the accident. I do not doubt that God and the weather will not be held accountable, but that the driver will not be seen again on this line.

Scarcely had I sat down to write this report than we were visited by Arthur Fowler, and – for once! – his illustrious father. That Sir John should encounter me now, of all times, when such a disaster had been visited upon my Railway! Sir John asked me briefly if the situation was secure, shook his head at the sight of the bemired engine, and then rattled in his cart back towards Braemore. He looked ill and I thought he had done well to come out in this weather. But such was fated to be my sole encounter with the greatest of engineers. What experiences we could have traded! Engineer to engineer, what a meeting of spirits! And yet we spoke not.

Memorandum to Mr. Kininmonth: When I met this morning with Mr. Gollan, I thought to ask him how this accident compared to the crash on the Penicuik Line. Was it as terrifying, was there as much damage, I wondered? Mr. Gollan looked at me puzzled, and then laughed loudly. "You did not believe that tall tale?" he asked, rather condescendingly as I thought. I confessed to him that I had. "Well," he smiled, "it was a grand invention, was it not?"

Needless to say, I was mortified with embarrassment at this revelation, for I had indeed believed every word.

Volume II:

From Talla to Jura
or,
The Island of Desolation.

Braemore – May, 1895.

During February, March and April of the year 1895, I further employed my skills as an engineer in resolving the problem of the descent at Braemore, so that the onward transport of passengers towards Ullapool might be achieved without inconvenience. The weather, however, was so atrocious that our progress was necessarily slow. Each attempt by day at creating a solid bed for the line was washed away by floods at night from the mountain, or sank relentlessly within hours into boggy ground. As a lasting reminder of the treacherous nature of the land, we had in our sight always the rusting hulk of the old steam-engine which had plunged into the bog in February: the very best efforts of navvy muscle and engineering mind had failed to extricate it. The wind howled almost without a moment of relief during the first two months of this early season, and April was to be remembered chiefly for the blizzards and sudden gales which fell upon us so rapidly from freezing blue skies and which within short minutes banished all the views to loch and wild mountain around.

In all this time, the navvies laboured silently. I was never privileged to see their faces, on those occasions when I walked among them to inspect the work. MacIvor and Gollan were far closer to these men than I. When the whistle blew to signal the end of a cold and wet day, the men would disappear as if into the Earth. Our distance from the Inn at Aultguish seemed not to act as a barrier to those men who wished to drown their sorrows. For those men too exhausted, perhaps, to trudge those weary miles at the end of such days, there was – I understood – liquid comfort closer to hand.

It had to be admitted, by even the most optimistic judge, that our excavations on the slope above Inverbroom seemed only to create a new river through the landscape, just another convenient route by which the infinite torrents of Wester-ross might reach the sea. After such tribulations, therefore, it was a proud moment for all when, on the last day of April, 1895, we stood at the head of Braemore and saw before us, leading down the left side of the glen and then curving round towards the head of the loch, the route which we proposed to ballast and make solid for our tracks. At last we could bring the railway to Ullapool!

On the very same day as we stood thus surveying our achievement, a letter came to me from the Board of the Railway Company, requesting my urgent attendance at their next meeting, to take place in Dingwall on the following Friday. I assumed – wrongly, as you will learn! – that the news of our efforts had reached our masters, and that further encouragement would be given to those who laboured in the wilderness for the great profit of the Great North-West of Scotland Railway Company and its many share-holders.

As if to lend some weight to my belief in the purpose of this summons, the third day of May dawned as sweet as any that a man in Scotland might see. The larks were up, tinkling invisibly in the mild sky, heavy bees crashed cheerily through the heather. When the train arrived from Garve not only did it afford the men an encouraging sight, but it was also ten minutes early, as if the very engine had been affected by the omnipresent feeling of spring. We arrived without incident at Garve, and I caught the next train into Dingwall, in time for the meeting of the Board, which was expected to commence at four o'clock precisely.

As I entered the Company's offices on Albert-street, I was suddenly struck by a cold feeling, a premonition of gloom. Outside, the sun shone and the pavements were busy. But when I pushed back the glazed heavy door and entered the chambers of my employers, I felt the dark dampness rush in around me. I shivered. The more so when I discovered that Mr. MacAllan, who serves as the doorkeeper and ancient messenger-boy for the office, was not present and that his small cupboard showed no recent signs of habitation. It was Mr. McGeorge MacAdam MacAulay who eventually emerged from the Boardroom, grunted coarsely when he saw me, and beckoned me in.

I had expected to see the entire Board of the Company. Instead, there was only MacAulay, sitting himself on the Chairman's heavy throne, surrounded by various ledgers and scraps of paper. Before him, on the vast polished table, was a pen in its ink-stand and a small tin strong-box.

"Mr. Kinninmoth," said MacAulay, scarcely looking up from his papers, "I will be brief. The Company is in a temporary financial embarrassment. The Board has therefore instructed me to halt the construction of the railway-line until new Capital can be raised."

He deigned at this point to look up at me, as if daring me to challenge his words. He made not the least attempt to offer me the respect due to a Railway Engineer; I, for my part, could not muster enough courage to demand it. Since my mind was benumbed by what he had just told me, I must have presented the aspect of a country idiot.

"Do you understand, Mr. Kinninmoth?"

I nodded and muttered some apology. Why I should have apologised to him, I can no longer say. In such situations as these, most men are mortal and seek the line of least offence. I find that it is not a simple thing to speak one's mind to someone who has the power of hiring and of sacking you. It was only on my way out of the offices, minutes later, that I summoned up internally the words with which I should have belaboured him.

"The Company does not expect to raise sufficient Capital until the autumn. Lady Matheson, Mr. Pirie and Sir Cosmo Coffin will spend the next few months engaged in this task. However, since Mr. Pirie is about to embark on a tour of France and Austria, we cannot expect immediate success. The Board has therefore instructed me to pay off Fairley of Inverness and the employees of the Company until we can re-commence our work." Here, Mr. MacAulay made a pretence of engaging in mental arithmetic, his narrow and contemptible head bent over some entries in a ledger. It was obvious to me that he already knew exactly how much I was to be paid: the man has never liked me, and must have dreamed of this occasion for months past. I will not give Mr. MacAulay the additional satisfaction of informing my readers how pitifully small my wages were to tide me over until the Board returned from its leisurely jaunts through the vineyards and pleasure-domes of France.

"The Company will continue to operate the railway service from Garve to Braemore," MacAulay informed me. He muttered to himself and then added, without looking at me: "I am under the strictest instruction from the Board to advise you that you may, should you wish, remain at Braemore Halt to occupy the post of temporary Station-Master, in recognition of past service." These last words were uttered between gritted teeth, clearly causing MacAulay some pain. But his parting shot brought him some relief: "But you may only remain there until the end of the month: a new man has been designated to take over the duties at that time."

As if in a dream, I took the wages, signed the receipt which Mr. MacAulay presented to me, and left the room. "Be so good as to close the street-door when you leave, Mr. Kinninmoth!" shouted MacAulay from his temporary seat of splendour. Throughout, the man had not even had the courtesy to give me my correct name!

For several hours I wandered around Dingwall, not knowing whether to return to Braemore, or whether to go straightway to Inverness to seek employment. The sun shone outside of me, and the cheerful people in the street talked in a language which, although my mother-tongue, I could not understand. All was as if through a glass. I stopped to take a cup of tea in the station-building, then determined to catch the next train back to Garve.

Our train pulled into Garve in the middle of the afternoon. It seemed a deliberate plan of MacAulay to bring me into Dingwall on a Friday, when he knew well that I would not be able to take the train back to Braemore Halt until the following Monday. Since the day was still mild, I set out along the stony road which led to Ullapool. As I reached the crossing of the road over the railway-line just short of Torr Breac, I looked up and down the road. There was no one in sight, beyond a few sheep. I made my way, therefore, on to the line and set the length of my stride to the interval of the sleepers. I marched nor'-westwards along my railway-line, my own achievement.

As I did so, what thoughts seethed through my mind! What a torrent of anger and of thoughts of retribution! I believe I spoke aloud, my fists swung out and my feet kicked viciously on several occasions. Anyone who might have seen me from the road would have been justified in reporting me to the District Lunacy Board.

What manner of world is it which allows the rule of Capital and of Capital's selfish worshippers to make or destroy the lives and ambitions of ordinary men? What society allows the manifest benefits, brought by a railway-line into the darkest spots of the land, to be started or stopped simply because they will make profits or make losses? Is it too much to ask that our Government and our rulers should think as decent men think, and allow the longer advantage to the poor and the weak to hold sway over the shorter advantage to plutocrats and possessors of material things?

By the time I had reached Aultguish, at a pace which must have startled the sheep of the moor and the larks of the air, I had, in my mind, cast down utterly the clay giant of Capital and smashed it to pieces with a Sword of Justice. MacAulay had been toppled into the Pits of Oblivion, and the Pirie and the younger Fowler had sunk beneath the Boiling Waters of Iniquity. But it was with a heavy heart that, at about ten o'clock, I finally reached Braemore Halt and the encampment. All was silent, and there was no sign of man, nor woman, nor any companionship. I retired to my bed, exhausted from my tramping.

I will not waste my readers' valuable time in detailing the events of the next few days; I will simply tell you that, on the Saturday, Mr. Gollan and Mr. MacIvor took their leave of me, intending to seek further employment on the rival railway which was now being built from Strome-ferry to Kyle. Many of the navvies followed them. Others vanished again into the hills and islands, to the south or to the west. Mrs. Macbeth was unapproachable; it could easily be surmised that she was brewing a potent curse against the Railway Company as she sat over her pots, stirring and muttering. Eventually, she too disappeared in the train back towards Garve.

I was left in sole charge of the station at Braemore Halt. As the train arrived, I performed with diligence the few duties laid upon me. But I had no one to cook for me and, more importantly, my mind was idle. Having lived and dreamed the construction of the railway for almost two years, it was an unutterable deprivation to stand idly for minutes or hours, to be incapable of taking the line down Braemore, to be not permitted to build the railway to Ullapool! For a day or two, I estimated the volume of useless piles of ballast, tapped iron rails with the hammer of futility, took measurements of despair. After a week of this, I was almost driven to despair. I took to asking travellers for their news, to reading their newspapers. More than once I made myself unwelcome to men of the cloth with whom I had sought intelligent conversation.

Among the passengers who arrived from Garve on the twentieth day of May was my old friend William Forbes, traveller in women's under-garments. He was in no hurry, so we sat and traded our news. When I outlined my present position, he eyed me keenly: "Now, can I suggest an enterprise which might attract you, Mr. Kininmonth? Although I am a native of Edinburgh, I have family in Peebles-shire. My sister, who lives in Innerleithen, has written to tell me of some construction works now beginning in that part of the country. It seems that the Edinburgh and District Water Trustees have received Assent to construct a reservoir in the Talla Glen, which will supply all the fresh-water needs of my native city. The waters of the Talla River are to be impounded, and a loch some two miles long will be formed. Water will be led from the reservoir to the city of Edinburgh by an aqueduct thirty-six miles in length."

Now, I had to confess that I knew as much of and cared as much for Peebles-shire and its villages as I knew of and cared for the invisible side of the moon. But my engineer's spirit was suddenly in the grip of an enthusiasm. What huge distances! What a grand social scheme, to bring the sparkling spring waters of Scottish hills to the very doorsteps, the very kitchens of the citizens of Edinburgh! A bank of drizzle passed relentlessly over us, accompanied by a cloud of tireless midges. I listened eagerly as Mr. Forbes continued.

"It seems that construction work on the dam will commence at the end of this month. But you may find it interesting, Mr. Kininmonth, that the first engineering task will be to lay down a railway between the villages of Broughton and Tweedsmuir, some ten miles, to facilitate the transport of materials and men. There – what do you think of that?"

My heart pounded, I felt the call of certainty. But I looked calmly at my old friend and shook his hand warmly.

"I think, Mr. Forbes, that I will leave as soon as I can for this place and try my luck with the Edinburgh and District Water Trustees! Thank you for your advice."

I did not think then to ask my informant where precisely

Broughton or Tweedsmuir lay: I trusted to my *Railway Gazetteer* to get me there.

I sent word to Dingwall that I wished to resign my post forthwith, and asked that my replacement should report for duty as soon as possible. As a result, I was approached the following week by Gilleasbuig Gillies, who had walked to Braemore from his home at Dundonnell to enter the service of the Great North-West of Scotland Railway Company. The man was taciturn in the extreme, and even when he did utter a word or two, he was impossible to understand. With the able assistance of his growling three-legged dog – named Albert after our Queen's late Consort – I was sure he would make a fine Station-Master.

That very afternoon, Tuesday, the twenty-eighth of May, anxious to be off to Tweedsmuir, I boarded the train back to Garve, to Dingwall, then to Inverness. Sparing no expense in my haste to engage in another historic engineering work, I immediately continued from Inverness by train to gain Edinburgh. In Edinburgh's huge cathedral of a station, over-looked by buildings of extreme grandeur, I obtained closer information on how to reach Broughton. It is a tribute to the advancing principle of railway engineering that I was able to reach the sedate village and meadows of Broughton barely thirty hours after leaving the wildest ancient rocks and bogs of the western Highlands.

For those unfamiliar with the situation of Broughton, I can tell you that you take the North British Line from Waverley Station (so named after Sir Walter Scott's brash young hero) to Eskbank in Mid-lothian, then through some bleak country to Peebles. From there you change on to the line operated by the Caledonian Railway, which will take you through Lyne and Stobo to Broughton. Should you so wish – and few do – you may continue on this train to the small town of Biggar.

Tweedsmuir – June, 1895.

Broughton is a comfortable village, pleasantly roosted at the foot of some fine hills. There appears to be much fertile farming land around it. A large estate lies to its south-east, and the railway-line to Biggar cuts across the middle of the town, near a cheerful stream which soon flows into the famous River Tweed. Arriving there quite late in the afternoon, I enquired after an inn; Mr. Johnston the Station-Master pointed out to me Burnside Cottage, which was owned by William Newbigging and run as a Temperance hotel. Mr. Newbigging, as a carrier, is enthusiastic about the new Water scheme, for he has found that his services at home and on the road will be much in demand.

As it happened, Mr. Newbigging was commissioned to take some goods up to Menzion Farm at Tweedsmuir on the morning after my arrival. I arranged with him that, for a modest fee, he would take me to Tweedsmuir, where I might expect to find the works-manager, Mr. Rankin. It was a dry enough day when we left Broughton, along the road which, my host advised me, led to Moffat in the high hills. Both knowledgeable and verbose to a fault, Mr. Newbigging told me all I ever wished to know about Broughton, about the Rachan Estate, about the projected railway-line, about the Talla Water Scheme, about − in brief − everything. If it did not impede the smooth flow of my narrative, I would pass on to you now my accumulated knowledge about the rival mole-catchers of Broughton, James Taylor and James Smith, and the long and bitter competition between them which did no credit to the small town, but seemed entirely to the advantage of the federated moles of Peebles-shire. No less scandalous, apparently, was the life of Mary Somerville, who opened and shut the level-crossing gates and much more besides.

What was of great interest to me, and therefore to my readers, was Mr. Newbigging's information on the projected railway-line between Broughton and Tweedsmuir. It would begin, so he told me, about a mile and one-half down-stream from Broughton, branching off southwards from the Caledonian Railway. It would be led through the wooded Rachan Estate and then, curving back towards the road on which we now travelled, would follow a course up the River Tweed on the meadows below the road. My guide pointed out the spot at which the railway would cross the River Tweed: we reached this after about two hours, as Mr. Newbigging's patient horse drew close to Tweedsmuir, not far beyond the Crook Inn.

Beyond the river, the projected path of the railway disappeared into the shadows of a great glen which opened up out of the sweeping hills. Up there, said Mr. Newbigging, was Talla. We descended between the fields at Tweedsmuir, and crossed a charming stone bridge over the Tweed. Since my guide had then to turn right to deliver to a farm up another glen, I alighted at the cross-roads. To my left, at a little distance, was a secluded church on a small hillock. Ahead of me stretched the Talla Glen: although there was no immediate sign of the new works, I could hear a distant noise and see the smoke from fires.

Although I arrived at Talla around noon, it was several hours before I managed to hunt down Mr. Rankin and to attract his attention. By then, I had been sent up hill and down glen by divers workmen and engineers, who exhibited a multitude of accents and dialects, but very little in the way of useful direction. I spent the entire afternoon trudging in frustration around the side of the Talla Glen, under the bare circle of the hills, up the north side to a farm at the head of the glen, where an agricultural man eyed me with great suspicion, down the south side and back to the encampment again.

By about four o'clock I had tracked down Mr. Rankin, but it was another hour before I could gain his attention, for he was an exceeding busy man indeed, rushing here and there, his pockets bulging with plans, a heavy notebook in his hand. It was fascinating to see him at work, talking to four or five different people at once, but never once losing the thread of each discussion, never once forgetting a question from perhaps five minutes previously. By the time he noticed me, I was in thrall to his efficiency.

"You, Sir!" he called over to me at last. "What can I do for you?"

I briefly introduced myself, and gave a swift summary of my experience on the Ullapool Railway-Line, and managed, within three gabbled sentences, to give a fair self-commendation. Or so I thought.

"Slow down, man, slow down! You tell me you have worked on the railway from Garve to Ullapool? How is it that I have never heard of such an undertaking? The extension of the Highland Line from Strome-ferry is the subject of many great reports. But – Ullapool? Are you being fantastical, man? Are you a Fictionist?!"

I was taken aback at this, and it must have shown on my face, for Mr. Rankin pointed his pencil at me in an interested manner.

"Come and see me this evening at seven o'clock, Sir, and tell me your tale again." With that, he turned his attention to a further clutch of emissaries and petitioners, and left me standing in the cold evening.

I had enough wit left to enquire of a curious by-stander where Mr. Rankin resided, and was advised that he held possession of a new wooden shed, humorously named "Victoria Lodge", on a hill over-looking the entire encampment. I moved up to a point some fifty yards from this shed then settled myself down to wait. When the hands of my watch showed six o'clock, the chaos which prevailed down below began to lessen somewhat, as work-men slid off into the gathering dusk. The silence of the glen began to return. At a half-past six, Mr. Rankin let himself into his "lodge". He emerged at seven o'clock promptly, obviously refreshed and smoking a pipe. I approached.

"Ah, well now, the engineer from Ullapool," he said, adopting a tone which, I confess, annoyed me. My face, once again, must have betrayed me, for he invited me to sit down on his doorstep and tell him my tale. This I did, in a few brief sentences, stressing the engineering difficulties of the Garve to Ullapool Line and my achievements in overcoming them. This time, he seemed more inclined to believe in the railway-line. I also told him, in more or less accurate terms, of the praise my work had received from Sir John Fowler himself and the local newspapers.

"In short, Mr. Rankin," I concluded, at last feeling some courage, "I believe that my engineering expertise can be of considerable use to you here at Talla."

Mr. Rankin puffed at his pipe for a few moments. At last he spoke: "My employer, Mr. Young of Edinburgh, allows me to take on anyone I feel is fit for the job. Now, I already have a well-qualified man working for me down at Broughton, where the railway-line begins, and I have no intention of replacing him. But it seems to me that we could make this job a shorter one by building the line from this end as well. The sooner the line is built, the sooner we can bring up the men and the supplies we need for the dam." He knocked out the embers of his pipe on the step. "Mr. Kininmonth, you will start your work to-morrow morning at eight o'clock sharp."

I leaped to my feet and thanked him profusely.

"I will not disappoint you, Mr. Rankin," I told him.

"Neither you shall, Mr. Kininmonth. Now, let me find you some quarters for the night and you can make more permanent arrangements for yourself in the morning."

At eight o'clock the following day, I sought out Mr. Rankin. My task was a simple one: to drive a track up the north side of the glen, just above the height to be attained by the dammed waters, as far as the farm at Talla Linn Foot. It was this farm I had reached the previous afternoon on my wild-goose chase, so I appeared intelligent enough to Mr. Rankin in asking questions about one or two land-marks on the way. This track was to be the foundation for a tram-way, or narrow-gauge railway, to transport men and materials to various points the length of the reservoir.

I did not pretend to understand the methods by which a reservoir should be constructed. To a simple man such as myself, it was a matter of building a dam of convenient height, thereby stopping up the waters, and then leading those waters by pipe in the direction of Edinburgh. Dam-building and pipe-laying were not in my field of expertise. The mechanical problems of impounding the rushing streams of Talla and Games-hope – such was the intention of the Trustees – were of interest but of no concern to me. My practical interest was in clearing the track at the height indicated. At the north-west end of this track, where the encampment now stood, I would join with the railway-line now being constructed from Broughton.

I soon found myself in the very thick of matters which I now knew well, after my embattled years in the Ross-shire glens. I had a team of navvies, with whom I could sometimes find agreement in the work that had to be done. But I frequently found myself regretting my Railway-Line at Braemore.

Among the men who were to work for me, I found two whose very presence was disturbing. Their name was Finlay – John Finlay was an elderly man, James of about my own age. I could find nothing to criticise in their work: even the efforts of the older man were favourably comparable to those of many of the younger men. But I noticed that few talked to the Finlays and none would seek them out. It seemed that this antipathy was shared by the Finlays themselves, who always sat apart at meal-times, and worked apart if they could. The pair, I was given to understand, were uncle and nephew.

Their outward appearance was such that I made it a rule never to be with them alone and out of sight of some third party.

Due to my elevated position as engineer, I had managed to find reasonably comfortable lodgings in the village of Tweedsmuir, with Mr. Yellowlees the school-master. It was in Mr. Yellowlees' house that I was given verbal portraits of all the signifying people of the area – Mr. Alexander Gunn, of Crook Inn; Mr. Carruthers, the farmer at Menzion; the Reverend John Dick; and many others. In return, I would tell Mr. Yellowlees – and his wife, a mouse of a woman who rarely spoke and never gave an opinion – of the day's events up at the encampment or in the Talla Glen.

"Ah, Mr. Kininmonth," Mr. Yellowlees would lament, "I have my doubts about the decency of this whole enterprise. There are many ill-educated men on the roads now."

"But, surely," I would reply, "the health of the citizens of Edinburgh, imbibing this pure water from your hills, is more important than any short interruption to your quiet village lives?"

"Oh, I cannot disagree with you there, Mr. Kininmonth. Sir Graham himself has extolled to me the virtues of a pure water-supply for those poor unfortunates."

(This was Sir Graham Montgomery, owner of various properties including the Games-hope and Menzion estates, also the Chairman of Peebles-shire County Council. His judgement of the whole affair might be favourably tinted by the promised sale of parts of his properties to the Edinburgh Trustees.)

"No, Mr. Kininmonth," went on my host. "But just think of the numbers of undesirable people who will be brought in to this part of the world! I am advised that it will be ten years before the reservoir is completed. Ten years in which we shall be overwhelmed by drunkards and vagabonds! We may never rest easy in our beds! Our churchyard will become full with the corpses of ne'er-do-wells! And we must surely see a police-station built in Tweedsmuir to guard us against all the thieves and rascals! Oh, Mr. Kininmonth, you cannot imagine to yourself how a Christian man fears for law and order in these dark days in Tweedsmuir!"

I sought to re-assure the school-master by telling him that my own experience of these vagabonds and rascals had generally been surprisingly pleasant. I told him of my recent life in the Highlands. While conceding none of my points, Mr. Yellowlees rewarded my contribution by commanding his wife to produce a fresh pot of tea and some home-made scones. (Mrs. Yellowlees, I might remark now, was the worst cook with whom I have ever boarded. Never a night went by without flames leaping from the kitchen range amid the pungent stench of carbonised meat or vegetable, accompanied by Mrs. Yellowlees' whimpers of rage and impotence. But her scones, however strange this might seem, were delicious.) In a warm flush of conversation, I then told him that there might, of course, be exceptions – take, for example, the two Finlays . . .

At this, Mr. Yellowlees threw up his hands in horror.

"My good Sir! You cannot mean that you are working with that James Finlay and his uncle? The Good Lord preserve us! What a wicked pair those two are, to be sure! Mr. Thorburn had to let them go, in the end."

It appeared from the jumble of half-finished anecdote and heavy-larded opinion which followed, liberally interrupted by more cups of tea, that the Finlays had a poor reputation in the county. The pair had turned up out of nowhere in the summer of 1893. It seemed that some letter of recommendation to the Earl of Wemyss, as land-owner, had accompanied them for they were straightway taken on as shepherds by Mr. Thorburn at Talla Farm.

At first, the pair had attracted little attention. They were found to be hard-working and taciturn. If there was striding about the hills to do, then the younger Finlay was the man to do it. If sheep were caught in a blizzard, then James Finlay would leave his fireside without a word, rescue the dumb animals from the snow-swept hills, and return to his fireside no further put out than if he had just poked his head out of the door. Even the uncle was capable of out-lasting the other shepherds or farm-workers when it came to hard labour.

But during the spring of 1895, Thorburn had begun to receive complaints from his neighbours that James Finlay was undertaking curious practices upon the bleak hill-tops over-looking Games-hope and Talla. From what Mr. Yellowlees told me, it seemed that Finlay, when he was out after the sheep, had begun to delineate shapes upon the barren moors, with stones from the drystane dykes which ran endlessly over the hills. At first, no one could make sense of the shapes he was setting out. It was impossible to see anything in his edifices that resembled either a round sheepfold or a straight line, which were the only shapes known to the people of that region.

George Thomson and his two brothers "up at the castle" at Games-hope were particularly enraged, for the demolition of the dykes by Finlay, to obtain his materials, allowed the Games-hope sheep to stray over to Fruid. On more than one occasion, there was violence, or the threat of violence, between shepherds on the hills over-looking Talla.

When confronted by Thorburn and asked to explain his actions, Finlay was enigmatic.

"It is the Island of Desolation," was his sole reply.

This reply had been too much for Mr. Yellowlees to bear. "Not in all my born days," he blustered, as his wife poured me more tea than I believed my body could decently cope with, "Not in all my born days have I ever heard the like! The Island of Desolation, indeed! Of course, Mr. Thorburn was fair affronted and told him so. But it was to no avail. Such is the hard-hearted nature and the unnatural pride of these men that James Finlay refused to do anything about the walls. Mr. Thorburn is a good man and his drystane dykes are the envy of all of Peebles-shire. I do believe, Mr. Kininmonth, that the times of radicals and of criminals are upon us, as the good Mr. Dick has oft-times said. Pass our guest another scone, my dear."

Aside from the outrage they caused with ill-considered dyking, the Finlays had made themselves few friends by introducing to the community a new kind of cabbage, which they grew in some shady ground by the farm. It was not like any cabbage anyone from these parts had ever seen. "Not one of the Good Lord's cabbages, if you understand me, Mr. Kininmonth. The Kernel Cabbage, the Finlays called it. Naturally, I have named it the Infernal Cabbage!" Mr.

Yellowlees laughed uproariously at his own wit, as a school-master often does.

Tweedsmuir folk regarded this cabbage with extreme suspicion. It was in all probability a plant cultivated by the Wee Man himself. The Reverend Mr. Dick had very divinely decried it from the pulpit, while Mr. Yellowlees had very rationally denied its very existence. Mr. Yellowlees' denial did not stop him from accepting a sack-full of them for the Casual Sickhouse at Menzion, with subsequent beneficial results for the inmates. "The taste was dreadful, but the infirm, Mr. Kininmonth, knew no difference," he explained. He ate none himself. "If the Good Lord had intended for me to eat this Kernel Cabbage," he argued, "He would have granted it to me in my own garden. I have a fine garden, have I not, Mr. Kininmonth?"

I readily agreed. It was only a shame that the fresh vegetables he grew there had to be sacrificed at night upon the smoking altar of the kitchen-range. Cabbage in particular will burn with the most appalling aroma. Nonetheless, red-currants, whose distillation into jelly we now enjoyed with scones, were a blessing of the Good Lord upon gardens in general and on Mr. Yellowlees in particular.

One Sunday, in late June, I attended the church service with Mr. Yellowlees. I found myself yawning surreptitiously and almost causing a scandal by nodding off in the middle of the Reverend Dick's sermon. His theme was "Christian Forgiveness", but it seemed this ideal only allowed for the forgiveness of other Christians of the Tweedsmuir parish, and was somewhat merciless on anyone – Christian or otherwise – from outside Peebles-shire. Fortunately for my relationship with Mr. Yellowlees, and for the reputation of the Water Trustees, whom I might have been said to represent in the tiny church, I gave every appearance of remaining awake throughout the morning.

After the third quarter-hour of the divine's sermon had commenced, my wandering gaze was startled by a familiar face. Over there in a dark corner of the mote-filled church, surely that was Mr. Rinck the itinerant preacher? Astonished, I sat up hurriedly and tried to lean forward without attracting attention – to no avail, for Mr. Yellowlees immediately tapped my arm with his hymnary and glared at me as if I were a badly-behaved school-boy. I studied Rinck surreptitiously; he shook his head pityingly at everything which the Reverend Dick had to say; he was in the company of a couple of like-minded souls, who kept behind him in the shadows.

I spent the remaining twenty minutes or so of the sermon in wondering what Rinck was doing here and whether he recognised me. As it was, I had no opportunity of renewing our acquaintance, since he vanished without trace, as soon as the church-doors were opened, whereas I was impeded by the necessity of accompanying my host in his stately procession from the place of worship to his home.

Over a bowl of luke-warm soup that might have heated only an Esquimau, Mr. Yellowlees asked me if I had noted the "radicals" in the church. When I confirmed hesitantly that perhaps I had, he confided to me, in the most sorrowful tones, that one of the "creatures of that man Rinck" was Charles Bicknell, erstwhile pupil-teacher in the school. "A promising young man, Mr. Kininmonth, but too easily led from the path of righteousness and into the slough of liberalism. But, you see, he is from Carlisle." And with that, as sufficient explanation of the fall from grace of the youth, he turned his attentions to potatoes and mutton blasted in the oven as in one of Mr. Bessemer's reducing furnaces.

Tweedsmuir – July, 1895.

I came across Rinck more and more frequently over the next few weeks, sometimes down in the men's encampment, on Sundays in the kirk, sometimes even striding out on the road or over the hills on some holy mission. I could not discover where he lived – I supposed it to be the smoky encampment. Almost always, he was accompanied by two or three dark-looking men, among whom was – as I soon discovered – young James Finlay. I had no chance of conversing with Rinck; he had greeted me briefly a number of times, but I never knew if it were my moral or physical welfare with which he was concerned.

One Sunday, early in July, having once more seen Rinck in the church, my curiosity was aroused sufficiently to wrap up warmly on a cloudy afternoon and go out in search of the man. My instincts advised me to proceed up to the hills at the head of the Talla Glen;

and I was right to do so, for I soon detected Rinck and two men — whom I soon recognised as the Finlays; they were walking away from me with some swiftness.

We reached the head of the glen, where Mr. Thorburn's farmhouse stands. The three men did not pause a moment, but turned towards a side-glen, which I now know to be Games-hope, where a clattering burn comes out of the hills. Apparently without taking any extra breath, they crossed a rather rickety bridge and proceeded to scale a huge hill which frowned over the left bank of the burn. I discovered later that this was a hill known as Erie Hill, no doubt the home of eagles or other soaring birds of prey. As we ascended — for I could not let up now — I felt my heart pounding and my insides churning. My breath began to falter. This pace could not be set by men, but by the Devil himself! It was not natural for men to so ascend such a steep slope as if it had been a stroll up Leith-walk!

Between the pace and the natural curve of the hill, I soon lost sight of the three men. Nonetheless, I pushed myself onward as best I could manage. Some sheep were startled by my laboured passage and careered with bouncing fleeces down precipitous slopes.

At last, as I felt a cold breeze signalling that I had reached some lofty summit, I stumbled abruptly upon James Finlay. I barely noticed him until he rose up before me from out of the heather, where he had been sitting. My stomach leaped in terror, for surely — I thought to myself — my last moment had come, and I would be left a bludgeoned corpse upon a hill which few men frequented. With this thought, I summarily fell to the ground, nauseous and shaking.

Nothing happened. I opened my eyes at length and beheld Finlay. "It is a fine day, Sir, but a steep hill," he said, as politely as if we had met in the gardens of Princes-street.

I muttered something and then stood up to recover some dignity. We were at the windy top of a broad hill, with the wide sky all around us. Finlay gazed down into the saddle which lay between us and another hill to the east. He was looking down at his drystane dyke. A continuous wall meandered around the hillside, eventually coming back on itself. It most closely resembled a gigantic stag with a panoply of antler and a shortened body. At its widest part, it must have been about a hundred yards in breadth. The antlers were many-branched and as complex in their design as a maze. The whole dyke was perhaps a mile or two in length, if a man was minded to walk the complete circumference.

I was more used to seeing either long straight lines in such dykes, or the neat safe circle of a sheepfold, and was astounded.

But I could not rest long in my astonishment, for I was then witness to a gathering of men and women upon this vast hill. Twenty, perhaps thirty, had already sat down around the tall unmistakable figure of Melchior Rinck; many of them appeared to be men from the Talla works; but a similar number were still arriving in small groups from other points of the compass. Young Mr. Bicknell hovered around the preacher. It was evident to me, a man who has read eagerly of the Covenanters in the works of Sir Walter Scott, that I was observing a gathering of the common people to hear the preacher. Finlay, I deduced, was standing sentry over this gathering, lest the Authorities came to crush it − I expected instantly the sound of galloping horse and scything sword, such was my dislocation from my time!

I decided to approach the crowd and listen.

Mr. Rinck was preaching a sermon based on the Second Book of the Prophet Daniel in the Old Testament, which deals with King Nebuchadnezzar's dream. I cannot tell you now the very words used by Mr. Rinck on that windy July afternoon, but must summarise some of the sermon with the assistance of notes which I scribbled down on my return home.

"There appeared to the King in his dream a huge and fearful image, which was shattered into pieces by a stone from a mountain. This terrible image tells us of the Ages of Man.

"The first Age is depicted by the golden head, that was the Empire of Babel; the second is the silver breast and arms, that was the Kingdom of the Medeans and Persians. The third was the Empire of the Greeks, which dazzled by its cleverness, depicted by brass; the fourth, the Roman Empire, which was won by the sword and was an empire of oppression. But the fifth is that Empire which we now have before us: it is also of iron and would like to oppress, but it is also of clay, as we see, stuck together by that plain hypocrisy which creeps and crawls over the whole Earth.

"For now a stone will come tumbling down upon the image, as a rock does from Carlavin Hill, and the iron and the clay and the bronze and the silver and the gold will be shattered into fragments and swept away entirely like the scree upon the hillside.

"Oh, dear friends, how splendidly the Lord will shatter the old pots with an iron bar. Crash, smash, crash, smash! For the stone from the mountain has grown large. You poor folk and you down-trodden see it much clearer than your rulers. Yes, the stone is large and has become what the foolish world long feared. God over-whelmed the world when He was young; so what shall He now do that He is so great and mighty?

"God will judge men in the last days, and His name will be rightly praised. He will free them of their shame and pour out His spirit over all that is flesh, and our sons and daughters shall prophesy and shall have dreams and visions. Therefore, a new Daniel must arise, and explain to you your revelations, and he must march at the head.

"Aye, but the stone torn from the hills is now grown large! Listen! The poor navigators and labourers see it so very clearly. Yes, God be praised, the stone has grown large! Now do as Christ has commanded. Drive out his enemies from the Elect, for you are the instrument for that. God is your shelter and will teach you to fight against His enemies, as is written in the Eighteenth Psalm. He will make your hands anxious for the battle and He will support you. The weeds must be uprooted from the vineyard of God in the time of the harvests, and then the beautiful golden wheat will gain firm root and grow straight. And the angels, who sharpen your sickles for you, are the serious servants of God, who refine the zealousness of God's wisdom. Listen to your dreams and strike down the false believers! For we are those who stand at the End of Time!"

There was much more of this, and great enthusiasm from the congregation. I believe that the sermon lasted equally as long as one of the Reverend Dick's; but here, either because it was so filled with conviction or simply because a cold wind had sprung up and the sky had clouded over, it was not possible to slumber. As the rain began, Rinck ended his sermon and, having passed out small pamphlets to those assembled, dropped down into the Fruid Glen. Then the crowd vanished into the moor and over the edge of the hill, back to their own hidden troubles in the twilight.

In the gathering gloom, I lost sight of James Finlay. I was left alone with my thoughts, but not for long, for the cold air and the dampness of the ground were seeping into my clothes. I did not wish to catch pneumonia, nor any chill which might put me at the mercy of Mrs. Yellowlees' broths, so I set off back to my lodgings.

"You'll have been out walking on the hills, then, Mr. Kininmonth?" asked Mr. Yellowlees, as his wife served up a mutton-stew with the consistency and taste of soap.

I prevaricated. "Indeed, Mr. Yellowlees, I had a very pleasant walk up Games-hope and climbed about the towers and gateways of the castle there."

It was only when Mr. Yellowlees launched into a lesson on Geology and the Border Ballads, lasting some two hours, that I came to realise that the 'castle' in Games-hope is only a formation of rocks out-cropping from the steep sides of the glen, and not a castle in which a baron or a lord might sit. I stood corrected, embarrassed, an errant school-boy found bearing false witness; but I fear I retained none of the interesting information he imparted to me. My spirit was with the Covenanting celebrants of Erie Hill.

Eventually, I found an opportunity to excuse myself, after so many physical exertions, and escape to my room. From my belongings, I un-earthed a great treasure which I had acquired in Edinburgh in May, while awaiting my connecting train to Peebles. This was a fine Order Book manufactured by Mr. Whyte of Edinburgh. I admit I was pleased with the purchase, for it gave me the opportunity to write down notes and questions on all the many mysteries of Tweedsmuir.

The "Order Book No. 55" contained an index at the front, divided into all the letters of the alphabet (excepting "I" and "Q"), and three hundred and thirty-four pages for notes thereafter. I organised my thoughts according to this excellent arrangement. Under "R", I noted, "Question: How does Rinck come to be here?" Under "F", "Investigate: What is the history of the Finlays?" Under "T", "Talla and Tweedsmuir – see pages 120 to 122", where I recorded my more recent observations. This is truly a fine organiser of thoughts for an Historian – I would heartily recommend it to others!

Pleased with my scientific categorisation, I also noted under "K", "Kininmonth – see pages 1 to 5." And on those numbered pages I set down all the things which had so far marked out my life. In a fit of Taxonomy, I wrote down another reference under "Y", "Mr. Yellowlees – see pages 50 to 51", but I did not dare note down any thoughts on those pages, for fear the man discover, and take his red correcting-pencil to, my Order Book. Recipes for soups and meat dishes were also omitted, although I was wilfully tempted to record these under "S" for Smoke. This did not prevent me from allocating pages for the Edinburgh and District Water Trustees ("E"); I found sufficient space (pages 201 to 229 inclusive) for Mr. MacAulay (there was a tab for "Mc" separate from "M", which I thought was a strong convenience; but I found the lack of "I" and "Q" disturbing – what if an Edinburgh shop received an order from Her Majesty? Or would occasional note-takers, such as myself, have no thought of "Iniquities", or "Injustices", or need for "Questions"? And why exclude "I" but include "Z"? I detected either some flaw in manufacture or some hidden arrangement of things which only shop-keepers would understand).

Tweedsmuir – Summer, 1895.

Throughout the months of July, August and September, my energies were taken up with the construction of the railway-line alongside the invisible loch. Apart from Sundays, I woke early at my lodgings each day, ate a hearty breakfast of burnt porridge, hard-boiled eggs and lacerating toast before departing to the scene of my labours. I would return, cold and usually soaked through, in the evening. On several occasions I had sufficient energy to make some notes in my Order Book and the pages were rapidly filling with questions, answers and observations.

I was pleased to note that our line advanced tolerably well along the side of the steep glen. It was difficult to imagine, looking down into the boggy deeps of Talla where the river twisted and rattled towards Tweedsmuir, that all of this would one day be covered by a serene weight of water, all for the perpetual health of the people of Edinburgh. What of the circular sheep-folds and the walls, the small huts which were dotted about down there? Already the earth-works for the dam had begun. The volume of water which would be impounded, and whose surface would lap at the very edges of my Railway, which was suspended so high in the air, filled me with awe. How mighty was Man upon Earth!

How mighty, yet how short-lived his exploits! In the last week of September, our brief stretch of line was completed. It had barely tested my skills, scarcely stretched my imagination or powers of planning. It was a neat enough line, providing a useful service. The ground under it was solid, the ballast tidy and the rails straight. I knew – I had gone over every foot of the way myself, day after day, delaying the hour when my work should be finished and I would have no more to do. I knew the railway would last just as long as was needed, and would then be left to rust into the ground. This was not to be the place where a Kininmonth monument would be erected by subscription.

There was no other hope here – I had finished the job asked of me by Mr. Rankin, and now I had to be paid off. To that end, there was a short and rather embarrassed interview with him in his shed on Saturday, the twenty-eighth of September. He thanked me, rather stiffly I believe, for my good work, and handed me a letter of recommendation with my final wages, then enquired after my future plans. When I told him I had none, he turned aside and began to toy with some paperwork, as if to dismiss me. Once more I had to scratch for secure employment: how low was the trade of Engineer debased and devalued in these forsaken hills and glens!

Having no plans for myself, I resolved to sit a while in Tweedsmuir to enjoy the surrounding hills and then to seek employment in the Dominion or the Cape, perhaps New Zealand. It is my belief that in those distant lands, my immortal works could yet be carried out.

I had hoped for a few quiet weeks of contemplation and rest, but gained only eight short days. For, on Sunday, the sixth of October, 1895, there was a fateful occurrence in the church at Tweedsmuir.

As was usual, Mr. and Mrs. Yellowlees and I were sitting wrapped in our own simple thoughts while the Reverend Dick benefited us with the full scope of his orthodoxy. As was usual, I saw Rinck and two of his co-religionists keeping out of sight at the side of the church: I noted that one of the two was the younger Finlay; the other I now recognised as the disgraced tutor, Bicknell. But I confess that, since my thoughts were many miles away, I did not at first observe what then occurred – I can only use deductive reasoning to present a clear picture of the drama.

Some twenty minutes into Mr. Dick's weekly revelation and judgement of the sins of other folk, Rinck stepped forward and made his way swiftly to the steps of the pulpit. His two friends joined him, then turned to face the congregation, while Rinck himself ascended to the pulpit and pushed Mr. Dick roughly to one side. It was Dick's high-pitched and panic-struck remonstration which called me back from my dreams; simultaneously, I believe, the souls of the remainder of Mr. Dick's flock migrated back whence they had wandered, and numberless truly were the expressions of outrage.

"Consider Mr. Dick, Dr. Lick-Spittle, the creature of the tyrants!" shouted Rinck in his thick accent. "He cowers before the very onslaught of God's Word, which rips through him, root and branch!"

After the initial astonishment of the congregation, some farmers of the district stood up as a body. But their eruption from the pews into the aisle was so badly executed that four of them fell together several yards short of the pulpit-steps, an entangled roaring mass of thick legs and ill-fitting suits, barring the way to their friends.

"Behold!" exclaimed Rinck, now the master of Mr. Dick's collar, "how the vermin wriggle and squirm in one heap, like the newts and the eels! Such will be the end of all those who try to serve two Masters, both God and Man! And now I will take this servant of the Godless to the ice-cold waters of the Tweed, and pass through him the torrents of pain and retribution, until he suffers the true revelation of the Fear of God alone!"

I am sure Mr. Rinck would have carried out his threat to bathe the Reverend Dick in the river nearby, had the farmers' wives not taken a surprising initiative; they stepped over the still-struggling bodies of their men-folk; gained the foot of the pulpit; thrust aside Finlay and Bicknell as if they had been two flimsy hat-stands in a tea-room; and stormed the short flight of stairs. Rinck, seeing the turn of the tide, wisely left Mr. Dick reeling into the arms of the on-coming phalanx of vengeful women, clambered over the edge of the pulpit and ran full-tilt down the aisle, closely followed by his complotters. They were out of the doors and into the Sabbath morning before anyone had the wit to stop them. Mr. Yellowlees threw himself into the aisle, too late to catch them – I believed his intervention was deliberately badly-timed.

Meanwhile, in the kirk, chaos ruled for several minutes, until, doctored and excited beyond toleration by the attentions of the women, Mr. Dick recovered more than fully and once again took command of the situation. As a result of which, our ears were assailed for a further hour and one-half on the wicked ways of radicals, Fenians, foreigners, sinners, Highlanders and navvies; much to the dissatisfaction of the men-folk in the congregation of Tweedsmuir. After barely thirty minutes, even the fidgeting of those women with roasts in the oven was beyond endurance, but they sat and coughed loudly until it was all over. I am sure that many felt, like myself, that we would have preferred the ducking of Mr. Dick to this ordeal.

At about eight o'clock in the evening of that fateful day, Mrs. Yellowlees and I were sitting quietly, trying to digest some under-cooked potatoes; the master of the house had gone out some time ago to share his accumulated learning with the Sunday Evening Discursive Bible Circle. Since the excitements of the morning, Mrs. Yellowlees had been nervous at the least sound, and the rain beating on the roof did little to calm her. So, when we heard the muffled sound of shouting and struggling outside the front door, she fairly screamed.

"My goodness, Mr. Kininmonth, who can that be?" she demanded of me.

I could barely formulate a guess.

"Shall we open it, Mr. Kininmonth, do you think? What if it is one of those Irish navvies come to murder us in our sleep? Or that man Rinck in his madness! Oh, Mr. Yellowlees warned us all that it would come to this!"

I tried to reason that, since we were not asleep, the Irish Navvy might not pursue his project, but to no avail. At length, since the knocking outside and Mrs. Yellowlees' whimpering inside both persisted, I stood up, marched to the door and flung it open. My breath left me involuntarily – what a sight greeted me!

"Oh, Mr. Kininmonth!" shrieked Mrs. Yellowlees, as she fainted limply into my arms.

Instead of some blood-thirsty gang of navvies, against whom I would not have been able to put up a fight, I beheld the wettest pair of figures I have ever seen. One I eventually recognised as Mr. Rinck, his mane of white hair plastered about his head, his clothes dripping as if he himself had fallen into the foaming Tweed. No less magnificent in moistness was the other figure, whom I at last identified as Mr. Yellowlees. The two men seemed locked in a deadly embrace.

"Leave me go, you scoundrel, or I will dash your brains out!" commanded Yellowlees, trying to prise Rinck's hands from his coat, without at the same time releasing his own hold on the preacher's clothing or his own walking-stick. From appearance alone, it was hard to tell whether the school-master was in the act of arresting Rinck or whether Rinck was in the act of murdering the school-master. Beholding this, I was faced with a horned dilemma, for I could condone neither the arrest nor the murder.

"Help me, man!" shouted Yellowlees finally. Some instinct, of which I am now deeply ashamed, made me respond without thinking. I laid Mrs. Yellowlees carefully on the rug before managing to free her husband's coat of Rinck's strong fingers. Almost immediately I had done so, however, I also had to prevent the school-master from thrashing the preacher with his stick, by stepping in between the two.

"Oh, Mr. Yellowlees, what is happening?" gasped his wife weakly, having regained her wits.

"I found this villain skulking beside our red-currant bushes and now I demand to know what he means by it! What do you mean by it, Sir?" continued Yellowlees, recovering his usual over-bearing manner in the comfortable light of his own porch. "Explain yourself before a constable is summoned. What were you doing out there on a night such as this? And don't try to deceive me, for I have considerable experience of the ways of criminals!"

"I came to speak with Mr. Kinnimunt," said Rinck. "And my purpose in speaking with him is not your affair, Sir."

Mr. Yellowlees almost exploded with wrath. "Not my affair, not my affair? – after your criminal acts this morning, Sir? The people of Tweedsmuir will not tolerate this behaviour, you blackguard! Your affair is my affair, Mr. Rinck – or whatever you call yourself!"

Ill-advisedly, I felt it was time for me to intervene, much to Mr. Yellowlees' indignation.

"Come, Mr. Yellowlees," I argued in my most reasonable tone, such as I reserve for growling dogs which might block my path and against whom I have no greater weapon than Reason, "if Mr. Rinck wishes to speak to me, surely he might do so. He has done nothing wrong. I expect he was sheltering in the bushes from the rain, quite innocently . . . "

"Innocently!" Mr. Yellowlees turned quite red. "Innocent people do not lay hands upon men of God in their very pulpits! Innocent people do not step out on wild nights such as this and threaten the lives of passers-by!"

I could not help but point out that Mr. Yellowlees had done precisely the latter. As I look back on that wet night, I marvel at how rapidly my wit functioned under those circumstances, and still smile at my own words. The man popped and rasped but could think of nothing else to say. Finally, I managed to put on a large coat and steer Rinck down the path, leaving the school-master of Tweedsmuir to pour a strong cup of tea upon the fires of his outrage.

When we had withdrawn from the house into the driving rain, some ten or a dozen yards, I turned to Rinck.

"For Heaven's sake, man, what were you doing in the bushes there?" I asked him. He did not reply but simply signed that I should follow him. There was no reason on Earth that I should do so; but follow him I did.

I was within a short time drenched to the skin, my heavy coat pouring with water. I could barely see, since water streamed from my hair and stung my eyes; but I did not miss the fact that, as we came to a copse of trees on the Moffat road, the younger Finlay came out of the night to join us. He pulled me solicitously into the shelter of a half-ruined out-house. Inside sat the elder Finlay. At that moment, I feared greatly for my life, and wondered whether Yellowlees had yet telegraphed for a policeman.

"Mr. Kinnimunt," said Rinck as a preamble, "had I listened to the faint-hearted Bicknell, who has this day succumbed to the Fear of Man and slithered back to England, I would not be meeting you tonight." Selfishly, I cursed the inconstancy of youth. Mr. Rinck went on: "I know you to be a man who acts from reason and not from passion, from thought and not from spirit. But that will change if the Lord permits you to suffer the living witness."

I thought to protest that a Railway Engineer such as myself could not act from anything other than scientific reasoning and the common sense of my upbringing; but I held my tongue and waited to see what I would be offered.

I shall keep my record of his explanations brief, for he rambled somewhat down the paths of the Prophets and in the by-ways of St. John's Revelation as the wind and the rain shook the very boards of our shelter. He gave me to understand that he intended a return to Ullapool, believing that he would have more success among the common people of that town than among the "thin-tongued vipers" of Tweedsmuir. There would be a "Citadel" built in Ullapool, a fortress in which the Godly could gather at the end of the world. "And you, Mr. Kinnimunt," he grasped my arm, "you will build us a railway."

My attention had wandered during this entire speech, but the final word immediately focused my attention. "A railway?" I asked. "But where?"

"From Ullapool to Inverness," he informed me. "The railway will be used by the Elect to reach our Citadel, and thereafter to help build an Earthly Paradise in that part of Scotland."

Despite some feelings of doubt, I confess that I paid close attention thereafter to everything that Rinck had to tell me. He advised me that he had some business to transact in Edinburgh and Glasgow, before he returned to the north-west, business that he felt would greatly enhance the prospects of the Elect and their railway.

"But first, Mr. Kinnimunt, we would ask you to help John Finlay here. He wishes to return to his birthplace, and needs someone to guide him there. I think that your knowledge of Scotland would be useful." I was flattered by this request, but asked where Mr. Finlay was born.

At this question, Rinck looked at me in some surprise. "Has Mr. Finlay not yet told you his story, Mr. Kinnimunt?" he enquired, eyeing me closely as if I were either a fool or a liar or both. I replied that I had no idea what was the history of the Finlays. At this, Rinck murmured something to James Finlay; who listened carefully, appraised me for several seconds, then nodded a consent.

"James Finlay here," continued Rinck, "will pass to you a book which contains the history of his family. We ask only that you read this book and, having read it, decide whether you will help us. Will you do that, Mr. Kinnimunt?"

I muttered "Kininmonth" at him, in the forlorn hope that he might at least pronounce my name properly, before agreeing to his terms. It seemed a small ransom to pay to escape from these madmen and retire to my own warm bed.

"And having decided, Mr. Kinnimunt," said Rinck, "you will find us and tell us your decision."

James Finlay passed into my hands a heavy package, tightly wrapped in some soft leather. He tapped my arm and urged me to look after this object with my life. "That book has the whole truth in it, Sir!" said he. "For my uncle's sake, take it and read it!"

I promised to do so.

And with that, Rinck and the Finlays melted into the night. It was close on eleven o'clock. The rest of the world was entirely silent. The wind had dropped, the clouds were clearing and there was a mortal chill in the air, under a watchful and threatening moon.

I made haste across the bridge into Tweedsmuir. Not surprisingly, for a damp Sunday night, there was not another soul to be seen or heard. I crept silently up to Mr. Yellowlees' door. Naturally, the door was firmly bolted and there were no lights to be seen. I could not hammer on the door for fear of scandalising the entire village, so I made myself as comfortable as possible in the garden shed, among the slaters, the seed-potatoes, the bulbs and ashes, with sackcloth for my blanket and Finlay's package for my pillow.

I fell again to a fitful and desperately cold sleep, turning over and over in my mind the events of the day but returning ever again to the most pressing question of all – How was I to explain my behaviour to the school-master?

Tweedsmuir – October 7, 1895.

The Student of History will not be surprised to learn that my dismal return to Mr. Yellowlees' fireside was not to be counted among the social triumphs of Mr. Kininmonth. Despite my uncomfortable situation, I managed to sleep until about seven o'clock, when I heard Mrs. Yellowlees opening the back door. In order not to startle her by a sudden eruption from the shed, of which she had a full view, I lay hidden for several minutes before emerging to creep around to the front of the cottage. Alas! her husband observed me from the window and my entrance was a sorry one indeed!

Mr. Yellowlees summoned me to his study, and I went, remembering similar occasions when I had followed my school-teacher as a wayward child, anticipating the pain of the tawse.

"You will be so good as to leave my house immediately," was the short instruction. "My wife has already packed all your belongings and you need only pay what is owed and leave!" He pointed sternly at the front-door.

I nodded, without daring to speak.

"You dare to say something, Sir?" demanded Mr. Yellowlees fiercely.

I shook my head.

"I say: you dare to say something, do you, eh?" he repeated, stepping up to me. "You mean to speak, do you? You wish to have words with me?"

I realised that he desired me to give him the satisfaction of an excuse for a lengthy tirade; but I gave him none, and retreated to my room to find my bags and the small amount of money that I owed for rent. The irate school-master took the money, counted it twice, told me three times that I "should be ashamed of myself", and then advised me that Mr. Dick had already summoned a constable from Peebles, and warned, "against his better judgement", that I had best be gone.

The seventh of October was a pleasant autumnal day. I would have gloried in its colours and in the busy finches at the berries, were it not for the fact that I found myself on the road, with no employment, no place of residence, and very little money. I had no idea where I should now turn, but took seriously the threat of summary arrest at the hands of the Peebles-shire constables; and made my way to the copse of trees where I had talked to Rinck on the previous evening.

There was no sign of any other living soul. I made myself comfortable behind a wall to order my thoughts. I failed in this attempt. Finally, I remembered the parcel which Finlay had passed to me. I carefully unwrapped it. I believe now that the wrapping and the strings which bound it were made from seal-skin. Inside I found an ancient, heavy and very abused Bible. At the back of the book was inscribed the name of its owner, "Reverend William Lunn, Shepherd of Souls on Jura, 1838".

I was at first confused: had James Finlay intended that I find not the truth, but "The Truth" in this book, not an explanation of their own history but an enlightenment on the condition of the human soul? Such an intention did not seem in his character. But when I turned the pages from Genesis onwards, I realised what he meant: for there was hand-writing in the margins of the pages, starting at Exodus, and continuing through the pages thereafter, with here and there gaps. I also noticed that the hand-writing was not all that of one person.

I settled down to read this annotated Bible.

And learned the most horrible story and example of human cruelty of which I have ever heard. Having read the pages, I copied out – word for word – this story from Exodus: I filled up pages 200 to 215 in my Order Book, and indexed these pages under "E".

[Exodus, Chapter 1, reading from Verse 1.]
This is a true history, which began in the Year of Our Lord, Eighteen Hundred and Forty, recorded by William Lunn [began the commentary, in neat and tiny writing]. In the northern-most part of the Island of Jura, in Argyll-shire, lies the village of Kenuachdrachd. These were hard times. The souls of Kenuachdrachd made their living with a few cows and with gathering kelp from the beach. But then the kelp grew scarce and my charges could not gather enough to sell. They went hungry. Corn was sent to them from the mainland, to keep them from death.

It was then that I decided that I should help these poor people, and made an arrangement with Captain George Harris, a native of the Isle of Man whom I met in Glasgow. He convinced me that an island named Kerguelen, on the further side of the world near to Australia, was a place of plenty, of high forests and of green meadows. Kerguelen, he explained, signified Caer-nan-Ghaellean, the Fortress of the Gaels, and it was so named because of the opportunities which it afforded the poor Scotch, Manx, Welsh and Irish. My knowledge of the Gaelic, together with some studies I have made of place-names in my native Galloway, led me to debate with him whether the name might not mean Fortress of the Young Men. But we agreed that the name was propitious, and that his ship would call at Lagg and take my people to Kerguelen. Many of that community and from other places in Jura had already gone, to America mostly, to seek out new lands and a living for their children. I was told by Captain Harris that here was a place where all my flock could become Godly men, without the oppressive rule of landlords and factors and taxes, but where we could live and worship and flourish in freedom: the Fortress of the Gaels for all time.

Many people agreed that this is what they should do. There were about four dozen of us in all, who boarded the big ship at Lagg on that April day in Eighteen Hundred and Forty, and who sailed down the Sound leaving the bald hills behind us for the last time. I remember that many a mother wept and many a grown man as well, as the last sight of Jura disappeared in the clouds. But the children were too excited to weep and ran about the deck and under the deck, exploring, amazed at every corner the ship presented.

It was on the first day of this awful journey that I found Captain Harris to be a fearful and a Godless man. He roared at the children if he saw them on deck and he was brutal to the sailors. Many a time I remonstrated with him and we shouted at each other, over the treatment of both passengers and crew, Captain Harris red in the face and with bunched fists, myself white as a sheet and arms waving. On one occasion Harris used his fist to end such an argument, and I had to retire below decks for three days while my swollen face returned to normal.

I cannot tell exactly what route we travelled, for I am a poor sailor and navigator upon the sea; but it was southwards all the way, through storms and flat calm, and heat and rain, for days and nights together. The ship rolled and turned even in the slightest swell, and many of us lay sick under decks, where we were tossed together. During one storm, which lasted for three days, the floor was slimy with vomit. My eldest charge, William Finlay, died in that storm, wild on his bed until the very last, when he suddenly sat up shrieking, then passed over. He was slipped over the side on the following day, his body to the waves, his soul to God. Two babies also died on that day.

After several weeks, we turned towards the east. I learned from some of the crew that the coastline which we could dimly see to the north was the Cape Colony. One morning, not long after this, I chanced upon Captain Harris. Harris had been drinking heavily and boasted to me that he would be a rich man after this journey was over, for he was to set up in trade in the China Seas, where, as he said, spices and slaves, rum and women were to be easily had. Such a confession shocked my sensibilities, and I remonstrated with him, calling him down for his un-Godliness. Harris was in no way moved by these words and laughed openly in my face. "Un-Godly, Mr. Lunn? I tell you, you are dealing with the most sinful man you will ever meet," he shouted; "for I have stolen this ship and no man will ever catch me for it!"

It seemed that Harris had obtained the ship by some trick, pretending to hire it for some short trip, but changing its name and appearance on the high seas, shortly before picking up his passengers from Jura. The whole act had been planned for many months. I had been deceived and implicated in all of this, for Harris had waited for our contract to be signed before he stole the ship.

Of course, I was horrified at this revelation, and mortified that the God-fearing men and women of Jura should be setting out for a new life on a ship which was captained by a shameless criminal, and I chastised Harris openly for it. But my words were like hailstones in summer – soon melted and leaving no trace upon the sinner Harris.

Over the next few days, we clashed more and more frequently

and violently. Had I not already been smitten once by Captain Harris, I believe I would have exchanged blows. As it was, words had to suffice. But Harris began to regret his rashness in telling me of his crimes, and had made up his mind to cut short this argument at the earliest opportunity, correctly fearful that I would cause his arrest on arrival in Kerguelen Island.

The winds and the seas in that part of the world were wild. A gale blew night and day and again into night, the waves lashed us from every side, and those of us who could still move had to care for friends and parents and children who were moaning in their cots. I led prayers for our salvation, almost incessantly.

It was therefore with great relief that, one grey morning, we saw land to the south of us, and saw that Harris was directing his ship towards that land. Some way off, on the horizon, we could just make out the sails of two ships disappearing to the east. Who they were we do not know.

It was by my calculation the twentieth day of July, and I called on my flock to rejoice that we had finally come through all our troubles, with the hand of the Lord upon us, and had reached Kerguelen in health and safety. Although it was July, it was not a summer's day. I observed Captain Harris, who seemed to me to have a mocking smile on his face.

All those who could bestir themselves came up on deck to see our new land. In all truth, it looked desolate and bare, unwelcoming. There was a huge mountain covered in snow which lifted itself up into the clouds and out of our sight. The coastline was rocky and waves crashed upon it. The cloud came down low from the mountains and obscured much of the land. After several hours, our ship tacked into a rocky inlet, where there was relative shelter. But there was not a tree, not a blade of grass to be seen. Wild birds swooped and dived and called like demons. An anchor was cast and we rode on the restless sea for a time.

I was beset by doubts, and took Harris to one side, and began to argue with him. "This cannot be the Island of Kerguelen, Sir!" I exclaimed, pointing at the most barren cliffs and headlands I had ever laid eyes on. "This land is no better suited for human habitation than Garbh Reisa." Harris simply smiled cruelly:

"Have you ever seen Kerguelen, Mr. Lunn?" Of course, he knew that I had never travelled so far and could only stay silent. But it was not difficult for me to believe then that Captain Harris had brought us to an Island of Sorrow.

It was not possible to land in that bay, which the sailors named Port Christmas, for a westerly gale was howling across the land from the sea beyond, preventing the ship from approaching the far beach. At around midday, therefore, Harris turned his ship south and eastwards again, and we sailed swiftly among rocks and reefs, with the land to the south appearing between the mist and the spray. We sailed for about four hours, fearing at every moment to be cast upon the rocks and to perish. At one time we sailed down a fast channel between a monstrous headland and a rocky island. At the head of the land to our right was a mountain which appeared briefly through the clouds. We passed through other rocks on which the sea broke terrifyingly. But the sailors were skilful. When night fell we were in a huge bay, where the water seemed calmer.

The ship lay at anchor all night, and in the morning we were told to get on the boats with all that we possessed. I protested again that this could not be Kerguelen, but Harris said nothing to me. He was occupied in moving the people from the ship into his two small boats, and in seeing them safely to land. The wind was rising again, and it was a dangerous business. Each time that I tried to speak to Harris, or to his first mate, I was brutally shouldered aside, and could get no answer. I was in the last boat to leave. As the sailors pushed away from the side of the ship, Harris leaned over the rail above us. "You are wrong, Mr. Lunn!" he shouted to me. "This is Kerguelen! And I am sure you will make it into the Gaels' own land, with your men of Jura!" With that, we pitched into the surf, now mounting rapidly, and headed for the shore. The sailors avoided our eyes, and none would reply to my desperate questions – until one, moved perhaps by pity, answered my pleas for some knowledge of where we were being landed. "This is the Island of Desolation. May God help you all!"

And with that blessing we were cast upon the shore of our new home.

I laid the huge book down on my knees and stared into the vastness of the sky above Talla. In the blank space, I tried to grasp the enormity of Harris's actions.

"Good heavens!" I muttered to myself, sitting up and striking my fist into my palm from outrage. "What kind of a fiend could put them all – man, woman and child – on such a desolate place?"

I had by now reached Exodus, Chapter Thirteen, for, despite Mr. Lunn's neat hand-writing, many pages were required to write down this small piece of history. It was scarcely appropriate that the Pharaoh should let the enslaved people go, just at the moment when the enslaved people were abandoned upon the Island of Kerguelen. Nevertheless it was so.

We were left on a land without trees, without beasts, without shelter, by a man who had stolen his ship and now proposed to make a fortune from sinful living in the warm seas of China.

But the eye of the Lord was upon us and His Vengeance came in a most strange circumstance.

No sooner had we been put ashore among those wailing families and friends, than the small boat pushed out into the waves again and made for the ship. But the wind, which had been strong enough until then, rose of a sudden to a gale and worse; it twisted and turned and began to strike up the sea before us into monstrous waves. The ship was tossing at its anchor like a piece of wood. The small boat was snatched up, driven sideways into some rocks and was smashed into a hundred pieces before our eyes. What became of the sailors we could not see, for the rain and the foam lashed into our faces and we had to seek shelter. And then the great thing happened!

I could almost imagine the Reverend Lunn's joy, across the years, as he wrote these words and saw the events in his imagination once more.

The Very Great Vengeance of the Lord Almighty came down upon the Devil in flesh, George Harris. For the wind blew stronger yet and a sea like a mountain rose up and crashed upon the ship and tore it from its anchor and sent it hurling across the bay towards the rocks! Oh! as we stood on the shore we knew that the Good Lord was with us, and I led my people in psalms to thank Him for these acts. And as we sang, Harris and those of his crew who could, leaped from their ship like the souls of the damned into the Pit, and they plunged into the foaming torrent and disappeared from our sight.

Oh! the ways of the Lord are mysterious, but glorious to behold!

Reading these words, I was carried along with the enthusiasm of the historian, and I could see now the waves, now the winds, now the drowning men in Harris's crew. I was swept to that veritable Island of Desolation and Sorrow.

No sooner had the Lord God emptied that ship of its heartless and sinful crew, than He bade the storms be silent and the waves be still, and a fresh breeze to come in the stead of the great wind. And, as Harris and his men pulled themselves out of the water on the shore of a small island out there in the bay, their ship, now purged of sin and grief, set its own sails and sailed peacefully out of the bay and at a steady speed towards the east.

The God-fearing souls of Jura were left on the main part of the land, and the sinner Harris and his crew on a small island, the two tribes separated by a sea in which the currents flowed fast. And never a boat for either of us. As the storm died away and the ship which had been our home disappeared fast behind a head-land, I led a prayer of thanksgiving, and then, turning our backs to the shore and to Harris, we left the shore in search of a place to build shelters.

I slowly became aware that my limbs were inordinately cold, despite the sunshine. I trudged around in a circle at the edge of the wood to restore some warmth to my extremities, thinking all the while of the outrage which had been perpetrated upon these poor emigrants from Jura. Just imagine, if you can! Driven from their homes by poverty and starvation, stowed in a ship like so many cattle or barrels of fish, refused the ordinary decencies of life for weeks on end, all at the whim of a man who had stolen and lied and invented Paradise to gain his end. And then this! – I have often wondered at the capacity of Man to be cruel to his fellows, at the depths to which a man can sink to satisfy the basest of desires. But to abandon, with malice and prior cold reflection – to abandon men, women, children upon an island so desolate that nothing grew there, to conspire to leave them there, surely to die in misery, without any sign of remorse! – ever-lasting damnation for such a man were too gentle!

And then this startling turn of events – this ship that set sail across the southern ocean, masterless, perhaps to sail into some serene Antipodean harbour to puzzle the colonials in the manner of that famously-abandoned *Marie Celeste* – despite my horror at the tale told by Lunn, this part of his story brought a smile to my face.

Still I thirsted for more knowledge of these tragic events. I noticed that Mr. Lunn ceased to write on the pages of Exodus, nor yet in Leviticus or Numbers, and it was only at Joshua, Chapter Twenty-Two, that I could continue my reading and recording into my Order Book.

> We found very little shelter. We found, some distance from where we had been landed, and protected behind a small hill, a place which we thought might suit to build some huts. And in the first few days that we were there, we built huts with our bare hands, digging rocks from the very hillside, collecting grasses and seaweed to fill the gaps as best we could. But how many times did we build up only to have a wind knock it down! In those first few days and nights, with a gale blowing without end, and the rain coming down upon us as upon Noah, we lost several small children and two old men, who died in the night, with only my poor words of ministration to comfort them.

I could read no further then, for I felt an anger and raw emotion which I could not control. I am a man whose throat tightens easily when confronted with suffering or with the tale of some tragedy or indeed when I gain a clear insight into great events, and it leads too often to secret tears, which I can never show to my fellows.

Noon-day had come and I dozed awhile under the sun, for my recent excitements had exhausted me. I slept for two hours, then I resumed my reading. Mr. Lunn had chosen to continue his story in the Book of Job.

When we had built enough shelters from the rocks and stones and had filled the cracks with moss, and had buried those who had died of exhaustion and starvation and fever, we began to arrange our lives. There was no wood which we could use for fires, but peat and seaweed aplenty. It became possible to cut and dry peat, using our bare hands for the most part, since we had few tools with us.

For food, we set out at the break of each day, men and women and children, to hunt down seals or birds or anything that had wings or scales or fur. After a whole day, it was possible to return home with nothing to show for the hunt. But we learned where the penguins were and where the fulmar and petrel. Seals were not easily found and less easily killed. We all joined in, from the youngest child to the oldest woman, for only thus could we find enough to feed us and keep us from day to day. I accompanied these parties if there was no sick person to attend to. Always one or two of the old people were left behind at our shelters to tend the fires and cut more peat.

It seemed that we had arrived in the worst days of winter. I tried to explain that the Southern Hemi-Sphere had opposite seasons to the Northern but I do not think many really under-stood. It was July when we left the ship, and in Jura the skies would have been blue and the days warm. Down here, the skies were dark, the days short, and the nights full of wind and sleet and snow.

After several weeks, the days grew longer and we saw the sun on several days. A more optimistic man might have named it spring. And then a thing happened which might have saved us all had it gone well. A ship appeared in the bay of the sea and a small boat was put out. We all watched from the shore, as the boat was rowed out to the island on which Harris and his remaining crew had been wrecked. We knew these men to be still alive, for we saw every day the smoke of their fires, as they must have seen the smoke of ours. We watched as the boat landed and then pulled away again, with several more men aboard. When the boat had gained the ship again, there was a delay of an hour or more, which we did not understand. I waved my arms furiously to attract some attention and our best men shouted and the women wailed. To no avail, it seemed.

At last, the boat put out again, with two or three men standing in it, armed with long guns. It came close to the shore but did not land. I called out to them to come ashore and to save us all from a certain death. There was a man in the boat, with long fair hair, who spoke few words of English. It seemed they were hunters after the whale, from Norway.

"I will not land," shouted the man in the boat.

"For the love of God, man," I cried, "can you not take away at least our poor children."

"No, Sir," said the other, "for if you have the plague, I will not land."

"The plague?" I shouted. "We do not have the plague. Please come ashore and see for yourself."

"I am sorry, Sir. Mr. Harris has told us your story," answered the sailor, "and I cannot put my ship at risk. We will ask another ship to come later in the year."

And with that, the boat put about and the ship left, with Harris and his men on board, never to be seen again.

"My God, man!" I exclaimed aloud at this point, beside myself with wrath. "What a monster! What a brute! A barbarian!" I have since thought of many other words to describe this beast, who had now condemned an innocent community to death, not once, but twice. What kind of tale had he spun to the Norwegians that they would thus sail off with him? How different it might have been had the small boat landed first on the other shore!

Was there no end to this man's monstrous behaviour? "Ah, sirs," he said to the Norwegians – I can see it all in my imagination – "those poor people on the far shore are victims of the plague which swept our ship some months ago. We were put across here by the good offices of Mr. Lunn, so that we might not contract the white death which they brought with them from Jura" – no doubt such a tale as he had been breeding for weeks on his desert island, far from the civilising influences of the fellowship of decent people.

So Harris had escaped from punishment by more falsehood; it must be supposed that his punishment came in the after-life, for he seemed a man destined to escape any chastisement or retribution in this life.

After a short turn round the wood, I continued to read.

Already we had lost about ten of the forty souls who had landed. We buried them in shallow graves and marked the graves with stones – babies for the most part and old men. And still we carried on. I, who had been a fit man full of hope when we left Jura, felt that I had aged beyond my years, my hair now almost white, as was my long beard. I tried to speak to my people with the words of comfort and of judgement from the Bible in which I now write and which was our only book of wisdom. But even I, in those months, sometimes wondered aloud to my friends whether the Good Lord had deserted us in our hour of need. I read in the Book of Job.

During our summer, we found the cabbage did much to keep us alive, for it seemed to keep our eyesight good and our skin healthy. The cabbage and the flesh of the birds, and their eggs – such was our food in that year and in all the years to come. But it did not close our doors to death or to sickness or to despair.

In the second spring on that island, I asked several of the younger men to go on a journey into the island, to see what they might find. We had until then walked for many miles along the shore-line, both east and west, in search of food, and had found other places where we might live. But no one place was any better than others. Water was to be found everywhere, as were the birds, the cabbage and the seals. Some glens were more sheltered than others, but our first place of landing seemed as good as any other. We had never been far into the hills behind us.

It was a morning of fog on which five young men set off. What a journey that must have been! They were away from their families for twenty days and nights, and they saw many lochs and many bays and rocky shores to the south, and places where fishing might be good. They saw long long hills abandoned by God. They saw bogs stretching to the horizon, over which they stumbled for hours, as in a slough. They saw distant mountains rising with snow on them, from behind hills which they knew they would not climb. They saw a coastline which was far far longer than all of the shores and hills of Jura put together many times. But they saw not one other living soul – not one.

I had to turn next to the Books of Nahum, Habbakuk, and Zephaniah. The writing here was not that of Mr. Lunn: it was far less confident and larger, the words encroaching upon the printed sacred text, with abundant ink-blotches and extraordinarily poor spelling and grammar (which I have here corrected, for it would be a shame to spoil my good prose with the ill-educated words of another; I have turned phrases, inserted punctuation, *et cetera*, as a good editor should). I assumed this to be the work of one of the poor exiles.

The whalers came back. Not that first year, nor yet the second. But in the third year after our arrival, a ship put down its anchor and a boat came out to our shore. We named that year the Year of the Doctor, for there was a doctor on the ship, a surgeon from Trondheim who spoke no English but managed to make himself understood to Mr. Lunn by signing and drawing on a slate. He seemed surprised that we had not all died of the plague which Harris had laid upon our heads, and was able to treat some of our worst sicknesses. Mr. Lunn asked if the ship could take some of our people off the island. But the surgeon told him that this was impossible, for the ship was about to set off on a hunting trip that was to last two years, and could take no passengers, nor yet even a letter.

But the Norwegian was most interested in our cabbage and he took as many as we could give him, in exchange for some bits of wood, some nails and tools, and two bags of grain, which could be spared. He also promised to return on a future voyage and trade with us again.

So our second visiting ship sailed off eastwards in the morning, leaving us once more to the desolation. I believe that this finally broke Mr. Lunn's heart, for he took to his bed and died soon afterwards. Thomas Campbell took the Bible to himself and read to us from the Book every night and twice on the Sabbath.

It was not until another two years had passed, in the Year of Grey Snow, that another whaling ship called. Once more it was Norwegian, and the Captain seemed to have knowledge of us. He came ashore and was warmly greeted. He brought wood and grain with him, which was most useful to us. He traded for cabbage and for salted eggs. And it was from Captain Sorensen that we learned of the war raging between Paraguay and Finland, and of the great tidal waves which God had sent upon Paris and Rome, destroying sinners in thousands, and he told us of the showers of meteors which had come down upon the wide plains of America and turned them all to infernos. When he told us these things, we were glad that we were in a quiet part of the sinful world, untouched by war or by pestilence, unpunished by the Good Lord. Captain Sorensen promised to return again in the following year, if he were spared, and to trade with us again, and to tell us if the world was faring any better.

And so he did, Captain Sorensen and other Captains, who traded with us and took our cabbage on their long journeys in search of the whale. And they brought with them news from the world, each time more frightening than the last: how Spain had been severed from its neighbours by a mighty movement under the Earth; how the Finns had defeated Paraguay and now had an empire stretching from Uruguay to Bolivia; how the Arabians in Africa had risen up and chased the white men from that land. Oh! we shuddered to hear of such evil, and such tragedy, and of the deaths of thousands. No matter how cold and how wet was our Island, it was at least beyond the horizon of all war-ships. Our friends promised never to tell of our island to any others, and promised to return to trade with us each year.

So we learned to grow cabbages in larger fields, and we stored eggs and meat for our friends, so that we always had something more to trade. The wood and the grain we received in return kept us from starvation and from the worst weathers of the winter. We now had new-born children to protect.

By the time I had read this far, dusk was falling upon Tweedsmuir. In the gathering darkness, I turned over in my mind these strange Norwegian tales of war and pestilence and catastrophe visited upon Mankind. I could only conclude that it was to the advantage of the Norwegians that the poor emigrants stayed on Kerguelen, to stock the whaling ships for their endless peregrinations in the southern ocean; and that for this reason alone, the Norwegians had fabricated such sagas and tales. My spirit grew heavy with thoughts of the wickedness of men against men.

I was by now cold and hungry. It was only sensible that I should find some shelter, and I decided to risk my liberty at the Crook Inn, some two miles up the road. I shouldered all my baggage and set off. On reaching my goal, I crept cautiously up to the very window of the Inn, from which poured light and the rather heady stench of strong tobacco mingled with beer, spirits, and steaming sweaty clothes. The inside of the glass was so completely opaque from condensed breath that I found it difficult to see anything, but concluded that I had little left to lose. I entered, pushed my way between rough labourers and farm-workers, purchased some bread and cheese and a warming tot of whisky, then settled down into a corner.

From where I did not stir for several hours. I fell to considering my position. It was obvious that I could never return to Talla; even were a constable not to arrest me for association with a known criminal, there was no one who would now give me either employment or shelter. Perhaps Mr. Rinck's apocalyptic scheme for Ullapool could offer me suitable opportunity for my skills. And I certainly had nothing to fear in taking an old man home to his place of birth.

Just as "time" was called, I decided almost on a whim to throw in my lot with Rinck and the Finlays, and to leave with them for Edinburgh.

On the Road – October, 1895.

By good fortune, the policies of the Crook Inn were extensive and included a dry stable which was not possessed by any horse. I lay down in the straw and slept deeply. On the following morning, it took me several moments to realise that the hand that shook me awake belonged to John Finlay. How he had found me in the stable, I never discovered. Perhaps he had been following me for the past twenty-four hours? He did not need to ask whether I was coming with him: he retrieved the package with his Bible, and waited patiently as I picked the worst of the straw from my hair and clothes. Then we crept from the stable and set off northwards.

On the approach to Broughton, the road passed above the works for the railway-line which was being laid towards Tweedsmuir. There were several gangs at work, and a man who might have been my colleague. The whole affair would, at any other time, have excited my professional interest: to-day, I shunned it.

As we came into the village, we were joined by James Finlay and Mr. Rinck, who had apparently taken refuge there the previous day.

"So, you have seen the way of salvation, Mr. Kinnimunt," said Rinck, obviously very pleased with himself. "And now we will make our journey together." I kept to myself my thoughts on the prospect of hours spent in his company. James Finlay kindly took my bag from me, and slung it over his shoulders. Thus lightened, I was able to march alongside them through the sun-lit October day.

Not another word was spoken until we crested the hill above Broughton. For the past mile I had been calculating in my mind just how Rinck and the Finlays expected to reach Edinburgh within the day, and hoped against all hope that this was not in fact what they projected. For, even at a pace of three miles per hour, I expected the whole journey to last at least twelve hours. But I could not aspire to maintain such a pace for any length of time. Already my boots were broken and very receptive to the water which still lay abundantly on the road's surface. We had travelled about ten miles in three and one-half hours, and I wished heartily for a railway-line to spring up beside the road.

We tramped along the muddy road which led under the side of the Broughton Heights to Blyth Brig. To relieve the silence, I asked Mr. John Finlay if he might tell me of his own life on Kerguelen. In reply, the old man gestured to his nephew.

I will make shameless use of a device favoured normally by Novelists by now setting down, as one continuous story, the words uttered by James Finlay; for, although he spoke fluently and well —

astonishingly so, given his lack of education, as I shall shortly tell — his was scarcely a model narrative. As an Historian, I feel that I must not fill these pages with inappropriate or superfluous words; I have, therefore, cultivated, as it were, James Finlay's story, told to me as we trudged wearily past Blyth Brig and up the long stretch of road towards Romanno Brig, past the wooded estate of Lamancha and on towards Leadburn.

"You should know, Mr. Kininmonth," began Mr. Finlay, "that I was born and bred far from here, on the Island of Desolation, which some men know as Kerguelen. I believe myself to be some thirty-four years of age, and I knew nothing of Scotland until two years ago.

"Kerguelen is a wild, wild place, full of wind and water. You can stand on a high hill in Kerguelen, and see only mile upon mile of wet ground and sea. On a clear day you can see the snows and the ice on the distant mountains, but little else. We keep low on Kerguelen, for the wind is stronger than any man, and it blows almost every day of the year. We never venture out on to the sea, for it is as treacherous as the Devil himself and never as pretty. Kerguelen is vast, far bigger than you might imagine. One time, my uncle and I walked as far round the coast of Kerguelen as we could, and we were away for fifty days, and still we could not see all of the island. And never could we visit the many islands which lay across the sea-water, for men are swept to their death by the tides.

"We were visited each year by men who came looking for seal-fur and for whale-oil. It was in the warmer months when we would see their big ships approaching our island. They came from Norway, from Portugal, from America, from Canada, from Africa. If they had visited us before, they would cast out their anchor in the Bay of God's Wrath. If they had never been to Kerguelen, we would see them sail up and down the coast, looking for a safe place, sometimes anchoring in the Sound to the south. Since the Great Whaling War between Finland and Paraguay, which destroyed many great cities and wiped fleets from the surface of the sea, we were fearful that there would be soldiers on such ships. But we were fortunate that they always came in peace. Very often they would bring us corn or pieces of wood, which were eagerly accepted. For such gifts, we were content to build up stores of seal-meat and fish for them to take with them when they went hunting the great and little beasts of the sea.

"They would bring us more news of the cruel world, of the Great Whaling War, of the Plague which struck down the nation of Spain and left it only to the rats, of the rise and fall of the Zetland Empire. We were glad, my uncle and I, that we were left in peace on a small island that few remembered. I tell you, Mr. Kininmonth," said James Finlay, shaking his head at me, "I do not envy my neighbours here, nor you indeed, for the cares and troubles which have overtaken Britain. You think that we may have been ignorant in our Island of Desolation. But each year we heard enough news from the sealers and whalers to allow us no regrets.

"It was our endless work to find enough food for these hunters. We laboured day on day, in capturing penguins and fulmars and other sea-birds in season, in killing seals, in salting and storing their meat for the visitors. We kept a field and traded the cabbages with the sailors, who were very keen to have such a thing with them on their long voyages. And in return they would furnish us with news and with wood and with sacks of corn. When I was a boy, there were other men came to Kerguelen – Englishmen, Americans, Danishmen. They anchored their ships in the far north of the island, in a place the sailors knew as Port Christmas, and in Cumberland Bay. We never saw these men, nor they us, but our whaling friends had talked to them. They said these men had come to study the stars in the sky.

"Finally, there were just two of us on the Island of Desolation. When I was very young, in the Year of the Fog, my mother and my father died along with many others, and my uncle and I were the only ones left. All those who have died are buried on the hillside, all of them, each under a white stone which was brought from the glens below the snow-fields. I have seen many stones there, Mr. Kininmonth; it seems to me there are a hundred stones there. My uncle built a wall around the place they are all buried, a long wall which keeps out the wind, built in the shape of our island. Not everyone who is buried there died in the Year of the Fog, but that was the worst."

When Mr. James Finlay had told me this much, it was growing late. I asked him why he had not come away with one of the ships?

He laughed at my innocence. "You have not been listening to me, Mr. Kininmonth! Why should we leave an island which was safe from the perpetual misery of the world? Why should we sail back into wars and pestilence and the vengeance of a wrathful God, when all that we knew and loved was around us on Kerguelen? We had food, we had shelter, we had the stones of our ancestors."

I was puzzled, for, despite all he was telling me, he had after all come away from his island. But I did not venture to interrupt him.

"It was about fifteen years ago, in the Year of Solitude, that they did not come in their ships. In the year before, some Canadian whalers had been, but they seemed poor, low men, unwilling to talk. They had returned from a long voyage on the sea without any catch. One of them told me that there were no whales left in the oceans, and few enough seals. I saw their poverty and he was telling me the truth. No ship ever came again after that. Ten – eleven – thirteen years passed without a visitor. We were left on our island, not knowing other than that perhaps all of God's people, and more besides, had perished in some great catastrophe. There was still food for us, and water, but our hut began to leak and to shake in the wind, and we had no wood or cloth to repair the damage. Once, I believe I saw from the Rock of Cuchullin a ship at a great distance, travelling fast to the east: we named that the Year of the Clipper, for sailors had once told us of fast ships which raced across the waters, never stopping for anyone. But we believed at length that we were alone on God's Earth. Sometimes we offered praise that we had been spared, at other times we lamented, and were cast down that we had been over-looked.

"Two years ago, Mr. Kininmonth, in the Year of the Frenchman, we were visited again by a ship. It was January, and a day on which we saw blue sky, and there was little wind. It was as if the Almighty had sent a sign, for days as calm as that were few. My uncle and I had walked on the hill over-looking the Small Isles which lay in the Sound to the south, for on such a day the green and blue of the sea and the sparkling waves can fill you with joy. As we sat with the sun on our backs, looking to the distant south, listening to the endless cries of the birds, watching the gannet plunge and rise, we saw a ship come silently round the low headland. It was a French ship, as we could see from the flag it flew.

"I tell you that we did not know what we should do. Thirteen years before, the Norwegians had told us tales of the blood-thirsty French, who had tried to capture the Telemark and been driven off after many great battles in the snow-plains and the mountains. You yourself will doubtless know of the deeds of terrible General Grenouille, and of his death in the claws of the mighty Norwegian Bear. We had been warned never to trust the three-coloured flag of the Frenchman. And there it was, Mr. Kininmonth, fluttering in the breeze!

"My uncle decided that it would be best if we watched, and waited, but did not go to meet them. We had a cave on the north side of the island where we could hide. We took some food and went there, even as the sun was at the top of the sky. For two weeks we stayed in the cave. At night, I went out to catch some puffin or sheath-bill for food, and to see where the Frenchmen were. They had encamped on ground on the south side of the Rock of Cuchullin, over-looking the great Sound, and did not seem likely to move from there. We thought they would go away again soon, but they showed every sign only of staying.

"One day, my uncle, without a word to me, simply walked over the mountain from our cave and into the French camp. I had no choice then but to follow him!"

In the dusk, we arrived at the hamlet of Leadburn. There is little more than an inn and a railway station there, both apparently shunned by humanity on that eighth night of October. We silently found our shelter in a shed at the station, and settled down for the night with whatever provisions we had brought for the journey. James Finlay did not think it appropriate to tell me any more that day.

I had had the good sense to borrow some of Mr. Yellowlees' candles when I left his house. Taking small comfort from the weak flame of one of them, I transcribed Finlay's history into my Order Book, indexed by "D" – "Desolation", and "W" – "Whaling"; that accomplished I lay in squalor at Leadburn and thought of the horror of the Finlays' situation. Mr. Rinck sat beside me, and scribbled his own thoughts in a notebook. Finally, I slept.

At about ten o'clock the following morning, we passed across the railway bridge at Auchendinny, a place which reminded me of a ludicrous story once tendered to me as good coin by my erstwhile colleague, Mr. Gollan. At this place, James Finlay began talking again.

"When I knew where my uncle had gone, I was stricken with a heavy heart. For, if he were eaten by the French, who have many strange tastes, I would be utterly alone. So I decided that I would also give myself up to the Frenchmen, and walked into their encampment.

"To my surprise, they treated us with great admiration and kindness. There had been astonishment among them when my uncle suddenly came down among them, for they imagined the whole land to be utterly empty of people. We were offered wholesome food, and clothes to replace those which we had worn for fifteen years now. Two men among them spoke English, and they asked us where we had come from, how we lived. I took them to our village on the other side of the mountain and they expressed admiration at the sight of our house, and took off their hats when they stepped within the walls where our family is buried.

"After a few days, in which they made themselves friendly to us, a man named Brassillon told me that they had come in their grand ship, the *Eure*, to claim this island for France. Immediately, I recalled what we had been told about the desire of the French to conquer the world, and I argued fiercely with him. But he could scarcely understand anything I said, and smiled politely. He left me and talked to the Captain of his ship. Then he returned.

"He advised me that we could either stay on the island, and become free citizens of the Republic of France, or we would have to leave. If we chose the latter, the Captain would see to it that we were returned safely to England. I told him that my ancestors came from Jura, but he persisted in nodding and saying, "Yes – Jura, England." But it was not a difficult decision to make – there was little left to keep us on the Island of Desolation; and we could never become subjects of the French tyranny, after hearing so many tales from our visitors from Norway.

"The Frenchmen were there for three months. With my help, they constructed stone buildings. In that time, they were always friendly to us, as if pitying our life on the island. My uncle gave them many walking tours of the land, and told them how we used to live before the Year of the Fog, and how we came to be on the Island of Desolation.

"In April, we left the Island of Desolation, the Island of Sorrow. We left our house, our ancestors, our birds, the Small Isles, and the Holy Mountain. All that we took with us was the Bible which had been brought from Scotland in the Year of Abandonment. They left some of their people and the French flag flying. The ship took us westwards, towards Africa, through terrible seas.

"One morning we came at last to an island which was high and green, a mountain climbing from the sea into the clouds. It was quite calm that day, and Brassillon called us out on deck into the sunshine. We looked at the island and the waves crashing on its rocks. The Frenchman called this the 'Island of Gough', and pointed out to us some ships which had also anchored off its shores. There were four ships there, each with a flag which my uncle knew to be British. It seemed we were to be transferred to one of those ships for our continued voyage.

"By the middle of the day, we stood on a ship named the *Polar Star*, watching the French sail to the north. The Captain of the ship was a Mr. Robertson from Peterhead, and all the ships belonged to the Tay Whale Fishing Company. They were now on their homeward journey. Captain Robertson paid us little attention, but there was another man with him, Mr. William Bruce, who listened carefully to our story. He was most interested in how we had lived, for, as he said, he wished to spend time himself in such desolate places. It seemed that, although no whales had been captured, Mr. Bruce had a great interest in all things which are to be found in the southern oceans.

"In June, we arrived back in Dundee. We slipped in to port at night, for it seemed that no one wished to admit that their voyage had been a failure. Mr. Bruce was kind enough to place us in the care of one of the men from the *Balaena*, who hailed from Peebles; and here we found work."

By this time, we had come past the village of Roslin, and through

Burdiehouse and Liberton; we tramped in silence, attracting the suspicious glances of the local people, until we reached the very suburbs of Edinburgh, at Newington. What busy streets we beheld, though none noticed us! A nation, it seemed to me, of shop-keepers and their boys, and of customers and their maids.

Since the Finlays appeared more and more bewildered at the size and the noise of the great city, it fell to me to conduct them through the streets safely, deftly avoiding bicycles and horses and carts. Masters of the bogs and mountains they might be, but I could show them the skills which a city-man learns from boyhood!

Newington – October, 1895.

Five o'clock was striking in the church on Clerk-street as we passed it. I had to consider where we could easily find shelter for the night which was already upon us. I first thought of my sister, Jessie, who lived in Rankeillor-street; but then I remembered that my mother would be at home also. My gentleman readers will no doubt under-stand when I say that I feared greatly to take my present travelling companions to two rooms presided over by my mother. Rinck clearly had no plan and seemed for the first time to rely on my native wisdom. Since we had very little money between us, I had to think of some abandoned shelter, somewhere that would be both dry and out of the wind, but beyond the gaze of the city authorities. I thought perhaps that the great halls of Waverley might yield some place, so we set off down Cockburn-street and mingled among the crowds on the Waverley-bridge, before descending into the gas-lighted halls of the North British railway station.

I had remembered, from my brief passage through the station some months earlier that the whole place was busy not only with hundreds upon hundreds of travellers, but also with an army of crafts-men, joiners, roofers and masons, who were engaged upon the great re-building work of the station, which is calculated to make Waverley Station the largest Hall of Travel in all of the British Empire.

Thus, as we descended into the station, we could see many boarded-up places where we might sleep. I looked around for the most suitable, and then I was inspired! I led my companions to the north side of the station, where the Canal-street station had been but a short time before. We managed to slip on to the new through-platform without being seen: there, on the other side of the railway-tracks, as I had remembered, was the almost invisible entrance I had been looking for. Due to the darkness, and the black soot caked on the stonework, the entrance was barely to be seen; if I had not known of its existence, then I should have missed it entirely.

We waited until the platform was deserted, then sprang down on to the tracks and ran over to the entrance. Once into the gloom of the tunnel which led off from the entrance, I stopped, partly to catch my breath and allow my heart to slow back to its normal pace, and partly to allow my eyes to accustom themselves to the darkness.

"What is this place?" asked Mr. Rinck plaintively from the darkness.

"This," I answered proudly – for I could not prevent myself from feeling satisfied with my ingenuity – "This is the tunnel once used by the Edinburgh, Leith and Newhaven Railway, which took passengers through to Scotland-street Station. It has been abandoned some thirty years now. It will take us under the very streets of the New Town if we follow it."

As it happened, neither myself nor my companions had any inclination to follow this black tunnel more than a few yards. Sheltered it was, and dry if you chose a suitable spot away from walls; but it smelled badly of smoke and soot, was noisy from the adjacent station, and uncomfortable in the extreme. After two hours in this terrible lodging, I began to think that my inspiration had not been a good one. The Finlays seemed completely inured to such misery; but Rinck seemed quite depressed; and I regretted even Mrs. Yellowlees' cooking and my warm bed at Tweedsmuir.

However, the night passed and we emerged into the daylight of Thursday, the tenth day of October. It was not difficult to escape to the main island of the station, for our clothes marked us out as working men, and we thus might have gained passage into any part of the station we desired. Trains were already running in from Morningside, from Leith, from Trinity, from comfortable towns such as North Berwick and Eskbank, bringing gentlemen to work in the city.

My stomach cried out from hunger, so I determined to find some breakfast. We made our way cautiously up to Jeffrey-street, where I purchased milk and bread in a dairy. We shared our meagre meal while seated on a wall over-looking the busy train-lines which fed Waverley from the east and south, with the General Post Office rising like a great fortress behind.

Apparently transfigured by our simple breakfast, Rinck now manifested great energy and determination. He proposed to visit some places in the town where he could arrange for the publication of his new pamphlet. Its title, he proudly showed me, scribbled down in his curious flowing writing on a pile of papers, was "The Miry Places and the Marshes Shall be Given to Salt". Did I wish to read it before he took it to the printer? I thanked him as politely as I could, but excused myself on account of a sore head. Whereupon he set off towards Leith.

I decided that it were best if the Finlays remain concealed until our business in Edinburgh was all transacted. I returned them therefore to the railway-tunnel. Having concealed them safely, I made my way to the premises of the Chiropody Supply Association, at number fifty-seven, Clerk-street. The Reader may, of course, surmise that my feet were causing me trouble; but no! this visit was so that I could pay my respects to my sister, Jessie, who worked at this address.

The offices of the Chiropody Supply Association were dull and lifeless. It was the kind of place where the eye found only packing-cases and odd displays of items of clothing, or medical devices, guessing at the purpose of which could only cause consternation. I would suggest that customers were few and far between, the passing trade of Clerk-street being unlikely to open the door and browse on a whim.

It was here that my sister had found employment for some five years, ever since my poor father had died. Jessie lived with my mother, as I think I have mentioned, at no great distance. As I entered the offices that morning, she was there alone. Mr. Morrison, the General Manager of the Association, often found opportunity to go on long circular tours of chiropodists' surgeries in southern Scotland to drum up trade, and so left my sister to mind the business on her own. Which she did competently enough.

"Alexander!" she cried, looking up from a ledger-book. "What a surprise!"

We greeted each other with sufficient warmth to indicate we were brother and sister, but without that tenderness which is described by such worthy authors as Mr. Dickens when dearly-loved siblings meet.

"And what are you doing in Edinburgh?" she asked, reasonably enough. When I hesitated in my answer, she looked worried and asked me whether I was out of a job.

"Oh no," I assured her, "I am only in town on an errand for my employer which requires my professional knowledge." What arrant nonsense! which my sister in her simplicity took as the truth, having little or no idea of the nature of my trade. As far as she knew, I was still employed in some capacity on the Forth Bridge. I changed the subject and asked after her health and that of my ancient mother. It seemed that Jessie was, as always, as well as the Good Lord permitted, and that our mother was, as always, full of complaints, both of the medical kind and of those directed against neighbours, shop-keepers and distant relatives.

After some few minutes at this, I came round to the reason for my call.

"Ah, Jessie," I said, coughing slightly, "I was wondering if you might be able to make me a loan of a few shillings, just to cover the expenses?"

She looked at me, for I had been in this position often enough before. "But did your employer not give you the money, Alexander?"

"Ah, no – this errand was arranged in such haste that he clean forgot to give me money and I clean forgot to ask. But he will make it up just as soon as I return to Dalmeny . . . "

She sighed. "So how much were you wanting?"

I told her that four or five pounds Sterling would be sufficient. She was aghast. "But Sandy!" she cried, using the shorter form of my name which she only employed when acting in the capacity of an older sister, "that's a small fortune! What on Earth do you need with such a sum?"

I spun her a story about requiring a licence from the Law Courts, and money to pay the lawyer, so that some engineering work could proceed. I admit that I made all of this up as I stood there, surrounded by bottles of restorative foot-balm and rolls of bandages, and prided myself later in my resolute inventiveness. Of course, she worried that perhaps my employer was going to make a fool of me, and have me pay all of his fictitious expenses, or that I would lose the money. But at last she agreed to find the money for me when she returned home for her dinner. I begged her to say nothing of my visit to my mother, and she retained enough good sense as to grant me that.

When one o'clock struck, Jessie closed up the office, and, locking the door, left me in Clerk-street. She would return at two precisely with the money. I wandered idly up and down the thoroughfare, which was slowly emptying of people as Edinburgh cooked its dinner. I peered into shop-windows and finally sat on a low wall in St Patrick-square, waiting for the hour to strike.

My sister was as good as her word. She handed me an envelope containing four pounds Sterling – goodness knows how many months it had taken her to save this small amount! – embraced me lightly and we parted. With a heavy heart, for I knew I had deceived one with whom I should be more honest, and a heavier wallet, I set off through the town to find my companions.

I decided, to avoid early detection, to enter the tunnel from the further end, at Scotland-yard. As I came down into the abandoned station, I wondered if there were lamps to be had in one of the sheds. Cautiously, I crept around the various damp buildings which, as night closed in, were disappearing into shadow. I found one building where the door was secured only with a lathe of wood, and easily effected an actionable entrance; I found immediately what I sought. I gathered together four lamps with some fuel and made my way into the tunnel where, by my light, I found the Finlays. For greater comfort, we moved our subterranean camp further to the north, to a spot which I estimated lay directly below the new foundations of the Portrait Museum. Rinck joined us later, greatly satisfied with his day's work, and illuminating us with all of it, at some length.

The Municipal Railways of Scotland – October, 1895.

It came to me in the early hours of the following day that I might be able to find further information on the true history of Kerguelen, and perhaps of Captain Harris, in the splendid Library on George the Fourth Bridge. I proposed this to my companions in the morning. The Finlays, having no idea what a library might be, looked blankly at me. Rinck had no objection. He himself intended to look out some people who might be of his persuasion. He also announced, as if it were quite in the normal way of things, that he purposed to nail a copy of a Manifesto to the great doors of St. Giles' Cathedral. I wished him well, thinking only that he might thereby attract to himself more attention than was absolutely necessary on a visit to Edinburgh.

And so, once again, we left the Finlays in the dark and went our separate ways into the bustling city of Edinburgh. I reached the towering edifice of the Carnegie Free Library at nine o'clock, just as it opened. It was blowing cold from the east, and I was pleased to enter the doors to find warmth and light inside. What a change from the rooms which I had most recently occupied!

Five hours passed swiftly in that remarkable place, surrounded as I was by learning. I sought books on the great expeditions to the southern – or Antarctic – seas. I found a book describing the expedition of Joseph Hooker in 1840. More than fifty years ago! Before even I was born, men were sailing in those terrifying seas with as much fear and foreboding as you or I might experience in walking down a country lane. I spent three hours immersed in the book, by Sir James Ross, describing "A Voyage of Discovery and Research in the Southern and Antarctic Regions", which makes some description of Kerguelen, and the very places mentioned to me by Finlay. Here, indeed, was proof that Finlay had been telling the truth! – for how else could he have described these far-away places with an exactness matching Sir James Ross's descriptions – of Port Christmas, for example, in the extreme north-west, which must have been the very spot where Harris first put in, but could not land. Hooker and Ross had built two observatories of wood at the beach-head, one to the north, the other to the south, for meteorological and magnetic observations, at the end of May, 1840. The party found that anchorage in a place named Cumberland Bay was far better, although more difficult to approach if the weather was not clear. Gales blew on forty-five of the sixty-eight days they were at Kerguelen. The crew had even eaten of the infamous Kerguelen Cabbage – here would have been the humiliation of Mr. Yellowlees of Tweedsmuir, who had mocked this as the Infernal Cabbage!

What I found most startling was that when Hooker and Ross had left Kerguelen in July, 1840, in two ships heading east for Van Diemen's Land, the voyage into Storm Bay lasted twenty-six days, even when driven swiftly by wind and current. Twenty-six days! – at that moment, the enormity both of the southern ocean and Captain Harris's planned villainy sank in. The poor folk of Jura had been abandoned a full four weeks from any other inhabited land!

I had taken with me Mr. Whyte's Order Book No. 55, for jotting down notes. I was busy copying down (under "K") the outline I give above, when something in Sir James Ross's account suddenly struck me: when their ship had first arrived at Kerguelen, the exiles had seen two ships upon the eastern horizon. Busily I flicked the pages of my notebook until I found what I had dimly remembered – that the Jura minister, the Reverend Lunn, had told his flock that it was the twentieth day of July when they cast anchor at Port Christmas – the very day of Hooker's departure. Amazingly, they had seen the two ships of the intrepid explorers vanishing over the eastern horizon! How very different might have been the fate of that community had they arrived just a day earlier, for surely Harris could not have anchored there, with so many innocent passengers, in the sight of Hooker and his ships. He would have been obliged to continue at least to Australia or Van Diemen's Land, lands of opportunity for able-bodied men and God-fearing natives of Scotland!

I felt a glow of deep satisfaction at my discovery: what a triumph for my system of cross-referencing, what a triumph for Mr. Whyte!

I searched in vain for any other reference to the Island of Kerguelen in the multitudes of books upon the shelves. It occurred to me that there might be something in Astronomy to shed light on the visit of

Hooker, but I could find nothing. Neither was there anything of interest about whaling or sealing. I also sought references in newspapers and journals to the Finnish Imperial possessions in South America, and other such matters, but to no avail.

It seemed that I had come across a part of the world which had neither history nor any chronicler. Was it possible that all of what I had heard was utter fabrication, a wild and mischievous invention? I hoped not.

The attendants in that grand library no doubt thought ill of me, and carefully avoided meeting my eye when I went to seek some advice. Dispirited, I took refuge among the tall stacks of books, until the early part of the afternoon; then went out again into the gloom of an Edinburgh street, over-looked by the County Buildings and the Police Office.

I decided to return to our miserable hiding-place by our original ingress, through Waverley Station. I had no difficulty in entering the low tunnel unobserved, and made my way in the darkness under Princes-street and St. Andrew-square. I was proceeding under the very vaults of the Royal Bank of Scotland when I became aware of a number of bright lights and voices up ahead. Not thinking of any other explanation, I called out – "Mr. Finlay, is that yourself?"

There was a moment of some confusion and then I beheld a group of men advancing rapidly towards me, bearing lanterns.

"There you are, Mr. Watson. You are d——d late, Sir!" one of the men in the group castigated me. "We were about to give up and return to the City Chambers. It was two o'clock, you said, that you would meet us. What the devil do you mean by coming so late?"

Before I had time to think, the man had grabbed my elbow, and was peering angrily into my face. Evidently, he took me for someone quite different. Rather than confess the true purpose of my presence in the tunnel, I decided to play him along. I apologised to him for my lateness, citing some trouble with "my book-keeper".

The man grunted. "Well, let us get on then, Watson. Here – this is Bertram, Clerk of Works; and this is Johnston, from the North British Railway Company; this is MacTavish; and these three gentlemen are my fellows on the Corporation, Councillors Clark, Scobie, and Gardner."

I shook hands with each of these gentlemen in turn, wondering what this group of City Fathers and public servants could possibly be doing in such a tunnel as this on such a day as this. I trusted only to an unwarranted optimism that I should extricate myself from this situation before too long.

"Mr. Finlay," snapped Councillor Gardner, a thin man with an angry tone in his voice, "can we move along – I have my own business to attend to after this!"

This more respectable Mr. Finlay agreed, and turned to me. "So, Mr. Watson, what can you tell us about building a railway to rival that of Glasgow?"

Sometimes my mind will perform miracles. I deduced from this one question the following, which might have astonished my supposed namesake, the medical chronicler of Sherlock Holmes: first, that these men from Edinburgh Corporation had agreed a meeting with me to discuss an underground railway; secondly, that the reason for this meeting was the rivalry between Edinburgh and Glasgow, now exacerbated by Glasgow's proud achievement, then nearing completion, of constructing an underground railway for its citizens; and thirdly, that Messrs. Finlay, Clark *et al* expected me to lay before them some grand engineering proposal.

I rose to the challenge, as you might expect, and led the party up and down a stretch of the tunnel under Edinburgh's fine broad boulevards. I had read a few things about the railway of the Glasgow District Subway Company, and I outlined the scope and extent of the works. I then contrasted this relatively small railway with the grander achievement of Edinburgh's own Circular Railway, which rapidly brought in passengers from far and near, above ground. I advised the good men who had sought my advice that this single tunnel was ill-suited to run modern railway engines. It was a tunnel which came from nowhere at its northern end and had only a single but flawed benefit – that it came into the main station of Edinburgh, but at right-angles. I concluded thus, eloquently, as I believe: "In summary, gentlemen, it is my firm belief, based upon sound engineering principles, that the citizens of Edinburgh would be best served by investment in the railways it already possesses, and has newly expanded, which lie above ground. It is my belief that the people of Glasgow are driven underground because they simply have no beauty to charm their eyes when they travel in the light of day. And, finally, sirs, it is my belief that this tunnel should be left as it is."

This was not what Mr. Finlay or his friends expected. Evidently, the real Watson had been engaged on the basis of advocating some grandiose and utterly impractical underground railway – I had come across such fantasists before, and valued them poorly. My clients muttered among themselves as I expounded the virtues of railways built above ground. They looked askance at me as I denigrated the cost, and the filth, and the impracticalities, and the dangers of railways running under the earth. Finally, they broke out in exasperation.

"What way is this to waste our time?" exclaimed Gardner, squaring up to Mr. Finlay. "I am away now to look after my medical supply business, as I should have done hours ago. Good day!" And with that he, and Scobie and Clark, stalked off down the tunnel to Waverley. Finlay and the Clerk of Works turned their wrath upon me and castigated me for several minutes. Then Finlay let loose a diatribe against Gardner and other "plowtering truss-makers". Finally, to my horror, they turned northwards and started towards Scotland-yard.

I attempted to head them off, for I knew they must surely come across our subterranean encampment, where trouble would fall upon us. But it was to no avail. The Clerk of Works had decided that they should see for themselves what lay at the northern end of the tunnel. As I kept up with them, I was torn between escaping southwards or staying with them to meet disaster. By the time I had decided that a discreet retreat was best, we had come upon John and James Finlay in their camp.

There was a great deal of confusion in the next few minutes. Mr. Johnston and Mr. MacTavish were at first astounded at the sight of these unwashed primitives and, not unnaturally, shied away from them. When they realised the two men were no physical threat, their natural habits of authority took over and they started to bully the intruders.

The Canals of Scotland – October, 1895.

It was a time to flee. James Finlay adroitly separated their discoverers from their lights, and, picking up such belongings as we had, we stepped post-haste towards Scotland-street Station, leaving the outraged magistracy of Edinburgh floundering in the dark, cursing and calling for assistance.

We stumbled out in a raw evening into the brambles and nettles which carpeted the station-yard. Thinking perhaps that we would not be pursued and that we had best wait for Mr. Rinck, we concealed ourselves as best we could. As the minutes and hours went past, we found that we were not disturbed. We spent the night in short slumbers, always expecting the heavy hand of the law to descend upon us from the darkness. Of Mr. Rinck, there was no sign at all.

In the night, old John Finlay whispered to me that he had a fear of dying in the great city and wished to return without delay to Jura. I readily agreed, keenly aware that there was no place for us in Edinburgh, and that we had best escape to some remote part of the land as soon as we could.

We were surprised in our concealment the following morning by two men with a cart and pair. They introduced themselves as employees of the great company of Asa Wass & Sons, of Fountainbridge. Etched upon the cart, but not the steaming horses, was a brief history and description of the business. "Established 1858. Cash Buyers and Sellers of the Following: Old Horse Shoes, Malleable Scrap Iron, Cast Iron, Cast Iron Borings, Brass, Gun Metal, Zinc, Pewter, Lead, Block Tin, and Other Non-Ferrous Metals in any Reasonable Quantities, Rags, Woollens, Bagging, Rabbit and Hare Skins." Mr. Young and Mr. Dickie were the two representatives of this company, and their purpose here, on this cold morning, was to clear some of the detritus on the ground. However, they were men of very cheerful disposition and in no way anxious to go about their legitimate business, so they shared a cup of tea with us. (James Finlay made the fire and Mr. Dickie provided the tea-leaves, the tea-pot and the cups – of exquisite china, it must be noted, although the pot possessed no lid and the cups were all devoid of handles.)

After our night of disaster, this was a heartening re-introduction to the better side of humanity.

Once our breakfast was completed to everyone's satisfaction, we were cordially invited to assist Messrs. Young and Dickie in loading their cart with sundry rusted metal frames and items of machinery. I had youthful memories of the "Patent Royal Gymnasium" on this very site, and supposed these hulks to be the relics of the old pleasure-ground. We undertook our work with some eagerness – I think its repetitive and physical nature took our minds completely away from our present position.

James Finlay's exertions soon meant that the cart was loaded and creaking, much to the dismay of the two cart-horses, who turned to peer from their blinkers at the unreasonable load they were now expected to drag back to Fountainbridge. Our two new friends were delighted to let us sit among the scrap, as we proceeded by way of Dundas-street and Princes-street to Fountainbridge. The trams upon the main thorough-fare astonished James Finlay to a large degree.

The yard of Wass & Sons was a busy, noisy place, full of men shouting, horses steaming and boys and women engaged in obscure tasks among piles of metal and rags. Seeing the activity, an idea occurred to me and I asked young Mr. Dickie whether Mr. Wass sent goods out of town.

"Oh aye, Mr. Watson," he replied eagerly (for I had adopted temporarily the name of the champion of underground railways for whom I had been mistaken the previous day). "Mr. McKelvie yonder is making for Falkirk this very day. It was Falkirk you wanted?" he asked, in that tone which implied a sure knowledge of our requirements.

Now, Falkirk was not a place I had ever wished to visit, but that morning its very name seemed as attractive to me as El-dorado might have sounded to the ancient Conquistador. Falkirk, therefore, it was.

What took me by surprise was that we intended to reach Falkirk by boat; for at the back of the Fountainbridge premises there lies the eastern end of the great Union Canal – a stretch of water, it should be noted, as long nearly as the railway from Garve to Ullapool.

We therefore embarked for our journey to the El-dorado of Stirling-shire upon a barge which lay moored behind the Wass yard. Its Captain, Mr. McKelvie, turned out to be as talkative as any man I have ever encountered. This was a mixed blessing, for the excitements of recent hours, and the exertions of the morning, and the puffing, steady pace of the steam-barge, lulled me to a deep slumber just after our ship had passed across the fields below the inspiring edifice of the new Craig-house Asylum; from whose many turrets and windows, doubtless, people far saner than I were gazing down in wonder. But McKelvie's words simply hummed past my ears, and neither of the Finlays seemed to pay any attention to his views on Mr. Wass, on the other travellers on the canal, the delays at the locks, the rich bourgeois of Polwarth, nor a myriad other items of debate. This lack of interest did not prevent McKelvie from talking energetically the full journey from Fountainbridge to Falkirk.

Mr. McKelvie was also the proud owner of a startling yellow hair-piece, worn much like a hat and tied firmly to his head with a sturdy black strip of leather. But this was indeed a wise precaution, for there was a wind howling across the plains of Scotland which must have chilled even the hardiest of the residents of Kerguelen. It was freezing cold, so I found a sheltered place among piles of iron below deck. The Finlays provided able assistance to the boatman by heaving coal for the small steam-engine, and in sundry heavy tasks, to which I was suited neither in body, nor in mind.

My awakening towards five o'clock had me thinking at first that I had slept past midnight; but I found that we were inside a long tunnel. When we emerged, we came suddenly in sight of the belching chimneys and famous red furnaces of Falkirk. The gloomy afternoon was lit up by the flames; it was as if we had come across a landscape of belching volcanoes. We passed close behind many of these huge iron-works, where the dark shapes of men scurried like ants, amid sparks and molten fire. There was a continuous roar of both furnace and machinery, and the whole landscape of Purgatory seemed to shake with the noise and to stink.

For about an hour we drifted amazed through this desolation until our barge reached its destination, and we disembarked at the Camelon Iron-works. The long-winded advice of Mr. McKelvie, whom I gave to understand that we were headed for Glasgow, was to find a man by the name of Wrightson, at the place where the Union Canal joined with the Firth & Clyde Canal, and through him a barge on its way to the west.

It may sound improbable, but this was as easy said as it was achieved. We found Mr. Wrightson in his small cabin over-looking the junction of those two canals, and he pointed us immediately in the direction of a barge tied up at the quay. I negotiated briefly with the boatman, Mr. Muir, who was willing to take us on the following morning. We spent the night under an up-turned boat.

On the morning of the thirteenth, I awoke with a fever upon me; this was hardly unexpected, given my exertions and exposure to the weather in recent days. I struggled to my feet and led the Finlays to our barge. Mrs. Muir saw my condition and immediately found me a quiet dry corner, where I lay down and spent the following three days in sweating and tossing and turning as one within the grasp of death. It is my belief that I do not sicken easily, but that when I do, my body is assailed all the more dangerously by agues and fevers; my mother frequently scoffed at such thoughts. But I felt then that I would die upon the canal. I believe I must have spent three days in the grip of hallucination, for I dreamed continuously of a march through the bogs of Kerguelen.

Mrs. Muir and her husband had two children, aged about six or seven years, who seemed unconcerned at the feverish imaginings and the words which must have poured from my mouth. Once or twice, when my brain saw clearly, they pointed out the passing land to me. They chattered excitedly as we drifted across the wintry fields to the south of the pretty town of Kilsyth. As we came up to the town of Kirkintilloch, they could tell me the names of all the coal mines, and informed me when we came up to the mouth of the canal which led off to Monklands; here we observed many boats passing up and down the canal. All these barges and their crews, it seemed, were known to the two boys, for there was much waving and yelling.

But for all this passing activity, we were as far from the highways of Scotland as Kerguelen was from the shipping-routes of the sea.

I awoke on the Tuesday drained, but with a clear mind again. As the day passed, we came around the north of Bishopbriggs, then passed through Maryhill. At this point, some of the greatest achievements of canal-engineering are revealed, which the Reader should not fail to inspect if afforded the opportunity. First, we passed that spur of the canal which penetrates to the very heart of Glasgow. Continuing in our westerly direction, we then came to a series of locks, named, for no good reason that Mr. Muir could suggest, the 'Botany Locks'. This took some time, but we were all pleased to have James Finlay, so active and with the strength of two men, to provide encouragement to the grumbling lock-keepers to get us through these basins at a swift pace. As we descended, we saw stretching before us an impressive aqueduct, some fifty or sixty feet above the vale of the beautiful River Kelvin. This bridge of water must have been a good one hundred yards in length, and for all that distance I marvelled that we could glide so smoothly over the glen many, many feet below. Although this canal was over a hundred years old, it still delighted the senses of an engineer; but the railways will undoubtedly last longer than such simple con-structions, which rely solely on the weight and natural properties of water.

As we traversed the aqueduct, Mr. Muir's two boys ran along the tow-path on one side of us, and even launched themselves up on their sturdy arms to peer over the edge of the stone balustrade. I shut my eyes in horror. Luckily, Mrs. Muir shared my anxieties, and, with a single shout and a brace of cuffs, brought them back to security in the boat.

Late in the afternoon, we came down near to the River Clyde, and reached our destination, the small village of Bowling. We descended through the final locks into the basin, over-looking by some thirty feet the huge harbour which has been constructed by the river. The cargo we had brought was to be transferred to some larger vessel on the following day, for onward shipment to Ulster. We disembarked here before the final descent into the harbour, thanking our boatman and his kind wife.

As we found our feet on dry land once more and were shouldering our baggage, two police constables emerged from the door of the high Customs House and came down the steps towards us. I thought immediately that the long reach of Mr. Yellowlees and of Edinburgh's Magistrates had finally touched us!

Helensburgh – October, 1895.

The two constables approached us as we stood shivering by the dock, gave us scarcely a glance, and advised us, in those ugly meaningless words, to 'move along quickly'. Relieved not to be placed under arrest, I was glad to oblige them, with John and James Finlay at my heels.

Where to move along to? – that was my next thought. For the sleet had begun again, night had fallen, and there was no place for rest. We came out on to the road which led, one way, to that city of deprivation and depravity, Glasgow, and, the other way, to the wildness of Dumbarton and beyond. How I longed for a warm bed!

Before we had come out on to the muddy, miserable road, we had passed under a railway bridge which bestrode the canal, just beyond the Customs House. The arches of this at least gave shelter, so we retired under one for the night. Our feet were buffeted by a wind which swept up the River Clyde, our ears felt the cold spattering of the sleet upon the brickwork.

On the following morning, I was required to make a decision. I fear my knowledge of the western part of Britain's coast is very sketchy, and I was in some doubt as to whether Jura might lie to the north or to the south of Oban. Our only hope was to make use of the railway-line which passed over our heads. I found it a hard thing to suggest – being a loyal employee of a Railway Company – but I proposed that we avail ourselves of an empty wagon or carriage in a passing train, and make our way westwards in that. I was certain that this railway could take us at least part of our way, for it ran through Crianlarich and so to Oban, whence I supposed we might sight Jura.

This proposal met with ready acceptance from James Finlay; his uncle seemed beyond caring. We therefore made our way through the silent village of Bowling to its little station, where I made a thorough examination of the Timetable posted there by the North British Railway Company. It was at that time barely seven o'clock and I found that there was a train due at twenty-three minutes before ten.

There was time for me to search out a shop that would supply us with three mugs of tea and a steaming meat-pie. I passed some upsetting moments in counting, and counting again, the meagre amount of money left to me, even after borrowing from my trusting sister. It was clear that we could not go on for much longer in this way. We had to balance the cost of travelling quickly, without meals, against the cost of travelling slowly, with meals. Although they trusted to my judgement, none of this seemed to make much sense to either Finlay, who had had no dealings with money all their lives.

In order that we could board the train unobserved, we moved slightly beyond the station at half-past nine, and concealed ourselves in some bushes. The train pulled in, there was some disembarkation and embarkation; the whistle blew, the train slowly got up steam and wheezed past us. Unobserved, as I hoped, we separately seized the handles on the doors to the goods-wagon, and hung on for dear life. The plan was that we should enter this van just as we pulled into the next station. All went well, in so far as none of us came detached, despite the raw nature of the day. As we slowed down into Dumbarton Station, James Finlay pulled open the door and hoisted us in. We concealed ourselves forthwith behind some parcels, and a rather elegant lady's bicycle; the far door was soon flung open and trunks and boxes were pulled out and heaved in. Luckily, no one saw us, and soon we were on our way, undetected.

This was no easy journey for me, although my companions seemed to have no cares in the world. I attribute this to the society in which they had lived, where there was no railway, no guard, no policeman, no magistrate to cut short a man's career with awful words of righteous condemnation. But it was not natural for me to feel innocent when travelling without a ticket. If we should be caught, what then? An engineer for a Railway Company found guilty before the Law of evading payment while travelling on a Railway Company's train!

It seemed to me, as our train rattled towards Helensburgh, that in the past few days, in trying to follow goodness and to bring comfort to the victims of an unnatural crime, I had without doubt found myself wandering fitfully in the County of Evil. I had not performed the work of Goodness well; nor had I undertaken the tasks of Wickedness with any measure of success. I was neither good nor bad, but a man who had failed to make good his intentions. I looked at myself – a bundle of damp rags in the corner of a shaking railway goods-wagon, somewhere west of Glasgow, with little money in my pocket; fleeing from crimes in which I had not participated; accompanied by two men who had no place in our society; and with no clear idea where I was headed.

As if to rub salt into my wounds, we were discovered at Helensburgh. The train rolled to a halt, the door to the goods-van was thrown open and a porter clambered in to retrieve the lady's bicycle. As he struggled with the bicycle, his eyes met mine in the gloom; for a second, I perceived that the sight had not registered; then he lurched backwards in shock.

"Mr. Macpherson!" we heard him cry as he leaped from the van, "Mr. Macpherson, come quickly!"

Mr. Macpherson turned out to be a very officious Station-Master with an exaggerated sense of his own importance. Rushing up to the scene in the goods-wagon, he refused to listen to any words I had to say, simply ranted at us and shouted at us and gesticulated. Such a proceeding proved very sore for me: for I am at heart an honest man, and cannot bear to be disbelieved, nor to have my reasonable words of explanation simply ignored by men whose minds are made up, nor to find no response to simple questions! It is a fault of mine that I feel such outrage, when dealing with utterly unreasonable men. I felt anger and frustration surge up inside me, and I began to shout back at him. At which point, the cowardly Mr. Macpherson retreated behind the porter, and blew his whistle to summon – I supposed – a policeman.

We did not wait to find out how close that policeman might be. We rose up out of our hiding-places, like three scare-crows, and fairly threw ourselves out of the van by the opposite door, across the tracks and into the bushes, leaving behind a great commotion and cry. We ran full tilt down the road, and round as many corners as we could hope to see, to leave all uproar behind us.

We came shortly to a quiet road, lined with trees, some cottages and a pair of comfortable villas. There was no pedestrian on the road, no carriage. A solitary squirrel darted up a tree at our approach, but this was the only sign of life. I believe it was the squirrel which put the idea in James Finlay's mind to seek food. He proposed that he should go and knock at the door of one of the smaller cottages and ask for some soup. John would accompany him. I did not dare to suggest that either or both of them might not receive a warm welcome; I was only relieved that Finlay had not suggested hunting down the squirrel for luncheon.

The cottage we chose was of pleasant appearance, having recently been painted white; smoke trickled upwards from its chimney. At the door we saw a lady of middle years, apparently smitten by untrammelled grief and lamentation: for her long fair hair streamed wild, as, by turns, she wrung her hands and shook her fists.

At the sight of us, the woman came running over.

"Oh, can you please help me?!" she asked breathlessly, and with a curious accent to her voice. "For these geese are gone in the house and I cannot chase them out!"

We passed into the garden through a rickety gate, which unhappily fell apart as I attempted to close it, leaving me holding a few sticks of wood. The woman did not notice this mishap, so I propped the sticks against the wall and moved on. The noise from inside the cottage was fiendish – had we not been told that these were geese in there, we would have perhaps imagined that the very portals of Hades had been opened up. So startled was I by a sudden crescendo in this demonic din, that I stepped back and accidentally put my foot through a cold-frame, which burst apart like a cannon-shot. The woman was intent on the commotion in the house and noticed nothing.

A man not given to second thoughts, James Finlay simply marched into the house, whereupon the commotion doubled in volume.

"How did they get in?" I asked, trying to calm the woman down.

"Oh, the elves have broken the door and the geese have escaped their house!" she cried, waving wildly in the direction of a rather ramshackle hen-house. "And then my cats did chase them, and they all ran in my house!"

At that very moment two cats, one very fat one, black and white, the other ginger, shot out of the door squealing, and disappeared round the back of the cottage. There was a brief pause, then, in great rushes, like a mountain river in spate, geese came flying out the door, closely pursued by a whirlwind that was James Finlay. In less than a minute, the cottage was apparently cleared of its unwelcome occupants. There was no sign of any elves, but I did not pursue this matter. The woman was rushing round her small garden, rounding up the geese, of which, despite immediate appearances, there were only six, and chased them back into the hen-house. John Finlay, I noticed, assisted her in this endeavour, and pushed the door closed behind them.

Once this was done, the woman ran into her house and fell to shrieking and crying, using words of a language which were quite unfamiliar to me. Tentatively, I followed her inside.

What an appalling sight met my eyes! It appeared as if the interior of the cottage had been struck by an Atlantic gale. Pictures had fallen from the walls, plates and cups lay broken on the floor, there was unmentionable dirt smeared on chairs and walls. A large china umbrella-stand had tumbled over, and spilled out its contents, but remained unbroken.

In the middle of this scene of domestic devastation stood the woman, crying into a huge pink handkerchief.

I stood at the threshold, rather embarrassed, unsure whether I should comfort her, or make a quiet retreat.

As I hesitated, she turned round and saw me. "Oh, what a catastrophe!" she cried in her curious accent. "All the nice things of my house!"

I mumbled some words and thought it best to try to bring order back to the house. I began to pick up those items of furniture and decoration which were not smashed beyond repair, in order to return them to what seemed to me to be the correct places.

I must note here that I do not think I have ever really understood the Fair Sex. It seems to me that, when a man does his best, perhaps in ignorance, to be kind and helpful, then his best is never good enough for a distraught woman. At least, that is the way it is with me. From my mother onwards, any woman I have had dealings with has found fault with my well-intentioned actions. So it was with my new acquaintance. She glared at my attempts to create order out of chaos for several seconds, then swooped down on me.

"No, not there!" she cried, shouldering me aside as I placed a picture-frame, with a photograph of a handsome man, upon the dresser. "Here, I must put back dear Glum." And she dusted the frame with her apron and placed it on a small table. "If you wish to help, then take that broom and sweep this floor."

I did as I was bidden. Peering from the small window as I passed along the floor, I saw that the Finlays had decided to repair the damaged hen-house. The maintenance of over-turned structures must have been a daily chore on Kerguelen.

After some considerable time, the woman seemed satisfied with the reparations to her domestic environment. "Now I will make some nice cups of tea," she said. "Forgive me," she held out her hand, hot from the house-work. "My name is Mrs. Snorrison. This is my house."

"And these were your geese," I replied, intending to make a joke, for I have found that most women respond more easily to a bantering attitude than to a serious one. Unfortunately, Mrs. Snorrison seemed not to be of the majority, for she burst into tears again.

"Ah, those horrible birds!" she railed. "I must kill them all – for me they are no good!" She snatched up a large knife from the table, and began to march out to terminate the existence of the unfortunate fowl. Scarce thinking what I did, I sprang forward to bar her way.

"No, you must not do that, Madam!" I urged, holding up my hands as she waved the steel blade distractedly under my nose. The woman was slightly taller than myself; in her despair she seemed not one to cross. Having found myself in her way, I could only hope to bluff my way to success.

She sighed. "Of course, you are right. Let us drink tea together, instead."

This seemed more acceptable. As she busied herself in the kitchen, she told me that she was an unhappy widow, who had come from Iceland to this part of Scotland ten years previously. Her husband,

Mr. Glum Snorrison, had come to seek employment in Bearsden as a topiarist, which skill he had learned in the old family business in Iceland. If I might be permitted to make a small play on words, subsequent events indeed proved "glum"!

The previous Christmas, Mrs. Snorrison told me, as the steam billowed out from her untended kettle, and filled the little scullery to the extent that we could barely see each other, a sword-swallower had passed through Helensburgh, putting on a show at the "big house" to earn his keep. It seemed they were on their way to meet a circus at Rothesay, that veritable Gomorrah of the West. Inebriated, no doubt, by the sight of the oiled fleshy thighs and flashing eyes of the sword-swallower's female assistant (for I have seen such things!), Glum Snorrison threw up his calling, and left home, geese and wife to go off with the sword-swallower for to learn this new trade. But barely had he arrived in Rothesay than Mr. Snorrison was struck down by an appalling accident; not, as might have been appropriate for a man who flagrantly deserted his wife, in swallowing a sword, or similar lengthy metallic object; but in being bitten by the circus bear; as a consequence of which Mr. Snorrison swelled up horribly and died.

From the little tears like diamonds which she shed, it seems that Mrs. Snorrison forgave her husband's temporary lapse of judgement. I, however, could not do so, and raged inwardly against that heartless wretch.

When the tea was brewed, I carried a tray outside, and we sat coldly in the watery sunshine of the afternoon: the Icelandic widow, the two exiles from Kerguelen, and myself — as rootless as any of my companions. I introduced the Finlays to the widow, and gave a short and rather romantic outline of our purpose — the return of the exiles to their home. Such a sketch perforce omitted to mention the unfortunate events in Edinburgh.

Suddenly, Mrs. Snorrison noticed the destruction of her gate, and then of her cold-frame. She blamed it on her geese, and looked for her steel instrument of fate. While I did not go so far as to correct her allocation of blame, I did persuade her to spare the innocent geese their lives; and assured her that James Finlay would repair the damage, just as soon as he had completed the securing of the hen-house.

As we sat at the table, John Finlay made a curious intervention. On learning that the widow hailed from far Iceland, he said: "Ah, lady, fortunate for you that you escaped from the war between your country and the Turks!"

Mrs. Snorrison looked puzzled; and I hastened to cover her confusion, for I deduced that this must be yet another of the tall tales which had been spun to Finlay by his captors on Kerguelen; a war between Iceland and Turkey being as likely as the famous winter expedition of the Mexicans which finally destroyed the might of Nippon, of which Finlay had also told me.

"I think, Mr. Finlay," I said tactfully, "that our hostess has not heard of such a thing . . . "

"Oh, but no!" interrupted the Icelandic beauty, much to my surprise and chagrin, "Mr. Finlay is quite correct in this, although I cannot think how he knows it! That war was many, many years ago, Mr. Finlay, when these Turks came and stole away much men and boys. It was maybe three hundred years ago. And these men and these boys never saw their homes again, but were sold into slaves."

This thought brought tears to the good lady's eyes. And for me, it brought a great feeling of unease: what if all the other stories told to the people of Kerguelen also had some basis in truth? What if there were wars and campaigns indeed between the most unlikely opponents, and massacres taking place in remote parts of the Earth? What if the *lingua franca* of the continent of South America was indeed Finnish? What if the stories we read in newspapers were undiluted invention, as much a fiction as this History is fact?

As the afternoon drew on, and we all finally retired indoors to the warmth, I began to feel an overwhelming urge to woo this woman, and to marry her, and to settle down in Helensburgh, where there was no more wandering, no more living in fear of the Law, no more bleak reminder of the Island of Desolation, no Finlay, no Rinck; just myself, a warm fire, a cup of sweet tea and a fine-featured woman of some maturity. On two occasions, I found myself about to blurt out some nonsense, some reckless declaration of attachment to her, which would doubtless have caused her to order me from her home. I realise now that all of this was an effect of my physical and mental exhaustion, and the strongly contrasting peace and delight of that small cottage. But even now, I wonder how it would have been, to save that woman from her lonely widow-hood, and to make a new life for myself by the gentle lapping waters of the Gare-loch.

What fanciful dreaming! What fiction!

We left that house with our stomachs full, our feet warm from the fire, and our pockets full of small parcels of dried fish. I had noted that there was a train due later in the day, which I expected would reach Helensburgh at about six o'clock. Although there was a danger that Mr. Macpherson or his police-constable might be on a sharp look-out, we decided to try again our chances at travelling ticket-less.

Our luck held this time as far as Tarbet, where we were again discovered.

The Station-Master at Tarbet was, in contrast to the Macpherson of Helensburgh, a kindly man, who shook his head sadly and asked us if we would "please vacate the goods-wagon, since passengers without tickets are not permitted to travel on to Ardlui and Crianlarich". We saw no reason to deny this polite man, and so climbed out. How pleasant it was to converse with one's fellow-man, rather than be bullied and cajoled and ignored – yes, even if the conversation was not to my advantage!

The Station-Master asked me whither we were bound.

"Go to Inveraray, then, and follow Loch-awe, then find the road to Craignish," was his sound advice, after some consideration. The man seemed to be a profound geographer, a walking gazetteer! "For I suppose you have no money for the train?"

Since he supposed correctly, we turned our faces to the west, down the road to Inveraray, which was pointed out to us.

I cannot hope to convey to you the awfulness of the days and nights we spent in our journey from Tarbet, through Inveraray, and down the interminable length of Loch-awe. The Reader might find it in his heart to forgive my swift passing over of the likely splendours of the mountains and lochs: I have heard that these are very beautiful places indeed. But we were, alas! no touring party. The weather broke foul about us. We did not have the energy to lift our heads from the mud and water which stretched out six or ten feet ahead of us, nor did our feet ever stray to admire the many wonders at the side of the road. At times, this all seemed so absurd that I laughed aloud; and had no sooner done so than regretted it, for the rain lashed in my face. I would step in a puddle or in sodden bog and find my feet submerged under several inches of instantly chilling water. We walked and we walked through this endless misery, with no idea and no care of where we went, our limbs following a law of their own, which demanded that one foot be set in front of the other, and then set again, until we reached our journey's end. My feet lost all feeling. When I examined them in the evenings, I beheld large white wrinkled and peeling masses of skin, and I concealed them from myself, horrified. Throughout these long days, I knew that my body was subjected to the dampest forces of Nature. But there came a time at which it no longer mattered how wet I became, for I could become no wetter; nor how cold I grew, for I was cold enough.

At length, towards noon on the eighteenth day of October, we came to the village of Ard-Fern, where there were a few cottages and an inn. We asked for directions, and were advised that the ferry to Jura left from the end of the road which continued to the south, at a place named Craignish.

The Finlays Depart – October, 1895.

At John Finlay's suggestion, we made the ascent of a hill to the west of the Craignish road, to spy out the land. It was not high, and in barely half an hour we stood on a windy top, gazing out across the sea to many islands. I did not know at the time what islands they were, knowing only that Jura was the large one which stretched for miles away to the south. But old John Finlay looked eagerly at them all, and named the others – Scarba, with its head in the clouds, Lunga, Shuna, Luing – all of them wild and black and cold. Far below us, waves heaved and crashed on the rocks.

Having regained the high road, we soon passed the gates of Craignish Castle and found ourselves at the end of the road; an impressive pier had been built here, jutting out into the wild waters of the sea. From its size, I imagined that the boats which plied from here to Jura must be very large indeed. But, on later consideration, I supposed the pier was for coastal steamers to deliver and uplift cattle, goods and passengers from Glasgow or Oban or other important places, passing Jura only on their voyages.

There was no one to ask, but our informant at Ard-Fern had said that the ferry to Jura would come towards four o'clock. We sat down to wait. John Finlay said scarcely a word, but gazed out keenly to the northern tip of Jura, where tiny houses could just be seen. When I asked him what that village was, he said it was Kenuachdrachd. I remembered that this was the name of the village which Mr. Lunn's emigrants had left behind them. Fifty-five years had passed since he had seen his village, and in the interval he had lived enough sorrow and misery, and seen more than enough of the world and of the heartlessness of men, to last him several life-times and most of the after-life as well.

As we watched and waited, a thick fog began to arise from the sea. It came very fast, and no sooner was I dimly aware that the far horizon had vanished and with it both Scarba and Jura, than the cloud was all around us, as thick as wool and bitterly cold.

I had no idea what o'clock it might be, for my precious watch had long since lost any accuracy. I took every opportunity to re-set it from clocks in stations and inns, finding that it lost between ten and thirty minutes each day. But at last a small shape appeared from the fog at the end of the pier which, on closer inspection, revealed itself to be a sail-boat with four people in it. The appearance of a frail craft from nowhere at the end of an empty pier built on a gigantic scale, was disturbing to the eye.

James Finlay ran down to the boat and engaged the people in it in conversation. I strolled as far as the landward end of the pier and waited for the outcome. Two of the people turned out to be passengers, who disembarked, one bearing over his back a huge lumpy canvas bag containing something the size of a croft-house. They looked at me curiously, and acknowledged my greeting with a nod, then passed on up the road.

The boat was indeed the long-awaited ferry to Jura, and we three boarded. There were no other passengers: which was indeed fortunate, for the boat was scarcely nine feet from stem to stern, and barely wide enough for us to avoid sitting in each other's laps. A short mast was mounted in the bow, with two sails attached to it, the larger of which swept to the rear of the boat and rose to perhaps twelve feet above our heads. It was no pleasure-yacht, and I feared for our safety. The ferry-man was a small-framed man, who looked at first too frail for the job; but I watched him work at the tiller, and realised how much power he exercised over his craft. His assistant was a wee boy of perhaps eight years of age, whose sole task was to sit at the very bow facing backwards and stare at us wide-eyed and wordless for the entire duration of the crossing, as if trying to read our strange histories; or perhaps waiting for us to tilt him overboard into the lapping waters.

In such a craft and on such a day, we crossed the Lethe, if I might be both fanciful and Classical. But this was no Journey of Forgetting for me, and for John Finlay it was a Journey of Remembering. The crossing took perhaps three-quarters of one hour, during which time we saw nothing except fog. Our pilot seemed to know his direction. About half-way across we must have come close to some rocks, for we heard the crashing of waves at no great distance. But were not ship-wrecked. Throughout the journey, John Finlay sat close to the ferry-man and talked in a low voice to him, doubtless about matters of long-gone Jura and Kenuachdrachd.

At last, the sound of whispering surf was heard and we came surprisingly to a shore. Our pilot eased his boat in beside a jetty of flat rocks and we clambered out.

On the island itself, the fog had lifted somewhat, allowing us a view to some croft-houses, huddled under the lee of a hill, and the dim outline of a larger cottage on flat land to the north of our landing place. The clouds drifted past at no great height.

We made our way up from the shore to the crofts. They were low and thatched, each with smoke issuing from a chimney. Stacks of peat were piled up at the gable-ends. There were perhaps four or five in total; other buildings, now fallen into ruin, showed varying degrees of disuse – some still had wisps of thatch, others no roof and no door, the remainder still barely showed their walls above the reeds and the bracken. More than one had a rowan-tree growing from the hearth. Once, this place, with its uncivilised name, had been the home of a thriving community; now it was the last refuge of a handful of impoverished families.

A few members of these families emerged from the cottages as we approached, looking at us suspiciously. We had no money and nothing to trade except our wits and John Finlay's history. Had we been in some busy town, such as Moffat or Dunfermline or perhaps Dingwall, then I think that we would have had to fend for ourselves and find accommodation in the hills. But no sooner was our situation explained; partly by John Finlay, who now lapsed into the Celtic tongue, struggling apparently with words which his mouth had not formed for half a century; partly by our ferry-man, Mr. Campbell; than two or three women stepped forward and offered us food and shelter. Which we gladly took.

There were merely five cottages with occupants, and I counted fourteen residents in all – three houses contributed a handful of dirty children and the remaining two were singly occupied by suspicious ancients.

In the few days which followed, James Finlay was able to repay the kindness of these people with all manner of hard labour – shifting peats, carrying stones to repair walls, collecting kelp – all of which he undertook with the greatest of grace and willingness.

I was pleasantly startled to find that I could be of help to these people by repairing a bridge over a burn which rushed down from the hills above: would that Sir John Fowler could have seen me then, a true designer and builder of bridges! The original bridge was a simple affair – four planks of rotting and greasy wood embedded in mud; but two days of work saw the erection of a rather grand design with a solid sub-structure, using stones from the abandoned crofts firmly founded in the soil, and a wooden platform carried over it. The whole of which presented a most splendid and thrifty monument to modern engineering principles. When Jura has its own reviving railway, my successor will be able to run a railway-line over it! I believe that the great Thomas Telford undertook certain projects upon Jura and is praised particularly for his pier at Lagg; now the world can take note that a bridge by Kininmonth exists on Jura, which will probably outlive the last of the community of Kenuachdrachd.

John Finlay spent his days in sitting round the fires with the old men and women, and the younger ones too, talking to them in their language, by which I was excluded. I supposed that he was telling them of his childhood in these parts, of the exile of his family and neighbours to Kerguelen, of his life there and of his escape. Goodness knows what view of history he might have passed on to his listeners: what sea-battles between Patagonians and Swedes; what forced marches of the brown warriors of Ceylon upon the hill-forts of Bolivia; what cataclysm ripping open the land from Amsterdam to Zwickau; what plague of locusts upon Belfast?! (I apply these marks of exclamation and question, knowing, as I do so, that perhaps any or all of these things might be found to be true, were I to go out into the world and cross oceans and see things for myself.)

In the late evening of the last day of October, I sat with the two Finlays and a huddle of the last inhabitants of North Jura, watching a peat-fire slowly burn itself out in a miserable fireplace. The older man was now turned into himself; over the days he had talked himself into silence. He took no sustenance. It was clear that he was in very poor health.

I remarked on his uncle's condition to James, who merely shrugged. "It is time," he muttered; I found his remark disturbing. What did he mean, I demanded to know. "It is time for him to die," he said simply. "He will soon find the islands of the sea." I neither knew what he meant, nor what to say: this forsaken place was not one to which a doctor could readily be summoned. I confess that I could do no more than set a watch upon John Finlay, expecting every moment for him to fall out of his chair or slump backwards in rigor mortis – I had a very uncertain idea of the instant of death.

November 3, 1895.

In the small hours of Sunday, the third day of November, I was rudely shaken awake. "Come quickly, Mr. Kininmonth!" someone was shouting in my ear. "They have taken my boat and gone to Corryvreckan!" I opened my eyes and, by the light of the lantern he held above me, I saw Mr. Campbell in a state of extreme agitation. "They have left too soon, they will be lost!" I kept to my bed, still half-asleep, and wishing only that this worried man would leave me in peace.

Mr. Campbell, however, grasped my shoulders, pulled me from my couch of heather, and pushed me out of the door. It was a clear night, and a huge full moon cast its light far over the landscape. Campbell pointed me up the hill to the north, towards a path leading over a saddle. "That is the way we must go, Mr. Kininmonth," he said. "There is nothing else we can do but watch out for them!"

With that, we set off. From the other cottages, people emerged excitedly, and soon the entire community had picked up its skirts in the midnight hour to hurry up the short hill. After perhaps a quarter of an hour, we reached a vantage-point over-looking the dreadful Gulf of Corryvreckan. By then, I had lost my strength entirely, and had such a stabbing pain in my left side that I could scarce breathe, let alone speak. The Jurans seemed no worse for the experience, so I supposed they must undertake such strenuous exercise as part of their daily lives; two of them assisted me up the final slopes of a rocky outcrop, and we reached its summit together.

I believed then, as I stood gasping and scanning the waters, that an artist designing a railway poster to publicise the Fastness of Purgatory would have here a worthy subject. For I had seen the volcanic fires and smokes of Falkirk; I had seen the wasted land-scapes of Lanark-shire; I had witnessed ice and snow on the wild mountains of Ross-shire, which I never hoped to see again; but now I looked out upon a stretch of water which, I believe, can have no equal anywhere in these Isles.

Under the silver light of the moon, as far as I could see to the west and to the east, the water flowed like pitch; the blackness was in the water, not in the night; here and there were huge expanses where it seemed to shimmer with tiny dancing waves; in the centre of each of these was a blank, swirling area, which was alike to a cauldron on the point of boiling. Dark water seethed and turned on itself, with small pockmarks on its surface, but the whole as easy and as powerful as Death itself. These were not the whirlpools of which I had heard so many things, for I was told by Mr. Campbell, who now squatted beside me in our eyrie, that the infamous whirlpool lay over by the threatening cliffs of Scarba. No, what we looked at was simply the Atlantic Ocean in foul mood, grim and silently threatening, defying any sane man to come out upon its waters.

"The tide is not yet turning, Mr. Kininmonth," Mr. Campbell advised me. "Your friends should have gone out later."

I did not grasp what he meant and told him so.

"If you wish to come out of the Gulf without harm," he explained, "you should go in about half an hour before the tide turns against you. Then, the tide is slack. And if you are too late, then you will only be swept back out again."

I nodded, dimly comprehending what it was he told me, finding it rather irrelevant.

"And Mr. Finlay has gone in too soon and will be in the middle of it all when the tide turns and the sea moves," he completed simply. "Look! There they are!"

He pointed away off to the east, where I could now see the small boat come round the point. It was not Mr. Campbell's ferry-boat, he told me, but a smaller one he had; even at that distance, I could see James Finlay's large frame plying away at the oars, and the boat scudding out into the scarred open sea.

Like a madman, I began to wave and shout. This was fruitless activity. The rest of the audience to this race between Frail Man and Mighty Nature simply stood silently. After a few minutes, by which time I had shouted myself hoarse, I realised the futility of my attempts to warn the Finlays of the rashness of their action.

And so we just stood and watched. The small boat gradually and inexorably advanced across the huge boiling expanse of the Gulf, heading directly, it seemed to me, to the whirlpool. James Finlay rowed on tireless, and behind him I could just make out a tiny figure wrapped in a blanket.

I do not know how much time had passed before Mr. Campbell noted quietly that the tide was turning; we watched the Finlays come ever closer to Scarba, then, as if the thread had snapped which attached them to our world, vanish abruptly in the shadows. I observed two old women put up their shawls, as if resigned to some overwhelming fate. Slowly the people of the village turned to retreat down the hill, until only Mr. Campbell remained with me on that cold and draughty rock. There was nothing to be seen, except moonlight and shadow and the black water hundreds of feet below our view-point.

Jura – November, 1895.

And that was the last I saw then of the Finlays. On the following day, when the sun was up, we went back up to our view-point. A mist came in from the ocean and gradually blanketed our view, until we could see nothing of the huge cauldron except drifting cloud. Neither in the remainder of that terrible third day of November, nor on the following day, did anyone or anything re-appear from the sea. I was left to picture for myself what violent, hopeless death had met them in the Gulf of Corryvreckan, where the maelstrom devours men and boats without trace. Mr. Campbell talked of going over to Scarba when the weather cleared, but he had to wait for his brother, who lived further south at Lussa, to come in a craft which was more suited to such expeditions.

On the fifth day of the month, when all hope had vanished and I accepted that the Finlays had probably gone out in that boat in the full knowledge of what awaited them, I decided that it was time to leave this community, and to find again some threads of my own life. If he were not now languishing in an Edinburgh gaol, perhaps even now Rinck awaited me at Ullapool.

The day dawned blustery and the waves pounded on the shore. Mr. Campbell had proposed on the previous evening that he should take me back to Craignish in his afternoon ferry. His proposal seemed quite comfortable in the evening; but on the morning, my second thoughts must have stared out clearly from my face. Mr. Campbell came to me in the late morning, announcing that "the wind will get worse", and that he intended to make his crossing early. He asked me if I still wished to go. Knowing that the only alternative was a long and miserable walk to Lagg, and then the uncertain comfort of the ferry from there to the bustling port of Keills on the mainland, I decided that, where Mr. Campbell could go, so could I go.

Without fear, without hesitation, without shivering. But not without a considerable amount of inner doubt. Had I been a believer in a God of Reason, I would have prayed to Him to ask for forgiveness and, consequently, a safe journey; but the Almighty exerts His Will untroubled by the pleas of men; so I prayed not; and we set out through the crashing surf.

The journey from Kenuachdrachd to Craignish was one which, by a blessed fault in the memory, I cannot recall in much detail. An old woman and her son from a croft some miles to the south had joined us for the crossing. Together we tossed in the waves, and seemed never to escape from the magnetism of the shore, for many a long hour. Once out into the open sea, our boat alternately plunged into the huge chasms which opened up in the water, or was flung high and sideways into the streaming air.

One single vision remains clear in my mind, and to this day I feel a thrill of terror in my lower innards as I see it again: as we towered on the peak of a heaving wave, I beheld the grim rocks of Garbh Reisa and Reisa an t-Sruith below us, terrifyingly close. It seemed for a brief moment, until I concealed my head in my hands, that I had reached the end of my allotted time, that my bones would crack upon these reefs, and I would ever so briefly have my entrails spilt under the skies, before my separated limbs were washed away into the tumultuous seas. For the forces of the sea simply do not know the thin nutshells of our boats, and we were likely to be smashed on the rocks as easily as the waters themselves, and the noise of our passing and our cries would be as nought amid the din of the spume and the green seas.

I do not think it unreasonable to propose that engineers, such as myself, have an ultimate duty to construct objects which keep fellow-men from danger. It is the duty of a marine-engineer to build great ships and tend to the engines which bring them safely across the widest seas; it is the duty of a railway-engineer to build railways which stride across country infested by Midge and scoured by blizzard; it is the duty of a structural engineer to build bridges and viaducts and supporting walls to ensure that no person has to come into unnecessary proximity with the elemental forces of Nature. At the close of this nineteenth century, it is an anachronism that people, and most especially railway-engineers, can come so close to death by drowning.

I could only admire the skill of Mr. Campbell, who steered us a course through this nightmare with the calm of a man who has seen far worse. And so at last we came within reach of the pier at Craignish, for which sight I had never felt so grateful.

Having remained utterly unconcerned throughout the crossing, the old woman and her son set off up the road without another word, as if disembarking a Circular-line train at Waverley. Mr. Campbell seemed at least to understand why I must have appeared so white; he clapped me on the back, as I staggered to my feet, and clambered up on to the jetty. I clutched a solid wooden pile and watched the ferry-man set off back into the maelstrom, considering myself fortunate not to have suffered a fate as bleak as that which must have over-taken the Finlays near their Island of Sorrow.

A Post-script.

The Reader might well ask, as I have reached the end of my second Volume, how I returned from the end of the land at Craignish and came back to the solid ground and calm airs of Braemore, where I now sit and write these lines? But I have decided that I will not itemise the travails which I under-went over those weeks in journeying from Craignish to Braemore; in which I saw more of the slavering jaws of dogs and the angry brooms of bristling matrons than I care to remember. For I was without money at all, and had not shaved for weeks; my clothing was damp and it stank; my hair was wild and heavy with the salt of the sea. My eyes were dark with grief and exhaustion; my face must have been a mask of hunger, for I ate but irregularly. Such attempts as I made to beg – yes, a man of my skill reduced to that, I may now confess! – were usually rebuffed. Where exactly I found food, I cannot advise the Reader without fear of legal reprisal.

A man outcast in our society, for whatever reason, is treated as one who has failed. In the space of these long days, I saw enough of the fear of respectable citizens for those of their fellows who have 'failed', that I sometimes wonder whether I can make honest conversation with such citizens again. I am not ashamed to have had to beg; I do not conceal my reduction to penury; I am proud to have lived as the poor and the vagrants do; for their self-esteem is far more moral than the comfortable disdain of the well-to-do!

In my journey, I passed the continuing works to bring the Skye

Line from Strome-ferry to Kyle, and admired greatly the fact that the Highland Railway Company seemed to have no trouble finding the Capital to invest in such inspired engineering.

I came at last to Braemore on the thirteenth of January, 1896, to discover that Mr. Gilleasbuig Gillies and his three-legged dog were no longer at their post. Finding the station deserted, I called upon my friend, Mrs. MacMahon, who told me that there had been a drunken altercation between Gillies and two servants from Braemore Lodge, during a violent Hogmanay celebration. Their argument centred around the relative merits of three- and four-legged creatures. Insults were traded; heads were broken; Mr. Arthur Fowler had demanded Gillies' dismissal; MacAulay had complied; Gillies and his dog had been banished without appeal to Dundonnell by the Destitution Road.

Seizing my chance, I availed myself of a razor belonging to Mrs. MacMahon's son and of Mr. Gillies' official hat and whistle; gave myself the veneer of respectability; and assumed my duties once more. The Board were advised of my self-appointment to the post of Relief Station-Master by letter despatched with the next train. Given my record of employment, the Board did not balk at this *fait accompli*, and were pleased to pay me a pittance.

I continue to execute the duties with a smartness and courtesy that our passengers would not believe possible on a railway-line north of Edinburgh. In the hours which elapse between trains, I have reviewed the notes in my Order Book, and have set down upon paper, kindly donated by Mr. Hector Fraser, the grocer and dry-salter on Shore-street, the history of my travels from Talla to Jura in 1895. I greatly regret that, when the Finlays sailed into Corryvreckan, they took with them their Bible. This book, which contained all proof of the tragedy of the community upon Kerguelen, was now doubtless at the very base of that insatiable maw of the ocean, the words of ink washed into the dark ink of a sea which none can read. It was fortunate indeed that I had copied out all the words which had been written there by various hands, and had them safe in my Order Book; but, at the same time, unfortunate, since I can now no longer produce the singular and incontrovertible evidence for a history which some will find hard to believe.

Volume III:

From Braemore to Ullapool
or,
The Citadel of the Elect.

April, 1897.

In the night of the eleventh of April, in the Eventful Year of 1897, the temporary station-buildings at Braemore Halt at last gave up the struggle against the elements, and with a prolonged groan and a ripping sound – which acted as a warning that gave me time to jump nimbly from my bed and dash out into the black night – began to buckle and vibrate in an alarming manner. Not for long, however, for the force of the gale soon detected this weakness, picked up the four walls and the roof of the building, and hurled them up into the screaming air. As if conjured away by an Illusionist in the Empire Palace, the Braemore Halt building vanished utterly and rapidly into the night, leaving its sole occupant, Mr. Alexander Auchmuty Kininmonth, quite exposed to the elements of an equinoctial storm. I stood there, dressed only in the thick woollen socks knitted for me by Mrs. MacMahon; these covered the thinner socks without which I never retire for the night. Luckily, I had managed to grab one of my blankets in my hasty departure, and I pulled this closer around me as I sought shelter from the tremendous gale which raged above my head. And in my left hand I clutched my boots, which I had thought to seize in passing out from my now roof-less and wall-less bed-chamber. Rain, sharp as needles, drove from the sky. The wind howled and boomed, like an express-train coming through the tunnel at Haymarket. I had the good fortune to wear also an old woollen waistcoat over my plain cotton nightshift, and a muffler, for it had been a bitter day. There was precious little shelter to be had, apart from an enclosure built from old railway-sleepers, which held the Halt's supply of coal. I hurried over to the enclosure and huddled down behind the protective wall, as the rain cracked over my head.

I had no idea what time it was, for, although I kept my watch safely in the inside pocket of Mr. MacMahon's old smoking jacket, which I had had the good judgement to wear that night, there was no light at all by which to examine it. (I might add that since my return to Braemore, it had, like myself, regained some of its accustomed equilibrium.) I might have been at the foot of some grim Fife-shire mine-shaft for all that I could see. Every so often, I could hear ominous smacks as tremendous gusts of wind roared up from Loch-broom and swept across the Dirrie More. I did not doubt that Sir John Fowler's woodlands were being made to suffer that night. The storm had been building up since five o'clock, and I had sheltered in front of my stove listening helplessly as it reached a pitch, then receded briefly, like waves upon the exposed beaches of Jura. All evening and into the night, I had sat expecting momentarily that a tree, or a rock would crash through the roof, or that the tiny frail window would shatter.

It was no great surprise, therefore, to find myself exposed to the storm in the middle of the night, and it was some relief to find shelter in the coal-store. The wind came directly from the north-west, and with such power that the rain had no opportunity to fall vertically upon me. So I remained relatively dry, and thanked my habit of retiring for the night warmly dressed in a pair of Bedford cord trousers, which keep out the worst of the cold.

There was no question of any sleep that dreadful eleventh night of April. I had had none to that point when my home was rent asunder, and would certainly have none until day broke again. I tied on my boots securely, pulled my blanket closer, adjusted my woollen night-cap and considered what I would do next. In truth, there was precious little I could do, at least until light returned to the world.

My options were limited, as I soon discovered when reviewing them. A man who has spent fifteen months as Relief Station-Master at the smallest and quietest railway-halt in all of North-West Scotland does not accumulate great wealth in either the financial or the social sense. I knew as few people then as I did in January of the preceding year. My savings were pitiful, and those which I had contrived to put aside were intended for paying back my dear sister's loan of four pounds Sterling, which she had made before my last adventure. Not that I had actually paid her back anything, although I firmly intended to do so.

The Great North-West of Scotland Railway Company had not as yet made any additional Capital investment in its line from Garve to Ullapool, with the result that I still languished at Braemore, which represented the grand terminus of that useful engineering project. I had had two visitations from the Board of the Company in the past year, which I had, at the time, taken to signify the imminent re-commencement of investment, and therefore an end to the hiatus in my career. But each time my restless expectations were disappointed. Hence, I now philosophised coldly, the demise of the station ticket-office and accompanying room, which I had become used to call my home.

When, at last, some light was shed on the devastation by the arrival of daylight, the storm began to abate little by little. And with its abatement the rain began to fall more and more vertically upon me. There was a shred of tarpaulin, which had once served to cover the coal, and which, by some beneficent miracle, had not vanished eastwards in the night. Filthy though it was, and scanty in the protection it afforded, I held it taut about my ears and awaited succour.

When there was sufficient daylight to see more clearly, I stood up to survey the scene. Huge clouds raced past, covering the bulk of the mountains around. The wind was still very powerful indeed, and I could barely keep my balance. Of the walls and roof of my home, there was no sign whatsoever; I assumed that the rotten pieces of wood from which it had been constructed were scattered far and wide over Glen Glascarnoch. Apart from the solid railway-line, and this pile of coal on which I now sat, there was no indication of human endeavour around me. Such is the flimsiness of Man's Achievements!

I considered it futile to sit shivering at my post. Although a train might be expected from Garve to-day, at twenty-five-past two precisely, I questioned whether it could run at all, let alone find paying passengers. For I could see at least two places to the east where streams had burst from nowhere and had over-run the track. Further down, where the Black-water rushes so powerfully even at the height of summer, I could only hazard a guess at what raging torrents might have broken loose.

I resolved, having consulted my watch, which still ticked warmly in my innermost pocket, and found it to be at or about eight o'clock, to seek the nearest congenial habitation and await instructions from

Dingwall. I decided that the Fowler residence would be my preferred port of call, since Sir John, as Member of the Board, might be expected to assume some responsibility for my present situation and the continued running of the railway.

I turned my face to the west, therefore, and struggled with my head down towards Braemore Lodge. It was a mere half-mile to the house from where my home had stood, but the force of the continuing gale was still such that it took me a good twenty minutes to reach it. What kind of picture I must have presented to the man who opened the door in answer to my knocking, I can barely imagine: I was still dressed in my night attire (although the man was not to understand that immediately), and was clutching various scraps of railway detritus to my body. He must, I suppose, from his startled look and subsequent snarl, have considered me to be a vagrant, in search of charity.

"Away ye go!" he exclaimed, shaking a threatening fist at me. "I'll set the dogs on ye!"

It was with some difficulty that I persuaded him of my real identity and then of the destruction of Braemore Halt. Even so, he was not impressed.

"Sir John isnae here," he informed me. "And young Mr. Fowler isnae here. They're nae here the gither!" And he closed the door in my face.

There was little I could do but turn away. I was not to be permitted to know when the Fowlers, younger and elder, were to return. Whether Lady Fowler was at home, I had not an inkling; but it would have done me little good to request an audience with her.

I made my way, with considerable assistance from the bullying gale at my back, down the track to the gate-lodge, and out on to the road which linked Ullapool with Garve; in that direction, at least, lay the main offices of the Railway, and in that direction, also, the daily train from Garve.

As if with seven-league boots, I strode along the muddy road, dodging puddles and leaping over burns, which had boiled up from their courses. It was an odd sensation, this effortless striding, and disconcerting, too: I felt like a puppet, strung up and manipulated by an unseen master. At a distance of about a mile east of the now obliterated station, I came across a large piece of wood, which I recognised as the board previously nailed to two posts, announcing BRAEMORE HALT. It now lay sadly in a swollen gully. Some distance further on, I came across my Station-Master's cap, sodden, muddy and worthless. Sadly, I picked it up and wrung some water from it – but it was far beyond repair.

The gale still blew, though the rain had all but ceased, when I came in sight of Aultguish House, surrounded by its hedge of short pine-trees. As I lurched towards it, I noticed a pony and trap emerging from its gates and turning in my direction. Someone was evidently out and about.

After only a few minutes, thanks to my speed rather than the pony's, we came abreast of each other. To my surprise, I beheld the bulky figure of Professor Cardew-Smith holding the reins, his body muffled up to an undue degree and his head wrapped in an enormous green shawl, which might have kept an entire family warm. With a shout, the Professor reined in the pony.

"Ah, Sir!" he exclaimed. "I was just on my way to see you. You have survived the night, then?"

I assured him that I still lived, and thanked him for his concern, wondering all the while why he should have been on his way to see me.

"Climb aboard then, Sir; we shall have some toast and tea, in front of a roaring fire!"

I needed no second asking and sat beside the academic as he manoeuvred the trap in a full circle on the road. This was a delicate operation and I closed my eyes, imagining at each moment that we would all end up in one of the foaming ditches. But Professor Cardew-Smith's driving skills more than rose to the occasion.

"Yes, Sir," he repeated when the animal's head was safely pointed back to its stable, "we were concerned for your safety in the night. I told Mr. Mackenzie to get the trap ready for me. But here you are, safe and sound!"

It seemed that the Professor's concern was genuine. This, I admit, even now startles me. The Professor had used the facilities of Braemore perhaps twice in the previous fifteen months, and had never once acknowledged my existence. Yet here he was, at some personal discomfort and at the risk of catching pneumonia, for which even Mr. Beecham's pills might provide no cure, venturing out solicitously. I stole a glance sideways at the man as he carefully guided us back to his house. His ruddy face was almost concealed in the monstrous shawl; a steady drip of rainwater splashed over his spectacles and down his nose. And he seemed jolly enough, talking all the while of monsoons in India and of Scotch winters.

When we arrived at Aultguish House, there followed several minutes of frenzied activity as I was ushered in, provided with a hot bath in the luxurious tub I had once admired as an intruder, given a warm dressing-gown and slippers, and then seated in front of porage, tea, toast, and Mr. Keiller's raspberry jam – which confection, I confess, is my Achilles' heel. The Professor, meanwhile, sat and warmed himself by the roaring grate and fired questions at me about the fate of the buildings at Braemore; and made arrangements with his man-servant, Mr. Mackenzie, to ensure that the train from Garve was halted at his front-door, should it ever come this far. To that end, Mr. Mackenzie's youngest son was posted at the window of an east-facing bedroom, furnished with a huge tin whistle, the like of which I have never before seen, and lectured sternly not to fall asleep, but to blow the whistle loudly as soon as there was any sign of the train. At which signal, everyone was to climb the embankment and interrupt the progress of the train. It was very well-arranged and I anticipated much excitement, as did the young lad.

The Professor was a highly likeable man, and not at all as I had once imagined him – neither aloof, nor inward-looking, as I had envisaged that a man might be whose passion was for things long dead or far-away, or both. He told me some amusing stories about young Arthur Fowler, which I do not think it is proper to repeat here. That the Professor was eccentric to a high degree cannot be denied. I noted that he adopted unconventional dress-habits. Divested of his enormous shawl and the all-enveloping Mackintosh overcoat, he remained still a large and powerful man, of about seventy years of age. He wore, I was interested at first to note, Highland dress, with a kilt in green tartan and a skean dhu tucked into his sock. It was only when I sat in a low arm-chair opposite his high one that I was paralysed to note that he wore no under-garment beneath the kilt.

Not expecting anything of the sort, I was puzzled at first by what my eyes beheld as I looked in his direction, then mortified; and, finally, horribly hypnotised.

Nonetheless, we passed a splendid morning, while outside the gale began to blow itself out, returning only infrequently in short bursts. The Professor treated me to a lengthy diatribe concerning a fellow academic, Maudslay by name, whose work on deciphering Mayan hieroglyphs struck Cardew-Smith as infantile. In the course of the morning, my Professor shewed me examples of this fascinating subject, such pictures as I had never seen before and whose primitive complexity struck forcibly upon my spirit. I believe, had I stayed more than a day in that house, I could have rivalled Professor Maudslay himself in my enthusiasm for – and ignorance of – these images!

I wanted to ask him more; however, as I had had in the past year but little opportunity to make any conversation at all, let alone intelligent observations, now I struggled even to find suitably laconic answers or interjections. This, fortunately, did not seem to weigh the Professor's judgement against me. I was invited to stay to lunch, as the train from Garve was expected soon. My clothes now having been dried in the rear of the house, I changed back from the loaned dressing-gown and slippers into more suitable garb. My Station-Master's cap had been washed and dried, but truly now possessed no semblance of authority at all; I stuffed it into my jacket-pocket. After an excellent lunch, we sat in the study, and, holding huge tea-cups in our hands – which I must suppose had been made for a race of giants, although Professor Cardew-Smith cradled his as any afternoon lady might hold a daintier one – embarked on a debate on the basic distinctions between the languages of the Western World and those of the East. Struggling with the terms *"satem"* and *"centum"*, I found myself slipping into the very foundations and darkest basement of human communication. Here I wandered dizzily, adrift in eternity, when suddenly I was shocked back to the Modern Age by the loudest blast on a whistle I had ever heard. As I wiped tea from my waistcoat, I realised that the boy Mackenzie must have been alerted to the imminence of the train from Garve.

As one man, we all rushed out to the gate of the house – myself, the Professor, the boy, Mr. Mackenzie; threw ourselves across the streaming road; over the photographed embankment; and took up bold positions on the track. Although I was the one solely authorised to stop the train, the Professor saw nothing untoward in standing forward to command the on-coming train to halt. Which it did, with considerable releases of steam from both the fireman and the engine.

I thought it best that I should myself talk to the crew of the engine and explain the situation, since mine, at least, was a face they recognised. In truth, there was not much to tell: simply that the station-buildings at Braemore Halt were no more. Which, when I now considered it in the calm light of day, was not really very much to report, and scarcely cause to arrest the "Ullapool Flyer", as the locals had drily christened the little train, from its painful ascents of the glen. I could read in the eyes of Mr. Campbell, the fireman, that he estimated the vanishing of the Halt as much as he would the minor trouble of sheep on the line.

"You would do well to climb aboard, Mr. Kininmonth," he concluded soberly. He eyed my companions with some doubt. "But your friends will no be wishing to join you, I expect?"

The Professor and his household confirmed this expectation, and soon we were on our way to the end of the line, leaving my rescuers behind at the side of the track. During the short journey to the crest of the glen, I tried to elaborate and embroider upon the terror of the night and the utter devastation at Braemore; but my graphic account did not meet with much interest. For his part, Mr. Campbell told me that the line was pretty solid all the way back to Garve, although the river at the Torr Breac gorge was at levels he had never seen before. This news, at least, relieved me, for I was now conscious that I had expected further mortification in the collapse of some of my engineering works, under the force of the storm. A weight was lifted from my spirit, and almost I felt inclined to go along with his more objective view of the destruction at Braemore.

When we pulled into the terminus, the only rational act I could undertake was to collect the tickets of the half-dozen travellers, extricate from the goods-van such items as needed forward despatch to Ullapool or to the farms, and thereby give out the semblance of normal service.

Waiting for us at Braemore was not just the usual half-hearted collection of carts and carters, huddling relatives and excited passengers for the return journey; but also Sir John Fowler, who had miraculously been advised of the situation by his coarse servant. A kindly old man, as I had learned recently, he waited until the immediate business had been addressed after the arrival of the train, then took me to one side to enquire after my state of health, my state of mind, and how I thought we had best proceed. With each of these three questions, I was buoyed up, for he dealt with me almost as an equal. I took the opportunity, not unnaturally, to advise him that all of my engineering works back down the line were as solid as Cromarty rock. He expressed satisfaction with this state of affairs, but returned rapidly, nonetheless, to the immediate problem – how to part the passengers for Garve from their fares and how to charge for the freight and baggage? I proposed that a letter from Sir John, to the Station-Master at Garve, which I myself would take there, would be the best; the letter should advise that all fares be collected at Garve, for both the outward and inward journey; until such time as suitable arrangements could be re-constituted at Braemore. Sir John considered this to be a sound proposal; he decided, additionally, that I make my way to Dingwall with a further note from him, to present to the Board of the Company; and retreated to his Lodge to write such notes.

The train being delayed while Sir John was absent, the few passengers who had laboured up the Brae to the terminus sat grumbling in the carriages, and seemed to have little or no interest in the fact that I had lost my home; for them, the interest was purely in the destructive power of Nature; many of them, in particular Mr. Macrae, merchant of Shore-street, were of the opinion that the station should have built something more solid. I could only agree with them, but did not voice this opinion aloud.

Two solemn boys of about ten or twelve years of age, whom I took to be Sir John's grand-children, brought the promised letters. The train being due to depart at five minutes to three, we set off some twenty minutes late. I chose to travel with the fireman in the cab of the engine, so that I could run my civil-engineer's eye over the state of the line and make a sensible report to the Board – to what end, I had no idea, beyond thinking that any knowledge I could acquire in the present situation might be of personal value to me. In fact, the line was solid all the way down the glen, although the river was terrifyingly high, and almost black with peat and soil, which had been torn from the banks by the rushing of enormous volumes of water. As I had been advised, the river at Torr Breac was stupendous, alike to the famed Niagara Falls in Canada from lithographs which I have examined. The crashing waters were deafening, even over the labouring of the engine.

Having dropped the first missive at Garve, we arrived in Dingwall where I braced myself for an unpleasant meeting with McGeorge MacAdam MacAulay, a man whom, above all others, I most despise. I took some strength from Sir John's second letter, as I stepped in through the door of the Company's offices; and was immediately cheered by the sight of Mr. MacAllan, back in his accustomed position as doorkeeper and messenger-boy, from which place he had been missing on my last visit to these premises. I greeted him warmly, and his running eyes and toothless mouth showed some signs of reciprocal pleasure.

I was shown into the presence of MacAulay, who greeted me curtly and held out his hand for Sir John's letter, once I had announced to him what it was. However, I made so bold as to withhold it from him until first I had given him a summary of the recent storm, in as colourful language as I was able, and with great emphasis on my own resultant destitution. The man was unable to contain himself for long, however, and he came close to wrestling me to the ground in his desire to lay hands on the instructions from Sir John. Having gained possession of it forcibly, he ripped open the envelope and devoured its contents.

What a pleasure it was for me to watch his expression change, from one of contempt for my person, to one of consternation at what he read, and then to a momentary grimace of emotional agony, until he forced himself to bestow on me a rather forced smile. "Well, Mr. Kinnimoth," he croaked at last. "It seems that Sir John Fowler is appreciative of your sense of responsibility to the Railway." He looked at the letter again, searching for his next words, for he would not have been able to find them in his own mind. "The Board should thank you for your efforts to keep the Company's business running smoothly." Having exhausted his own depths of patience with this reckless vote of gratitude, he folded the letter once more, locked it in a drawer in his desk, and walked to the high windows of his room, hands clenched behind his back.

"What is the Company to do, then, Mr. Kinnimoth?" he said at last, without deigning to face me or to use my correct name. He paused, presumably for greater effect. I made so bold as to suggest that "perhaps it would be up to the entire Board to decide that question", implying, thereby, that MacAulay might not be the most important man in the Company. He took this suggestion badly, but was careful not to show his wrath.

"Certainly, it is a question which I must put to the Board, Sir," he said. "There will be a quorum of the Board in Dingwall to-morrow, and we must wait until then. Be so good, Mr. Kinnimoth, as to present yourself here to-morrow, at five o'clock, and you will learn what is decided. Good-day." And with that I was expected to leave his presence.

Which I did gladly, stepping out into a Dingwall evening which was as wet as it was gloomy and cold.

At ten minutes past five o'clock on Tuesday, the thirteenth of April, I received from Mr. MacAulay the news which obviously pained him, that I was to be re-instated as engineer on the Railway-Line from Garve to Ullapool. The matter of not having proper facilities at Braemore, either for the collection and dispensing of tickets, or for the correct handling of luggage and goods, was to be resolved by my suggestion (although doubtless presented by MacAulay as his own) as regards ticketing, and by Sir John's offer of using the gatehouse of his Lodge as a temporary Goods Office. And – to my great surprise – I was restored to my position as engineer. Admittedly, my deep sense of satisfaction was tainted by the fact that my wages would be considerably below those any reasonable engineer might expect from any reasonable Railway Company, and that my only colleagues would be those as I could afford to pay myself. But at least I had been restored to the grand design and project to which I had laid claim for almost four years!

My instructions were to continue the survey for the extension beyond Braemore, as far as Ullapool, in such detail that the Company could, as soon as Capital came free, engage a contractor to complete the railway in the shortest possible time. MacAulay did not go so far as to say that Capital would ever become free, but he certainly gave heavy hints on this matter.

As soon as the timetable allowed me, I made haste back to Braemore, and came to an arrangement with my good friend, Mrs. MacMahon of Achindrean, according to the terms of which I would pay her some of my wages for board and lodging, to which she would apply a discount for "conversation". Further, she recommended to me young James Campbell, the thirteen-year-old son of her neighbour, whom she extolled as a bright lad and who could serve as my assistant at a very modest wage. At the end of these negotiations, which were the best terms I could hope to obtain anywhere, I would have shelter, food, companionship, and someone to grumble about; and I would be left with an amount not exceeding eight shillings per week. I determined to save one half-crown for my mansion in Strathpeffer; one half-crown to repay my debt to my long-suffering sister; and to spend the remainder on frivolities for myself – such as books, strong spirits, maybe a patent medicine for my unmentionable complaint. I determined on a simple and undemanding life, and to work through this period of surveying with patience, in expectation of recognition by the world when at last the Railway was through from Garve to Ullapool.

I will admit freely that, after two evenings of Mrs. MacMahon's "conversation", I wondered if I had made the right decision, or whether it might be preferable to seek lodging with young James' father, Thomas Campbell, a man who barely uttered a dozen words from dawn to dusk, and who kept himself to himself from dusk to dawn. But I am a man of my word, and found it easy to retire to my room early in the evening, with the excuse of being tired. And so the spring days passed.

May, 1897.

During April and May, the weather around Loch-broom was mild, and many were the days when I worked with my hat and jacket off, taking delight in measurements and survey, under a sky which was so high that such larks as sang were as the angels. I remarked as much to Miss Keir, who took the school at Leckmelm, when she stopped one day to talk to her alumnus, Jamie Campbell; she was a tall, handsome spinster in her early forties; but she had no time for me, snorting impatiently in response.

Jamie rewarded my landlady's confidence in him, and rarely had to be told anything twice as we measured and tacked our way from the foot of Braemore and down the Strath. On such days as he wanted to be fishing in the river or climbing a tree, he would drive me to the edge of tolerance by behaving as one who is either a dedicated fool or a practising sophist, taking my commands so literally as to render them nonsensical. But those days were fortunately small in number, and we got on well enough, I respecting his need for some freedom, and he respecting my need to get a job done, and the two of us together teaching each other important matters in life. Jamie had a younger brother, William, who was six years old. William stood close by us when he could get away from school and his mother, and studied our endeavours with a serious eye. William was a charming boy – oh! would that children never grew up and became corrupt in their souls with the cynical ways of experience! Even in his brother Jamie could be detected the first signs of cunning, of antipathy towards fellow-beings, of the desire to be a victor even where there was no conflict. It wearied me sometimes.

It was in early June that my idyll was interrupted by the return of an old acquaintance. Mrs. MacMahon mentioned the name of Preacher Rinck when she returned one afternoon from Ullapool. She had encountered the man standing on the corner of Red-row and Quay-street, where he stood preaching to passers-by before the Caledonian Hotel. At first amused, Mrs. MacMahon had gradually been attracted by the man's manner of speech, by the way he appeared to talk directly to each and every person who passed; and in the end she had felt such a profound sense of unease at what he said, that she broke off and came away.

"Alexander," she told me that night as we sat down to our supper in the kitchen, "you know that I am a sensible woman, do you not?"

I candidly confessed that I did, knowing her to be none other than that in most respects, inclined to be less than charitable to fools and charlatans.

"Well, then," she continued, while pouring the tea, "when I tell you that this man seems to talk straight into my heart, you will think I am odd, will you not?"

I was cautious here, for I knew something of Mr. Rinck's powers of persuasion; but I confessed readily that I would have considered any such statement by my landlady as decidedly out of character.

"And yet," she continued as we munched our way through toasted cheese, "that is precisely how he seems to talk to me – of the sinful ways of this world, of the greed of the powerful, of the laziness and vice of the men who run our country, and of the way in which the poor of the Earth have been held back and not fed the Bread of Knowledge. With every picture he showed me, it was as if a scale fell from my eyes."

I must have looked horrified at her, at this demonstration of a woman in her more-than-mature years being caught up in the web of Rinck's religion. She caught my look and laughed loudly.

"Oh, Mr. Kininmonth, you look so appalled! Maybe you should come with me next time Mr. Rinck is due to preach, and judge for yourself."

I muttered some placatory phrase at that, all the while determining not to venture anywhere near Ullapool while Mr. Rinck walked its streets. I had retrieved my Railway; I was no longer in thrall to his fantasies of Citadels and Apocalypse.

June 19, 1897.

Notwithstanding all my secret intentions, when Mrs. MacMahon proposed to me on a Saturday in June that I should ride with her into Ullapool, I had not the courage to refuse. For I thought that it would have offended the lady, one whom I could still call my friend –

and I had few enough of those left in the world! And so I joined my landlady in her small trap and we made the short journey into the town. Young Master Campbell had in mind some expedition up near the Falls, into which I did not enquire closely; it was a perfect afternoon for such an activity and, as I squeezed into the cart alongside Mrs. MacMahon, I could only envy my apprentice's freedom. With the passing of the years, how difficult it is suddenly to cast off the heavy clothes of inhibition and the mud-caked boots of habit, to be fancy-free and reckless!

It is but a few miles from Achindrean to Ullapool, and the road in June is quite passable. I took the opportunity, as we rattled along, of showing Mrs. MacMahon the line which I envisaged would be followed by the extended railway. When the line had come down from the heights of Braemore (where all sign of our labours of two years ago had vanished once more beneath bracken and mud), it would pass behind Mrs. MacMahon's policies at Achindrean. Here I had now effected a change in my original scheme, which had been to cross the river there; I proposed that the railway-line should continue down the west side of the glen, at the point where the level ground of the Strath joins with the steep slope of the hill; the line would then pass to the rear of Garvan and Auchlunachan, and finally of Mr. Arthur Fowler's residence at Inverbroom; just beyond this, the line would traverse the meadow in a diagonal due northwards, and bridge the river just where it flows into the loch. I envisaged some form of bridge there which might complement Sir John's famous lenticular bridge of wrought iron at Achindrean, which I admired every day as I passed to my surveying work.

Having crossed the river, I advised my companion, the line would pass by Inverlael, Ardcharnich and Leckmelm. At each mention of a farm or lodge, Mrs. MacMahon made some wry comment on the likely reaction of the occupier to having a smoky railway-engine pass by his door. The Mundells, tenants at Inverlael, might welcome the excitement; but she doubted whether Sir Arthur Mackenzie of Inverlael would be over-joyed at the proximity of the line. As for Mr. Alexander Pirie, in his fine town-house in Queen's-gate in South Kensington, he with his 'private halt', she laughed long and loud at how "affronted" he would be by the reality of a locomotive thundering through his Leckmelm grounds. She thought that William Murdie, Pirie's stableman, would have something to say about the effect of steam-engines on his horses, but elected, as a lady, not to imagine what words he might use to express his opinion.

We came into Ullapool at about half-past three, and left the pony in the care of Mrs. Jamesina Mackenzie in Argyle-street. Mrs. MacMahon then took my arm and led me in her determined fashion to the junction with Quay-street, where already a small crowd had gathered around the preacher.

At first, in the excitement engendered by this, my first brush with crowds of people for many a long day, I thought irrationally that the good people of Ullapool had set out flags and bunting to welcome the preacher. But it was only as we passed the Bank House, with a large banner hung before it inviting the Good Lord to "Save The Queen!", that I was reminded that our Monarch's Jubilee celebrations were due shortly, and that all the flags and the newly painted house-doors were in preparation for some expensive jamboree.

At the junction with Quay-street there was considerable bustle, as idlers and enthusiasts gathered to hear the preacher, mingling thereby with crowds of people purchasing provisions for the coming week; men with ladders and rolls of brightly coloured cloth, to hang in front of the main buildings of the town; and last – but not least – what appeared to be a vast platoon of men marching up and down in some semblance of military precision, under the orders of a diminutive captain with a bright red face and a stentorian voice. Since few of the passers-by paid any attention to their line of march, dogs, children and old women were constantly becoming entangled in the body of men, disrupting their parade and manifestly upsetting their leader. These, Mrs. MacMahon advised me in a tone of some derision, were the Ullapool Volunteers, under the instruction of Mr. Coleman.

The whole scene was one of utter confusion. In the midst of it all, however, stood the figure of the preacher. He was elevated above the crowd upon a chest, which had been used by John McQueen of Glasgow for packing Spanish Canary Seed. As we hurried up, for my landlady wished to miss none of his sermon that day, he was talking to the crowd around him, comprising about twenty people and three promiscuous dogs, in a voice which barely rose above a whisper. It is most remarkable that, despite this, all those around him could hear what he said, as if there were but two of them in a secluded hermitage. From where we stood, which was a good five yards from the man, the cacophony of barking, screaming, shouted orders, tramping boots, trotting horses, wailing babies, the gulls of the sea – all seemed to fade to a dull background hum, and his clear voice reached our ears. I do not know how this happened: some observed later that it must have been the Voice of God Himself whispering in our souls. I am not a student of the Voice, so I cannot pass comment, although I am sure some demonstrable scientific effect was thereby displayed.

Mr. Rinck's sermon lasted for an hour at least, investigating at length the need for men to "Fear God Alone", and to experience the True Suffering of the Spirit in dreams and visions, in order to reach salvation.

"So, my dear people of Ullapool, hold fast to your dreams! It is in the true apostolic, patriarchal, and prophetic spirit that one waits for visions and overcomes them with painful sorrow. Therefore, be not astonished that our Ministers, and our Landlords, and our Estate-owners reject them, as is written in Job, Chapter Twenty-Eight. For when a man has not learned the clear word of God in his soul, then he needs visions. From this I now conclude that whoever in ignorance and out of a worldly understanding decides to be an enemy to all visions, to reject or accept them all without exception, saying that false dreamers have done great harm to the world by ambition or pleasure-seeking – he will come to a bad end and stumble over the Holy Spirit."

By about four o'clock, most of the inhabitants of Ullapool seemed to have gathered around him. Mrs. MacMahon and myself were thus in the centre of a vast and muttering throng; for some said that what Mr. Rinck said was right and proper and that the Wrath of God should be visited upon us; and others said that he was insulting to Queen Victoria in the very week of her Jubilee; and yet others argued among themselves as to whether the Reverend Macdonald of the "Parliamentary Church" in Red-row – who was, no doubt, listening to all of this from some secure station – was the embodiment of

Godlessness in Ullapool, or whether the Reverend Macmillan in the Free Church had visions or no. The parade of the Ullapool Volunteer Company had long since dissipated.

Finally, Constable Hutchison, representative of the police force in the town, made an appearance, looking fiercely from over his moustache, and suggesting gruffly to those on the outside of the crowd that they should get about their business. At this, Mr. Rinck raised his voice from above the level and low tones he had used before.

"My friends!" he called. "Should not every servant of God have the power to teach his parishioners in such a way that they can be educated in the ways of the Lord? Do not obey this spiritless man! For the Fear of Man is the work of the Godless, and your spirit will dry up and you will be struck down by the stone! I call upon you to fear only God, your Father, for then the fear is pure! This man tells us to be about our business? I ask you: what is more pressing business to-day than the business of the Lord?"

But I must report that there were many that day who decided that the sight of Constable Hutchison in his Godless wrath was more to be feared than the righteousness of the vengeful God. And so the meeting broke up. Mr. Rinck stepped down from his packing-case and sought refuge in the Hotel nearby.

June 22, 1897.

The celebrations of our Queen Victoria's sixty years upon the throne could not be ignored. All work ceased on all the surrounding estates so that everyone could be shepherded into Ullapool to shout "Hurrah!" In truth, most were in excited mood more from the prospect of having a holiday, and being able to celebrate with their companions, than at the thought that our monarch had reigned so long.

On the morning of Tuesday, the twenty-second of June, large numbers of people made their way from the countryside around Loch-broom into the town. I encountered my friend Professor Cardew-Smith from Aultguish, together with his household, the young Master Mackenzie being equipped for the occasion with the famous tin-whistle tied with a patriotic ribbon.

From the Dirrie More, from Strathbroom, from Dundonnell even; from Isle Martin and Achiltibuie, from Inchnadamff and other far-flung places, carts and traps and people on foot came in, and people came in boats across the loch. Ullapool had probably never seen so much of humanity gathered upon its decorated streets in its few sad years of existence.

Mrs. MacMahon had arranged that two carts be cleaned up for the occasion and we all made our way along the road, reaching the town shortly after two o'clock.

The Ullapool Volunteers again were much in evidence, led in pomp by Captain Roderick Macrae, cleansed of the usual marks of his cattle-dealing business; the hundred or so men marched down Argyle-street, up Mill-street, along Pulteney-street, down Quay-street, along Red-row, along Shore-street and up Mill-street, round and round, emerging unexpectedly from now this junction here, now that street there, followed by a gang of small boys hooting and marching and throwing stones at cowering cats.

Meanwhile, polite society was also parading itself. Apart from Mr. Arthur Fowler, together with his wife and family – which I now saw for the first time in its entirety, three girls and two boys between the ages of about three and twelve – my companions pointed out to me: Mr. Cameron, owner of the mill; Mr. Tusk, the Admiralty Officer; Mr. Hay Mackenzie of the Bank; the Reverend gentlemen Macmillan and Macdonald; and the medical Dr. Lamond. Seeing them strutting about in their parochial glory, in the company of their rather plain families and dull friends, I was forcibly struck by Mr. Rinck's remarks of three days before: these people seemed so shallow of spirit and not worthy of being the keepers of their fellow-men. These people were not to be feared!

Many events had already started that afternoon, and many more were planned for the evening. There was an acrobat in Red-row, and a card-sharp upon Market-street; there was a family of tinkers selling brightly-coloured trinkets outside the Argyle Hotel, and another selling flags in imitation of the Union Jack on Mill-street. Considerable quantities of beer and spirits were being consumed within the two hotels, while small children were well-provisioned in the matter of sweets and bright red confections on sticks, considerable portions of which adhered to passers-by. There were groups of fiddlers and several lone pipers, each surrounded by a jigging crowd. Down by the shore, the illustrious Alexander Grant of Inverness, who happened to be a guest of Major Houston at Braes, was demonstrating his latest patented invention, the Vibration Rod, with which he could cast for fish a full twenty yards further than any man previously. I was inclined to go down and seek a demonstration of his innovation: but already a cluster of men surrounded him, and I am not one of those who will flock to view a novelty. (I heard later that Mr. Grant also played "God Save Our Queen!" with the vibrations of his rod, a concert I would dearly have attended, not out of loyalty to our Sovereign, but out of pure engineering interest.)

At four o'clock, Games were to be held on the West-terrace, under the direction of Dr. Lamond, Mr. Hay Mackenzie, Mr. Stuart and Mr. Gauld of Leckmelm. This grand event, with the promise of prizes for all and sundry, attracted those who could still walk for more than ten paces. Accordingly, there was a great drift towards the west of the town, where chairs and benches had been set out for the ladies, and lanes for runners marked out with the ubiquitous ribbons. Races were to be run by small boys, small girls, larger boys, and there was a "Jubilee Challenge Cup" to be presented to the fastest adult male. There were novelty races – a "wheel-barrow race", involving one person on their hands being pushed, as it were, by another grasping his heels; a "sack-race", which seemed to require that grubby boys clamber into coal-sacks, donated by Montague Fowler from his coal-store at the Pier, and race amid a cloud of choking coal-dust until grubbier still; and a race which seemed designed to place the participants in the most humiliating circumstance, involving the balancing of a large potato in a small spoon while simultaneously negotiating an obstacle course composed of logs, tethered cattle and barrels of beer (at each of which latter, a large draught was pressed upon the contestant), with a prize of a sack of potatoes donated by Arthur Fowler.

Finally a Grand Tug of War was to take place between the men who lived to the west of Quay-street, generally regarded as the "low" end of town, and those higher beings inhabiting the east of the town. Since there was already some animosity between these two quarters of town, there was a general expectation of an enthralling contest.

However, it was not my lot to spectate this final event, nor indeed much more than the minor races in which children from the school seemed to run about at random in great delight, as a prelude to the more serious competitions. For I was called by Mr. Rinck to a higher purpose.

Mrs. MacMahon had been invited to a banquet of cake and wine at the Drill Hall in Pulteney-street, presided over by Mrs. Fowler, Mrs. Mackenzie and Mrs. Macdonald, wives of the aforementioned luminaries. Since none other of her household was invited, we parted and I wandered around the town, finally attracted as if by a centripetal force to the rooms of the Caledonian Hotel, which were full to bursting with men laughing and sweating. One room, however, had been set aside for a more sober and thoughtful group, and at the top of this room stood Mr. Melchior Rinck. Curious to learn what he had to say about these jolly celebrations, I slipped in at the back of a crowd of serious-faced men. And found myself in the midst of a conspiracy!

You need not be reminded, dear Readers, just how much I have striven in my life to remain on the right side of the Law, and have only strayed a few times beyond the boundaries of decency as a result of circumstances forced upon me. I need only remind you that my involvement with Rinck's escapades at Tweedsmuir was accidental; that my travels without ticket on the railway were a result of impoverishment; that my reduction to beggary after my stay on Jura was in an attempt to climb once again back into respectability; earlier in my life, when I — no, we need not go into such matters of wild youth in this volume! Perhaps on some other occasion. But to return to my story: by virtue solely of stepping into a room which I had supposed to be filled with spirits seeking solace in the Fear of God, I found myself cast among those who sought to turn the whole world upsides-down.

And even as I discovered this fearful truth, I confess I was strangely attracted. For — I reasoned — what could it harm the world if the poor of the Earth and the downtrodden finally gained equality with their rulers, and the hypocrites who now handed out wine and cake, and who slept at ease in their Bank Houses, while around them people thirsted in a spiritual desert? What was the harm that a Kingdom of the Elect was being proclaimed in Ullapool, as a beacon which might shine out to signal to humanity to cast off its chains, and rise up and seek light, on the very day when the Worldly Kingdom and Empire were celebrated?

Such were my thoughts on the Jubilee Day. For, in his corner, Mr. Rinck spoke quietly and outlined his plans for turning this day of Godlessness into a day of Revolution – there! I have said it! For truly the world would revolve, and the high and mighty would be cast down, as in the dream of Nebuchadnezzar, and the poor and the starving and the deserted would cast off their Fear of Man.

I will not outline such plans as were laid there that afternoon, for they were soon put into effect, and you will shortly see how they fell out. Suffice it to say that Mr. Hay Mackenzie, the Agent of the National Bank of Scotland, figured largely, as the Arch-Enemy, in the plans for the uprooting of Godlessness and Corruption. There was general agreement on this from another part of the Hotel, for Mr. Mackenzie also functioned as Chairman of the Western Lighthouse Lodge of Good Templars, a Temperance Society which battled against drunkenness and debauchery on the grim Saturday nights of Wester-ross.

I was standing in interested observation of these desperate men when my eye was snagged, over a veritable tide of heads and a sea-storm of tobacco-smoke, by the eye of Mr. Rinck. He made, as I recall, no motion of his head, nor of his hands, but silently summoned me to join him. Those of a more learned disposition might explain this curious phenomenon by the experiments of Mr. Mesmer; others, of a religious nature, perhaps as an Act of God; myself, I can only surmise that in the amorphous cloud of human relationships, there are invisible lines of communication between spirits with an Affinity. How else can we explain that device dear to novelists of the romantic pre-disposition, "Love at a First Glance", which some of us have experienced? How else can we explain the certain knowledge of close friendship which assails us after perhaps only a moment's conversation – doubtless a friendship that lasts but one month or one year before souring, but precious enough in its time?

This summons from Mr. Rinck was something in the same line – not, I hasten to clarify, as a matter of Love or Close Friendship, but more as an 'Affinity'. It is possible, I believe, to have an Affinity with another human without thereby being in love or becoming a close friend. Perhaps one can have an Affinity with the Wee Man himself, without thereby feeling other than disgust and hatred for his works and ways?

On arriving at Mr. Rinck's side, I joined a desperate band, whose members wore determined expressions, which certainly had nothing to do with the imminent Tug of War. From my later knowledge, I can say that convened there were: Kenneth Ross, a tailor; Mr. Macrae, a shoemaker; Alexander Lamont, a spinner at the mill; Roderick Fraser, a piper; his brother, Charles, a driver for the mails; a number of the Mackenzie clan, tenants at Leckmelm; and an equal number of Campbells from Inverlael.

It being shortly after four, we proceeded to Corry-hill, a small elevation at the east of the town. On the top of this, a bonfire had been prepared for the evening. The main combustible in this bonfire was an old fishing-boat, named the *Commodore*, and in and around and on top of the boat had been piled all manner of wood, coal, tarpaulins, old clothes, and other material.

"It is time," said Mr. Rinck, when we had reached the top of the hill and were gathered around the pile, "It is time to light the fire. Not the fire which the Godless have intended should be lit here, to celebrate the wicked ways of the fifth Age of Man; but the fire which will signal to all the Elect and all the down-trodden of the Earth that they should cast off their chains and break the bread of God and feed themselves with it. For no one has broken for them the bread of knowledge and offered them the wine of freedom, but rather they have been kept in a prison and made to starve! Now is the time to cast off the Fear of Man and to submit to the Fear of God alone!"

There seemed to be general agreement that such a time was come, and several stepped forward to ignite the bonfire. But Mr. Rinck stayed their hand.

"It is written in the visions of John that there shall be forty-two months during which the wrath of God will rain down upon the world. After six times seven months, the Kingdom of God will be established upon the Earth and the Godless shall have perished and the Elect will be raised up. And a New World will have arisen. At the end of the year nineteen-hundred, after many trials and many punishments, a new century will dawn and a new age for Man!"

With that prophecy, Mr. Rinck laid hold of a burning torch, held for him by Charles Fraser, and thrust it into the pile of wood. Expecting a huge conflagration, we all stepped back hurriedly. Unfortunately, the torch had not been placed efficiently, and there was merely a small sputtering, some smoke and then silence. Mr. Rinck glared at Mr. Fraser, and would have said some cutting words had not young John Mackenzie, a sea-faring man who seemed adept at any manner of practical matters, nimbly extracted the torch and re-applied it at several more welcoming spots in the edifice, much as if arson and fire-raising were his profession.

Almost instantaneously, the *Commodore* began to smoulder and to burn, and all the tar began to smoke and to spark, until soon there was a great roaring blaze upon Corry-hill. At the intensity of the heat, which Mr. Rinck interpreted for us as the heat of the wrath of God, we gradually moved backwards below the brow of the hill.

After several minutes, the whole thing was burning in the bright afternoon sun and a huge column of smoke spiralled upwards over the heather. While we were transfixed by the flames, young John Mackenzie, who thereby proved himself to be a most sensible man, had been keeping an eye on the town below. After several minutes, he advised us that a large crowd of people was heading our way from the West-terrace, attracted no doubt by the unexpected burning of their Jubilee Bonfire, and perhaps with some thoughts of retribution on their minds, fuelled by drink and false patriotism. We considered it best to absent ourselves from the scene, and made our way down the east side of the hill.

When we reached the foot, I took it into my mind to join the crowds now arriving from the Games and attached myself to the running, yelling mass that rushed up the hill. Mr. Hay Mackenzie and Constable Hutchison were in the vanguard.

Realising that no power on Earth could extinguish these flames, the figures of Authority roundly and ostentatiously condemned "the dastardly deed". "Our indignation knows no bounds," declared the

Reverend Macdonald, when he finally arrived, ten minutes after most others, at the summit. "What manner of man should thus sully our Glorious Queen's celebrations with such villainy?" he enquired. There was much sage nodding from the assembled grocers and dignitaries, and it was left to the Reverend Macmillan of the Free Church to state out-right that the force behind this act of terror must be none other than Mr. Rinck himself, that Worm sent into Eden to lead the people of Ullapool astray from the righteous paths of God. There was general agreement on this.

Mr. Arthur Fowler proved himself at this stage to be a man of determination. He submitted that another bonfire be built straight away beside the slowly-subsiding remains of the old one. In the company of his brother, the Reverend Montague Fowler of no known parish, and many light-headed but able-bodied men, he descended the hill to search out the material for another fire. The Tug of War had apparently been forgotten, and all energies were now channelled into the building of a new fire. It seemed that Mr. Rinck's hopes of lighting a blaze to overwhelm a Godless society had diminished and finally sputtered out – as indeed did the real fire atop Corry-hill after an hour.

I confess now that, partly to ensure that my passive role in Rinck's act of retribution was not suspected, partly out of sheer enjoyment in a communal activity, I greatly assisted the plans of Messrs. Fowler. We located another old boat lying derelict on the foreshore, evicted from it a family of crabs, cleared it of sea-weed and dragged it to the top of the hill. This feat, equal perhaps to that of those Ancient Egyptians who built huge pyramids in the deserts of Arabia, was achieved in less than two hours, the boat being dragged through the streets and up the hill by sheer force of muscle and the enthusiasm inspired by Arthur Fowler. What a cheer went up when we hauled the rotting timbers of the *Albert* over the crest of the hill! (The Reverend MacMillan ordered that we change the name of the vessel to the *Phoenix*, to avoid any disrespect to our Queen. Accordingly, and with a bottle of 80/- ale, she was re-named.) All of the town had by now gathered here to watch and to help. New materials for the blaze arrived from below, and by close on seven o'clock we had before us a flammable pile, at least equal in size to the first. As well as new materials, sundry barrels of beer and bottles of stronger refreshment also arrived from below, so that restitution was pleasant enough. In the course of all of which, I had entirely forgotten my part in the earlier affair, and was momentarily pleased that our Queen had reigned long enough for us to celebrate communally in such a fashion.

You may consider me to be an unprincipled man, to thus leap from one crest of morality to another, from righteous indignation at the falseness of our nation to a wild celebration of that very same nation's Monarch; to abandon comrades and to take up with their opponents, within the space of scarcely an hour! I ask you: what man does not live his life in much this manner?

Leaving a guard of perhaps twenty of the least inebriated Ullapool Volunteers, under the command and watchful eye of Captain Macrae, the crowds descended once more to the town, to while away the time in eating and drinking until the Grand Display of Fireworks. Food was to be had in any number of places in the town, and it was possible to eat well at no personal cost. I therefore did so.

At a half past nine, a general shout went up, and the Display of Fireworks began. Sir John Fowler had provided a rather magnificent supply of rockets and fountains of fire and exploding cones, all of which were set off without major accident, except to the property of Mr. Munro, the Inspector of the Poor, in whose garden a small shrub was set ablaze by a falling rocket. There was considerable mirth about a "Burning Bush seen in Ullapool", but this irreverent jollity was rapidly quashed by some stern looks and pithy words from Mr. Macmillan, who considered that the words of the Good Book were not to be applied to Mr. Munro's garden.

At a half past ten, the crowds had assembled once more at the top of Corry-hill in the twilight, and Mr. Hay Mackenzie's young daughter lit the new bonfire. It was a wonder that the wee thing was not instantaneously carried off to Heaven at the tender age of two, as the blaze had been liberally doused with spirits to counter-act the dampness of the sacrificial *Phoenix*. But she was snatched quickly from the explosive force of the fire by alert on-lookers and suffered nothing worse than a few singed curls.

And so the night passed; it was several hours past midnight when the Achindrean party arrived home. I understood that Professor Cardew-Smith did not reach Aultguish until noon on the following day, due to an unsuspected desire to learn the pipes from Charles Fraser, an endeavour which lasted all night and ended, without any great success and only after the intervention of Constable Hutchison and his lieutenant Mr. Macdonald, at nine o'clock in the morning.

June 26, 1897.

On the succeeding days, until the Saturday morning, all was quiet. Heads which had been sore began to revive in the sweet June airs; the lingering smoke from the bonfires gradually dissipated; men and women and children returned to their various duties in the fields and on the sea. Although I did not return to the town, I understood from Mrs. MacMahon that great labours had been undertaken to clear the streets of all evidence of the celebrations and return the town to its usual grey aspect.

What befell on the Saturday, dear friends, is now still quite terrifying to me!

Since Wednesday, stirred up by the Authorities in Ullapool, investigators had been gathering evidence about the premature blaze on Corry-hill. As a result, Alexander Lamont, under the threat of being dismissed from his position at the mill, confessed to being among the conspirators, and had advised Constable Hutchison of Rinck's leadership in the affair and of the other participants. As it happened, he did not know my name, only those of his fellow-citizens, and one or two of the estate-workers.

Word reached me of this when I ventured back into town on the Saturday afternoon. My reason for going there was simply that the Ullapool Volunteer Company was holding its Annual Shooting Competition on that day, and young Jamie Campbell, my assistant, had expressed a desire to be present at this gala event, having himself a queer ambition to join the Company. All innocent of the investigations at that very moment reaching a climax, I foolishly agreed to accompany him, Mrs. MacMahon kindly lending me her pony and trap for the excursion. Little did I know that I had but a Single Journey ticket on that trap!

We came into Ullapool to the crackle of distant gun-fire, which emanated from the field behind the Drill Hall. A small and largely male crowd had gathered there for the event, and Mr. Mackenzie (by virtue solely of his position as Agent of the Bank, he seemed to be the most important citizen of Ullapool: thus the God Mammon holds sway in our Land) was much in evidence at the giving of prizes.

When faced with the actuality of the competition, the vaporous enthusiasm which had inspired me to accompany my assistant soon disappeared, and I advised my young companion that I would meet him later in the day. I wandered off. The afternoon was brilliant, and I felt my very soul grow soft and malleable, forgiving and companionable. I decided to seek out Mr. Rinck and find his news, perhaps tell him of the terrible fate of the Finlays. I therefore directed my steps towards the Caledonian Hotel, where I enquired after the preacher. Mrs. Mackenzie, the owner's wife, muttered something in reply, and I saw that a number of the customers in the bar edged away from me. Not understanding the significance of this, I persisted with my questions. Finally Mr. Mackenzie emerged from some back room, took me to one side, and gave me intelligence of the latest events: that Mr. Rinck had left the town the previous night, thus evading capture; that most of my accomplices in the adventure were under lock and key; and that the police were even now seeking out those who had been implicated but not yet named! My heart thumped and I could feel sweat break out upon my brow! Was I, yet again, to become a fugitive before the Law?

"My advice to you, Sir," said Mr. Mackenzie in conspiratorial manner, and with the ease of one who has no personal sacrifice to make, "is to follow Mr. Rinck from the town and to seek refuge in the hills until all this is forgotten."

I sat down heavily in a chair. Mr. Mackenzie studied my face seriously and nodded to himself. Evidently my appearance confirmed his every suspicion.

"But where has Mr. Rinck gone?" I asked, after some moments of reflection. "Has he told you?"

With a gesture of triumph, the inn-keeper produced from his apron a rather crumpled piece of paper, which he now presented to me. I took it, and noted with some surprise that it was addressed to me – or at least to "Mr. Kinnimunt". I opened it. The message was brief.

"If you hold true to the ways of the Elect, you will join me in my exile. Brother Mackenzie at the Caledonian will give directions."

And so it was that as twilight began to creep over the hills from the east, I found myself setting out on the road to the north. A boy was sent from the Hotel to look out for Master Campbell and pass him a note for Mrs. MacMahon, in which I explained the situation in as roundabout a manner as I could contrive. I left Ullapool with only the clothes in which I had dressed that morning, and coins to the value of three shillings and sevenpence three-farthings in my pockets. Mrs. Mackenzie gave me some broth and bread before I left, and lent me a blanket which smelled very strongly of the stables from which it had been plucked.

I had directions from Mackenzie to follow the road north to Ardmair. A carter took me with him as far as the turning of the road to Achiltibuie, and then, at about nine o'clock, I was left to proceed northwards, firstly to the hamlet of Elphin, and then to Inchnadamff.

It was a fine night, and I was more concerned with putting distance between myself and the investigating Authorities of Ullapool than in resting. As a result, I made good progress for the ten or so miles which lay ahead of me. The hills and the desolate countryside looked so strange to me in the dim light of a waning moon; there was not a sound except the occasional rustle of a small burn, coming down from the low ridge of hills to my right, and the padding of my feet upon the road. Away to my left, I glimpsed the silvered pinnacles of Stack Polly, and was reminded of the rocks which will tumble down and smite the Godless. On reaching Elphin, I had a sight of the shapes of Suilven and of Canisp, which resembled ancient recumbent monsters in the measureless night.

At about two o'clock in the morning, I came finally to a gap in the hills which Mackenzie advised me led to Mr. Rinck's refuge. A river ran down from the gap, and some cloud was beginning to obscure the stars and the moon, so I chose to rest for the remainder of the night in a small clump of trees, which grew beside the road. My feet were glad to rest, but I could not sleep.

I turned over in my mind the various madnesses which had

brought me to this exile. What reason was there for any of it, except that I had found an Affinity with Mr. Rinck's ideas and had followed them, more out of curiosity than persuasion? It was a juvenile foolishness, more simply a desire to distance myself from the main Celebrations, which had led me to participate in the burning of the *Commodore*. Although no crime had been committed, it was certainly not the part of a representative of the Great North-West of Scotland Railway Company to be found fire-raising on the shores of Loch-broom; I took some comfort in thinking that, with the passage of time, the whole episode would be forgotten, and all those implicated would be able to settle back into their lives. For now, however, discretion should direct my foot-steps. Unless there was some unexpected visitation, it was unlikely that Mr. MacAulay in Dingwall would hear of my enforced absence for a few weeks. My only fear was that Constable Hutchison should be an avid follower of Conan Doyle, and, following some deductions of his own, might arrive on Mrs. MacMahon's door-step. For this would surely reach the ears of Mr. Fowler, and thence reach Dingwall, and my career would certainly be over! However, I consoled myself with my supposition that Constable Hutchison was no Dr. John Watson, far less a Mr. Holmes!

Scarcely had I settled down to rest than dawn crept over the hills again. The clouds now extended over the whole sky and it was cool. At about five o'clock, I must have drifted off to sleep, for it was well after nine that I awoke, hearing voices on the road, which passed by some ten yards from where I lay concealed. I looked cautiously between some bracken and saw two men heading south on the road. They were soon out of sight. A few minutes later, a shepherd passed with his dog. But I remained undisturbed.

Presently, I gathered up my blanket, and made my way into the glen. There was a sharp climb up beside a waterfall, behind which lay a very stony and enclosed valley. On both sides, sheer slopes hung over me. The path led beside the water for about half a mile. I came across a most curious natural phenomenon: there was a small pool formed in the lee of a steep bank of the burn. From holes about three inches in diameter in the river-bed came spouting up a number of springs of water, evidently channelled there from under the hill. I stood and watched this simple wonder for several minutes, utterly forgetting my present predicament in the interest and solace which it provided. I was transfixed by this sight of water emerging into water, of a spring bubbling under and into a river, and marvelled at the hidden workings of Nature, of the fascination of the most basic things in the world, water and rock.

Shortly after this, I had to ford the burn and make the steep ascent of a slope to a cliff whose base lay about a hundred feet above the water. Already, from the ford, I could see that there were three or four caves at the pedestal of the cliff – these I understood to be my goal, and my home for the next few days and nights. As I crossed the rushing, rocky burn, the sun broke through the low cloud and a hot day promised.

Clambering up to the ledge, I came face to face with none other than James Finlay!

I gaped at him. "But surely . . . ?" I could not complete my sentence, for it would have been in poor taste to tell the man he was dead and at the bottom of the ocean! "Were you not . . . drowned?" I finally managed to ask.

James grinned at me, and was about to answer, when Melchior Rinck's voice came to me from around the corner of the rock. "Oh yes, indeed, Mr. Kinnimunt," continued the voice. "James Finlay was indeed drowned. But not in the way you think. He was cast under the waves of suffering and drowned by the spirit of God. But, as you see, he lives now! He is my Prophet of the Wild Places. Come and talk with me, Brother Kinnimunt." Finlay beckoned that I should approach and together we ducked under a lip of rock and into a cool dry cave.

Mr. Rinck lay in exile in his chosen cave upon a bed of heather, surrounded by books and wrapped in good blankets. As I entered the cave, he set down a small leather-bound volume and greeted me.

"Do you feel, Mr. Kinnimunt," he enquired, "that within you the truth begins to bubble up, like those springs down in the valley?"

I supposed from this greeting that Mr. Rinck had been watching my ascent of the glen. However, I had no ready answer to this rather profound question. It was not a question which could expect a simple affirmative or negative; it was not a question which I could possibly answer with a brace of well-chosen sentences; it was not, indeed, a question I would have expected ever to be asked in my life, and so I had no answer to it. To be polite, I stammered some sort of response, but I fear it did not meet with my interrogator's approval.

"Do you not think, Mr. Kinnimunt, that that stream is like the Torrent of God's Grace, which comes dropping down to us from the times of the ancient Prophets?" Mr. Rinck looked at me with his burning eyes. I mumbled some agreement.

"And that each new spring which bubbles down there feeds the Torrent anew, just as the new Prophets bring fresh revelation to God's people?"

As I could only nod my head, Rinck sighed. "Sometimes the inner motion to truth is slow, Mr. Kinnimunt. Be patient." He turned back to his reading, saying, with a dismissive wave of his hand: "James Finlay has been tested by the Lord and has suffered the trials of the turbulent waters. The spume of the Lord swept over him and yet harmed him not! And he has proved himself to be one of the Elect, who fear only God alone. It is my habit, Mr. Kinnimunt, to keep by me men and women who can prophesy, who can bring forth the Word of God from their dreams and visions. Brother James is such a one, for he has suffered the whirlpools of isolation, and the reefs of misfortune, and the tides of desolation. He will tell you of his turmoil and his salvation."

Finlay led me out of the cave. My residence was not to be as palatial as that of Mr. Rinck; I was quartered in a cave some ten yards further round the cliff, which was at first sight draughtier and cooler than that of my fellow-exile. Finlay explained to me that Brother Rinck – as he wished to be addressed – preferred to live in solitude during his exile from the Godless, and that both he, Finlay, and I would hereinafter reside in this secondary cave. And here I was told the most extraordinary story by Finlay, which I could only believe because I knew him to be incapable of telling an untruth.

It seems that the two Finlays had somehow managed to creep past the dreaded whirlpool at Corryvreckan and had rowed under the very cliffs of Scarba out towards the west. They had only just escaped with their lives, for the raging waters had all but swamped their tiny boat. Once beyond Scarba, James Finlay, under instruction from his uncle, had turned the boat to the north, and as daylight came upon them had reached some small islands which were known to John Finlay as the Garvellach. The Garvellach are rocks in the midst of the ocean, beaten by wind and rain. They had been used in ancient times by such saints and heroes as Ossian might have described. Some small ruins still survived, and in these the two Finlays sought shelter from the storms. To them, it must have seemed like a return to Kerguelen. For several days, they lay sheltering; James Finlay caught birds and fish for food. Then old John Finlay had died, and his nephew had buried him in among the stones of an ancient graveyard, over-looked by the cliffs. (Finlay told me later that he had buried the Reverend Lunn's Bible, along-side the old man – for those who wish to brave the violence of the waves, that proof of the suffering of the Finlays must still be there.)

Now alone on these deserted islands, James Finlay waited for a break in the weather, then set out once more in the small boat, rowing ever northwards. More by good fortune than by good navigation, although the castaway suggested the involvement of the Hand of the Lord, Finlay ended up one evening in a bay over-looked by the small town of Oban. The sight of so many lights terrified him and he rowed on further.

To cut a long story short, and allowing for the gross deficiencies of Finlay's and my own knowledge of the area, it seems that Finlay had rowed over many days, past abandoned hamlets and lonely islands, under the precipices of huge mountains, through storms and sunlight, to the very mouth of the great Caledonian Canal. Here he found himself a berth on a boat, and finally disembarked at Inverness, where, by an almost impossible chance, he had stumbled across Rinck haranguing a crowd of self-righteous disbelievers. On moving on from this City of the Plain, Rinck had brought Finlay to Lochinver, and then, on his own return to Ullapool, had left him at the caves as a sentinel of his secure hide-away.

"And now Brother Rinck chooses to have me as his prophet, Mr. Kininmonth. For that, I am content." At the end of this incredible tale, Finlay grinned at me, looking as little like a Prophet as anyone I had seen. "Are you hungry?" he added, after he had shown me where I could make my bed. "Can I get you some food or water?"

I readily agreed that my stomach was feeling the need for sustenance. Almost like one of the street-conjurers who had entertained the crowds on the Jubilee Day, Finlay produced from a large bag some bread and cheese, along with a knife.

There was a man, he informed me, at the Inchnadamff Hotel who was of the Elect and who would keep us supplied with food when we needed it. This was some consolation to me, I confess now, for the past few hours had scarcely convinced me that my exile would be comfortable and full of joy. Food, at least, I might have; and a roof over my head, albeit one which my ancestors had abandoned some thousands of years ago; all that remained for my immediate needs was a bed. Once I had greedily eaten, James Finlay indicated where, at the foot of the slope, I might gather sufficient heather to make myself something to lie on. Accordingly, we both clambered down through the rocks and cut large armfuls of heather, with which I struggled back up to the cave. Seven journeys sufficed both to make a reasonable mattress and to exhaust me utterly, and at about ten o'clock I threw myself upon my bed, prickly though it was, covered myself with the blanket, and fell profoundly asleep.

There I lay, hidden away, almost under the earth, unseen from a road which few travelled, in the quietest corner of the kingdom. At least I could feel safe . . . until about three in the afternoon, when I awoke to the sound of voices from near at hand.

I lay for some time, trying to determine whether the voices were those of the marshalled forces of Law and Order in Ross and Cromarty; or whether, as I hoped, they might be friends. After several minutes, I decided that, since no voices were raised in anger and since the voices continued, they must belong to persons who meant no harm. Cautiously I eased myself from my bed and stood up, in order to present myself "next door". Ill-advisedly, as it transpired, since I had quite forgotten that the ceiling of the cave was barely five feet from the floor. There was a terrific crack inside my head, and I must have shouted in pain, before falling back upon the bed, clutching my skull, which I believed to have been split from stem to stern. When I opened my eyes, Finlay was beside me.

"You will have stood up too fast, then?" he enquired quite unnecessarily. I could barely speak, let alone nod, and sat on the ground clutching my head, now and then drawing my hands away and examining them for the tell-tale traces of gushing blood and spilled brains. Rather to my surprise, there were none such. Finlay gave me a drink of cold clear water and advised me to sit quietly for a while, until the pain eased. Withdrawing for a moment, he returned with some pamphlets in his hands.

"Brother Rinck believes that you will rise above your pain if you read these works of his," he said.

Dazed, I took the gift from him. "Who is talking to Mr. – Brother Rinck?" I enquired.

Finlay only shook his head. "That will be some of the Elect, Brother Kininmonth. Now, you sit here and rest. Perhaps these books will ease your pain?" He sounded neither convincing nor convinced in this hope.

I rested back against the cool rock for a few more minutes, and then examined the pamphlets which I had been given for solace. The titles scarcely promised easy healing: the first I picked up was "The Express Unmasking of the Soft-Living Doctors of Edinburgh by Your Brother Melchior Paracelsus Rinck"; another was "A Highly Called-For Speech of Defence of the Spiritual Salvation of the Elect Against the Pernicious Rumours of the Godless Professors in Aberdeen: Written by a True God-Fearing Servant of God". I put the latter to one side, and picked up "A Shocking History and Judgement of God Which Will Fall Upon the Godless Flesh in Westminster: A Very Profitable Lecture by a Humble Philanthropist"; and last came the thickest of all, "The Fear of God is the Beginning of Wisdom: Brief Notes for Common Men from their Godly Friend".

I confess that I sighed and did not immediately open the yellow covers of any of these short pamphlets. All were in closely set type and much dog-eared from frequent usage. On a June afternoon, such as the one which I could see outside, in which the lark sang and the burn bubbled freely, I praised my God in other ways.

Having finally determined that my skull was still whole and that the worst I need expect was a throbbing pain, I crawled cautiously to the entrance of my new home and ventured out. From the neighbouring cave there emerged a constant stream of talk and tobacco-smoke. Finlay was stationed between me and the visitors to Mr. Rinck, so I decided that I would take a stroll up the valley a little, to where the cliffs began to curve around. Scarcely had I begun to move in that direction that Finlay came up behind me and advised me that Brother Rinck did not wish me to show myself during the day. "There may be spies and enemies about, Mr. Kininmonth," he explained, looking significantly up to the crest of the hills, as if he momentarily expected to see a host of constables spring from hiding, wielding truncheons and warrants for Mr. Rinck's apprehension.

"Surely you do not think – " I began, with a short laugh, which died on my lips when I realised that Finlay was actually convinced of the danger; but who was I to judge – perhaps he had indeed some power of foresight? I returned to my cave. There was nothing else to be done: I picked up one of the pamphlets at random (the slimmest of them all), and settled down to read it. It was the "Highly Called-For Speech of Defence . . . "

I recall some of what was written about the Professors of Theology at King's College in Aberdeen, against whom Mr. Rinck seemed to hold a large and indomitable grudge:

> Our professors would have us bring proof of the spirit of Jesus to their high school. But they will fail completely, for, learned as they are, they do not wish that the common man with his doctrine should be their equal, but rather wish to judge belief with their stolen scripture. Therefore, you, the common man, must have knowledge yourself, so that you will no longer be misled.
>
> They come along with their insipid and stale mugs and say quite barefacedly: See, I believe the Scripture! And then they get all jealous and annoyed, so that they grunt from behind their beards, saying: Oho, this one here denies the Scripture! And then they want to stop up the mouths of everyone with their slanders, for they want to give cheap satisfaction to the high motion and heartfelt misery of the Elect, or just to cast it to the Devil without further ado.
>
> The Son of God said: The Scriptures give a witness. The professors contrariwise say: The Scriptures give belief.

The poor man cannot learn to read, because he is troubled for nourishment, and they preach unashamedly that the poor man should let himself be skinned and scraped by the tyrants. So how can he learn to read the Scriptures? "Yes, dear Mr. Rinck, you are raving: the Professors have to read beautiful books, and the common man should just listen, for faith comes through listening." Ah yes, they've found a nice trick there, which would put much worse scoundrels than ever before in the place of the judges and landlords.

The weeds must now suffer the winnow. For the time of the harvest is now here. Dear brothers, these weeds now shriek from every corner, professing that the harvest should not be here. Oh, the traitors betray themselves!

The balmy breeze which came up the glen from the west, carrying the sweet scent of heather and the sounds of bird and water, combined with the soporific effects of the words which floated before my eyes, soon had me fast asleep once more, dreaming fitfully of fields of corn, in which all humanity scythed and reaped and baled and winnowed.

And so the days of my strangest exile passed. Finlay provided me with my meals, some further details of his adventures, and sustenance for the soul in the shape of these endless pamphlets, whose titles were as long as the contents were uninteresting. Every day, some member of the Elect in Ross and Cromarty would ascend to the caves to hold exclusive conference with Mr. Rinck. Every day, I would listen to the mumbling voices and rage silently against captivity, until, after a week, I determined that I should be better returning to face the consequences of my foolish actions in Ullapool. Every day, I would get off the bed of heather and promptly crack my skull against the roof of the cave, until my head throbbed from morning until night.

And on the very morning when I had finally decided that I would return along the high-road, and, in expectation of a new life, took care not to stand up to my fullest height – on that very morning I turned round deliberately to step outside: and found myself unexpectedly face to face with Mr. Rinck. The shock caused me to stand bolt upright.

As I clutched my head again, Mr. Rinck squatted down and looked at me. "The pains of exile are like blows to the head, Brother Kinnimunt. They are sent upon us to test our souls and our readiness to face down the Godless. Take all comfort in this."

It was with some effort that I restrained myself from advising Mr. Rinck that I took no comfort at all in rendering myself helpless each morning due to the proximity of the roof of my shelter.

"Let us sit and talk, Brother," proposed my fellow-exile. "Come and join me."

With mounting annoyance, I followed him along the narrow path and entered his cave. The weather had been hot and dry all that week, and the air outside was already warm, despite the early hour. Finlay was preparing a pot of tea – the first I had seen in all that time. I supposed that Mr. Rinck enjoyed this as a daily breakfast, while I supped on bread, cheese and water.

Whether it was the prodigious supply of warm tea, or whether it was the fact of enjoying some human company after all these days, I found that the summer of exile suddenly acquired a golden tinge. Who was I to care about the forces of the Law? Who was I to take heed of what others thought of me? Here I was an Exile and perhaps one of Mr. Rinck's Elect, the sun shone, the waters sprang down the glen, and there was not a care at all in the world.

"Brother Kinnimunt," began Mr. Rinck, after we had commenced on a second pot of tea, "on our imminent return from exile, we will build an Earthly Paradise here in Ross and Cromarty, upon the dissolute ruins of the old world."

I dared to ask for clarification of the word "we".

"You may think that we are few in number, Brother," he continued, "but consider this: Gideon had such a firm, strong belief that he overwhelmed a large world, and countless enemies, with only three hundred men. The Fear of God creates the holy spirit, so that the Elect may be unharmed by the Fear of Man."

I dared again to ask just how few in number we might be.

"I do not deal in numbers, Brother," Rinck replied, rather sternly. "How many men and women does it take to let the light of truth shine into this miserable world? Does it take a thousand? Ten thousand? Or a dozen? Or just one?"

I conceded that a dozen would be ample, but perhaps even one would do. Mr. Rinck nodded his head, satisfied.

"The numbers will be sufficient unto the day, Brother Kinnimunt. Already we have good men and good women scattered throughout this land, and, at a sign, they will rise up and crush the Godless in their Banks and their Hunting Lodges, and smite down the Sinners in their Mills, and cast down the Clay Giants from their pedestals! Oh yes, oh yes!" Rinck's eyes shone at this vision.

I could think of little to say. For all I knew and cared, the Godless world which Mr. Rinck described could burn to ashes to-morrow. There were perhaps one or two people whom I would like to see preserved, and I secretly made it my task to ensure that they would be so saved.

"Now, Brother Engineer," said Mr. Rinck, turning his penetrating eyes to me, "I have a task for you. You will remember a talk we had at Tweedsmuir?"

I assumed that he referred to his proposal that I should assist in building a railway for the Citadel of the Elect.

"Indeed, yes, Brother Kinnimunt," continued the preacher. "Now, I urge you to return to your daily work and your normal life at Ullapool. We wish that the old world be burned upon the bonfire and from the ashes there should arise a new city, a Citadel of the Elect, and a new world where men and women live in harmony and fear only God alone. And in this new world there will be new buildings and new railways and new roads. There will be great works of engineering. Universities shall arise in which only the Will of God, as revealed in visions to the Elect, will be taught. There shall be no money with which one man may enslave others. There will be no guns and no swords, only plough-shares and looms. There will be no hunger, either for food or for knowledge. In the Kingdom of Ross and Cromarty, which will be God's Realm upon Earth, all misery will be replaced with joy."

He stopped there and looked at me. "What do you say to that, Brother?"

I said that it sounded indeed like an Earthly Paradise; but that I felt there was danger in returning to Ullapool so soon.

"Trust in me, Brother, for I have sent word to Ullapool that no one should name you to that Godless man Hutchison, far less to the arch-enemy Fowler. You will fear no man as long as you fear the Lord and walk under His protection."

All this seemed very pleasant, and I was prepared to believe it, if only to be able to return to my comfortable lodgings at Achindrean. It is my confession that from that moment I was under his spell, that I could not have refused him had he asked me to put down my life for the people of Ullapool – which, for all I knew then, was what he did indeed ask of me. It is curious: with my rational, engineering mind, I knew the man to be slightly ridiculous, with his curious accent, his tangled white beard in which traces of an old supper were still to be seen, in whose eyes shone a strangely alluring light, such as would have had him promptly placed in custody, and taken to the Poor Asylum, in any civilised part of the realm. But the heat of the moment, the power of his words, the thrall into which some other part of my nature had placed me, told me that I must bow to this man.

"And when you return," continued the preacher, "you will set out the plans for the Kingdom at Ullapool – all its buildings and roads and schools and railways will be your design. Every house in which the Elect shall dwell will be from your drawing-board. Every train that brings the poor and the dispossessed to the Citadel at Ullapool will travel upon your railway. Every ship which arrives, bringing the suffering and the meek from over the ocean, will tie up at your piers.

"And, Brother Engineer, as you will henceforward be known," continued Mr. Rinck, "you will build for the Brotherhood of the Elect such a Citadel as has never before been seen. I have been sent a dream of how it will look: it will be built upon the spot where the Bank House now stands, in the pernicious Argyle-street. It will be built of granite and will shine in the sunlight far and wide. It will have seven floors, one standing upon another. There will be on every floor seven rooms, each with seven windows. At the pinnacle will be a glazed room, two and forty cubits square, in which the Shining Light will always burn, to be seen from far and wide. The raging waters of the mountains will be diverted to the upper floors of the Citadel, and will flow down in torrents through every floor, as a sign of the living Word of God, which runs through us all." Mr.

Rinck stopped here and looked at me. "Can you do this, Brother Engineer?"

Faintly and excitedly, I nodded, already sketching in my mind drawings for the tremendous aqueduct which would be required to pass the waters through this new Wonder of the World. And the opportunity for completing my Railway and designing a New Ullapool – such a chance came but once in a generation to engineers! Myself, Kininmonth – a New Telford!

"Indeed, I can do this, Brother Rinck," I managed to say at last. "When do I start?"

Mr. Rinck looked at me most earnestly. "I have told you, Brother Engineer, that a man of God must keep by him companions who can dream dreams and suffer visions. Brother James is one who has travelled the seas of abandonment, and he will be our pilot through the storms to come. You, Brother," he gripped me by my shoulders and stared into my eyes, "will be the architect of our Citadel, and you will draw your plans according to the Word of God alone, which will come to you in dreams and in prophecies. Now, you must leave here, to-day, and return to your work. But it will be best if you do not appear in Ullapool before anyone who might recognise you, for the Fear of Man is still strong in that town. Stay away from the town as much as you can, and draw up our plans for the Earthly Paradise. When we are ready, we will come for you."

July, 1897.

I returned to Achindrean on the morning of Monday, the fifth of July, 1897. My journey back from the wilderness was no less dangerous than my outward journey, for I had to be sure of meeting no one when I came to Ullapool. I did not have the good fortune, this time, of riding upon a cart, and had to make the entire journey on foot. However, I reached the hill above the town at about two in the morning, and passed through it, without incident. A dog barked, a cat slipped out ahead of me. But not a light was there to be seen, far less any sign of human life. The sheep in the fields found me of great interest as I passed. Foot-sore and exhausted, I reached Mrs. MacMahon's house at close on five o'clock, as the birds began to stir.

Mr. Campbell, young Jamie's father, greeted me suspiciously as I approached the house, and followed me with his eyes as I let myself in. I had decided that I had best wait in the kitchen until the mistress of the house came down, lest she had already let my rooms to another, or wished to have words with me on the subject of my sudden absence. As I waited, I reflected on that other morning, when I had crept back to my lodgings at Tweedsmuir in the middle of the night. I seemed to be making a habit of keeping strange hours!

Johan the maid was rightly disconcerted when she came down shortly thereafter to make up the fire, and persisted in exclaiming over my appearance, even though I asked her to desist. She ran about, encouraging me to impossible tasks: "Oh, Mr. Kininmonth, look at your beard!" and, "Oh, Mr. Kininmonth, just see the back of your coat!" and, "Oh, Mr. Kininmonth, do you no think you're like a bogeyman?", until I decided to step out into the back yard where some chickens were scratching, paying no heed to my state of dress.

Mrs. MacMahon's lack of surprise and concern at my bedraggled re-appearance was wondrous, and I was glad of it. She asked Johan to heat water for a bath, and laid me a magnificent breakfast. By ten o'clock, I was as a hero refreshed. Taking the time to comb my incipient beard, and slightly to adjust the styling of my hair, I then went out into the heat of the day to whistle up young Jamie, and – as it might seem to any casual passer-by – to continue my surveying work for the railway from Braemore to Ullapool.

But already my eye was seeking out suitable sites for grand buildings! On the shores, I perceived new and busy harbours. In gaps in the hills, armies of workmen constructed schools or light-railways. I looked at that hunting-lodge over yonder and saw it torn down to make way for clean settlements for the poor and the dispossessed! In very truth, it was as if I was in the grip of prophecy! By day, I worked for the Railway Company, by night, I worked for the Greater Good of Mankind, and dreamed of an Earthly Paradise.

I did not venture into Ullapool throughout the long hot month of July. Such errands as I needed there – and they were few – were undertaken on my behalf by Jamie. The young boy was very compliant to my wishes now – I think he imagined that I was some

Master Criminal, in hiding from the very Government of the Land, sought after by patrols of cavalry, and perpetually living in fear of capture and loss of liberty. To some extent, I have to admit, this latter surmise was true; but as the days wore on, I felt that no ill would befall me.

Once a week, I received a visit from Mr. Aird, the watch-maker of Quay-street. Mr. Aird was of the Elect and was in communication with Mr. Rinck. He would come in the early morning, in order to be back at his shop by nine o'clock. He had little to tell me, except once, when he brought news that the famous magnate, Mr. Andrew Carnegie, had passed through Dingwall during the previous week, but had not dared to come near the rebellious town of Ullapool: this was taken as a sign that the Elect would soon gain the upper hand. "For the Fear of Man drives wild through the souls of such men, Mr. Kinnimoth," whispered Mr. Aird, with an air of revelation, "and the Rich shall not enter the Kingdom of God in Ullapool!"

Mr. Aird asked, on each visit, after my "Grand Plans", in order that he could pass word of my Divine Works back to the preacher at Inchnadamff. I told him honestly that I was making great progress and that all the draft plans would soon be ready.

Since I have touched on the subject, I should like to digress for a few moments and take you on a Grand Tour of the Citadel of the Elect at Ullapool and the surrounding Garden of Earthly Paradise.

In my earliest enthusiasm, I had thought to keep to the spirit of Mr. Rinck's instructions, which made considerable reference to the Revelation of John in the Good Book. However, when I considered the New Jerusalem in a more practical light, I could see likely engineering and architectural obstacles. For the city to be twelve thousand furlongs square, would mean that it would simply not fit upon the islands of Britain. I determined to correct this amateurish error in calculation, and to think more reasonably of a city of some fifteen miles from end to end, which would comfortably stretch from Braemore and up to Inchnadamff. I made some other adjustments to the plans: the walls could not be made of jasper – even if I were able to identify a reputable local supplier of that material – nor could I argue for them to be piled up a hundred and forty-four cubits high – by an engineer's good Imperial Measurement, some two hundred and sixteen feet. The twelve foundation-stones (of jasper again, of lapis lazuli, chalcedony, emerald, and many others) were never in my reckoning, and I intended to replace them with simple and impressive granite, grey or pink, in the manner of the grander edifices of Aberdeen and London. I knew that the Island of Mull might supply suitable material. Perhaps there would also be room for something pleasing with quartz; but certainly not for sardonyx, or chrysolite, or the like. As for the twelve gates of pearl, I had reduced them, after an hour's thought, to a dozen gates of honest cast-iron, which would have to be painted regularly in the manner of the Forth Bridge, perhaps in gold, perhaps in red lead.

The centre of the New Kingdom of the Elect was the Citadel, which would arise from the rubble and ruins of the Bank House in Argyle-street. Such would be the destruction of the premises of the National Bank of Scotland that not one stone would be left standing upon the other. Instead, there would be a building which would be constructed of solid granite, to the height of eighty-four feet, like a fortress, with but one grand entrance, supported on twin pillars. At the top of the seven successive storeys would be a tall and tapering temple, made of cedar-wood, glazed with three layers of the finest glass, to keep out the howling winds and the winter storms. And on top of that, in the manner of the grand Stevenson light-houses, a revolving light, magnified an thousand times by polished lenses.

Stretching far behind this Citadel, to the north, and supported upon the widest arches, there would be a granite aqueduct, joined with the Citadel at its top-most floor. There would be thirty-five such arches, each a hundred and fifty feet wide. A water-channel would be supported by the arches, drawing the clear crystal waters from Loch-achall in the hills behind Ullapool, a mile distant. There was nothing beyond my powers as an engineer.

The "Water of Life" would thereby enter the Citadel, to cascade down a central stair-well, through each of the seven floors, before finally being forced underneath the building, and along Argyle-street, as a living water-way. The banks of this water-way would be lined with silver birch and other trees of life, and the mud of the road would be replaced by well-tended lawns. This plan fitted pleasingly with John's Revelation.

On Argyle-street, Red-row and on Pulteney-street there would, of course, be built: sundry schools for the poor, houses for the homeless, etc., hospitals for the sick, colleges for higher learning, bath-houses, and such-like.

At the point where Argyle-street joined Quay-street, a large pool would be excavated before the Caledonian Hotel, fed by the channelled living water, with a diameter equal to the entire width of the cross-roads. From here, the water would then flow down to the sea in a series of dramatic descents. But before it reached the sea, it would pass through my grandest design, the terminus of the Garve to Ullapool Railway.

Under one vast glazed roof, magnificent in its cast-iron and steel arches and decorations, there would be no fewer than four platforms at which trains could arrive and depart. There would be a spacious ticket-hall in ornate oak, There would be a spacious and echoing luggage-office, such as even the condescending Station-Master at Waverley would envy. There would be a panelled and cushioned waiting-room, for all classes and both genders of passenger, for this would be a democratic railway. And finally there would be, still under the one roof as if it were another set of platforms, the quays, at which ships from far lands and from the nearer islands might tie up and transfer passengers to land, or to a train, with the minimum of inconvenience. I expected that a light-railway might be built across to Ardmair and beyond, to Inchnadamff, and so other platforms could later be added under the roof.

Through the centre of this great edifice the running waters would flow into a narrow channel of pure quartz, before they plunged spraying into the sea over a weir.

The twin railway-lines would come into the Station along Shore-street, from the east. As they neared the Station, a number of premises would have to be demolished, to allow for the two lines to split into four to feed the four platforms. There would also need to be room for a turn-table for the simple manoeuvring of engines. Any carts or horses which previously used either Shore-street or Quay-street would be diverted up Mill-street, where a wider road would have, perforce, to be built.

Such was to be my design for New Ullapool. And since St. John prophesies that there will be no need of the sun, neither of the moon, to shine in it, I began to draw up plans for public lighting of the streets, by day and night. These lights would be powered not by gas, but by electricity generated in turbines driven by the waters of life as they cascaded down the Citadel: electricity from water would be the power of the Elect! Perhaps I could patent some method of transmitting this electricity to my Railway? Truly, I felt in those days that my mind was on a plane above all around me, and that I was the man of vision expected by Rinck!

I also understood from John's Revelation that there were to be, at the End of Time, some hundred and forty-four thousand Chosen Ones. I determined, from the outset, that I would simply lay down the outline of the required huge city, under-pinning it, as it were, with the necessary railway, water-supplies, drainage and sewerage, the lines which the streets would follow, the places where schools would arise, and so on. I reasoned that if the ground-plan was correct, then the construction of the City would logically and of itself be ideal. I read also that there were expected some two hundred million horsemen at the time of the Apocalypse: now, this number would require an acreage of grazing and stabling which I felt that the north-west of Scotland could not support; advancing a rational argument, I supposed that perhaps two thousand horsemen would be a more-than-sufficient number for the company of Angels of the Lord, and so I allowed only for the lower figure.

I would sit pains-takingly for hours at my plans, inventing and setting down the names for my hundred and forty-four streets in my best writing. Satisfied with my work, I then decided that a new Society would require new measurements, and in the small hours, by lamplight, calculated the dimensions of each building in "cubits", the length of each street in "reeds", the capacity of the public cisterns in "baths".

In my enthusiasm, I thought again about the unborn generations of Kininmonths, and of how they would remember their famous ancestor for his works at Ullapool. So much better that, than lying forgotten and unknown behind the veil of the passing years!

As I hereby interpreted the words of John the Prophet, in the long summer evenings of Wester-ross, I was as happy as a man who has left behind all the cares of the world and ascended to the heights of a wooded mountain, from which all of his world could be viewed, paltry and impermanent in comparison to his soaring spirit. The warm months of July and August passed swiftly in this almost dream-like state, and I managed to forget my own troubles, and the fact that I might still be a wanted man, whose portrait was pinned to the walls of the police-station in Ullapool, alongside that of Mr. Rinck and many another dastardly fugitive from the Law. In August, I despatched young Jamie Campbell into Ullapool on two occasions, on some pretext, to spy out the situation and to see, if he could, into the house of Constable Hutchison. But he returned from these expeditions without any positive proof either to set my mind at ease or to encourage me to flee to the south, perhaps back to Talla.

In the end, I determined to enter the very nest and lair of the Ross and Cromarty Constabulary, and see for myself how the land lay.

September, 1897.

Thus it was that the night of the eighth of September, being a Wednesday, was fateful for your narrator. It was a night which seemed designed with precise measurements for the plan I had in mind, which was to enter Ullapool without being seen, to determine for myself, by subtlety and subterfuge, whether Mr. Kininmonth was still a hunted man, and then to retreat as if I had never been there. I admit now that I had no clear idea at that time how I was to make my determination; I had a vague notion of asking subtle questions in the Caledonian Hotel, or of skulking around Mr. Hutchison's residence in Market-street; I understood from my young apprentice that, when not on duty, the constable frequented the Argyle Hotel, in which I could scarcely make myself known.

Notwithstanding this lack of clarity in plan, I ventured forth at six o'clock, intimating to my friend Mrs. MacMahon that I intended to return towards midnight. It was a cold evening; the fog, which had settled around the loch during the afternoon, was damp and thick, wafting occasionally in the sharp bursts of wind that came down from the hills, but then closing in around me again. For this reason, and in order to disguise my appearance a little, I had borrowed the all-enveloping coat of Mrs. MacMahon's son, a seafaring man whom I had never met. My landlady supposed him to be gadding about the South Seas at that time, having recently received from him a brief letter written at Madras. I had no reason to imagine that, in those latitudes, he would have cause to regret having left his coat behind in Strath-broom. I also took the precaution of enveloping my head in one of the sailor's hats, a musty and over-large example of the chandler's art. However, it concealed most of the top of my head, inclusive of my eyes, and I bore the inconvenience for the advantage it gave me in remaining unrecognisable. Finally, I took with me a storm-lantern, filled with enough oil to see me there and back, furnished with small doors with which I could conceal the light at any time from inquisitive passers-by; a facility which I found extremely comforting.

Thus, wrapped up against the weather and against the eyes of those who, in the words of Mr. Rinck, "feared Man more than they feared God", I set out briskly along the road to Ullapool, reaching my goal at about a quarter past eight. I came up against but two travellers on the road, and my ears were keen to their arrival long before my eyes, so I was able to hide behind the dyke as they approached. Once or twice, on my long journey, thunder rolled faintly above my head, but no lightning struck, nor did the rain come down. I reached the town *incognito*; it was as deserted as could have been hoped for by a man in my situation.

Just as I came up to the old graveyard, which over-looks the shore at the entrance to the town, I paused to tighten my boot-laces. My mother always advised me to keep my boot-laces tied firmly, for I might never know when I would need them that way. I imagined that her purpose in telling me this was entirely maternal, and did not for one moment encompass nocturnal escapades such as I was engaged in; but the principle was sound and I was leaving nothing to chance. What would have been my mother's two-fold affront had I been captured, while fleeing from the Constables, simply because my boot-laces had come undone! I placed my feet in turn on the low wall of the dyke, facing into the graveyard whose rocky hillock seemed to tower up measureless before me. Just as I completed the operation, I was aware of a sinister presence advancing upon me. A grey cat, of dimensions which at the time seemed utterly supernatural, was creeping down from the graves and heading straight towards me. As I caught my breath in horror, it began to run; unusually for any cat, it was running straight towards me, and I felt for an instant that the unravelling of my life was begun; that the cat was an emissary of Death, come to fetch me to the Other Side. I retreated in horror, hands held before me to ward off the evil presence. The cat – which I now believe had simply not seen me until that point, and was as surprised as I was at the encounter – suddenly darted off to the right and into the fog; leaving me gasping for breath and sweating with a passing terror. Dear Reader, it may seem to you a stupidity on my part! but I was seized by the raw horror of it, the tricks of the night in the fog, and the excitement of the moment. I believe that I cried aloud the instant I saw that feline monster bearing down upon me. I remained shaking for several minutes.

Fortunately, there was no one abroad to see my discomfiture, so I retrieved my lantern and made straight for the Hotel, as I had already intended, for to calm my excitement with a good glass or two of spirits. Within five minutes, I was standing in the noisy bar-room, among fellow-humans, the sweat of my brow mingling with the steam from the coats and the smoke of the pipes. My hand was still trembling when I sipped my whisky, and one or two of my fellow-patrons looked askance at me.

I dared not remove either my hat or my coat; as a result, I was more than comfortably heated within a couple of minutes. This heat seemed to send the spirits whirling to my head, and I took the time to sit down and look for anyone who might advise me. Mr. Mackenzie the landlord quite obviously saw through my disguise, but, with a small shake of his head and a furrowing of his brow, he discouraged mutual recognition. Of the other men in the bar, I recognised many but knew not one. There seemed little point in remaining here. For pleasure, I ordered another "nip" or two; sat for about half an hour imbibing the warm air; and then abruptly and quietly departed into the night, making sure that no one followed me. The fog still billowed around, now opening up an avenue of some fifty yards, now cutting off all visibility above two yards.

I determined now to creep up on the police-station in Market-street. How else, I reasoned with myself, was I to find out whether I was still the fugitive that I imagined myself to be? It was, as you will perhaps concur, a reckless undertaking; there may even be some who take the view that my determination floated high upon the strong waters taken at the Caledonian Hotel. I can no longer say who might be right in this matter. Whatever the cause for my decision, I hastened along Argyle-street, with the fog streaming around me, keeping close to the houses and listening for any foot-fall or voice. There was not a soul on the street that night. Holding my lantern before me, I passed the Bank-house, house of infamy that it was, crossed the road to avoid the lights of the Argyle Hotel, and finally reached the junction with Mill-street.

Those of you who have until now been advising me against my course of action will be pleased to discover that I never reached the police-station. My skills at avoiding detection under the very nose of the Law were not put to the test. For, having proceeded directly up Mill-street as far as the junction with Market-street, I heard the sound of a horse trotting along the road. My nerves still in turmoil after my meeting with the graveyard cat, I ran backwards with exaggerated rapidity − 'ran', note you, not simply 'stepped' − in order to conceal myself. In so doing, I fell against a rock that lay at the edge of the road and tumbled sideways to the ground.

What happened next was at the time beyond my comprehension, but I suppose it was like this: as I fell, the lantern fell beside me and was dashed open upon the stony ground. The oil therein sprayed out upon me, and then ignited, thus touching off small fires about my person, mostly upon my back and sleeves. I noticed this conflagration straightway and sprang up in a panic, clutching the broken lantern. As I dashed forward, in my vain attempt to escape the consuming fires, I ran full tilt into the horse, which was pulling a small trap with an old man asleep in its seat. To avoid an injurious collision, I leaped upwards and managed to fall quite upon the sleeping figure who gently slid away straight on to the ground (which accident, as I found out later, did him no harm at all, occasioning only a mild surprise).

As I landed upon the seat, the horse neighed in fright and began to gallop down the hill towards the sea. All aflame as I was, I managed to pull myself upright, and finally laid hold of the reins; as we came to the top of the sharp incline which led precipitately down into the sea, I managed to persuade the horse to cut around to the right into Argyle-street; which it did, with considerable noise, and (as I now understand it) a deal of senseless bellowing from myself. As luck would have it, a group of men was just then emerging from the Hotel: they watched stupefied as I drove down upon them from out of the fog, a dark figure blazing now quite fiercely, babbling in tongues. We rattled furiously down the length of the street. The shouts of the group at the Hotel attracted others as we proceeded. When we reached the cross-roads in front of the Caledonian, I could feel the heat now coming through the coat and decided that the sea was probably the better option after all. We veered once more, this time to the left, before the eyes of all the people in the Hotel, some of whom were peering from the windows, others spilling out into the street, as we thundered past.

My horse and I cracked down the final hill, rattled on to the wooden pier at which Mr. Macbrayne's boats tie up, and headed into the unknown. The horse and I saw the end of the quay emerge from the fog at precisely the same moment; for my part, I believe I let out a shout of horror, the horse − with good animal sense − stopped short, with the logical result that I was propelled rapidly over its head and into the lapping fog. Indeed, this moment and the next few constituted a graphic demonstration of the laws of physics − in the first place, of Newton's Second Law; in the second place, of the law concerning the arc described by falling bodies with a forward motion; and in the third, of the exclusive properties of water and fire. For I was no sooner in the air than under the water where the flames were extinguished.

I will pause here to reflect on this event, which lasted barely three or four minutes. For myself, each minute seemed to last a life-span. My only concern was to ensure that my brains were not dashed out by the mad careering of the horse; and then to extinguish the flames which were threatening to engulf me. But what can the on-lookers have seen? I will return to their wider perceptions later; for now, just consider: they saw, emerging from the grey fog without warning, a blazing figure driving a white horse, galloping past them in a fraction of a second, disappearing again shrieking into the fog. When people finally caught up with the horse, which now stood steaming at the edge of the quay, there was no sign of the flaming figure; and not a sound which might lead them to me.

For it was this way with me: the cold water not only doused the flames but in an instant brought me back to an objective assessment of my appearance to the world. How foolish, I thought, as I floated in the water, how foolish of me to be here, charred and soaked! What crass stupidity to be so caught out! What a donkey I was! This was no way for Mr. Kininmonth to appear to the world! And I determined that, as far as possible, the world should not find me out for the numb-skull I was. Shaking off the coat therefore, which was threatening momentarily to pull me under the waters and into oblivion (the hat having already been lost in my short flight above Loch-broom), I swam swiftly and silently to the east, away from the end of the quay, hoping to touch dry land somewhere near the Cemetery. I could hear the shouts of men and the high-pitched interrogative voices of women upon the quay; but the fog concealed me from their sight.

Ordinarily, I am neither a strong nor an enthusiastic swimmer. But that night I swam the two hundred or so yards from quay to shore with a determination and power that could be generated only from embarrassment. No one should find me out! What a simpleton I had been! What had possessed me to venture out that night? I raged at myself, and my anger kept my arms and legs moving and my breath coming strongly, until at last I found myself able to stand and walk across the slippery sea-bed to the shore, slightly to the west of the end of Mill-street. (You may ask how I had contrived to keep my bearings so well, at sea, in the fog, in the dark. I can only reply: "I have no idea." Perhaps there was indeed a Spirit or Angel looking over me that night.)

I emerged on to the street, dripping with salt water, teeth chattering, hat-less, coat-less, light-less – and terrified lest some-one see me. At a trot, I set off, away from the hub-bub at the far end of the street, and ran, until exhausted, along the road leading back to Strath-broom. Admittedly, I did not run for any great distance, for my legs soon gave way beneath me and I had to rest for several minutes below the cottages at Braes. After that, I could only walk for about five minutes at a time before resting again. I dared not rest for long, for I feared to catch my death of cold, which would have been a sure way for the people of Ullapool to discover my foolish behaviour. Social disapprobation is a powerful persuasion for clinging to life, as I am sure you know.

At what time I reached Mrs. MacMahon's residence, I cannot tell. My watch had stopped at exactly twenty-four minutes past nine – I supposed this to have been the time when I entered the water. It might now have been about two or three o'clock. The door was shut, but not bolted, and I was able to slip into the silent house and creep up to my room, where I pulled off my soaking, freezing clothes and fell into my bed.

There followed a period which now has for me the uncertainty of a disturbed night. I put down my vagueness concerning this time to the fever into which I fell as a result of catching a cold, and from which I only recovered after a week in my bed. There was no concealing from Mrs. MacMahon that I had lost both her son's coat and cap, and, indeed, the lantern which she had kindly loaned me for my adventure. Since I would offer her no explanation for the losses, her disapproval knew no bounds; which did nothing to assist my recovery. She barely spoke to me twice in the time I lay in bed – the first time to enquire after the lost clothing, the second time, eight days later, to demand to know when I expected to get out of my bed and return to work; and I believe that she placed all the inhabitants of the house under an obligation to shut any doors loudly and frequently; and if possible to shout, rather than speak quietly.

My confusion was not lessened, however, when I finally managed to get out of bed. For by then – this date was the nineteenth day of September – the whole district was alive with Apocalyptic rumour and fantastical speculation. These rumours and opinions were relayed to me by Mrs. MacMahon, who put aside her extreme displeasure so far as to bring me abreast of the latest news from Ullapool, when she returned from a visit there that morning. I will endeavour to set out the various rumours clearly, rather than rely on the good woman's very excited, confused and topsy-turvy recital of her understanding of the facts.

It seems that the group of people who had witnessed the final yards of my flight from the door of the Caledonian Hotel were those of the Rinck-ian party. What they had been privileged to see was nothing less than this: an Angel of the Lord come down upon the town of Ullapool, with vengeance in his heart and the power of God blazing in his wings. The Angel had ridden a Horse of Vengeance through the town as a sign that the Days of the Apocalypse were upon us and that the End of the Reign of the Godless had come. The Angel was clutching in his hand one of the Seven Flaming Torches, as a sign that the Sealed Book was about to be opened. As is the habit of Angels, he had passed through the land with swiftness, so that only the Elect had been granted a full revelation, while the poor-in-spirit had only had a sorry glimpse. And, having paid his brief visit, the Angel of the Lord had flown up over the waters of Loch-broom – interpreted as "the sea of glass" revealed to the sainted John – and had vanished once more from the sight of mortals.

In the opposing camp, those who had emerged from the door of the Argyle Hotel were of a more sanguine and worldly disposition; they recognised the horse to be that of William Donald, the aged father of the mill-manager; held the view that the figure driving the trap was that of a petty horse-thief; and considered the abrupt disappearance of the flaming man to be his deserved death in the cold waters of Loch-broom. But the patrons of the Argyle Hotel left themselves with an awkward question: why was the supposed petty criminal ablaze? The Caledonians hounded the Godless unbelievers with this question. The Argyles for their part offered up various ludicrous and imaginative explanations, but none were at all convincing and fewer still hit upon the simple truth. Even those citizens of Ullapool who were of an agnostic disposition were easily led to believe that although the horse was perhaps or doubtless William Donald's, the blazing figure which had ridden it had been of divine provenance. So that, in the space of a few days, as I lay sweating and burning on my bed, the vast majority of the people of Ullapool had been persuaded that their town had indeed been visited by the Angel of the Apocalypse.

Seizing the God-sent opportunity, on the evening of the ninth day of September, Melchior Rinck made his return from exile. He was greeted at the edge of town by a crowd of two hundred, hurriedly assembled by his supporters in the town, eager to hear his words and to prepare their souls and houses for the End of Time. Along with a half-dozen of his trusted lieutenants (James Finlay and Mackenzie of the Hotel prominent among them), Rinck led a disorderly procession to the cross-roads of Quay-street and Red-row, and there held a short meeting of preaching and praying. For the purposes of his sermon, he counted the welcoming crowd at exactly one gross, and announced that they were surely the progenitors of the hundred and forty-four thousand Elect Souls prophesied by John; and that the four horses on which the party had arrived from Inchnadamff were but a further sign of the Imminence of the Vengeance. All this, as a result of the visitation on the previous night by the Burning Angel. Rinck then announced that he would now convoke and convene the four-and-twenty wise Elders who were to usher in the new Age when the Rule of God, the Fear of God alone, would fall like a cleansing fire upon Ullapool, and all of the land.

Despite the misgivings of some in the crowd, who wondered aloud whether four-and-twenty wise men could be found at one and the same time in all of Wester-ross, the night continued with a meeting of the New Elders of Ullapool, much to the outrage and distress of the Parish Council, who were for their part called to an Extra-ordinary Meeting at the home of the Reverend Macmillan. As was often the case, the Chairman of the Council, Arthur Fowler, was away in London, and the Reverend therefore presided. Thus, at one end of the town, the representatives of the Old Order took their seats and passed resolutions condemning the riotous assemblies and provocative sermons of Mr. Rinck; at the other end of town, in the Caledonian Hotel, the Elders of the New Order smoked their pipes and passed resolutions condemning the perversity of the Rich and the Powerful, and all those who would have the Common People fear Man more than they feared God, and they most particularly vilified the members of the Parish Council.

Fevered as I was, I had no cognisance of either of those historic meetings, which signalled the parting of the times and a sundering of the town. Had I been able, I would certainly have wished to have been one of Rinck's Elders, for my sympathies – if not my scientific reasoning – lay with that party. But although I had had adventures enough for a man of my years, I was secretly disappointed not to have witnessed the concluding event of the evening: when the entire Constabulary of Ullapool, in the persons of Mr. Hutchison and Mr. Macdonald, was summoned by the Parish Council and ordered to arrest Mr. Rinck and bring him up before them on nebulous charges of Public Disorder, Sedition and possibly High Treason; when, simultaneously, Mr. Rinck had been persuaded by his New Elders to make representations to the Parish Council and now despatched three dozen assorted fishermen, inn-keepers, tailors and bakers, under the leadership of James Finlay, to Mr. Macmillan's residence in Mill-street; when the intrepid policemen, accompanied by a group of small boys, much in the manner of a pack of terriers, emerged on to Argyle-street at the east end; when, at that self-same moment, the Elect started down the same street from the west end: then there was an easy and bloodless victory for Mr. Rinck's party. Pride was hurt, in plenty, but there were no broken heads.

And Ullapool, on the ninth day of the ninth month of 1897, became the Citadel of the Elect.

Over the next ten days, as I lay unconscious of the excitement, the two parties vied for the support of the towns-people. Both sides understood that the Visitation of the Burning Angel lay at the heart of the struggle for power. And while Mr. Rinck and his supporters drew on the words of the Holy Book, particularly from the Prophecies of John, the Parish Council tried more worldly approaches. The walls of the town were soon decorated with notices announcing that the Burning Angel was no more and no less than an attempt by the "Disloyal and Republican Fenian Socialists" to bring down the rule of our Most Beloved Queen and Empress. Hand-bills were posted on every window, a new one each day, each with some tale more lurid than the last, all of which had evidently come from the mind of the Reverend Montague Fowler, whose sole claim to significance until then had been his ownership of the coal-store down by the Pier.

Mrs. MacMahon, on finding me returned to the land of the living, read out to me some of these hand-bills. I will not pass on all the stories contained therein; suffice it, for the purposes of illustration, to say that the latest of these stories went as follows:

The Rinck-ians had, some days prior to the fateful night, found in their midst a traitor, one Alexander Kinnimoth. (I began to suspect the hand of Mr. MacAulay in all of this, from the deliberate mis-spelling of my name.) They suspected this "promising and able engineer" of having become a spy for the Parish Council, and of being about to reveal to the Authorities of the town the refuge of Mr. Rinck. Mr. Rinck, it was now established, had been in hiding at Achiltibuie, and the brave Mr. Kinnimoth was on the point of leading a gallant troop of the Ullapool Volunteers to the charlatan's lair. But Mr. Kinnimoth was nefariously captured by Rinck, and held in a cave for several days, without food or even the comfort of a Bible. Then, on the night of the eighth of September, Mr. Kinnimoth had been ceremonially decapitated, his bleeding broken body had been tied to a horse, set ablaze and sent through the town as a warning to any other honest citizen who might oppose Mr. Rinck. The body of the loyal engineer had no doubt sunk to the very foot of Loch-broom, while the Rinck-ians had stood at the edge of the Pier, laughing madly and drinking spirits the while.

"But, Mrs. MacMahon," I exclaimed weakly when she had finished reading this latest nonsense, "how can they think I am dead when I am lying here, for anyone to visit?"

My landlady sighed. "Mr. Kininmonth," she advised, "you would do well not to leave this house until some of the excitement has died down. There are those who do not have time for Mr. Rinck: those people are ready to believe any nonsense which that young ass Montague Fowler cares to put about; and would certainly believe you to be a dreadful ghoul, returned from the Dead. And then there are those who believe Mr. Rinck to be the emissary of the Lord: those people may now believe that you have betrayed their cause and deserve to die, for they have a rage against any who might endanger their cause. If you appear in the town, you would most certainly walk in the Valley of the Shadow of Death, Mr. Kininmonth. For that reason I have told no one that you are here."

There was good sense in her remarks and I was grateful to her for her concern. I was overwhelmed by the guilt of having destroyed all of her son's clothing, and began to explain. At that, she held up her hand imperiously: "I have no wish, Mr. Kininmonth, to hear any disagreeable details. No wish, nor yet desire. You just get your strength back and let us wait and see what happens." With that, she – as one who I now hoped to be my reconciled friend – left me to mull over the consequences of my ill-thought actions, and to consider how best to appear in society when I was once more hale.

It was another three days before my fever had left me. On the twenty-second day of the month, I awoke to a glorious September morning, in which a silence filled with all the possibilities of human endeavour towered in the heavens above Mrs. MacMahon's house. As I gradually slipped out from sleep, I realised that my head was for once clear of pain. Cautiously, I sat on the edge of my bed, then stood up. I felt that I was whole again. With a feeling of renewal, I set about cutting off my beard and shaving all my stubble back to a fine smooth chin. Then I went downstairs.

No sooner had I sat down to my breakfast in the kitchen, served to me by Johan with the fuss which can only make a man feel that he has found a home, than there was a commotion to the front of the house. Johan went to investigate and then came running back, alarm written over her face: "It's Mr. Rinck, Mr. Kininmonth! Whatever can he want with us?" I was, in truth, much perturbed myself, for Mrs. MacMahon's warning had been troubling me since our discussion.

"Is he on his own?" I asked her in some trepidation, imagining that he, being half-American, might have called out a "Lynch-mob" for this visitation. I understand that the Americans delight in this executive form of popular justice, after the example set by Captain Lynch of Virginia; and have also perfected the "posse", with which to pursue those "on the run" (as it is termed) from justice. It was not beyond reason to suspect that Mr. Rinck might have convoked some similar League in pursuit of myself, a perceived agent of the Godless.

"There are two men with him, Mr. Kininmonth," said the girl, edging round the back of the table, away from the door. I should have wished to make a similar movement, but felt that it was my position as a man to put up a courageous front. As I sat there, shaking within, the kitchen-door opened and Mrs. MacMahon stepped in to ask me whether I would receive the visitors. I had no option but to agree and to accompany her to the drawing-room, at the front of the house.

To my great surprise and trepidation, Mr. Rinck greeted me like a long-lost friend. He advanced upon me with his arms out-stretched: "Welcome back, Brother Kinnimunt!" he exclaimed in that thick accent of his. He encircled me with his arms and clasped me to his bosom. His enormous beard scratched at the side of my head.

When I was finally released from his embrace, I saw that he was accompanied by James Finlay, who greeted me amicably, and a man, about forty years of age, clad in a long black coat and a curious wide-brimmed hat, whom I had never seen before and who said nothing.

"This is Daniel McManus," said Rinck, introducing his impassive companion. "Brother Daniel has a great interest in engineering, as you do." The silent man scowled at me by way of greeting.

Mrs. MacMahon suggested we all sit down, and then retired from the room. We all sat in the various chairs at our disposal; and then Mr. Rinck began.

Many were the subjects of our long conversation. But principally they were these: first, that there was a need to bring the railway-line with all due speed into Ullapool from Braemore, and this was my task, with the assistance of Brother Daniel; secondly, that I was to prepare a "Revelatory Chronicle of the Building of the Citadel of the Elect at Ullapool", for Mr. Rinck had heard that I was a man who desired to record all history in the making; and thirdly, there was some discussion of my plans for the streets and buildings of the New Ullapool, on the understanding that I should supervise their construction once the railway had been completed. Rather optimistically, I thought, Mr. Rinck proposed that the railway be completed from Ullapool to Braemore by the first day of January in 1898; which gave us precisely a hundred days to plan, progress and perfect the line. I expressed my concern, saying that I did not think it possible to advance the fourteen miles across rough terrain in such a short period, without a miracle. Mr. Rinck looked at me with strong disapproval, then shook his head sorrowfully.

"I see, Brother, that you are still weighed down by the chains of the Godless. Trust in the Lord to guide you; trust in your visions.

You will have many eager friends to help you and the Fear of God will be your spur."

With that, the subject was dropped. Talk drifted on to other matters, and I admit that I did not listen very hard, since I was applying my arithmetic to the task ahead. One hundred days would be reduced to about eighty-six, it being unlikely we would work on the Sunday of any week; eighty-six days divided by fourteen miles was about a furlong and a third per working day. One mile every week! Certainly, if we had been on the arid Great Plains of the America of the Plutocrats, we might have achieved this easily. Even with a veritable army of Enthusiasts, I despaired of success in Wester-ross. I knew the wild sodden country far better than Mr. Rinck, who had seen it only in an exceptionally warm and mild summer.

By the time I had made my final pessimistic calculations, in my head (my erstwhile school-teacher, Mr. Wardlaw, would have been proud of my skills in Mental Arithmetic!), the conversation of the others had passed on, and they were ready to leave. All three men had arrived on new bicycles, which had been placed at the disposal of the New Elders by William Macphail, merchant; Rinck decreed that these "Godly Bicycles" should be used solely by Visionaries. Accordingly, one was handed over to me, much to the disgust of Daniel McManus, who faced a twelve-mile walk home.

Arrangements were made for McManus to join me on the following day to make firm plans for the extending of the railway from Ullapool to Braemore. I discovered, to my secret horror, that the man was a Glaswegian! You might think it strange of me, but I have had an aversion to Glaswegians for some time now, finding in them all that is brash, insolent and disrespectful among civilised Scotsmen. Mr. McManus and I would probably not get on well together. In this fear, I was fully vindicated.

After Rinck's departure, I spent much of the afternoon in assembling the most significant of my thoughts, by means of a cycle-run up and down the high-road. I wondered at myself for having placed myself in a position where I was fooling one of two parties as to my loyalties – the Railway Company, who thought I was engaged in their business; and Rinck, who imagined I was entirely his – but did not care to consider which party was the dupe. Was I, perhaps, the real fool in this case: is this what was meant by trying to serve two Masters and thereby serving none?

As I pedalled along the road, I considered – not for the first time in those years, and not for the last – how I had come to be entangled in such a complex web of intrigue and conflicting loyalties. It would have been so easy to cut through all the ropes, and invisible threads, which now bound me and walk away – travel, like so many of my generation, to the Colonies and start again. But the truth is that, at my age, I was afraid to take such a step: I had work before me, which I knew I could do well if left to manage it; and in the end that is what mattered most to me: not the adventures, not the people, but the lasting pleasure of laying down a railway-line from Garve to Ullapool, which would be marked on the ground and on the maps for decades to come, and which would announce boldly that a man named Kininmonth had been here and built here.

Volume IV:

From Ullapool to Braemore
or,
The End of Time.

September, 1897.

Work began again on the railway on Thursday, the twenty-third of September, 1897, at eight in the morning, when I arrived on my Godly Bicycle (I confess it was the most comfortable machine I had ever ridden upon) at the house of Miss Kilroy, now the lodging-place of Daniel McManus.

From the very start, I realised that my fears about the man were well-founded.

"Let us begin," I proposed, "by reviewing the surveys which I have so far conducted; then we will proceed to the first stretch of construction. During each stage of construction, we will survey the next stage, and so on." I found this proposal to be quite sound and beyond any argument; having stated it, I felt content.

My colleague was of quite a different persuasion. His stated belief was that we need not worry too much about surveys, for the Good Lord would surely guide our hands and lay our tracks in the right direction, embedding them on the solid ground of faith.

"We must start building now, Brother Alexander!" he shouted, striking his fist into his palm. "Every moment in which we are idle is a moment passed to the Godless!"

I made it clear to him that I would not alter the methods I had adopted in twenty or so years of engineering. I asked him what experience he had had of laying down railways; he confessed that he had none, although he had studied many books at the Allen Glen's School. This, I retorted, did not carry much weight in the wild conditions of Wester-ross; if he wished to complain, he could go back to Brother Rinck. Otherwise, he was to follow my instructions. There was a considerable amount of grumbling and of kicking of stones in the road; in desperation, I cited my role as appointed "Visionary", and this finally silenced my new colleague; we agreed to adopt the scientific approach to the Godly Railway.

I had already decided that we must construct the railway from its terminus eastwards. We could expect no assistance from the eastern mainland – indeed, I expected we should meet all manner of obstruction from Railway Companies and policemen, when it was discovered that the railway was physically an extension of the Garve to Braemore Line, but spiritually a completely different line altogether. All our materials, all our labourers would come from or through Ullapool.

McManus and I made our way to the Caledonian Hotel, arguing all the way about the procedures to be adopted for our project. It was my intention to gain Rinck's support for my plans in advance, and so put an end to Daniel's ridiculous behaviour. I also needed Rinck to send a man of strong character to Glasgow, at the earliest opportunity, to seek out the materials which would be required – in particular the iron rails; and, if possible, a small locomotive. And, finally, I had to make arrangements for a party of able-bodied men to travel by night to the site of Braemore Halt and to borrow from there such rails and sleepers as still lay forgotten in the bracken beside the terminated line.

To my very great surprise, all my demands and requests were immediately complied with. There was no argument from anyone. McManus was to be despatched to Glasgow on the next boat, accompanied by Finlay, and armed with a letter promising payment; the details of which did not concern me. I had mixed feelings when this was decided: on the one hand, I should be rid of his unwelcome presence for a few days; on the other, I had no idea what unsuitable goods he might come back with. But I was in no position to dispute the decision. Further, a whole army of able-bodied men and boys was made available to me for all the other work. To complete my delight, Mr. Aird the watch-maker was invited to make repairs to the watch which had suffered from its immersion in the loch, and it is to his credit that it was returned to me, as good as new, within the week. (Would that the watch-makers of some of our larger towns were as assiduous in their endeavours!)

It was decided that I should organise the transportation of the materials from Braemore that very night. Having despatched young Jamie Campbell on a scouting expedition to Braemore, to seek out and mark the position of all the abandoned materials, I went with a dozen men to the junction of Quay-street and Shore-street to mark out the first furlong of the railway; this would be the easiest part of the construction, for we only required ballast, sleeper and rail to lay down over the existing road.

By five o'clock, all my preparations were complete. Work was to begin in earnest the very next day.

But first, I had twenty men with two carts pulled by strong horses to lead up to Braemore under cover of darkness. I knew that Jamie had found everything I required. So it was without much trepidation that I joined my gang on the road beside Achindrean. We came to Braemore at about ten o'clock. There was only a thin crescent moon that night and all was quiet, apart from the sighing of a cool wind, which came up from the loch. We passed the gate-house to the Lodge, with some caution, and came shortly afterwards to that scene of desolation, the Braemore Halt. Jamie, who had accompanied us, led the gang in the darkness straight to the area which was once used to pile up ballast and rails and sleepers, and which was now concealed from all human knowledge by bracken some three or four feet high, interspersed, as we found, by nettle and thistle of equal magnitude and ferocity.

It took a good two hours to load all the rails and sleepers we could find on to the carts, not because of the quantity but simply because it was almost impossible to see what we were doing. I had furnished myself with another storm-lantern, but dared not use it much; as a result, everyone felt their way through the undergrowth, exploring for iron and wood with bare hands. Many were the oaths and curses muttered that night.

Finally it was done, our two carts creaked and groaned back towards Ullapool. At each turn of their wheels I felt my heart leap into my mouth, convinced that I had heard a shout from the direction of the Lodge, certain that Arthur Fowler was following us with the forces of the Law at his back. It was with considerable difficulty that I forced myself not to break into a gallop as we came down the brae. With what relief did Jamie and I step aside at Achindrean, instructing the men to proceed to Ullapool and to leave the carts at the Pier!

But my relief was of short duration: no sooner had I seen Jamie to the door of his father's cottage than I heard shouting from the road, as of many men arguing. I deemed it necessary to be both inquisitive and cautious; therefore I crept back down the track to the road and, concealing myself in the inky shade of the bushes and trees, peered into the gloom westwards. There was scarcely anything to be seen. After several minutes, during which the commotion continued and I resigned myself to taking some responsibility, there was a final set of shouted insults and a figure on horseback started to trot towards me. Immediately, I pulled myself back into the hawthorn bush behind me, at great discomfort to my person. (The following morning, I found several large thorns embedded in my most sensitive areas of skin, and was in considerable mental anguish in debating how they were to be extracted. For a man cannot readily put his eye close to that part of his body, as is requisite for the extraction of thorns from the flesh; nor can he readily ask any member of the gentle sex, unless she be his wife – of which I had none, at that time; nor, without possible grave mis-understandings, can he ask another boy or man to do the necessary. My only recourse would have been to a doctor of medicine. Dr. Lamond in Red-row was a man whom, at that time, I was particularly anxious to avoid, since he was of the Godless party. What is a man to do, other than suffer discomfort, and spend endless hours in the privacy of his own room with three mirrors and a pair of tweezers? It was a fortnight before the last of the thorns was extracted and the infected skin healed.)

The rider came abreast of me, engaged in animated discussion. I found that it was the Reverend Montague Fowler, the younger son of Sir John, and that he was talking to himself. As he came up to me, he was noisily demanding "what the d—e" those men had been doing, and deciding that it was "no honest business, by G-d!" The Reverend decided, just as he passed me, that he had to answer a call of nature. He slid from his horse and, to my horror, advanced directly to my bush, all the while muttering to himself. He stood barely a yard in front of me, and relieved the pressure on his bladder on the leaves and grass around my boots. I closed my eyes and held my breath: how it was that he did not see me, even allowing for his inebriation, I did not know then and do not know to this day. After what seemed several minutes, the sound of his water ceased and he turned back to his horse, laughing aloud at a coarse rhyme about a fallen woman named Lilly, which I shall refrain from repeating here, insensitive as it is and hardly illuminating for the history I am writing.

When he had ridden up the road towards Braemore (and moved on to other bawdy rhymes concerning Nancy and Fanny and Peggy), I emerged from my concealment and went to bathe my boots and trousers in the cleansing waters of the river. And then I returned home.

The following few days were spent in trying to sort the wheat from the chaff among the large group of able-bodied men who had volunteered to lay the railway-line. I had at that time about forty men at my disposal, ranging from the strong to the puny, from the sober and eager to the weary and drunken. I was able, after one day, to find among them four men in whom I could place some trust to carry out my instructions sensibly and as near as possible to the letter. They all seemed capable of commanding a gang of men, either by virtue of stentorian voice or by quiet and kind persuasion. And so we got along. The great advantage which we had over any other similar gang of men was that almost all of them were there because they actually desired to have the railway-line constructed. I wondered if I was witness to the beginning of a society in which men would work not to increase the profit of others, but to increase the quality of their own lives?

By the following Wednesday, the penultimate day of September, we had managed to lay a furlong of track along Shore-street. The quality of the timbers and rails which we had rescued from rust and decay at Braemore was variable, but almost all the material could be used. Having laid a furlong of track, we saw our small stock-pile of material exhausted. But luck – or, as Mr. Rinck persuaded us, the Lord – smiled upon us; and our spirits had been raised by the return of McManus on the preceding day, having successfully negotiated with the company of William Baird in Coatbridge for a delivery of rails on the following Monday, and on the first Monday of each month thereafter as long as credit was given. In the meanwhile, two gangs of men were despatched to forage in the surrounding countryside: one, led by the carpenter Matherson, went in search of logs which could be used for sleepers; the other went to Mr. Cameron's quarries up by Loch-achall, and brought back innumerable cart-loads of stone for ballast.

All that was missing was a locomotive; our emissaries had failed to secure any such machine, either new or second-hand, from any of the usual manufacturers. McManus had visited almost all the works in Glasgow and Kilmarnock – Chaplin's, Dixon's, Marshall's, and all the others – but had met with the same response everywhere. It was our suspicion that all the owners of those works were fearful of selling to people who were not in the usual way of Railway Companies. It was McManus's stated opinion that these engine-works were "the Place where Satan has his Throne", as John had revealed in advance. However, with the aid of a subterfuge – and this came as no great surprise to me, it being in the character of Glaswegians to revel and to delight in subterfuge – Baird's of Coatbridge had been persuaded to sell us also an old wagon, on which materials could be transported. It was young Finlay's proposition that this wagon could be pulled along the rails by two or more strong horses.

On the Monday following, at two o'clock, a large boat arrived at Macbrayne's Pier, and was soon unloaded of its cargo of iron rails and a flat wagon, some thirty feet long. By dusk, the wagon – the first rolling-stock of the "Railway League of the Godly" (as it had been named) – was proudly positioned on the rails which had so far been laid. Two horses had been brought in from the fields, and an evening of sport initiated for the children of the town: the horses, being attached to the wagon, drew nigh on forty shrieking children up and down the line, the length of Shore-street, for a good hour. All of the people of the town (with the exception of the Reverends MacDonald and MacMillan, but not excepting the three otherwise docile children of the latter) came to watch and admire, regardless of which party they supported.

This great occasion also brought me into close proximity to Miss Keir, the handsome school-mistress of Leckmelm, who accompanied her charges to view the day's events. She came up to me with a brisk air and introduced herself, blushing in a most charming way. "This is excellent work, Mr. Kininmonth," she said, unable to hide the school-mistress in her soul. I could see the flush spread to her ears and admired greatly the way in which soft curls of her light-brown hair, here and there streaked with grey, were brightened by her skin. I was, I admit, rather overwhelmed by the pleasure of standing so close to her, and could barely stutter any sensible words of conversation. We talked one-sidedly of matters which the other barely understood – I of the technical aspects of railway-building, she of the pleasures of children. In those brief ten minutes of our meeting, all the world seemed to fade away. When she had to leave, she gave me her gloved hand; I held it for as long as I could, and longer than I should, feeling an unaccustomed tremor in my stomach and a breathlessness most unsuited to my years. Perhaps I over-stepped the bounds of common decency. Looking back now, what petty things disrupted me! But those of you – perhaps all of you – who have at some point – perhaps more than once – been affected by Love, or Infatuation, or Reckless Admiration, will understand the power of such feelings – against which we are as sand in the boiling ocean – over the Mind. There is no escape, just the constant painful burning of certainty and uncertainty, like the embers of a fire in the grate, with brief flares of passion and determination, soon dying away to nothing in the choking smokes of dark despair.

But, in all the time of the building of the railway, this day, the fourth of October, was the easiest and happiest moment for Ullapool, and for myself.

On the following morning, work began with an enthusiasm which I had never experienced before and have never experienced since: the men of the gangs were almost running to get to their labours and to advance the line eastwards to Braemore. I noted that their numbers were already being increased by people who had arrived from the north in the previous days. Mr. Fraser, who worked as the mail-driver, had, to my surprise and his own, emerged as one of my four lieutenants; he it was who dealt with the hiring and firing of the labourers. He told me that word of the Citadel was attracting many of the poorer sort of Ross and Cromarty to Ullapool, where they perceived salvation and the beginning of a new democratic society. Word was also reaching the islands to the West, he said, and he expected many more to arrive in the coming weeks, now that the harvests were finished.

The only discordant note in that day's proceedings was the

insistence of Daniel McManus on leading the gangs to the head of the line, singing the words of the Ninety-Seventh Psalm from a scroll, and bearing aloft a huge white flag painted with a rainbow. When I asked tentatively what it meant, he turned to me, his eyes blazing with passion, and told me that Brother Melchior had permitted him to do this; that he meant to begin each morning and end each afternoon by leading the gangs out behind the "banner of the Godly" and singing one of the psalms, "by which they may instruct themselves in the way of the Lord. Brother Kinnimoth, have you not read in the Revelation of John, Chapter Ten, that a mighty angel came down from Heaven, clothed with a cloud; and a rainbow was upon his head, and he sware to all men that there should be time no longer, that the mystery of God shall be revealed from the scrolls?" I kept my peace, for it was not my place to interfere in my colleague's fantastic notions: the men would soon enough let him know if he went too far. Already it was rumoured that Daniel McManus intended to present himself as the "Angel of Cromarty", a prophetic Daniel of the League of the Righteous.

Thus, day after day during the month of October, except the Sabbath, McManus, his scroll and his painted flag led the way along the ever-growing line from Ullapool, his whining voice tunelessly singing from the Psalms, while behind him trudged forty, fifty, sixty men with their tools of trade.

Some notes for the "Revelatory Chronicle".

It is my duty to bring together all materials which are thought necessary for the publication of the "Revelatory Chronicle of the Building of the Citadel of the Elect at Ullapool". I have already kept to one side the pamphlets which Melchior Rinck prepared during these months. When the time comes (or the End of Time, maybe?), these will be included as appendices or bound together in a separate companion volume. For September of 1897, for example, I have listed the publication of the following three titles by a man named Robertson, who lived in Market-street: first, "Torrents Rushing in Cromarty – the Poor Man Rises Up and Seizes Hope"; secondly, "The Seven Thunders Which I Have Heard, But Am

Forbidden To Write Down, For They Are Sealed Up For Ever";
lastly, "The Citadel at Ullapool – How Man Will Come to Fear
God in Forty-Two Months". Each of these was handed round
enthusiastically, until the cheap paper on which it was printed fell
apart. Luckily, Mr. Rinck ensured that I always had a clean copy for
my Chronicle. (I confess that I rarely read much beyond the titles,
which were, to my engineer's mind, always more interesting than
the body of the text.)

Perhaps more important than these small publications were the
efforts of Rinck and his companions to organise the civil government
of Ullapool. From the very first day, the four-and-twenty New
Elders sat in their room at the Caledonian Hotel, of which the door
was removed from its hinges so that all might witness the wise
discussions taking place therein. Mrs. MacMahon told me one day
that she had been to attend one such meeting, and barely saw
anything of what was going on inside because of the thick clouds of
tobacco-smoke; and could barely hear one word that was spoken for
the din of the crowds pressing around the door-way. The official
Parish Council was grandly ignored by the New Elders; and as long
as this was the case, the decisions made by the New Elders generally
held sway in the town. There were a few parts of the town which
adhered to the Parish Council – these being first and foremost the
establishments of the two Ministers, that of Mr. Mackenzie of the
National Bank and those of one or two additional members of
established society. But, increasingly, any decision made by the New
Elders was obeyed by the majority of the people, with far more awe
and respect than any decision ever made by the Parish.

Among the formal pronouncements made in September of that
year were: an ordinance, dated the tenth of the month, requiring
that all house-holders give "one half of all that is excessive to them"
into the "Common Purse", and that all the estate-owners yield up
all their land to the same fund – both instructions proving highly
popular among the poorer people, but impossible to enforce; an
instruction, on the same date, that the National Bank of Scotland
entrust all the funds held by their Agent in Ullapool to the body
known as the New Elders, for the greater good of the community,
and the furtherance of the Will of God; further "amicable and

Godly" calls on the Agent of the National Bank to yield to the authority of the New Elders; several dictates throughout the month, requiring the intransigent representatives of the Church of Scotland and the Free Church of Scotland to stand down from their pulpits and allow the common men in their congregations to preach; a number of mandates relating to the divine purpose of bicycles; and, on the last day of the month, a passionate attack on the "Jezebel", the Church of Scotland, for seducing decent men into fornication and idolatry (Revelation, Chapter Two, Verse Twenty), and on the Free Church, "Babylon the Great, the Mother of Harlots and Abominations of the Earth", which was "drunken with the blood of the saints" (Revelation, Chapters Seventeen and Eighteen).

October, 1897.

What progress we made during the month of October! By the end of the first week, the line had passed beyond the old grave-yard at the corner of Mill-street, and had rounded the corner which led out on to the highway. I had decided, early one morning as I lay in my bed turning all the projects over and over in my mind, that, in the present circumstances, it was far better to lead the railway over the road which already existed than try to blast a new way over rock and moor. This thought was no sooner mentioned to Rinck than it was ratified by the Council of New Elders; and immediately condemned by the Parish Council, whose responsibilities included the upkeep of the highway between Ullapool and Garve. However, the New Elders had more than enough men and women behind it to enforce its decision, while the Parish had to content itself with loud denunciations and a strong letter of protest.

In order to lessen the tumult and outrage caused by my decision, I determined that the existing road should be shared equally between the new railway-line and the carts and horses. To that end, almost every yard and chain of the road was widened, to allow the railway to run on the north-east side of the road, and the other traffic to run on the south-west side, the two carriage-ways, as it were, being separated by a fence, for the avoidance of terrible accidents such as might occur should a horse or child be frightened by the approach of the locomotives. In one or two places, existing dykes had to be knocked down and re-set a yard or two back from the road. In the old days, such actions would have required the intervention of Inspectors, officious Clerks of Works, Writers to the Signet, representations to the Houses of Parliament. In the New Age, all it took was a firm knock on the door of the Lodge or the big House – whose owners at this time of year were generally absent – and a gang of men with hammers and spades.

Thus we progressed from the town at the required rate of three halves of a furlong per day, and by the end of the month we had progressed almost three miles out of Ullapool, to the very edges of Leckmelm Wood. The remarkably mild weather of the summer months had been succeeded by fine, dry days, and there was little to hinder our progress. At the end of each day, I was utterly astonished to pace out just how far we had come in the previous ten or eleven hours: what must be the joy of the American railway-engineer as he sees the miles gobbled up by his gangs as he crosses the Plains! Here, by the shores of Loch-broom, there was little to complain about: our only significant problems were with two steep gradients, the one leading up towards Braes, the other at Corry Point, in both places the ascent being upwards of one hundred feet in half-a-mile, being a gradient of about one in twenty-five.

Do not imagine for one minute that I was lax, or did in any way imperil the solid principles of engineering, in my efforts to make steady advances! Every foot and every yard was inspected by myself personally; every bolt was tapped by myself, every sleeper thoroughly examined for correct alignment, every cubic foot of ballast tramped upon; and in the first days I had to take my supervisors (and on one famous occasion, Daniel McManus, who vociferously resented my intrusion) to one side, and gently point out some shoddy workmanship which would have to be taken back and put right. But such occasions grew fewer as the men began to learn the trade and the tricks. I discovered that a few men had worked on railway-building before, and two or three had been under me between Garve and Braemore, although I failed to recognise them. I indicated to my supervisors that advice should be taken from these experienced men when I was not available to answer questions; and in that way, everyone under my command began to learn the basics of good railway construction.

The long wagon which we had acquired from William Baird & Sons proved invaluable, being tirelessly dragged up and down the line by a team of uncomplaining horses, transporting sleepers, rails and ballast from the field below Braes, where we had stock-piled all our materials. Hour after hour, it came and went, its screeching wheels announcing its arrival and departure. On those stretches where the gradient was exceptionally steep, it was necessary, when ascending the slope with a full load, to hold in reserve a supplementary team of horses, and when descending the slope to ensure that the horses followed the wagon, and that a rudimentary brake was applied. For this last piece of equipment, I commissioned Donald MacLeod, the blacksmith in Pulteney-street, and he came up with a most ingenious design which could have been patented and made the man his fortune; as it was, he was content to see the pleasure which its installation gave John Mundell, who hitherto had continually lived in dread of seeing his proud horses crushed under the weight of a wagon out of control.

McManus, I should mention here, had taken to riding out on the first such wagon-load each morning, still with his rainbow banner held high, reciting from his beloved scroll another psalm, 'as a rider riding forth, conquering and to conquer'. I had my Godly Bicycle; he had his Divine Chariot. Striking his pose thus, gazing evangelically into the ascending sun, he was unable to see that the trudging gangs which followed him were utterly oblivious of him.

Such was our progress that, in the final week of the month, we again ran short of iron rails; and since the next shipment was not due until the first day of November, we had to content ourselves with the laying of ballast and the manufacture and transportation of the sleepers to the head of the line. On the last Friday of the month, the entire Council of New Elders paid us a visit, arriving on the wagon at about eleven o'clock, to the cheers of the navvies. Daniel McManus marched forward to greet them, and gave a long and impassioned address, which he had obviously prepared some time in advance. "Behold!" he proclaimed, "the former things are passed away! We are making all things new. We are making a new Heaven and a new Earth!" As is ever the way with Glaswegians, he took upon himself the role of leader, guide and poker-of-nose into all matters relating to the construction of the railway, which he either mis-understood or of which he was quite ignorant. I held my peace and allowed him to get on with it.

During this visit, James Finlay, whom I had come to regard as a kindred spirit (for were we not two brothers visited by prophecy?), engaged me in some conversation. He made gentle mockery of McManus and his ignorant enthusiasm; I had harsher words to say, but it was not in Finlay's nature to be so sharp. "He will find himself out, Mr. Kininmonth," he explained. I enquired of him if he relished his role as Mr. Rinck's prophet; he laughed quietly and told me that he was simply a dreamer, and if it pleased Mr. Rinck to hear his dreams, then so let it be. But then his expression turned gloomy when he told me that he frequently dreamed of Kerguelen, the Island of Desolation, and of the families he had left buried there. "That was no place to build Paradise, Mr. Kininmonth, and I wonder if it is any better in Ross and Cromarty?" To lighten his mood, I did my best to enumerate some of the advantages which our adopted terrain had over that frozen desert island: I admit that I found it a difficult task to find many. But Finlay regained his composure and shook me by the hand: "You are probably right, Mr. Kininmonth: you can see things which I cannot. I believe I dream too much of the past and not enough of the future."

The New Elders were greatly delighted with our progress, and departed on their wagon back to town, leaving McManus bounding around like an excited dog. In those few short weeks, I had come to regard the man as my necessary "MacAulay", a Ross and Cromarty Nemesis, but in this case one more to be mocked than one to be at all feared. I was confirmed in my judgement by a rather surprising source: towards the end of the month, Mr. Fraser came to me and said he had been approached for employment by a man who claimed to have known me in earlier years. Intrigued, I went back up the line and was startled to find my old friend Mr. MacIvor, whom I had last seen at Braemore in the spring of 1895! I greeted him as a long-lost brother and asked if he had come to assist in the great project. He confirmed that he had, although I detected in his voice an under-tone of disapproval – not that such a note was unusual for the man, since he had always been the voice of my conscience, when we had worked together. He explained that he, like many others, had just been paid off at Kyle, where Mr. Best had completed the extension from Strome. Most of the men had gone south to pick up work on the new Mallaig Line, but he had heard of the line we were now undertaking and sought to try his luck with us, "if we would have him?"

I confess that I was delighted, and said so in as many words. In order not to offend my four newly-trusted supervisors, I appointed MacIvor to the head of a separate gang of men, who were to go back over the line inch by inch, checking for any slippages of the ground or the ballast, correcting any deficiencies, ensuring that the line held true. By having him in the rear, I could now concentrate whole-heartedly on the land in front of me.

Of course, Daniel McManus was in total disagreement with me. "What kind of a man have you brought to God's work!" he spluttered, shaking his Bible at me. "I have just heard the man blaspheme and take in vain the Name of the Lord! You must cast this serpent from our midst this very instant!"

In my indignation, I was very short with Mr. McManus. I told him that I would rather hire ten MacIvors, if I could lay hands on them, than one thousand pious men who knew nothing of railway-building. McManus stormed off in the direction of Ullapool, leaving me agitated and feeling sick in my stomach; but since nothing more was said of the matter, I believe that he found no sympathetic ears at the Caledonian Hotel into which to pour his vitriol.

In the course of the next few days, MacIvor and I conversed on our past two years, both of us being brief – I for the obvious reason of not wishing to appear driven by whimsy and short-lived enthusiasms, he for the obvious reason that labouring on a railway-line through Midge, bog and rock for two years is not a topic for sparkling conversation. MacIvor also urged me to consider the building of the "Godly Railway" as an act of folly, which could only end in tears.

"It is a ship of fools that you sail in, Mr. Kininmonth, a ship of fools," he told me, shaking his head.

I asked him what he meant by that.

"A ship of fools, Mr. Kininmonth. It is leaky and patched with seaweed; it has sails made of Bible paper; the crew are moon-struck and the Captain has his nose buried in his books. The ship will founder at the first storm, Mr. Kininmonth."

At the bottom of my heart, I knew that his words rang true; nonetheless, I argued with him, pointing out that there would never be a railway from Garve to Ullapool if we left it to the devices of the Great North-West of Scotland Railway Company. I also asked him simply to look about at his fellow-workers and to tell me in all honesty whether he had ever seen anything at all being built with such pride and eagerness in all his days. And he had to confess that he had not. But he warned me to "watch out for myself", for the Government would not tolerate our actions for much longer, and it was best not to get on the wrong side of the Law. I forbore to tell him just how often I had been there in recent years. And so we left it.

It was on the day following the visitation by the New Elders, Saturday, the thirtieth of October, that a huge storm came out from the ocean and smote us. At the noon hour, the sky to the west of Ullapool turned ever blacker, and those who were stationed upon higher ground reported that the ocean had all but disappeared in a storm. At half-past the hour, the air became suddenly still, and then there was the sound as of distant racehorses; this aural phenomenon soon revealed itself as a most terrible downpour of rain. The force with which it fell upon the Earth surprised and amazed us, even although the blackness of the heavens warned us of its power. Within seconds, every man who could not shelter was soaked to the skin; the small burns and dried tracks of burns on the hillside were foaming and bursting with water; the roadway was turned into a river. After several minutes, there was a re-doubled energy apparent in the tempest; the rain ceased but was almost immediately succeeded by a storm of hailstones, which crashed through the trees and bounced from the earth like living insects. This lasted some ten minutes, in the course of which all human conversation was killed, and men crouched under whatever shelter they could invent from tarpaulins, hats, pieces of wood and the surrounding trees, staring in wonderment at the scene around them.

When the hail abated, there was a sudden stillness – or, to be more precise, there was no sound to be heard other than the rushing waters which tore down the hillside and across the road and down to the loch, whose shores now bubbled with the on-flowing mud. We gazed around us and, as the waters began to subside almost as quickly as they had arisen, we perceived that great damage had been done to our works.

Naturally, Mr. McManus had much to say about this. He strode around, with his black-bound Bible held open, declaiming passages from the Revelation of St. John pertaining to the plagues sent by the Lord; it seems that the Angel of the Lord frequently sent hailstones for to punish Mankind.

I had no time for this. The rain and the hail which had fallen were in some way our payment for the weeks of dry and hot weather which we had experienced during the long summer. And the ferocity of the forces of Nature was such that in many places our neat piles of ballast had been penetrated and pierced and pushed aside by the waters. At one place, above Corry Point, the road had all but disappeared under a landslip from above and the entire line of rails had been pushed aside. It was always my contention that the road, which was the responsibility for many years of our Parish Council, was in a poor state of repair; and there was ample vindication of this when I saw how easily the road was over-run by the uncultivated land of the hill above. Had the road been in a better state of repair, then the depredations of Nature would not so easily have torn it apart; had that been the case, then my Railway-Line would certainly not have been so badly affected as it was now.

In the space of thirty minutes, damage had been wrought which I expected would take all our men some two weeks or more to set right.

No sooner had I reached this profoundly upsetting conclusion than I was approached by Daniel McManus, in his highly excited state.

"Do you see, Brother Alexander?" he exclaimed, brandishing his Bible at me. "The Seventh Angel hath made a visitation upon us and smitten us down with hailstones, as it is written! 'And there were voices, and thunders, and lightnings; and there was a great earth-quake, such as was not since men were upon the Earth, so mighty an earthquake and so great. And the great city was divided into three parts, and the cities of the nations fell. And every island fled away, and the mountains were not found. And there fell upon men a great hail out of Heaven, every stone about the weight of a talent; and men blasphemed God because of the plague of the hail; for the plague thereof was exceeding great.' Do you not see, Brother, the vengeance of the Lord is upon us!"

MacIvor was with me at that time. He stood with a grin upon his features, wringing the waters of the storm from his beard. When McManus paused to catch his breath, MacIvor leaned towards him. "And what of the first six Angels, Mr. McManus? Are they delayed at Garve Junction? Where are our malignant sores, and our seas of blood? Why are we not burned up by the sun? What of the great darkness, and the drying up of all the rivers? Should they not have come upon us by now? Or can the Lord not count, that he sends seven before six and five and four?" As McManus puffed and huffed, unable to think where to start remonstrating with his interrogator, MacIvor continued: "Mr. McManus, if you lift up your eyes, you will see the mountains standing, and if you look out to sea, the islands are still there. Don't trouble yourself with such a small storm, man! You with your Glasgow ways might not have seen a wee storm like this before. But you can be sure it is not the End of the World just yet."

"You are assuredly a damned and sinful man!" exclaimed McManus. "And you will see the wrath of God upon you, and the mark of the beast will be etched upon your brow before long!"

With that, he turned and strode off. MacIvor shrugged his shoulders and pulled out his pipe. "Well, Mr. Kininmonth," he said, "we've a bit of work before us now, Angel or no Angel."

It was true. But it was work that we could not easily start until the earth had dried some, so we abandoned our work for the day; and for the month.

Further notes for the "Revelatory Chronicle".

Of particular interest among the many actions of the New Elders in the month of October was the establishment of a "New College", which was instituted with the worthy aim of educating the common man. The New College was ordered much as a great University is ordered, with teachers, and students, and courses on every topic imaginable. Classes were held at almost every hour of the day or night, on every day of the week, including Sundays. Until such time as a College building of chrysoprase should be erected in Argyle-street, the New College was set up temporarily in Montague Fowler's coal-store down by the Pier. This seemed right and just to me, since the coal-store had served no purpose until now. The published curriculum was greatly influenced by Mr. McManus, who conducted at least one class per day, and sometimes two; but I reflected that if he expended his energies in the coal-store, then he might have less to expend upon troubling me.

I attended a class one evening. It was led by Charles Aitchison, a short dark man, with the looks of an otter, who crouched behind his lectern and glared upon those assembled before him. Aitchison worked at Mr. Cameron's mill, and generally smelled of spirits, which surely qualified him for the lecture he was to give on "Death and Resurrection".

As it was, his lecture did not last long, for it was readily interrupted from the floor. No sooner had Aitchison broached the subject, and quoted some words from St. John, than an undisciplined discussion broke out on who would arise in the first resurrection, and who would have to wait until the second resurrection. It was the belief of Mr. Elder and Mr. Lachlan Mackenzie, bakers, that the Bakers of the Earth would be included in the first resurrection, and that, logically, Grocers and Dry-salters would have to wait an additional thousand years. Messrs. Fraser and Thomas Mackenzie, grocer and dry-salter respectively, violently disagreed with this supposition, and, indeed, reversed the hypothesis, to the detriment of both Bakers and Inn-keepers. Mr. Mackenzie of the Caledonian Hotel had words to say on this. Then there was a spirited intervention on behalf of the Tailors of the Earth from Mr. Ross. And so the discussion raged.

It was Mr. Gilbert McBoyle, a man with whom I had had until now no dealings, who contrived to bring the discussion to a rather untimely conclusion. It should be explained that Mr. McBoyle was a carpenter and undertaker, a man with whom one hopes to have no business whatsoever. He was of a rather smooth appearance, with gleaming dark hair, which seemed to have been burnished upon his head, rather than to be a natural growth. His smile was one of many teeth and little sincerity. McBoyle sat quietly listening to the raised voices and the mounting disagreement around him. In a pause in the proceedings, just after Mr. Aitchison had stepped from behind his lectern, to shake the Tailor-faction by the collar, and brandish his fist in the faces of the Shoemaker-sect, Mr. McBoyle stood up slowly. Since the seats around him had never been filled, he stood out from the crowd.

"It is my belief," stated Mr. McBoyle quietly, "that the Undertakers will be first." His words caused an engulfing silence. "For who else has the skill to unwind the dead from their shrouds and unscrew their coffins when they rise again?"

Of course, this proposition turned the already tumultuous "class" into a dog-fight. Everyone turned on McBoyle with fury, united temporarily by their disgust at his presumption. I slipped out when violence broke out, not being attracted to physical demonstrations of wrath.

During this month, also, more tracts were published. I list here the titles of these: "The Name of the Beast is Montague Fowler. An Explanation of the Revelation of St. John, Chapter Thirteen, Verse Eighteen" (I read this pamphlet with some interest, for it contained a fascinating mathematical proof that the numerical value of the letters of the man's name did indeed add up to "Six hundred three-score and six"*); "The Kingdom of Zion is Established in Ullapool – A Timely Call to the Common Man of Scotland"; and, "How Much Longer Can the Godless Poke Their Snouts in the Trough? – An Answer Given by the Seven Flaming Torches".

Mr. McManus published a pamphlet this month entitled: "Humble Notes on the Practical Building of Railways: How the God-Fearing Are Rewarded and How the Godless Are Punished", which was many

---

* *Mr. Marjoribanks writes:* Mr. Kininmonth enclosed several pages containing his own algebra proof, and several other proofs he had deduced. But I fear they are too complex for me, and I have chosen to omit them from the text, since it is a maxim of Dobie & McIntosh that we should not publish what we cannot understand. The original papers are, I believe, in my desk and available for study.

things, but never about building and neither practical nor humble. Although it purported to describe the construction of my Railway out of Ullapool, the author contrived to mention my name not once. To all appearances, the railway was the work of the divinely-inspired Mr. McManus alone. Mr. MacIvor understood my anger at this criminal misrepresentation, but cautioned me to silence, pointing out that those who were interested in the railway would already know my part in it; and that those who had no interest in the railway would never read the tract. I was hurt and enraged by McManus's insolence, but decided that MacIvor's advice was quite sound.

I noted from some of the publications by Rinck that he ever relied on the "true saintly visions of some tested Brothers" – this surely included myself and James Finlay. But apart from the increasing length of Finlay's beard, I believe I never saw two men less fitted to the role of prophet.

November, 1897.

In stark contrast to those glorious days of September and October, our progress in building the railway-line during November was grim and unrewarding. The damage which resulted from the storm at the end of October was considerable, and we laboured for most of November to try to repair it. I found it necessary to send almost all of my gangs to work from the start of the line forwards, examining and repairing the holes which had appeared, buttressing the slopes which were in danger of cascading into the loch, lifting and re-laying the rails. It was work which I had to supervise personally, except where I could rely on MacIvor to make decisions on my behalf. McManus was of no use at all to me, since he spent most of his time striding around with his Bible, proving to his own satisfaction that we had indeed been visited by All The Angels Sent By God To Punish Us; more helpfully, he frequently absented himself to the New College.

We were in no way assisted by a sudden change in the weather in the first week, which obliged us to work in bitterly cold conditions. On several days, snow fell at an alarming rate, and covered the ground on which we were endeavouring to work. The cold, the snow, the shortened days, the over-cast sky, and the perpetual misery of working on the damp shores of Loch-broom – all these things became a penance, and it was noticed that the number of men in the gangs began to drop day by day. I despaired of advancing the line by a single yard in the course of the month. It seemed that our credit with Baird's was still good, for another shipment of rails arrived promptly on Macbrayne's boat at the beginning of the month. But the rails simply lay piled up at the Pier, for there was no place to which we could move them until all the repairs had been completed.

To add further insult to our injury, news came at the end of the first week that the railway-line which extended from Strome-ferry to Kyle had been opened to traffic, on the second day of the month, amid much ceremony and rejoicing. It was now possible to travel from Dingwall to the Island of Skye in little more than four hours, on any one of the three trains per day. But what hope did I now have of completing my Railway? Everything was set against me – the weather, the materials, the season, the railway to Kyle! In the dark mornings, when I awoke in Mrs. MacMahon's house, with the sound of the wind dashing the sleet against the rattling window, many was the time that I wondered whether I should take the trouble to get out of my warm bed and pedal those twelve bleak miles; I would arrive grim-faced at the workings, when I should have arrived full of enthusiasm and good cheer to encourage the dwindling band of taciturn labourers. The only man who kept my spirits up was MacIvor, whose mood rarely varied, unless it tended to great humour and good cheer when he had had a violent argument with McManus over some obscure verse in the Book of Revelation, of which my friend seemed to have an intimate and unsettling knowledge.

I knew now that it would be impossible to reach Braemore by the start of January; it had been an improbable dream from the out-set; I am an optimist when embarking on the first days of a job, and I cannot help but think that all will go well. But, at the end of the month, when we should have reached perhaps Inverlael Lodge, I had barely thirty days at my disposal; I was necessarily less sanguine, estimating that we might attain Leckmelm House by the end of December – a mere third of the distance required!

At least I was not troubled by either McManus or the New Elders, for they had other matters on their minds, and did not subject themselves to the discomfort of an inspection, relying only upon my written reports – which they may or may not have read. A railway-engineer seems fated to submit reports of his progress to his employers and yet to receive no acknowledgement that they have been read or understood.

On the twenty-ninth day of the month, by which date we had well-nigh recovered our position of the same day in October, I was summoned by a letter from Alexander Mackenzie to attend a meeting of the New Elders. The meeting was due to start at half-past seven o'clock, and I set off for the Caledonian Hotel as was usual. On my way down Argyle-street, I came across a great commotion at the Drill Hall. This was a nest of the adherents of the Parish Council, and a place that no Rinck-ian had ever penetrated without receiving a bloodied nose, or worse. An attempt had been made in August to "liberate" it, on behalf of the New Elders, but despite an invigorating series of assaults by a phalanx of the young men and women of the town, led by that master-tactician, James Finlay, the attempt had been beaten back. Some credit in this is due to a young gentleman named Talbot Clifton, tenant of the deer-forest at Rhidorroch, whose bold organisation of the Volunteers (or such of the Volunteers as still supported the Parish) was grudgingly admired by all.

It was obvious, even from a distance, that the Drill Hall was that night not the stronghold of the Parish Council. Suspended above the door of the Hall was a huge banner, made up, it seemed, from bed-sheets sewn together by the labour of a dozen seamstresses, painted with a rather splendid arching rainbow and the words below it: The Great Hall of the New Elders. Underneath the banner, and guarding the narrow entrance to the Drill Hall, stood a gang of about a score of men and women, of all ages and aspects, some holding smaller versions of the banner flapping above their heads, other holding lanterns, all shouting defiantly at a small group who stood off at a short distance. This group comprised the Parish worthies – the police-constable sheltering the Reverend MacMillan, and flanked by a number of respectable men, among whom I recognised Mr. Tusk and Mr. Coleman; and in front of all of them, a small pack of respectable matrons, who had abandoned themselves to shrieking Fury.

I approached cautiously, ready to turn back at the first sign of animosity. Mr. Coleman was explaining agitatedly to Mr. Tusk that the hall had been hired for the evening by a man purporting to be a "Mr. Harris", a traveller with magic-lantern pictures illustrative of an educational journey to Van Diemen's Land. But it was he, Mr. Coleman, who had belatedly discovered the awful truth of the false arrangement, and had alerted the constable and the minister. I edged past the two men; and was relieved to see on the piquet my friend, James Finlay, who waved me cheerfully through. Trying not to quicken my pace, and failing rather poorly at this, I passed through the screaming women before me, who were hurling abuse at the screaming women behind me, and entered the Hall.

Inside, Chaos reigned. Men, women, dogs and children milled around everywhere, obviously delighting in the possession of a fortress of respectability and authority. The children screamed and threw themselves about, the dogs barked. Men stood around in groups and puffed on their pipes. At the far end of the room, there was some semblance of peace and quiet: a small platform was raised there, large enough to hold perhaps two drill-instructors; gathered at the foot of this plinth were some figures I recognised – Rinck, McManus, Miss Keir the school-mistress, Mr. Mackenzie of the Caledonian, and others. I made my way to this group, intending to converse with Mr. Mackenzie, who had, after all, summoned me to this assembly. As I came up with them, Mackenzie abruptly leaped up on to the platform and began furiously to ring a heavy hand-bell – which all the men in the room immediately recognised as the bell used in Mackenzie's bar to signal "time" – and to call for order; there were some irreverent hoots of laughter at this, and some rather inevitable witticisms, but gradually the noise died down. Children and dogs were slapped, gathered up, or shooed out of the Hall, and the Assembly commenced.

The Elders of the Citadel were provided with chairs, and twenty-three were seated around the foot of the platform. Since I was now close to the front of the crowd, I had a good view of all of them. I had not until now known who our Elders were. One or two faces were unknown to me, but a bone-boiler, who was standing next to me, made me a roll-call.

Since I have not mentioned it before, for historical accuracy I should now give the names of the Elders: first and foremost, Melchior Rinck; then: Alexander Mackenzie, of the Caledonian Hotel; James Finlay, visionary, late of Kerguelen (who remained throughout this meeting on guard outside); Miss Keir, school-mistress of Leckmelm; Miss Duncan, school-mistress of Strath-canaird; Kenneth Ross, tailor of Shore-street; Kenneth Macrae, shoemaker of Shore-street; Alexander Lamont, spinner at Cameron's mill; Roderick Fraser, a piper; his brother, Charles, a driver for the mails; William Aird, watch-maker of Market-street; Peter Cameron, quarrier; Annie Campbell and Ann Stewart of Auchlunachan; Donald Campbell of Leckmelm; Duncan Campbell, tailor of Ardcharnich; Hector Fraser, grocer of Shore-street; Lachlan Mackenzie, baker of Shore-street; Roderick Mackenzie and Sandy Maclean of Leckmelm; Duncan Matherson, carter; John Mundell of Inverlael; Gilbert McBoyle, undertaker of West-terrace; and Daniel McManus, of no known profession, of Glasgow.

The meeting opened with a speech from Mr. Rinck. What he spoke of is not important, but he concluded that the proof that the Elders and people of New Jerusalem were righteous was in the easy victory they had gained in securing the Drill Hall for their meeting.

Rinck then asked Mr. Mackenzie to run through the order of the meeting. The first item, much to my immediate consternation, was for me to explain my failure to progress the railway-line. All eyes turned to me. I stood up and gave some faltering words. At this, McManus shouted out: "The traitor cannot defend himself!"

At this sally, my innate pride burst out. "I hear you cry out, Brother McManus," I said, as calmly as I could, although a molten fire of outrage was blazing in my chest and head. "If you spent more time working on the railway, along with our honest labouring brothers, instead of skulking here in Ullapool, you might under-stand our situation better!"

I think this arrow hit its mark, for there were murmurs of agreement from those around me whom I knew from the work on the line. One or two of the Elders whispered among themselves and grinned at McManus, whose face had turned pale.

I pressed home my advantage. "If the Elders would care to come to-morrow to see the damage done by the storms, I will explain it to you. And perhaps I can call upon our learned engineering Brother McManus to explain what he would have done differently?" Some open laughter burst out among the crowd, and McManus applied himself to a notebook, in which he scribbled furiously.

Mr. Mackenzie saw the mood of the crowd and declared the discussion on this item closed; he passed on to the next item, which happened to be a proposal from Mr. McBoyle, the undertaker.

Mr. McBoyle, whose knowledge of engineering was limited to the mechanics of lowering coffins into six feet of earth, stood up to make some of the most risible proposals I had yet encountered. In summary, and stripping away his well-groomed verbiage, he proposed: the construction of a bridge across Loch-broom, between the Pier and Aultnaharrie, where the ferry-man now plies, for the purpose of opening up a coastal route to the south; and the building of a huge balloon which would be able to carry passengers and materials safely to and from Inverness, and so avoid the need for an expensive and dangerous railway passing through the territory of the Godless.

Mr. McBoyle set out his proposals; no sooner had he finished, and retreated like a smiling wolf into his corner, than McManus bounded out of his seat and gave his enthusiastic backing to both ideas, labouring the point that either one of the projects would mean that no railway to Garve would be required. He argued that the bridge to Aultnaharrie would be "as the rainbow which God sends as a sign to His Elect"; that it would arch across the "Deep Waters of the Burning Angel", as a wonder for all to behold; and most particularly, that it would avoid the muddy necessity of constructing a railway-line over unforgiving moor and bog, through the lands of the Godless.

My heart was still beating fast from my easy victory over McManus, and I felt as if my voice was crying out to make itself heard. Once more, as McManus called for a vote on the proposal, I found myself stepping out on to the floor, and, with words which

I can no longer remember, I poured scorn and derision upon the proposals, with easy eloquence. I pointed out the difficulties of building even the smallest bridge over a burn, let alone a bridge over a deep and mighty loch. I drew the attention of the learned Brother McManus to the hill, the bog and the rock which lay behind Aultnaharrie, over which some road would need to be driven to reach the next loch. I reminded Mr. McBoyle of the direction and strength of the prevailing winds, which would make it easy for an intrepid balloonist to reach Inverness, but almost impossible to return to Ullapool; I asked jocularly whether perhaps Mr. McBoyle was proposing that his black carriage should drive to Inverness to retrieve the balloon after each trip? (This sally raised much laughter.) I reminded the Assembly of the progress we had made on our railway, despite the adverse weather and the occasional absence of some of our less-than-ardent workers. Finally, wagering that I had talked McBoyle and McManus down, I repeated McManus's call for a vote to be taken, and felt enormous satisfaction in seeing the proposals defeated almost unanimously.

I noted that from the platform Miss Keir gazed upon me, and presumed to think it was with admiration. I felt myself – oh, arrogant pride! – beginning to enjoy the Assembly, and the power I seemed to wield from my simple professional knowledge, which, in this community, was far above the understanding of most people. However, my moment of glory was out-shone by an old woman – yet another of the Mackenzie clan – who stood moaning loudly at the back of the Hall, surrounded by her ancient sisters. When Mr. Mackenzie of the Caledonian asked the reason for her distress, the old woman was led to the front, where she delivered herself of the story that she was possessed of the Second Sight, as all would witness, and that she had looked out upon the waters of the loch that very evening and seen many things. "Oh, strange things indeed, sirs!" she advised us, wheezing and moaning. "Dreadful things that an old woman should not live to see!" At this, a number of her cronies, who had pushed their way through the crowd to ensure their share of attention, began to shriek, and rend their hair, and clutch each other around the neck, agreeing that old women such as they should not live to see terrible things.

It took little prompting from the crowd to persuade the old woman to share her visions with us. It seemed she had seen a wide plain of burning fires, tall broken trees and ruined palaces, smoking fields and broken bridges; across the plain, from the glens and the cities, came many great monstrous trains, belching steam, and making a noise like a hundred winter tempests. In the carriages of every train were thousands of men, the very flower of youth, laughing the while and singing psalms of joy as they rattled across the plain towards the scenes of devastation. And of a sudden the trains had been smitten by dragons from the air, and had been struck asunder by fires; the widow Mackenzie had seen bodies spilled open upon the earth, and brains dashed out, and fountains of blood erupting, and "many young men lying dead, and their sweethearts tearing their hair for grief and growing old without bairns". "Ochone! Ochone!" cried the old woman, and her cronies joined in.

There was considerable disturbance at this demonstration of superstition, and, here and there, shouts for the railway to be abandoned to avert a tragedy. Others, however, decried the whole performance as nonsense and called for Mrs. Mackenzie to be taken back to her bed to sleep until sober. The Assembly was in uproar. Some dry wit shouted: "Give her a bicycle!" My earlier energy for standing up to speak suddenly evaporated in the face of this nonsense.

At last, Rinck stood up and called for calm. When he could make himself heard, he explained that the Lord frequently sent visions to the Godly to give them understanding; but warned that the Devil sometimes sent visions to tempt us and to test us. He himself had trusted companions who received visions from God sometimes, and dreams from the Devil at other times; and since Rinck knew how to probe these dreams and visions, he would sit with the old woman and determine whether hers be sinful or righteous. Until then, he said, the building of the railway for the benefit of the righteous would continue, "under the guiding hand of Brother Kinnimunt". The sisterhood was visibly delighted with this judgement, having obtained for themselves an interview with Mr. Rinck, and having easily been the most interesting turn of the evening's entertainment.

Other items came up for discussion, but as they were mostly dry, and theological, and not of an inflammatory nature, the crowd began to disperse in twos and threes, dogs and children first, then the men and the women, until at ten o'clock there were so few people remaining that the outraged officers of the Parish were able to re-take the Drill Hall.

Even more notes for the "Revelatory Chronicle".

On the fifteenth of the month, the New Elders decreed that the street-names and the names of important landmarks in the Citadel, the New Ullapool, should be changed. This decision was prepared in an ordinance published on the previous Saturday: "How the Godly Must Wipe Out the Names of the Beast". It was argued in this document, a copy of which I have retained, that the names given to the streets of the town were Godless, since given by the Godless men who had first built the town many years ago. The principal streets were: Mill-street, Shore-street, Quay-street, Argyle-street, Red-row, Pulteney-street, and Market-street. Such names, it was argued, showed that the spirits of the founding-fathers encompassed no more than the narrow circle of their mortal existence. The name of "Red-row" also contained a dark hint of the Red Dragon, which threatened the Church of the Godly. As for "Pulteney" – no one apart from myself knew that he was Thomas Telford's patron; the street-name had to be changed simply because no one knew its origin.

It was time, argued the New Elders, to raise the merely physical in the Citadel to a spiritual plane. Thus, Mill-street was to become "The Road of the Wheat and the Chaff"; Shore-street was to be known as "The Terrace of Terrifying Torrents"; Market-street, "The Road of the Cleansing Enlightenment"; Argyle-street, because of its location on the plan for the New Ullapool, was to become "The Steps to Divine Fear"; while the Argyle Hotel, due to be demolished for the imminent erection of the Citadel itself, was to be closed down and called nothing at all. Loch-broom was henceforth to be referred to as "The Deep Waters of the Burning Angel", a proposal which I heard with some pride, since I had been that Burning Angel. Finally, New Ullapool was to be "New Jerusalem".

This was one of the most violently discussed of all the ordinances of the New Elders. Especially among the adherents of the Parish Council, and also among the residents of the smoking-room of the now-anonymous Argyle Hotel, were the proposals held in the most profound disrespect. Mrs. Jamesina Mackenzie of the Argyle admitted to her private dwelling – now that it was no longer a permitted public house – anyone who cared to take refreshment with her, and, in ill-concealed defiance of the ordinance of the fifteenth of November, continued to talk loudly of "Loch-broom" and "Ullapool", with cronies who persisted in residing in "Mill-street" and "Quay-street". But even among the Rinck-ians, the old names died hard, and most had great difficulty in referring to streets and locations by their newly-approved names. It was said – although I cannot verify the truth of such reports – that people who had lived in Ullapool all their lives got lost on their way home, as they strove to grasp the new geography, and that tradesmen gave up their deliveries to houses on whose doors they had knocked every day for years, because some customers persisted in using the new names.

For no reason at all, I was suddenly brought in mind of the Reverend Lunn's question – as to what the name "Kerguelen" might mean: Fortress of the Gaels or of the Young Men? Was Rinck trying to conceal the ordinariness and tedium of Ullapool behind the name "New Jerusalem", a name which shone brightly in dream and prophecy? Could Ullapool become a second Kerguelen for the poor people of Scotland, a paradise turned to a prison for its inhabitants?

It was only some time later that I learned, with no real surprise, that the author and instigator of this ordinance was none other than Daniel McManus, a man who seemed to have nothing better to do with his famous learning than to dribble sand into the great wheels and pistons of common tradition, when he should have been pouring oil on the engine of democratic or socialist change.

I should also note in this "Revelatory Chronicle" that Mr. Hay Mackenzie left the town towards the end of the month, taking with him his family and the books of the Bank. It was widely rumoured that all the cash deposited at the Bank had already been smuggled out of town by Montague Fowler. On the third Sunday of the month a yacht had sailed into the loch; those who had seen it before knew it to be the elegant play-thing of another brother, Mr. Evelyn Fowler; since the yacht was only ever seen in the month of June, and exclusively when the weather was fine, its arrival provoked some surprise; discreet activity was noticed between shore and yacht in the evening, and by the following morning the boat had gone, sailing out past the Summer Isles before a north-easterly. That same day, the Bank-agent left with his family for Braemore Halt on a conveyance driven by Arthur Fowler's coach-man, Murdo Mackenzie, whom many thereafter treated as a pariah and an out-cast.

December, 1897.

It was on the first Sunday of December, two days before I celebrated the completion of my forty-fifth year, that a most disastrous event occurred, an event which would ultimately lead to the complete abandonment of my building of the railway.

On that Sunday, McManus stood up, in his small and rather grand pulpit at the cross-roads outside the Caledonian Hotel, to preach a sermon which, although I did not hear it, had a profound effect on my professional life. The pulpit had recently been carpentered for McManus by his fawning crony, the execrable Gilbert McBoyle; it was, it has to be admitted, a rather fine piece of work, and was furnished with two wheels, like a barrow, which allowed it to be trundled out from McBoyle's shed every Sunday afternoon, where it was assiduously polished and waxed during the week.

The sermons given by McManus each Sunday afternoon were rather poorly attended, most people having little patience for the man or his ideas. Nonetheless, there was always a small band of some dozen enthusiasts who stood around the foot of the pulpit as he ranted on, for upwards of an hour, expounding on texts from the prophets of the Old Testament or the Revelation of John from the New. Of the enthusiasts, perhaps one half faced outwards from the pulpit, like a guard of honour, while the rest hung on McManus's every word and shouted "Amen!" or "Ochone!" at any opportunity. Prominent among those who stood facing outwards was the oily McBoyle, smiling upon all who passed and nodding at every point made by the preacher behind him.

McManus's band wheeled the pulpit to its usual location; the Glaswegian mounted and called on witnesses to hear him, as was his practice. For his text, McManus had chosen the entire five chapters of the Lamentations of Jeremiah, which he recited aloud to his audience. It seems that McManus had learned all of the verses by heart, for his performance was simply perfect. From the moment when McManus wailed, "How doth the city sit solitary that was full of people!" all the way through to, "Thou art very wroth against us", a full three hours elapsed. By which time, McManus was almost hoarse and his band of 'Enthusiasts' were worked up to a passion of wailing and gnashing of teeth, and small boys were hiding for very fear of the emotions aroused. A small dog, whose heart was set cold against the Lamentations, had the temerity to answer a call of nature against the lower reaches of the pulpit, and barely escaped with its life under a barrage of stones and curses from the audience.

Having delivered himself of the Lamentations, McManus paused for two minutes in utter silence, his face pointing into the grey sky, as if seeking a word from God. And then he said: "Such is the darkened vale into which the New Jerusalem has been led! Such is the fear in which we live! Such are the souls of the people! See what is come upon us! O ye faithful Elect! Let us now say unto God, 'Thou hast seen my wrong – judge Thou my cause.'

"It is time to cast out the snakes, who flicker out their forked tongues, and smile sweetly upon us, and fix us with their eyes so that we might be led into their mouths and utterly devoured. It is time to establish the true Citadel of the Lord in Wester-ross!"

Word of McManus's preaching passed through Ullapool like a snell wind, and soon people emerged from their houses, wrapped up against the cold, to hear what he had to say. The larger the crowd grew, the more McManus warmed to his theme. He condemned Rinck and almost all the New Elders as treacherous charlatans and Godless men. He railed against the construction of the Citadel and of the railway leading to Braemore. He cried down the Wrath of God upon all those who sought to retain the old ways and the old names, and all those whose heart was not utterly dedicated to the Godly Revolution: "For he who is not prepared to render up his life to God is one who must stand on the side of the Godless. He who does not fear God alone, he who serves two Masters, will finally be found in the battalions of the Godless!"

Rinck himself did not put in an appearance at this remarkable sermon, but most of the New Elders had quickly gathered; bitter recriminations were soon flying backwards and forwards. But McManus was not to be stopped. His voice increased in pitch as he sought to overcome the shouting and the heckling, ignoring any questions or challenges put to him.

What McManus proposed was the establishment of a New Jerusalem on the south side of Loch-broom, on the peninsula which was bordered to north and south by the sea-lochs, to the west by the mighty ocean itself, and to the east could only be approached by the narrow track which led from Dundonnell, or the path which led from Letters. Such a citadel would be secure from attack; in such a fortress, a small number of the Elect could wait in safety until the Day of Judgement. "The Lord calls upon me to prophesy against Gog, for the Lord will set his judgement upon Gog and all the priests," proclaimed McManus. "Let us move to our chosen Land, O ye faithful people of Ullapool, and let the Lord build for us a Citadel on that Land!"

Not only was the Lord to build a Citadel and a fortress, in which the Elect could await the last trump and the final punishments of the Lord, but in so doing He was also to find new work for the labourers to engage in. "Can you not see, those of you who are blinded by the treacherous priests and the abandoned whores of the Railway Companies, can you not see that the railway which is being built towards Braemore is the road down which the Dragon will slither and crawl and render you unto ashes? Can you not see that to join our railway to the Fowlers' railway at Braemore will join our hopes to the hopes of the Godless and bring us to destruction so much more swiftly? Let us abandon that railway before it is too late! Let us use our arms and our pick-axes and our spades to build us a Citadel in which we may be saved!"

McManus, to the great applause of McBoyle and sundry others, called on all the labourers on the railway to bring their tools on the following day to the Pier, and to take transport with him to the further side of the loch, and there commence the great work of building the "True Citadel of the Elect". Those who wished to know of the true Citadel were urged to turn their eyes to the Book of Ezekiel, from Chapter Forty onwards, where the measurements of the Citadel and of all things in the Citadel were clearly set out by the Word of God. Those who wished to learn more, advised McManus, could follow him now to the 'New College', where he would spend the rest of the day in revealing the new Citadel as it was set out in the Book of Ezekiel. (Later, I had the time to study this chapter of Ezekiel, and found it very precise in its plan of the Citadel – which was much smaller than anything Rinck had chosen to build. In this, and this alone, McManus was a modest man!)

And with this convocation, he stepped down from his movable pulpit, and led the way to the erstwhile coal-store. McBoyle led the band of supporters which followed him, two of whom were eager to wheel the pulpit. Rather surprisingly, a considerable number of citizens also went along, either out of idle curiosity, perhaps spoiling for a brawl, or maybe even touched by McManus's oratory.

As I have noted, I passed my Sunday in ignorance of all this. More precisely, my day was spent in splendid misery, repeatedly revolving in my thoughts two matters: the matter of Miss Keir; and the matter of the Citadel at Ullapool. I pondered that day on what the Citadel comprised – in sum total: a saloon-bar; an undertaker's shop; and an abandoned coal-store by the Pier. That even was Mr. Rinck's enduring Citadel! That even was the grand goal of my Railway-Line! It brought an engineer to the edge of despair.

As for Miss Keir, I knew not how to act; for she might be offended were I to proclaim my passion for her; or, if I said nothing, she might be turned cold by my apparent lack of interest. Not having the experience of some men of my age, I trembled between two extremes of inaction.

Thus, on the Monday, when I made my way to the head of my Railway-Line through the cold rain of the early morning, I was already in poor spirits, having barely slept in the preceding two nights. I knew that Mrs. MacMahon had discovered one cause of my distraction, for she urged me in maternal fashion, as I left her house that morning, to "snap out of it and go and see the woman!" When I turned back to deny any such cause, the front-door was shut firmly in my face.

Arriving at the head of the line at about half-past seven o'clock, I was rather puzzled to find that so few men had turned up for work. Under normal circumstances, I should expect upwards of thirty men already there, either huddled in grey groups under the trees, or standing around in cheerful gangs, depending on the clemency or otherwise of the weather, invariably smoking their pipes. It always took some organisation on my part, and that of MacIvor and my other supervisors, to coax, wheedle and threaten the men to knock out their pipes, shoulder their tools and set to work; either our urging, or the arrival of McManus, if he arrived first; for the men wanted, above all, a quiet life.

But this morning I could discern barely a dozen men sheltering under the trees, and of my supervisors, only MacIvor, Fraser and Matherson were in attendance. While we sat and waited for re-inforcements to arrive, MacIvor told me of the events of the previous afternoon; and Fraser was of the opinion that some men had decided to go with McManus and some had taken the opportunity of McManus's declaration to give up work altogether.

Fraser was correct: we waited for an hour, and no one else came. Our numbers comprised myself, three supervisors and fourteen navvies. I had no idea whether I could expect a wagon-load of materials to arrive, since it was unclear where Mr. Mundell's loyalties now lay. Leaving MacIvor to organise our meagre workforce, I went with Mr. Fraser into the town to determine for myself how the land lay. We exchanged but few words on the road. When we came to the junction of Shore-street and Mill-street, we could see a crowd up at the Pier, and so directed our feet towards the commotion.

My arrival at the Pier was greeted by Daniel McManus, who commanded the centre of the stage, with a shout: "Behold the Godless Engineer, yon Cycling Hypocrite! See how his sinful brow is marked with the Mark of Sin!" Everyone turned to watch me, and I deemed it not advisable to approach any closer, contenting myself with distant observation and the recognition of faces. To my relief, I could not see Mundell among the crowd of 'Enthusiasts', but Fraser pointed out to me more than a score of men who should at that moment have been wielding spades and pick-axes on my Railway.

Spades and pick-axes were here in plenty, and several small boats were being loaded with men and boys and women, for ferrying over to Aultnaharrie. Already one crowded boat was leaving the Pier, to the shouts and cheers of the remaining crowd. By a trick of fate, the sun broke through the clouds and a huge rainbow arched over the dark waters of the loch. McManus made the most of this "sign of the Lord". At length, both he and McBoyle, along with two other men and a woman, embarked in a boat and set sail under the rainbow. One of the men was Alexander Lamont, one of my absent supervisors.

To my bewilderment and sorrow, I saw that the woman was none other than Miss Keir!

When six or seven boats had thus departed for Aultnaharrie, and the first of them could be discerned grounded on the far side, the crowd which had been at the Pier began to disperse. Several men, in whom Fraser recognised our navvies, were approached by him, but they sidled off without meeting his eyes or responding to his questions, or else were insolent in their replies. For my part, I felt it safe to approach the end of the Pier and strike up conversation with those who were left and who were not hostile to me. If anything, the men and women standing there rather pitied me, or illconcealed their amusement, in the all-too-human expectation of my impending troubles. I had confirmation from these idlers that the boats which had set sail carried those who wished to build a Citadel on the south side of the Loch; that McManus and McBoyle had now been joined in their endeavour by Miss Keir, Mr. Lamont and – rather to my surprise – Mr. Coleman the drill-instructor, who had been tricked out of his own 'citadel' barely a fortnight ago.

My natural inclination was to judge the new venture by the people it attracted. That Coleman, who, until recent days, had been a loud-mouthed, red-faced and embittered opponent of all things to do with Rinck or the Common Man, should now have taken up the cause of McManus and McBoyle, immediately inclined me against the group. That Lamont should have joined them merely confirmed my barely conscious judgement that he was a man I could easily dispense with.

But the betrayal by Miss Keir was a hard blow. I was over-whelmed by a feeling of aimlessness, that nothing was worthy of my endeavours, either now or in the future. I trudged wearily to the very edge of the Pier, sat myself upon one of the huge wooden columns which supported it, and gazed out over to the south side, which the last of the boats had now reached. A phrase of MacIvor's came into my head – "a ship of fools". It seemed that a whole flotilla of such ships had now passed across to the other side!

As I watched, a great swathe of rain came in from the west, obliterating the rainbow and obscuring the entire hill above Aultnaharrie. I sat, and was soon drenched by the pitiless down-pour, and cared not. Around me, the Pier was now deserted, such men and women as had remained now vanished back to their houses or their trades.

I seemed always to be a pawn in the hands of others, my life buffeted this way and that because someone else in my immediate circle had claims above my own! The Board of the Railway – I was their servant, and it mattered not one whit what I wanted to do to build their railway – the Board's decisions were paramount. The elder and younger Finlays and their terrible abandonment, which had wrested me completely from my berth and cast me adrift as an outlaw. And now Rinck and McManus, whose wild ideas for the establishment of one or more Citadels of Salvation in Wester-ross had completely crushed any hopes I had ever entertained of completing my Railway. It seems there is no rest or respite for myself in all of this – I must always be re-acting to the desires of others, a servant to my fellow men! Even my attempts to record my own thoughts, my own actions, my own achievements – in my own work of literature – have come to nought, for there is no space for that in these volumes! What are those things they call "Free Will" and "a man's own life"? Not for me, it seems.

I have little memory now of the remainder of that day, the sixth of December, on which the "Enthusiasts" embarked upon their rebellious enterprise. I do recall returning to the most advanced point of my Railway, and of conversing briefly with MacIvor and my remaining colleagues. The weather was, I believe, abominable, and little progress was made by anyone. The whole site turned slowly into a field of slippery and greasy mud. When all light faded at about three in the afternoon, we called a halt, and I retired to Mrs. MacMahon's for a hot bath and some cups of sweet tea. My landlady seemed to have a telegraph to all parts of the Strath and already knew the full story of the Exodus of the Enthusiasts; I was relieved that she did not make any fuss about it in my presence, realising, as she must, just how these events would have upset me.

On the morning of my forty-fifth birthday, I awoke early. The sky was a soft blue and the sunlight reflected brightly from the hills around. There was a frost upon the ground and hoar upon the fence-posts, but even as I breathed in the fresh air at my window, the frost was turning to vapour which floated upwards from the out-houses and the trees. This was no day to lie in bed, nor one to consider despairingly the blocked cutting into which my train had rolled. I determined, there and then, to try to weld together the pieces of my life, under the winter sunlight.

Having broken my fast and received the congratulations of Mrs. MacMahon and of Johan – and, if I may add without being indiscreet, a quick kiss from the latter, which cheered me tremendously – I dressed warmly, took a walking-stick, and set off into the morning. Contrary to Mrs. MacMahon's expectation, I directed my steps not to the northern side of the loch, but to the rude track which led down the south side. As I looked in panorama at the mountains around me, I saw the old lady standing at her doorway, hands on her hips, either puzzled or exasperated. I waved gaily to her and then headed towards the manse and the church at Inverbroom, then onwards, as the day progressed, towards Letters, Rhiroy and – my final goal – Aultna-harrie. My good humour sustained me past numerous small crofts and houses, each of which had a snarling Cerberus to greet me as I swung past. The sky remained cloudless, and, although it was still frosted and the puddles remained iced over on this shaded side of the land, I carried my jacket over my arm from the heat which my energetic stride generated. I considered myself in 'good form' for a man in his middle-years.

On the north side of the loch, I could now and again see the workings of my Railway, now silent and abandoned. When I came to a point in line with the northern end of Leckmelm Wood, I passed a small croft and the track – such as it was – gave out; I flung myself with some energy on to one the many sheep-tracks which led onwards across the bog and heather.

I had calculated that it was near eight miles from my lodgings to my goal, and I made good time; at close on eleven o'clock, I came around a bend in the hill and beheld the camp of the Enthusiasts.

I confess that I laughed. I had set out that day with a suppressed but insistent idea that I would come across a vast city of Medeans and Persians, spread over the Plain; instead, I came across a tiny group of make-shift canvas tents and a few small smoky fires, around which some people huddled. It seemed to me that even the tiny remnant of my work-force on the far side of the loch made a better impression than this. I smiled to myself and folded my arms for a few moments of self-satisfied musing, such as a man can afford on his birthday, if at no other time in the year. The camp was situated well up the hill, some eight-hundred yards from the ferry-man's small house by the shore. There was a good track leading from the ferry up the hill and across to the far side of the peninsula, leading – as I knew – to Badralloch and Dundonnell.

Once more, I was forcibly struck by the similarities between "Kerguelen" and this "Earthly Paradise"! This was the undrained wasteland on which McManus presumed to build his Citadel!

It was in the best of spirits, then, that I cut across the waste-land of bog; after a while I set foot on the track and strode up the hill towards the small encampment. It lay some fifty yards to the right of the track, next to a burn which flowed from a lochan to the north-west. As I turned off the track once more, two people approached me: one was McBoyle, the other Miss Keir. McBoyle, after barely four-and-twenty hours out of his natural surroundings of the winding-cloth, the oak and the brass, looked discomfited and haggard; his normally smooth and burnished hair stood wildly from his head, and his usual gleaming smile had been replaced with a rather sour expression. Miss Keir, on the other hand, seemed like a wild flower which had languished dusty and neglected indoors but was now restored to its proper habitat – she was ruddy, she smiled and positively strode across the earth beneath her feet. I was glad to see that she was sensibly wrapped in a brown woollen blanket, notwithstanding that the bottom few inches were dark with damp mud.

"Mr. Kininmonth," exclaimed Miss Keir, "have you come to pitch in with the Elect in God's good work, then?"

I shook my head and explained that I had only come to see how the small band were settling in. McBoyle, whom I now suspected of harbouring inappropriate feelings for Miss Keir, snorted and advised me, in disconcertingly civilised tones, to return "to the forsaken town of Ullapool", if that was all I had come for. He took Miss Keir's elbow and attempted to lead her back to the camp. But the school-teacher brushed off his hand, as one would a cleg, and asked me how I could still continue in such a mis-guided manner. I did my best to explain, but, as is usual when I am beset by strong feeling, the words stopped in my throat and came out half-strangled and, no doubt, incomprehensible. Miss Keir then asked McBoyle to leave us alone – which he did with an obsequious and utterly fantastic little bow, such as would be proper at the bed-side of 'Venerable Age, Expired' – and then came up to me, inviting me to walk a short distance, "for I have something to show you which may yet change your mind".

I was, as you might imagine, delighted at the prospect of an intimate conversation with the lady, and even more so by her confident dismissal of McBoyle, who now stood glowering at us from the shelter of one of the tents. However, my pleasure was short-lived, for we soon came upon the thing which she wished to show me.

It was none other than Daniel McManus, who was enthroned in an old leather arm-chair at the side of the track, some hundred yards further from the point where I had left it. The arm-chair was in poor repair, much of the horse-hair emerging in tufts all along the splitting seams, its feet embedded in the mud, and all shine that it might ever have possessed already matt from exposure to the elements. McManus sat bolt upright in the chair, his feet planted firmly on the ground, in his hands his Bible, in which he was (to my mind) rather too obviously absorbed as we approached.

"Ah, Brother Kinnimoth," he called out when he looked up and saw us, "welcome to the foundations of the Citadel of the Lord." He grandly swept his arm across the expanse of bog and moor which encircled him. "Am I to believe that you have come to offer your engineering expertise in the cause of the Righteous?"

Miss Keir looked at me expectantly, causing me to think twice before replying. She gazed at me in such a way that I believed truly that I had only to say one word to McManus and then she would be my companion in life, and the wife for whom I continually searched. One word, and I would strike off on another roadway, with new companions and new hopes. But at that moment, I caught another glimpse of the miserable camp lost on the high moor, which, even at that glorious mid-day, looked so frail and fragile. No, if I was to win Miss Keir for myself, I must draw her to my side, rather than throw myself to hers.

"I regret, Mr. McManus," I therefore replied, "that that is not the purpose of my visit. I came simply to see how you were established, and for some fresh air to fill my lungs."

"Of which we have plenty, Kinnimoth," replied McManus, as Miss Keir took the several steps that led her from my side to a position behind the arm-chair. "For the Lord has blessed us since we began our work here – behold! have we not cool airs and warm sunshine and the pleasant waters of the lochs around us? Consider this – it is the middle of winter and yet we are able to proceed with God's work. His Citadel will be built before the spring returns, and our enemies will be confounded and put utterly into disarray!"

"Well done!" exclaimed Miss Keir.

"And lest you doubt me, Mr. Kininmonth," continued the new prophet, "let me tell you that I will sit here, under the Eye of the Lord, upon this humble seat, both day and night, until His work is done. And when the Citadel is built, I will arise from this place and walk only among the Elect."

I was momentarily confounded. "You mean to sit out here in the cold and rain, until the spring?" I exclaimed.

"Yes, of course," snapped Miss Keir in the tone of voice which I supposed she reserved particularly for the dullest of her small charges in the school. "That is what Brother Daniel will do. He will sit here under the protection of the Lord, and when the Citadel is built, on this very spot, he will arise and lead us all into the Fortress of the Righteous!"

I shook my head in disbelief; and then shrugged. It was not for me to advise this man of his idiocy; surely one single winter's night, exposed to the raw winds and the needling sleet, would knock some sense into him.

"And now, Mr. Kinnimoth, since you have not experienced the true torrents of belief and the icy waterfalls of truth, turn your steps again to the North Side, and go. But take this message to the worthless Rinck: that the Elect will shortly prevail, and the Lord will march down from Ben Ghobhlach with His army and will wreak His vengeance upon the Earth. And the people languishing in Ullapool will eat the heads of asses and the dung of doves! Now go!"

With these strong threats, McManus dismissed me, and opened again his Bible, and ostentatiously applied himself once more to his studies. Miss Keir, walking at some distance ahead, led me back down the hill, leaving the prophet in his arm-chair. Not one word was spoken. She stopped at the head of the path leading to the camp and waited with eyes averted until I had caught up, had faltered, had mumbled a farewell, and had proceeded down towards the ferry-man's house.

For the rest of that day, my head whirled with contradictory thoughts of where my allegiances should lie, of whether I should have set my passion for a woman above my desire for an easy life; I knew I cared not one whit for Mr. Rinck's Citadel, nor for Mr. McManus's Fortress, for it was certain that neither of these would ever be built. Had I been a younger man, I would perhaps have thrown in my lot with McManus simply for the sake of finding the smile upon Miss Keir's face. Had it been the middle of summer, or a high day in spring, perhaps my advancing years would have yielded to temptation. But not now, not to-day, and not while my stomach contracted with hunger, for it was now past noon, and I had, in my earlier enthusiasm, forgotten to bring any baps along with me to eat.

I determined, therefore, to make shorter work of my return journey, and called the ferry-man, Mr. Mackenzie – yet another of the clan – to take me across to Ullapool by the shortest route. I had to wait an hour, since he was at his broth, and, at all events, as he explained, he had high expectation of a party from Dundonnell "shortly". I whiled away the time with an inspection of the shore, which was dull in high degree. Towards half-past one, two men arrived from over the hill, the ferry-man rose from his broth, and we set off across the loch.

On arrival at the Pier, I determined to have a celebratory meal at the Caledonian Hotel, and within minutes was lapping up a good soup, and washing down plenty of bread and cheese with a glass of beer. I confess that I also indulged in a small nip of whisky as well, and felt as comfortable there as I had for many a day. When the time came for me to leave, and I stepped out into the afternoon, the sun had been blocked off by the height of the mountains on the opposite shore, but the brightness of the day still dazzled me. It was with a rather faltering step that I proceeded down the road past Braes, but I stopped for nothing until I arrived home, as the night came on.

The remainder of that week was spent at the head of the railway, making poor progress. I had little enthusiasm for the work, and even less to impart to my supervisors and gang. I came home of an evening and read in the books of Mrs. MacMahon's library, chiefly the exciting works of Mr. Robert Stevenson. These works, although full of the most unlikely events and absurd co-incidences, entertained me and diverted my thoughts away from the gloomier paths they might otherwise have taken.

On the evening of the fifteenth of the month, Mrs. MacMahon greeted me with great excitement as I came home.

"It seems, Mr. Kininmonth," she said, "that the Railway Company is continuing to build in your absence. From Braemore Halt downwards!"

I looked at her, I confess, blankly. Of what was she talking? I was the one who built railways from Garve to Ullapool!

Eventually I was persuaded to believe that a host of men had arrived on the train from Garve that morning, had erected a veritable village of huts, complete with mess-hall, and had begun to off-load all the materials required for the building of railways. I found all of this still rather incredible, like one of Mr. Stevenson's Romances, and set out almost immediately, stopping only for my supper, and to bundle myself up in warmer clothes, for the night was damp and raw. Before I left thus precipitately, I sat down for two cups of tea and a buttered scone. On such a night, it was fortunate that I had so fortified myself. When my stomach had quite settled and my digestion had commenced, I ventured out to round up young Jamie Campbell, as my guide and companion.

As we ascended the road to Braemore, Jamie explained to me that he had had two days of wild freedom – after Miss Keir had defected to the Enthusiasts, thereby abandoning her small troop of scholars to their own devices. However, authority and good sense had intervened, much to Jamie's disgust, and a replacement teacher had arrived: Mr. Ross, a man – it seemed – of vicious temper, red face and hands itchy to lay the tawse upon his charges. Jamie had felt his wrath twice already, and he poured forth to me his indignation on this ignoble manner of receiving an education.

My mind was rather elsewhere, and, although I mumbled encouragement and outrage at all the appropriate points, Jamie soon perceived my distraction and desisted. Which was to the good, since I wished to approach Braemore Halt – yet again! – with the utmost caution and silence. We crept past the Lodge at the top of the brae, and came upon the settlement which Mrs. MacMahon had quite correctly reported. There were, as far as I could determine in the dark night, some two dozen huts or tents erected, and a merry fire burning before each of them. There was the sound of men's voices, some singing, some arguing, some engaged in a dull hum of talk. One or two figures moved around in the gloom.

I heard footsteps behind me, and a man of about thirty years of age greeted me. Re-assuring myself that I had come this time with no criminal intent, I faced him.

He wished me a good evening and asked if I had come to see what was happening? I conceded this. Would I like to come and share a mug of tea with him, he inquired? I detected from his accent that he came from Aberdeen-shire. "Bring your son along too, and we'll get him warm by the fire," added our host, playfully punching Jamie on the shoulder. "Reminds me of my own lad," said the man wistfully.

When we were comfortably seated before a crackling fire, clutching warm mugs, and breathing in the bitter smoke of our host's pipe, we learned all that we wished to know. This was as follows: the men, some fifty of them, were sappers, attached to some Highland regiment whose name, since I take no interest in military affairs, immediately escaped me. They had received orders to come here and construct the railway to Ullapool, since there was unrest in that part of the world which required the despatch of troops and horses by Her Majesty's Government.

"It seems, Sir," explained our new friend, whose name was John Duthie, "that the engineer in charge of building this railway as far as here has been killed by the people at Ullapool, and so the task of completing his work has fallen to us. Kincorth, or some such, was his name."

"Kininmonth," I muttered almost involuntarily, casting a warning glance at Jamie, who now sat open-mouthed staring at me.

"Aye," said Duthie, "that would be it. Seems he was kidnapped by a madman and murdered. The constables have not managed to arrest his murderers, but the Government is determined not to rest until they have all been captured."

Duthie told us other things about the men in the camp, about their commanding officer, and about the strengths and weaknesses of the engineers who directed their efforts. But my mind was racing on: if they were intent on completing the railway, then it could only be with the intention of bringing Law and Order to Ullapool in the greatest possible strength – and keeping it there. And the reason for that was surely to capture Rinck and all his supporters and to pass judgement on them. Where did that leave me? – on the one hand, officially murdered and beyond resuscitation; on the other, still stalking the streets of Ullapool, known to all its citizens as Rinck's Engineer, alive in blatant disregard of the official position!

In order to appear merely curious and not intensely interested, I asked Mr. Duthie how they proposed to bring the line down the steep hill of Braemore. His reply did not surprise me, it being that they would simply lead it down the line of the road, on the north side, until the level of the Strath was again reached. There was no thought of cutting across to the south side, let alone of employing such imaginative methods of descent as I still cherished. But I said nothing of these alternatives, fearing to draw attention to myself as a man of engineering capabilities. As it was, I was exposing myself somewhat with questions which were of more than the ordinary level of intelligence.

Having discovered all that I required, and more than I really desired, I excused Jamie and myself on the grounds that his mother would be worried at our absence, and was bidden a jovial good-night by Mr. Duthie. We re-gained the Dirrie More road, and made haste to get back to Achindrean, Jamie babbling on in annoying manner about my supposed death, the presence of the soldiers, and other topics of great interest to a thirteen-year-old boy, but of little to a forty-five-year-old man. I marched on, deep in my own thoughts.

I slept little that night. I was awake throughout most of it, hearing the grand-father clock downstairs strike mutedly each and all the hours. At around three in the morning, I rolled over and over in my mind how the Board must be laughing at their good fortune, how the loathsome MacAulay must be rubbing his hands in delight: to have killed off his hated Kininmonth, and to have the railway taken to completion by the military, at no further expense! Was my professional life now at an end?

At about six o'clock, I finally lay on my side and fell into a deep sleep, which was interrupted at eight by Mrs. MacMahon demanding to know if I thought it was the Sabbath? And even if it was, which she strenuously denied, was I not ashamed to being lying abed?

December 16, 1897.

That day, yielding to a burning curiosity to see the men working at Braemore in the day-light, I once more headed up the brae and walked slowly past the Halt. There was a thick mist blowing at that height, but between the swirling clouds I could see that already a huge store of steel rail and ballast had been delivered, and that, even as I crested the hill, another train was arriving with further materials. The men pitched into their tasks of unloading the train, of marshalling the stores, of tidying the site, with an unbelievable sense of urgency such as Braemore had never seen before. While the site was being arranged, another gang of men was already advancing along the line out beyond the spot where it had been halted these past eighteen months.

Taking care to keep myself concealed in the mist where I could, my cap pulled down over my eyes and my shoulders hunched up, I stopped only as long as I could observe without being observed. After a few moments, I walked onwards in a daze. I calculated, as I wandered along the Dirrie More, that these men could complete the line to Ullapool in less than three months – sooner, indeed, since they would join up with the line emerging from Ullapool in good time. It was a thought scarcely to be borne. My feet now led me where they would: I had no desire to return to the Strath, far less to come past the site of such industry so soon.

After an hour or so of aimless strolling, with the mist now thicker than ever before, to the degree that I scarce knew where I was in that familiar glen, I found myself at the entrance to Aultguish House. As I hesitated at the gate, not sure whether I should go in uninvited or whether simply to pass on, I glimpsed the young lad Mackenzie, the son of the Professor's man-servant. He saw me and waved cheerily, then ran round to the kitchen-door and shouted to his mother that "the Railway Man" had come to visit the Professor. With that, I plucked up courage and walked up the short drive-way to the house. As I approached the house, the front door was thrown open, and the Professor himself stood there, in his kilt, and noisily bade me come in and let him get back to his fire-side to "demolish Faulmann". Albeit puzzled, I needed no second invitation, and, just as once before, was presently installed before such a fire as might have driven a loco-motive participating in a Race all the way from Aberdeen to London. (Readers will recall the event of 1895, when this enormous distance of some five hundred and fifty miles was travelled in a little over eight and one-half hours; had the fireman had the direct supervision of the Professor at that time, I am persuaded that even this exhilarating time might have been exceeded.)

Spread over tables and chairs in the Professor's study was a profusion of thick books, scraps of paper, rolled parchment bound in black ribbon; a number of oil-lamps provided sufficient illumination; here and there a pile of paper had slipped to the ground, and was in grave danger of being consumed by the crackling spitting fire. Hastily, I moved those piles which I considered to be at greatest risk of conflagration, only to be told by the Professor, in no uncertain terms, that I was to touch nothing. I was to pay attention.

I did so.

"As you are well aware, Mr. Kininmonth," said the Professor passionately, brandishing a thick volume at me, "Faulmann made no mention of Cuneiform script in his *Buch der Schrift*. Look at the man, will you? – not the faintest idea of the science of phonetics, a very rudimentary grasp of the determinative syllables! No, no, no, Mr. Kininmonth," he went on, shaking his finger at me in cheerful remonstration, "you will not pay any heed to Faulmann of Vienna. You are naturally interested in the Cuneiform?"

Tentatively, I agreed.

"Well, it is fortunate that I was looking through some of my collections when you arrived. Sit down there and have a look at this wonderful example of Akkadian script – I think it should be dated about 2500 BC. What do you think?"

I gazed down in wonder upon several sheaves of paper with those tiny marks I had seen on the clay tablets which I had once held in my hand in this very room.

"But primitive, very primitive! How these people managed to last so long with such a dreadful mode of transcription, I shall never understand. Look at this other example here." He thrust a piece of pottery under my nose, covered, similarly, with those outlandish markings. "Now, you see these symbols here? Read phonetically, as you are well aware, this says 'anak-sadu-sis'. I am driven almost to despair by the sloppiness of it! What they meant by 'anak-sadu-sis' was of course the name of the king, Nebuchadrezzar. What do you think of that then?"

"Surely you mean Nebuchadnezzar?" I asked, plucking up the courage to appear wise.

"Don't be dull-witted, man! Nebuchadnezzar is a corruption, introduced by those idiots when they translated the Bible for King James. Rezzar! Rezzar! Nebuchad-rezzar, that's what it says! And you can only tell that by the use of this tiny determinative symbol here, which indicates our man. Do you see?" He thrust his large finger at a tiny marking on the pottery. "The determinative is the key to it all – a text can be read in so many ways, but if you find the determinative mark – *fiat lux*!"

Professor Cardew-Smith regarded my amazement, then laughed uproariously.

"But of course, I was forgetting you know nothing about this. I am sorry, Sir. Let me explain."

And in the course of the next half-an-hour, he informed me how the ancient Persian priests used to record their accounts by means of this script, made with tiny wedges of wood or ivory upon soft clay. The script had been used to record history and poetry, had been employed in the service of different languages – those of the Hittites, the Sumerians, the Medeans and the Persians; it had been used in Babylon (a name which, I was advised, came from the Akkadian *bab-ilu* meaning "the Gate of God") and by the Pharaohs of Egypt. I was much taken by the fact that all the Professor's subjects were familiar to me – he had brought to life the books of the Old Testament by rendering them as History! Hittites, Sumerians, Chaldeans – they were real people, real kings, real slaves, engaged in living and dying, writing and trading, building and farming. What I had previously considered as legend or religion, I now found to be rooted in historical reality.

Professor Cardew-Smith showed me different symbols, and illustrated on spare sheets of paper how the tiny impressions had been abstracted from the original pictures – a ram or an ox, for example – which had grown from recognisable pictures of these animals; or those symbols for a man or a woman, which (I blush even to relate it here) were developed from rather crude depictions of those parts of the body which most distinguish the genders. I was intrigued to see that the symbol for a king was simply the symbol for a man with an additional mark which represented a crown – what little separates a king from a pauper!

At about eleven o'clock, the Professor having abruptly decided that he required a nap before luncheon, I was ushered from the house. The mist was thicker even than before; but, with with my brain groping manfully through the even mistier problems of determinative marks and lost tribes, my feet carried me effortlessly back up to Braemore. These were uplifting thoughts, which unaccountably cheered me; I even waved to the military men labouring at their tasks as I passed, and shouted a greeting. Mrs. MacMahon, when she let me back into her house, was much astonished and pleased to see the change which had been effected in my mood. I told her of my visit to Professor

Cardew-Smith. Since Mrs. MacMahon had several strong opinions on the Professor, I was able to sit peacefully, taking a bowl of thick, hot soup, while she speculated on his past, his interest in Colonial matters, his relations with the polite society of Wester-ross and, above all, the scandal of his bathroom.

Thus passed in a whirl of excitement and revelation the sixteenth day of December, 1897. In all the days I spent in that part of the world, I count it among the most pleasant, being among the most inspiring and thought-provoking. As I sat and puffed at a pipe in the evening, I reflected on the use of an alphabet which was, for the most part, utterly impenetrable to all but the enlightened few, and which even then required you to read all of the words prior to making sense of any one of them. Was there not a lesson here for the likes of Rinck and McManus? Was there not a lesson here for my own self? What was it that told me I had made sense of anything – of the construction of my Railway, of Miss Keir, of the episode of the Burning Angel?

Looked at from a slightly altered perspective (with a different "determinative", to use the Professor's term), would it not be possible to draw quite divergent conclusions from each and every event? Melchior Rinck sees the same words as you or I or Sir John Fowler, but places his own determinative mark at the head of the words and takes his own meaning. Daniel McManus places two determinative marks there and draws an even stronger conclusion. I, for my part, would be inclined to place three different marks in different places, and still not know which one was the correct one.

I considered also such ancient history as had been revealed to me that day. The fact of the historical reality of such as Nebuchad-rezzar (I remembered this name well, in order to have a point to score against McManus, should I require it), Bab-ilu, the Assyrians, the Medeans and the Hittites shook me profoundly. I had lazily considered these all to be simply names in a book; but now I found that they were real people, with cities and priests and trade, like any other, vying with each other for power. And I began to view the Books of the Old Testament in a far different light. I determined that I should read the Bible now as a book of History, not as the proof of Rinck's enthusiasms.

Two nights later, I have now to report, a strange encounter was made. Those of you who have been paying close attention to the narrative here set down will have noted that the "Burning Angel" of Ullapool, the news of which had been greatly noised abroad to my eternal consternation, was none other than myself, caught in an unfortunate series of accidents. You will, therefore, be more than a little surprised to learn that I had an encounter with a real Angel, who claimed to have been that self-same Burning Angel!

I was in Ullapool on the evening of the eighteenth day of December, having spent the day at the railway in fruitless planning and speculation. The gang of men who now turned up for work had dwindled to a mere two or three, and they were insufficient to do more than keep the existing line clear of mud and snow. The rails rusted which were piled at the head of the line, and no useful labour was being undertaken. Everyone around Loch-broom now knew of the work being done at Braemore, with the result that those who had not crossed the water to join the Enthusiasts, and still maintained an interest in the project despite the schism, were cast into abject lethargy by the thought that the railway would soon come to Ullapool from Braemore, rather than the other way around. I stayed in the town to listen to gossip and to try to learn some of the more scandalous rumours surrounding Rinck and McManus, both of whom appeared to have passed beyond rational activity. I understood, from a man who had that very day been across to Aultnaharrie, that McManus in his arm-chair was poorly, racked by a tremendous cough, the very skin on his face cracking with the cold, but still determined to sit there until his Kingdom was established. And Mr. Coleman, the drill-instructor, had long since abandoned this new encampment to return to Ullapool, now twice the enemy of change that he had ever been, claiming to anyone who would listen that he had been on a mission of "espionage" ordered by the Government.

As the night grew late, I set off homewards on the Godly Bicycle. At the corner of the old grave-yard, however, I was astonished and slightly perturbed to see sitting on a grave-stone a figure with huge wings, which vibrated in the cool breeze. The figure was clutching in her hands a burning flame. I could not see how the flame was contained, but it seemed to live simply in the palms of her hands (for it was incontrovertibly a female figure, regardless of its tremendous height, and the wings). I attempted to hurry past, no longer having the confidence in myself to deal objectively with strange manifestations. (I recalled a story, told to me by my mother, concerning a young man, in excellent health and with the most promising of prospects, who had been in the south part of Edinburgh one stormy St. Andrew's Night, and had had the misfortune to come across just such a figure as I now beheld, and – to cut a long story short, which my mother rarely did – who now lay in the Edinburgh Cemetery at Warriston, under a grave-stone with an epitaph stating that he had been "struck down suddenly while walking in a Suburb of Edinburgh". At the age of six, I was told this story and it had made a great impression on me, to the degree that I was most unwilling to pass by the gates of grave-yards and cemeteries at night, lest some similar accident befall me, a reference to which would necessarily be included in my epitaph. The very Latin word *suburbium* even now holds layers of darkness and impending doom, which I cannot quite shake off in the clear light of Reason.)

"Be not afraid," called out the figure as I made my way past, "but step aside and speak with me!"

The voice was deep and sweet, strangely accented and comforting. Although my legs and heart screamed at me to continue my flight along the road to Braes, I felt myself obliged to dismount and turn towards the figure. Observing her more closely, I saw that she was much taller than me, perhaps six feet and three inches in height, with the tips of her wings fluttering over the back of her head.

"Speak your name," said the figure.

I replied that I was known as Alexander Kininmonth.

"I shall name you Kinnymott," said the figure rather grandly. "And you shall name me Ingeborg, the Burning Angel."

I was about to protest on two accounts, but then stopped my words before I spoke them.

"Be not afraid," said the Angel again, in a manner which I considered to be rather patronising, "for I give you into no harm. I have come not to burn, but rather to bring peace to your heart. Come closer . . . come closer." She gestured gently with her hands, in which yet the fire still seemed to live, impossibly, for I could see no container that would prevent the fire from burning her skin and causing her to cry out in pain. I approached her cautiously, picking my way slowly between the sharp head-stones. As I came close and looked up at her, I could see that her face was indeed that of an angel, so sweet and so noble. Her hair was of bright gold. She enfolded me in her arms – I forgot briefly the flames in her hands and gave no heed to possible injury to my back, nor to the likely damage to the overcoat, which Mrs. MacMahon would not forgive a second time – and, lowering her face, she kissed me full upon the lips, which felt as hot as if they burned me first from without and then from within. The kiss lasted several seconds, almost long enough to become immodest, long enough for me to wish it to continue for ever. And then the Angel thrust me back with such force that I tripped upon a slab and fell to the damp earth.

"Begone, the Kinnymott! Away, mortal sinner, and tell the world that you have been in the embrace of the Burning Angel and been found unworthy!"

And with that she came down from her seat and flew with giant strides into the night. The remains of the Angel's fire had been scattered upon the ground, where a dozen tiny flames now flickered and slowly died as I watched them. Long after the last trace of fire had vanished, I sat there and wondered what I had just seen. Perhaps there was indeed a Burning Angel – but, no, that could not be!

Disturbed, afraid, puzzled, I made my way home and retired to bed, reflecting on those embraces which might be modest, and those which might be immodest. Should the immodest embrace of an Angel be considered as 'beyond modesty'? Should the modest embrace of an unworthy person (I had not yet encountered a Devil, except in the shape of MacAulay, and the thought of his embrace was not one I could contemplate at all) be considered immodest? How would a rational man consider, for example, the immodest embrace of Miss Keir? I tossed and turned all through that sleepless night, remembering, pursuing fantastic notions, and considering greater and lesser questions of Morality.

On the following Monday, I determined to venture once more to Aultnaharrie. First, I wished to see if my new-found perspective on life had affected my view of Miss Keir. Secondly, I was curious to see if any engineering progress at all had been made. As it turned out, the answers to these questions made me a happier man than I had been for many a week.

To the accompaniment of Mrs. MacMahon's critical words on the subject of honest daily toil, I left the house on a frosty morning, with my breath freezing almost in my throat, and set off down the south-side of the loch as I had done once before. It was a splendid walk, which made me rosy-cheeked; I felt cleansed both inside and out as I came round by the ferry-man's house at Aultnaharrie. I noticed, with some degree of satisfaction, that there was as little activity in the encampment here as there had been at the end of my Railway on the far side of the loch. I was greeted upon my arrival by Miss Keir, whose eyes were red – I thought at first from the raw cold; but I soon discovered the reason.

Daniel McManus was dead.

It seems that he had succumbed to the cold of the season as he sat out, day after day and night after night on that bleak hill-side, with no protection other than his own misguided faith. He had contracted a fever which swiftly and surely passed into his lungs, burned through his organs like wild-fire, and then stopped his heart. He had died the previous night, still in his arm-chair, for they had been unable to loosen his grip on the arms of that sodden, benighted piece of furniture. (I observe here that my own grand-mother used to fasten herself to her chair in a similar fashion, after her husband had died. She was no more to be moved from her seat, if she was comfortable, than a dead man. Only the repeated inducement of a cup of tea with a scone, at the table, could sometimes dislodge her. In both cases, that of McManus and that of my grand-mother, Death Himself proved not to be too strong a force for them to resist. My grandmother had expired one Saturday afternoon, between the hours of four o'clock, which was when I had brought her last cup of tea, and six o'clock, when she would normally demand her soft-boiled egg. Unfortunately, she was of very heavy build and, my father being out of town on business, we could not move her from the chair. It was not until Monday that the undertakers came for her, since nothing could be done on the Sabbath, by which time her body had unfortunately moulded itself to the shape of the chair, with the result that chair and occupant both had to be carried down the stairs by the grumbling undertaker and his wheezing assistant. My mother had thrown a black cloth over my grandmother, for propriety, and various neighbours and relatives called in during the Sunday, to have, as they said, "one last cup of tea" with the shrouded corpse seated there. But for McManus, there was no cup of tea.)

Even as I arrived, to be unexpectedly and very warmly greeted by Miss Keir, who pressed my hand repeatedly as she led me to the largest of the tents, McBoyle was performing those rites in which he was greatly skilled. McManus lay in state under a soiled canvas, which was originally striped green with white, and was last used to inclose a cocoanut-shy at the time of the ill-fated Jubilee Celebrations. I admit that McBoyle had performed some miracles in preparing the man to meet his Maker, for McManus looked both serene and at peace with the world – something, I should remark, if I have not already done so, which he had never been during his short life.

I gathered from Miss Keir, who kept by my side, and linked her arm in mine, that McManus was to be ferried back to Ullapool, and would thence be shipped to Glasgow on the next boat which Mr. MacBrayne consented to send in our direction. We wondered aloud just how much MacBrayne would charge for such a passenger, for he was not a man noted for charging half-a-crown when three shillings would do. The school-mistress also whispered to me that McBoyle had designs upon the leadership of this small community, and hinted, with a blush and a tremor in her voice, that he had perhaps designs upon Miss Keir herself. Hit hard in my heart by the helplessness of a woman who had been much in my thoughts in the preceding night, I immediately vowed to her that neither of McBoyle's ambitions would meet with success. Miss Keir whispered her gratitude, and her large brown eyes filled with tears once more.

McBoyle soon completed his preparation of the deceased for the last journey across the dark waters to the gloomy sunless realms of Glasgow. It seemed that a ceremony was called for, on the site of McManus's greatest folly, one which our esteemed undertaker was to lead. A small group of the Enthusiasts clustered around in the freezing air to hear McBoyle recite the words of Lamentations, tonelessly and without feeling. He called for the Lord to take into

His arms the beloved Brother Daniel, and then with some sense of urgency to turn His attention to those who remained and who wished to carry on Daniel's work – to wit, the construction of a Fortress in which the Elect might conceal themselves when God's Wrath was finally visited upon the Earth.

I was rather taken aback when a fierce argument then broke out between McBoyle and a couple of surly individuals, who had been his trusted companions in Ullapool, and the larger majority of the remaining group. The latter simply wished to give up McManus's risible attempts to build a Citadel, and proposed a return to Ullapool and the bosom of their own families. Miss Keir stayed out of the argument at first, but I sensed that she had had enough of life on the exposed mountain which over-looked the loch. At length, when both parties had exhausted their arguments, and two punches had been laid by one of McBoyle's men upon the nose of Mr. Lamont, and McBoyle was taking off his jacket with the intention of extending the discussion by more violent means, Miss Keir intervened.

Those of you who have not forgotten your school-days will probably remember just how terrifying an outraged school-mistress can be, how your bowels can turn instantly to ice at her words, what a longing to hide can be provoked by gimlet eyes, what shame and embarrassment will hotly spring to your face as she scythes you with her tongue! Just so it was with Miss Keir, whose performance was both magnificent and irresistible. McBoyle was stopped dead in his tracks, and within less than a minute, he was profusely apologising to anyone who cared to listen; at the end of two minutes, he had been silenced altogether; and at the end of three, even those whom Miss Keir was not chastising were inwardly begging her to stop. At the end of four minutes, there was no question but that the camp would be abandoned, there and then, and that we would all – some fifteen men and women – accompany McManus across the water, and abandon all the forlorn hopes of the 'Enthusiasts'.

Before the darkness came, at about three o'clock, McBoyle had, in the manner of Professor Galvani, sufficiently roused himself as to send over the loch for a coffin of good quality, in which the poor devil McManus could be transported. The whole party had abandoned the camp at one o'clock, and all had been ferried over as twilight fell. As for myself and Miss Keir, once the cold, damp crossing of the loch had been effected, we strolled along Shore-street for several minutes in pleasant and educational conversation, before going our separate ways at the junction with Mill-street. I had high hopes of making a reconciliation with that admirable woman.

Miss Keir, it should be observed for historical accuracy, having lost her position at the Leckmelm School, was now obliged to take up residence in Ullapool at the house of the dreadful Miss Kilroy, who had subjugated my own person and that of Mr. Forbes three years previously; this lady now had a vacancy; I believe it was Miss Kilroy herself, who had become even more embittered over the years and was known to be of the McBoyle party, who turned Miss Keir against me and shattered such delusions as I constructed for myself from my pipe-smoke during the long walk home, on that nineteenth day of December, 1897. There were those, Mrs. MacMahon principal among them, who told me that Miss Keir was a flighty woman, taken to wild and strong passions, which burned fiercely and as quickly died away, like one of the Jubilee fire-works. That was a judgement which, although I might see how it was easily arrived at, I did not share.

I met with no more Angels that night, although I looked eagerly minute by minute.

It has to be said that the collapse of the rival "Enthusiastic" adventure on the south side in no way improved the prospects of my Railway on the north side. All activity there had simply ceased, my Railway petering out from a proud and relatively straight road of iron and steel into a muddy and ice-bound channel dug through the fields. My readers may find it troubling, and will no doubt shake their heads in pity at my attitude, when I tell you that, in those strange days, I was not greatly concerned!

Final notes for the "Revelatory Chronicle".

It is not possible for me to continue with these notes for a Chronicle, insofar as I no longer have any enthusiasm for any party to this ill-judged scheme to institute a Paradise in Wester-ross. McManus, before his untimely and senseless death, published no more tracts, for which we may all breathe a sigh of relief. Rinck, never one to miss a chance to score points, issued several leaflets explaining how the Whore of Babylon came before men such as McBoyle and McManus, and had tempted them with the promised delights of "women of a certain class" – among whom we must suppose was included Miss Keir – and had had their lips smeared with the honey of easy salvation, only to find it turn to the bitter gall of damnation. Rinck exulted in the demise of his rival in his "Judgement of God Upon the False Daniel: A Word of Warning to the Elect on the Dangerous Path which Leads to Wisdom. Together with Some Prophecies by the New Elders of Wester-ross on the Swift Fall from Dis-Grace of an Untested Prophet"; which ran to more than just "A Word", but to at least eighty-seven pages of closely argued vituperation upon McManus, McBoyle and any other soul unfortunate enough to have had dealings with the "Untested Prophets".

The final episode to report in this momentous month, as far as concerned the events surrounding the Citadel of the Elect, was the arrival on Christmas Eve of an old man and woman from the parish of Achiltibuie. The promise of the past few months had so greatly inspired them that they had received a vision (some said the old man had been out on the hill, attending to his whisky-still, when the vision came) that the Messiah would arrive in Ullapool on Christmas Day. To that end, and in order to greet the Messiah with honour, they had sold every single possession they had, including their cow and a couple of dozen sheep, in order to buy finery and regalia to present to "Him". The old man had made a trip to Edinburgh to acquire from Charles Jenner a length of regal blue velvet, a gilded crown and a jewelled sceptre, which – to the surprise of many, perhaps, but not of regular patrons of Mr. Jenner's limitless establishment on Princes-street – were readily available from stock. He returned to the north-west with the finery in a back-pack; his wife had sewn the velvet into a grand cloak; and the pair had arrived in Ullapool and presented themselves at the Caledonian Hotel, announcing their expectation. I was not present at this strange scene, but I understand that Mr. Rinck made a public display of this demonstration of the power of vision, and had entertained the old couple lavishly.

Alas for their eagerness, there was nothing untoward in Ullapool on the following day, except for the entertainments provided by a travelling troupe of Danish actors who, having taken a wrong turn at Garve on their way to the Isle of Skye, were now wintering in the town. I declined to mingle with the noisy, drunken crowds of men and young women who flocked to see this troupe, but I was advised that the entertainment boasted: a family of Fire-Eaters; the "World's Only Bird-Woman"; a man who could walk on nails; a Brahmin Magician who could make sixpences appear from the ears of Mr. Elder, the perplexed baker of Pulteney-street (and continued to make them appear, while the rowdy crowd howled with laughter at Mr. Elder's expense); and the "Penultimate Unicorn in the Western Hemisphere". I myself enjoyed the entertainment only "by proxy", through the disjointed reports of young Jamie – I had often told him, to no avail, that a facility for telling a simple story from start to finish, without interruption, was a valuable social asset – who was of an age to be easily influenced and excited by such things. I, for my part, rested at home with Mrs. MacMahon and Johan, and played parlour-games which were peaceful and undemanding, as befitted a man of my more mature years.

Let me just mention that on the first day of January, 1898, Mr. Rinck presented to the world his infamous "Solemn Testimony and Prophetic Announcement by the New King of Cromartie", in which it was demonstrated that the "Kingdom of Cromartie" was now in the hands of the Elect, and that Rinck himself was now the Vice-Regent, ousting the young Countess of Cromarty, while the Lord Himself was King. It was in this pamphlet also that Rinck referred once more to the Revelation of John, and announced that the Day of Salvation for the Elect – and only for the Elect, let it be noted, for those who had not been baptised in the Spirit and excoriated by the Living Word would not benefit – would fall on the eleventh day of the second month of the New Year, that being two-and-forty days into the year. Six times seven days would elapse before the Apocalypse started; and six times seven days would it last; and at the end of the twelfth week, the Martyrs and the Purified-in-Spirit would rise again.

I took exception to Mr. Rinck's recital from the Seventeenth

Chapter of the Book of Revelation, in which reference is made to the curse "MYSTERY, BABYLON THE GREAT, THE MOTHER OF HARLOTS AND ABOMINATIONS OF THE EARTH", understanding as I now did that Babylon was a city, "the Gate of God" for the ancients, and not a woman of loose habit. However, I did not feel strong enough in my acquired knowledge of the antique civilisations to challenge Rinck on this matter, much though I desired to.

Rinck followed the publication of this pamphlet with another tract, dated the sixth of January, entitled "The End of Time and the Beginning of Time: A Vision of the New Godly World", in which Rinck not only predicted the numbers of those who would survive the Apocalypse, but also the ratio of men, women and children. Of the hundred and forty-four thousand who would still be alive on the twenty-fifth of March (Mr. Rinck's previous flocks in Tweedsmuir, Chicago, Muenster in Germany, and other parts of the known world, would contribute to the final total), three-and-thirty thousand would be adult males, six-and-sixty thousand would be adult females, and the balance would be children of mixed gender. Therefore, announced Rinck, it would be necessary for a man to take to himself two wives. The Reverend Macmillan was outraged almost beyond words, and advised all decent women to stay within doors. Mrs. MacMahon was greatly intrigued.

January, 1898.

The attentive Reader will have noted that this fourth volume of my History has scarcely advanced the railway from Ullapool to Garve any distance which signifies. But let us take the opportunity afforded to all, great and humble alike, by the turning of the Year, to reflect on past achievements. Consider this: since August 1893, the railway has been built from Garve as far as Braemore; had it not been for the incompetence and chronic incapacity of the Board of the Railway Company, then I might by now have brought the line the full distance to Ullapool, as originally projected. But, if one bears in mind the troubles and travails against which I have had to labour over the four years since that promising beginning; and if one takes into account the mile or so which has been added at the north-western end of the line: then I am certain that historians will look back at this human endeavour and find me not wanting.

Such were my reflections, as I sat up with Mrs. MacMahon on Hogmanay, while all around me a jovial crowd drank and danced, made music and joked. As the fumes of whisky lulled me into a state of warmth and restfulness, and I sank deeper into the arm-chair which I now called my own, I found myself reflecting idly on Rinck's proposals for the marriage of two women to every man. I will draw a veil over the course which my thoughts took for a space of twenty or so pleasant minutes, and will embarrass no one by revealing whither my phantasy led me, or by indicating the role which Miss Keir played in this Romance. However, I think it is to my credit that I did not lay claim to more than one wife in that blissful reverie.

In this, and like remembrances of Angels and Alphabets, I spent a warm and comfortable evening. How little did I, or anyone around me, know then that the peace of the glen and the merry spirit of the community would so soon be shattered!

The first day of January being a Saturday, there were few people who stirred themselves that day to open a shop or an office, or to step out into their fields for any other than the most pressing business to do with sheep and cattle. Many were the sore heads which required the purgatives and solace offered by the clear blue air of the day. Nor was the following day, being the Sabbath, any less quiet and peaceful. It was on the Monday, the third day of January, that the subjects of The Queen in that part of Britain set again about their habitual tasks; and on that day, also, I determined to venture out as a man of my profession and see what I could do to improve the world about me. The day was filled with sleet and heavy cloud, through which the watery sun would nevertheless gleam for whole minutes at a time, before being obliterated for an hour by the next squall from the ocean. I cycled down to the head of the line at Leckmelm; the sight which greeted me there rapidly turned my spring of optimism and well-being into a desert of despair and a bog of bitterness. I saw an abandoned site, which the depredations of the winter weeks had over-laid with the mantle of neglect, of rust, of mud, of hopelessness. I thought to myself that even if I were to find myself an enthusiastic gang of men, led by MacIvor – whom, I now realised, I had not seen for several weeks, and whom I supposed had packed his bag and pointed his beard in the direction of some new works, perhaps on the further side of the country – yes, even with those handy labourers, I would have to start again on this line as it came out of Ullapool, for there was little of permanence in it.

With these oppressive thoughts dragging themselves gloomily through my mind, I stood for several minutes in the churned earth. I did not hear any sound, and was thus abominably shocked to feel myself slapped on the shoulder, while a well-kent voice insinuated itself into my left ear: "Well, Mr. Kinninmoth, your enterprise is not much to look at, is it now?"

It was MacAulay. I looked at him in some bewilderment at first, suspicious when I found him to be on his own, instead of appearing as the fawning courtier to some greater figure, like Sir John. I noticed his horse tied to the low-hanging branch of a tree, and looked round for any signs of companions.

"No, Kinninmoth," sniggered MacAulay, clapping his left hand with the pair of black woollen gloves he held in his right, an insolent leer on his frost-pinched face, "I'm quite alone, as you see. But not as alone as you, I expect?"

"What do you mean, Sir?" I exclaimed, perceiving some veiled threat in his words, and preparing to defend myself. The pugilistic arts are not ones which I had until then admired, and my understanding of balance, of where a punch might land most effectively, and – more importantly – how to defend my nose and mouth against the punches thrown by an assailant; such understanding was defective in the extreme.

"Och, calm yourself, Kinninmoth," laughed MacAulay, "I've not come here to harm you. After all," he lowered his voice and winked at me, a horrible sight, in which his entire narrow mouth lurched to one side to allow the muscles of his face to control his eyelid, "After all, Mr. Kinninmoth, you're already a dead man! Killed, I believe, by the followers of Mr. Rinck on the eighth of September last? Would that not be you, Mr. Kinninmoth?"

"How could it be me," I snapped angrily at him, "when you see me here, before you, in the flesh! Here," I took the liberty of pushing him on the chest, so that he stepped back in alarm, "does that feel like a ghost to you?"

"Have a care, Kinninmoth, have a care!" warned MacAulay, brushing invisible specks of mud from his coat. "You are swimming in waters far deeper than you suspect. These are not the small annoyances you used to dream up for me when you worked for the Company; these are matters of State; your name has reached our revered Queen herself! Have a care!"

My astonishment showed on my face, I suppose, for he then laughed out loud and strutted up and down for a few moments.

"You have no inkling, Sir, of what you are about, have you? Oh, I have you at last, you rascal! I have my revenge for all the trouble you have given me! Oh, but this is sweet!"

With these and such-like expressions of his mean joy, he laughed until he almost showed colour in his face, and then was over-whelmed by a fit of coughing which I hoped would be the end of him. But he recovered, blew his nose violently through his fingers, then wiped his eyes with the filthiest piece of cloth I have ever seen emerge from a gentleman's pocket.

"Here is where you are, Mr. Kinninmoth," he explained. "On the eighth of September last, you were put to death by Rinck and his followers, as a spy in their midst. An awful death it was – disem-bodiment, defenestration and having your head chopped off." (I repeat MacAulay's words as he said them to me – anyone with any wit and education will realise that he most likely meant disembow-elment and decapitation.) "And then being burned at the stake, like any piece of carrion. What a grisly end for such an educated man, eh, Kinninmoth? No, as I said to Mrs. MacAulay at the time, it couldn't have happened to a nicer man!"

I silently wondered to myself what manner of woman could possibly have allied herself to such a man in marriage, and pitied her, for it was likely that she had been trapped into matrimony by some black-mail or dishonourable act on the part of her husband.

"Well, it's more than you are worth, Kinninmoth," he went on, "but the Government in Westminster and The Queen in London have been struck with pity at your awful fate, and are even now taking steps to bring the rascals to Justice. And what Justice it will be, I expect! No more than they deserve – strung up on the gallows like socks on a clothes-line, every one: now, who shall it be? Mr. Rinck, of course, and Mr. Mackenzie, and what's his name – McManus? – and maybe that fair school-mistress, Miss Keir . . . "

Although I knew that the man was simply provoking me out of a mis-begotten sense of humour, I could bear no more of his taunting. I struck out at him with the flat of my hand and fetched him a resounding slap upon his left ear. He staggered back, pale as a fetch.

"You devil!" he shouted. "Alive or dead, I will have you for that! Yes, you, and that Jezebel, Miss Keir, and that woman, MacMahon, if I have to!" He spat carefully into his handkerchief, looking anxiously for traces of blood or broken teeth: of which, naturally, there were none. After a few moments, he looked craftily at me. "Well, we'll see, Kinninmoth, we shall see. Alive or dead? The Chief Constable thinks you are dead, Robert Cecil, the Earl of Salisbury, thinks you are dead, our beloved Queen herself thinks you are dead – and you know she has a soft spot for Highland laddies, eh, Mr. Kinninmoth? So the Army has been sent in to track down and arrest your killers. That being the case, who am I to stand in their way?"

"But what about Sir John Fowler? Or anyone at all in Ullapool?" I blustered. "Any single one of them would be able to swear that I am who I say I am! The Queen would listen to Sir John, surely?"

"Alas, Kinninmoth," MacAulay shook his head sadly and mockingly, "Sir John has determined that he will stay out of this affair, since it is too close to home. In any case, he has shut up Braemore and gone to Bournemouth, I believe, for to keep warm in the winter. I don't expect you will be able to reach Bournemouth without trouble. Protesting will avail you nothing, my friend," he continued, smugly. "We need you to be dead, don't you see, Kinninmoth? We need you dead!"

I was aghast. All that this miscreant was telling me had the ring of truth to it. If it had been officially decided, in the very highest offices of Government, that I had been murdered, then how could I prove otherwise? And how many innocent – and not-so-innocent – people were to be punished for this supposed crime! Oh, how I bitterly regretted stumbling in the night in Mill-street! From that simple human act, I repeat, from that all-too-human slip, what a story of Angels had been spun, and how that story had spawned other stories, a lie as mother to other lies, and then, finally, how the off-spring had come back to mock me, in my disgrace!

MacAulay obviously felt that his work was now done, for he pulled on his gloves, rubbed his left ear ostentatiously, and turned to his horse. "Well, it will be small comfort to you, Kinninmoth, but rest assured that you will be avenged before the month is out!"

Within days, I had ample proof that what MacAulay had told me was true, for the platoon of army-men, who had been working up at Braemore, emerged over the brow of the hill on the sixth of January, bringing the line down into the glen; such was the rate at which they worked that, by the twenty-first of the month, they were bringing it past Achindrean! They appeared to be possessed of almost Herculean powers, and their engineer was – as far as I could tell, when I lingered in disguise near the workings at sundry times of the day or night – quite as competent as I.

My disguise had been designed by no less a person than Mrs. MacMahon, who seemed to understand the peril in which I might stand; I now went abroad as a friend of her son, a 'Mr. Lunn', returned from the sea; and although some might have argued that a sailor should not look so wan and bloodless, and my mother in particular might have sat me down in front of some potted heid and a strong cup of tea to improve my complexion, the disguise sufficed. I had already determined to grow myself a beard, and, despite some unwillingness on the part of my face, some tufts of beard were sprouting about my cheeks, ears and chin, much to Johan's amusement and childish delight. Mrs. MacMahon's kindness in those months was truly Christian, for she looked after me as a son; I was forced to all the subterfuges I could imagine to persuade her to take any money from me as rent.

On one occasion, my disguise was put to a severe test, when Mrs. MacMahon received unexpected visitors. A horse and cart drew up one Saturday afternoon, while we were sitting having a cup of tea in the kitchen. The maid, on answering the door, showed into the drawing-room "two gentlemen", who turned out to be the Reverend MacMillan from Ullapool, and his colleague, the Reverend Sutherland of Clachan, to whom Mrs. MacMahon attended straight away, having, as she did, an innate respect for "the cloth".

It was fortunate that I had had few dealings with these two men, else I would have felt most uncomfortable when, yielding to some impulse of the sort which always made of Mrs. MacMahon a dangerous companion, she blurted out to the ministers that "a family friend" was home from the sea, and I was called in to make polite conversation. Introduced as "William Lunn", I was obliged to spin them ever more bizarre tales of my voyages in the South Sea, and my encounters with ill-mannered savages and the unconverted heathen. My audience was extremely attentive, following my words avidly; for I have always noticed that men will attend to you if you feed their prejudices. Warming to my theme, and oiled with fresh cups of tea, I told the two men anything which my imagination came up with – desert islands, buried treasure, cannibals, human sacrifice, albatrosses – "yarns", as I termed them, of the Stevensonian sort, all of which made their eyes round and rounder. Finally, running short of the Phantastical, I decided in desperation to tell them the history which the Finlays had recounted to me many months previously, about their abandonment on the Island of Kerguelen, and their subsequent failures to be rescued until the Frenchmen took them off. But, whereas my invented tales fitted quite neatly within their narrow circle of belief, this true story pushed the two Reverends beyond the furthest frontiers of their credulity, and they began to raise their bushy eyebrows, and to question me more closely as to my credentials. At this point, Mrs. MacMahon came to my rescue with some smoothing banter, and I was despatched in disgrace back to the kitchen.

But the most remarkable, and for me most comforting, aspect of their visit was that they had not one slight suspicion that I was other than 'William Lunn', home from the sea, and that for them I bore no resemblance at all to the late Alexander Kininmonth.

When the railway reached Achindrean, I determined to pay a last visit to Melchior Rinck, to try to apprise him of the dangers into which he had wandered. On Monday, the twenty-fourth, therefore, I set off into town to seek him out. It was some time since I had last paid a visit to Ullapool – indeed, I had not been there since the day of McManus's final voyage home. I found that much had changed. The streets were far quieter than of late, and there was little evidence of a Citadel of the Elect under construction, beyond some tattered bills affixed to the outside of the coal-store. Everyone went about their business, perhaps with less enthusiasm than was usual, but quietly for sure.

I made my way as of old to the Caledonian Hotel, and found that it was deserted. The man at the bar informed me, with a hint of irony in his voice, that Mr. Rinck was to be found at McBoyle's establishment on West-terrace. This news rather astounded me since, when I had last seen the two men anywhere near each other, they had been implacable enemies. However, having reflected that there is nothing so strange as the day-to-day alliances of men in politics and religion, I resolved to root out the two men straightway.

The Joiner and Undertaker's business on West-terrace was a rather grand affair, having two windows in which, as it were, the tools and fruits of Mr. McBoyle's trade were presented to the discerning public. In the left window was a simple vase, in the Ancient Grecian style, filled with flowers which had withered and died at some time in the summer of 1887, to judge from their appearance. The vase stood on a rather dusty black velvet drape which was so hung as partially to conceal a screen made of highly polished pine. A block of wood was propped up, indicating that funerals could be conducted "in any part of the Parish of Ullapool", and that "the finest coffins are made on these Premises"; "Personal Supervision" was promised. In the right-hand window were some pieces of wood and two rather handsome cabinets, which were advertised as "some of our Handiwork". A slightly yellowed card stated that "pulpits, communion tables, ministers' and elders' chairs, fonts, lecterns, organ screens, etc." were "our Speciality".

I pushed my way into the gloomy shop, which had a stuffy smell hinting of death, dust and decay. A small bell rang above the door as I closed it, followed by a profound silence. I could hear my boots squeak as I approached the counter. Somewhere far in the distance I could hear murmuring voices, as of bees in a hive. The seconds ticked past, each fully measured by the sombre clock on the wall. I cleared my throat rather noisily. There was no interruption to the murmuring. I tip-toed back to the door, opened and closed it, this time with some force: the tiny bell leaped wildly into the air and crashed to the floor.

Within seconds, McBoyle was at the door which led to the back of his shop. His face was a rather fascinating mixture of outrage, obsequiousness and startlement, as he detected, first, the bell still rolling on the floor, secondly, a customer, and then, finally, the customer as myself. I waved my hand at the bell and tried to explain that it had fallen down on its own.

"Ah yes, it does that sometimes," he agreed in an oily manner, "if you open the door rather too suddenly. I'm sure we can have it fixed in no time. And what can I do for you, Mr. Kinnimoth? I trust there is no sad occasion for your visit?" This last question was put in the blatant expectation of my denial. But he was disappointed.

"No," I said, picking up the bell and placing it between us on the counter. "I am told that Mr. Rinck is with you. I had rather hoped to have a short word with him, if he is free?"

McBoyle denied that Rinck was anywhere on the premises. "But it is not often that I have the pleasure," he smiled rather too widely, "of meeting a man already dead. Are you perhaps in search of a memorial-stone? Perhaps I can interest you in a simple one made of Mull Granite." He indicated a featureless slab of pink stone which stood rather grandly in a corner. "And what epitaph would you like inscribed? 'Here lies Mr. Kinnimoth, civil engineer, whose works brought economy and profit to a small community?' That has rather a grand sound to it, has it not?"

I had no wish to joust with the insolent man. "No, Mr. McBoyle, I am not here to place any orders with you. I have come on an important matter which concerns myself and Mr. Rinck alone. So, if he is not here, I will be going." I straightened my hat and turned to the door.

No sooner had I made this declaration than the door to the back-shop opened once more, and the tall, imposing figure of Rinck came through.

"Brother Kinnimunt," said Rinck, "I never thought to see you in Ullapool again. Had you not left us to follow the roads of the Godless?"

I shook my head. "I have not once left this part of the world, Mr. Rinck. I have laboured long and hard at the task of bringing the railway to Ullapool, in accordance with the wishes of the New Elders. But since Daniel McManus took his own congregation to the south side – " and here I looked hard at Gilbert McBoyle, who gazed blandly back at me – "since then, I have found it hard to keep the men of Ullapool interested in the construction . . . "

Rinck interrupted me with a brusque wave of his hand. "Enough of that, Brother. There will be no railway. Leave that thought alone. Let us consider not what great buildings and wonderful railways might have been, but let us look into the souls of men and women, and consider how we may bring to our world the Fear of God alone, so that greed, terror, violence, inequality and the Fear of Man may be up-rooted from our midst and we may live as God intended us to live, fearing Him alone and having no fear of other men. Are you ready for that, my friend?"

I hesitated, looking at my boots, wondering how to divert the discussion to the matter to which I wished to alert him.

"Brother," continued Rinck, advancing upon me, with McBoyle hovering behind his right shoulder like some sleek hoodie crow. "Is there anything more important here on Earth than to ensure that men and women should not be subject to each other, that their slavery be ended, that their ignorance be burned away by the bright shining light of Godly wisdom, that small children may eat and learn, regardless of the wealth of their parents, that every boy-child and every girl-child may have health and wisdom throughout all their days? Tell me, Brother, can there be any more important matter than that? Is there anything more important than that which is happening here, to-day?"

There was, in truth, no sane answer which I could give to these questions. For surely, these were precisely the things which I wanted: an end to ignorance, to needless sickness, an end to abject poverty and indescribable wealth, an equal sharing of the fruits of the Earth among all those who were deserving. Nothing could be more important than that. And yet, and yet – I wanted to tell Rinck that the glorious goal to which he and I aspired was not to be attained in 1898, in Wester-ross, by the people who surrounded us, nor by the expectations he had of Divine intervention. It was too much to expect, too late, too soon, too little.

In answer, therefore, I shook my head, struck dumb by the impossibility of rendering up a simple response.

"You shake your head, Kinnimoth," sneered McBoyle. "You have, then, something more important to do?"

McBoyle's voice was like oil being poured on the slow-burning fire within me.

"And you, McBoyle, where were you when McManus went over to the south side of the loch?"

I marched up to the undertaker and shook his little door-bell in his face. But before I could do any harm, Rinck placed himself between us.

"Have patience with Brother Gilbert," he advised, "for he has seen the error of his ways, and has experienced the sharp pains of enlightenment, and has been washed by the torrents of uncertainty, and now walks among the Elect again. Brother Kinnimunt," he continued, leading me by the arm to the front of the shop, where we might peer over the wooden partition and the musty arrangement of flowers, "tell me why you have come to-day."

I took a deep breath and explained as well as I could the significance of the railway now being built down from Braemore, and the warnings given to me by MacAulay, and how I feared that great harm would come upon us all, if the soldiers once reached Ullapool, and found it still in the hands of the New Elders.

To my disappointment, but not to my very great astonishment, Rinck smiled more and more broadly at my tale of woe, until at last he burst out laughing and clapped me on the shoulder.

"Well said, Brother!" he laughed. "But none of this is a surprise to me. You think little of me if you imagine that I did not know what the soldiers are up to at Braemore; let them come! I expect them to be here on the forty-second day of this new year, and with them they shall bring the Visitation of the Lord upon both the Godless and the Elect, and we shall be those who have reached the End of Time."

"Amen!" murmured McBoyle from his corner.

"And now, Brother Kinnimunt," continued Rinck, gently but firmly directing me towards the door of the shop, "look into your own soul to see what you must do next. Search long for the pain which will tell you that which is true, and avoid those moments of ease which will tell you only that which is false. You must cast off your fear of Men, Brother, and fear God alone!"

And with these words in my ears, which were the last addressed to me by Melchior Rinck, I stepped out again into West-terrace, and found myself among the future clients of Mr. McBoyle.

I wandered aimlessly along the quiet streets until I found myself yet again at the gates to the small grave-yard over-looking the bay. I pushed back the gates, entered, and found myself a comfortable spot to rest and to reflect. Perhaps I would be visited again by an Angel, who might tell me what it was I should now do, and kiss me full and long upon the lips.

Should I flee this wild corner of the kingdom, and set myself again on the roads which normal men followed? But I could not do so as Alexander Kininmonth, he being murdered and dead, charred and drowned many fathoms deep in the loch. Should I stay here and await the events of the days yet to come? But I could only do so either among people who had no premonition of what was about to befall them, or among people who rightly thought that I was no longer of their persuasion.

I looked around: there was no Angel come to embrace me, nor any ghost to terrify me, nor any grey cat to chase me. I was alone. I reflected that I could as well place an order with McBoyle, as he had suggested. I considered for several dismal minutes what my epitaph should be: "In Memory of Alexander Kininmonth, Civil Engineer, and Author of the 'Abridged History of the Railway Between Garve, Ullapool and Lochinver', who died at Ullapool in January, 1898." It did not resonate; and I could rely on McBoyle, either through ignorance or through malevolence, to mis-spell my name. Perhaps I should simply ask for: "Here Lies a Railway Engineer, who worked in these parts briefly".

Dear Friend, we must all have experienced those moments when our grasp on life evaporates in a moment, and a great panic strangles our throats, until, even as grown men, we feel like howling? Such a moment as that came upon me then, in the gloom of an early afternoon, in January, in Ullapool, Citadel of the Elect.

February 11, 1898.

Many of the events of the eleventh of February, 1898 will in time be documented in the history-books, and there will be scarcely a school-boy who cannot tell something of the bold attack by Major Beuzeville Byers upon the seditious rebels of the Citadel of Ullapool. It is my purpose here to give an "eye-witness" account of that fateful day, from the early-morning hours, up to twenty-four minutes past nine o'clock in the evening. It is my belief that this account will be the first from inside Ullapool; all other accounts which might have been published in the newspapers and scandal-sheets (but which are unaccountably missing), or in the despatches of Whitehall, would simply recount events as they were reported by the Army. By the Army or by the newspaper-men who had assembled on Evelyn Fowler's yacht in Greenock and who arrived off Ullapool at about eleven in the morning of Monday, the fourteenth of February, far too late for them ever to have witnessed anything but the subsiding dust of the assault; which delay probably would not prevent each and every one of them from boasting of their assault on the barricades, alongside the bright young officers in Major Byers' troop.

In the days leading up to Friday, the eleventh of February, the gap between my Railway-Line leading from Ullapool and my Railway-Line leading from Braemore grew ever narrower. On the afternoon of the tenth, the gap was closed, as I discovered when I walked that way out of more-than-idle curiosity. Every fifty yards along the line, two soldiers were posted on guard-duty, and I was frequently looked at with considerable suspicion as I sauntered down the road from Achindrean to Ullapool, trying to appear at once native to those parts and aimless, and certainly failing in both. An up-lifting thought passed through my mind as I considered that it was, at that moment, physically possible to board a train in Garve and reach Ullapool within less than an hour, without stop or hindrance. Indeed, that it was possible to board a train in London, Edinburgh or St Ives, and not have to disembark before pulling into Quay-street, on the shores of Loch-broom. That should have been a moment for a Railway Engineer to savour!

But there were no garlands, no platforms groaning with illustrious figures, no photographer from Aberdeen to record this glorious day for posterity. Only some hard-faced soldiers and some black-faced sheep.

I continued my walk into town, saddened and oppressed by the thought that the hour of my greatest achievement would pass by unmarked. I reached the Caledonian Hotel, which I regarded now as my second place of residence, at about five o'clock.

The next few hours passed, I now regret to say, as if in a haze. I confess that I drank more than was good for me, and that I fell in with a pack of carousers, with whom I had nothing in common. They were for the most part workmen and craftsmen of the town. One, in particular, struck me as an interesting man, partly because he seemed more thoughtful than his companions: this was Thomas Jarvie, who, by a most curious coincidence, worked for McBoyle as a carpenter. Mr. Jarvie introduced my palate to a number of malt whiskies which I had not tasted before, and after several of these, in the heat of the saloon-bar, amid the din and the laughter, I dropped into a state resembling reckless somnambulance.

At length the landlord called out that it was "time" to close up; after several repeated calls of that kind, and perhaps an hour or two later, Mr. Jarvie and I stumbled out, at the tail-end of a boisterous group, and found ourselves under the bright stars in a deep black sky. Most of the group then disappeared into the night, singly but clearly with a purpose. Mr. Jarvie and I considered these figures and laughed quietly. My companion then invited me for a "night-cap", and we made our way, not without mis-hap and some damage to my boots in a ditch which opened up under my feet in an unforeseen manner, to McBoyle's shop in West-terrace. Mr. Jarvie urged me to be as silent "as the wee, wee mouse", and we crept into the back-shop, through a side-door, to which my companion had the key. When a lamp had been lit, I was at first rather shocked, but then unaccountably entertained, to find myself in a room full of coffins in various stages of completion. This was where Mr. Jarvie spent his days.

Advancing upon a very small coffin, the child-like size of which brought a lump to my throat and tears of despair to my eyes, Jarvie opened the lid and extracted for me a rather pleasant bottle of whisky, whose contents we proceeded to compare with all those others enjoyed that evening, until sleep overcame us.

When I awoke, cold and horribly uncomfortable, it was still dark, although there was enough light from the moon through a sky-light to tell me where I was. Having laid myself under an oath to tell the full truth to my Readers, I find myself embarrassed to reveal that I had been reclining in a pine coffin, which rested on two trestles in the middle of the workshop. I could just discern Mr. Jarvie, asleep in a corner under a pile of blankets or similar cloths. My limbs ached. I realised, as I sat up, that I still exercised very little control over my legs or head. In short, I was a pitiful drunk. With considerable difficulty, I managed to clamber over the side of the box, causing a commotion fit to wake any corpses who might have been sharing the "guest-room" with me (but leaving Mr. Jarvie quite undisturbed), and to fall upon the floor; from where, after a space of several minutes, I was able to reach the door and step outside. My head was spinning, my mouth full of the sickly taste of malted grain.

It was about five o'clock. It was so cold that the breath seemed to freeze in my lungs. Hastily, I covered up my mouth with a muffler and inhaled as best I could through that; this precaution is one I would heartily recommend to anyone caught out on a cold night, for it certainly removed some of the sharp edge of the air. My eyes were streaming, and my feet were frozen; but already my brain was beginning to function again. I told myself that I had to keep moving, both to expunge the effects of the spirits and to ensure that I did not die of the cold, as I believe it is possible to do, on nights such as these. (When I was twelve years old, my father, returning one evening from his work at Bethune's, the Masonic Furnishers and Regalia Manufacturers of Clerk-street, had told us how a drunkard had been found that very morning in the Gardens of Princes-street, frozen solid. It was my sister who informed me on the following day, after consulting with school-friends, that the man had been found frozen against a tree, where he had been answering a simple call of nature. I spent the next few weeks in arranging my leisure-time so that I might go down to the Gardens to see if any more such fascinating victims of their own depravity – which is the point my father had wished to make – were to be seen against the tall trees; and, if so, what aesthetic there might be in the icicles thus formed; but I was always disappointed. Since then, however, I have had a fear of the shame of being found dead in such a public place.) On that cold morning of the eleventh of February, I prayed that I would not be found in such a position, for my sister and mother would find the disgrace hard to bear.

The simplest plan which I could elaborate for myself, after rejecting countless other proposals, which, regardless of their circuitous routes, led inexorably and improperly to the house of Miss Keir's lodging, was to walk back to Achindrean, if necessary falling foul of Mrs. MacMahon. Better, I thought, to be alive and condemned as an unrepentant fool by that indomitable woman, than dead from the bitter cold and be twice condemned as a drunkard. I therefore marched off in unsteady fashion; my legs obeying a rhythm of their own.

As the road slipped away behind me, I gradually warmed up and found my head becoming clearer. On two occasions, I thought I could hear the sound of a train, and stopped stock-still to listen; but, hearing nothing more, I decided that it was just a persistence in my ears. Shaking my head to clear it further, I walked on.

When I reached Leckmelm Wood, at about a half-past seven, I realised that I could indeed hear a train: it was no sound emerging from the fumes of my intemperance. An engine was coming down the track from the direction of Braemore. Without a pause for sober reflection, I leaped over the dyke at the side of the road and ran the short distance to the point where the two lines had been joined. It was now less dark, although the sun had by no means appeared over the hills to the east.

My hearing had not deceived me: as I stood there, rocking slightly and trembling with the cold, I could distinctly hear the sound of an engine approaching down the track. There was nothing to be seen. Now and then the sound vanished utterly, as the engine disappeared behind some small hill, or rounded a hidden bend. I knew, from my surreptitious inspection of the track on previous days, just how it marched across the fields and touched the side of the road, leading the straightest route – as I would have led it – towards Ullapool. At the point where that line joined mine, both tracks lay about ten yards from the road, there being some flat ground on which we could yield to the rare luxury of not hugging the road so closely.

And then suddenly, as I watched through streaming cold eyes, the engine appeared before me, barely fifty yards away, steam pouring from its chimney, the lamps at its front glowing in the gloom. Even as I caught sight of it, the engine slowed down, and there was a terrible screeching of brakes, which must have been heard as far as the town itself, and probably out beyond the Summer Isles. I retreated to the dyke, and crouched down safe in its shadow.

The engine – from its shape apparently requisitioned from the Strome Line – drew four carriages, in which lights glowed dimly, and a large goods-wagon: considerably more than its usual load. Bringing up the rear was a small guard's van. When the engine was nearly up to the point where the two lines joined, it stopped to allow the engineer to climb down, accompanied by several figures from the first of the carriages: officers of the Army. Some short discussion ensued. It seemed that the debate was about the advisability of proceeding down a stretch of track which no engine – and certainly none pulling such a heavy load – had travelled before. I admit to feeling a sense of outrage and injustice at the question even being asked, but I held my tongue: nothing was to be gained by springing out at them, self-righteous and murdered inebriate that I was.

At length, the Army men won the day, and it was decided to proceed slowly. Everyone climbed back in and the brake was released; with much squealing and puffing, the engine set off again. Acting on an impulse, I waited until the last carriage had passed me – I now saw that each carriage was full of soldiers – and ran forward to clamber up on to the back of the guard's van.

What a sense of magic overwhelmed me as we proceeded ever so slowly towards Ullapool! It was the culmination of my dreams over the past several years: to be riding on a track which I had laid, on a train which came from Garve and would pull into Ullapool! Freezing though I was as I hung on to the handle at the back of the van, my heart sang and a smile transfixed my face. I laughed out loud as we crept along yard after yard of track, each yard confirming that, despite my doubts about the quality of the ballast, and the slope of the ground, and the precision of the laying of the rails – the line held! Every so often, I would peer around the side of the van and look to see where we had come to: we came out beyond Leckmelm Wood and on to Corry Point, where the gradient grew steeper. The engine laboured hard to pull its load up the slope, but the line held! Behind me I could see no evidence of slippage, or of displaced rails, or of anything untoward which would offend my professional eye. I thanked my wisdom in appointing MacIvor to inspect these rails. At Braes, the slope ran down again and I could hear the engineer cautiously applying his brake to prevent any disaster – but the line held! We came safely, if roughly, down the track: I made a mental note that, if the world ever came back into its usual ways at the end of these troubled times, I should have to examine once more the quality of the ballast and the alignment of the rails just at this place.

The sky had lightened considerably by the time we ran into Ullapool, at exactly twenty minutes past eight o'clock by my watch. To my disappointment, the engine did not enter the town, but pulled to a halt some yards short of Shore-street. Even before it had properly halted, there was an eruption of activity from the carriages ahead of me: doors slammed open, men shouted, a bugle sounded, orders were barked. From the goods-wagon, I could hear neighing and the sound of hooves, as horses were led out into the cold air. Cautiously, I peered around the side of the van and saw that a force of some hundred soldiers was marshalling on the road beside the loch. Already they were forming up into lines and their officers were mounting the horses, which shied and bridled nervously.

I deemed it best to come away from all this activity as soon as I could, and crept around the further side of the train, cut through the trees, and then climbed over the wall into the small glen at the side of the old grave-yard. I was not noticed.

It was obvious that the soldiers were here on serious business, and that there would be arrests, perhaps even shots would be fired, possibly men would be killed. My throat seized up with panic and I shook uncontrollably. What was I best to do? I could not simply walk away, for I knew that some great Act of History was about to unfold, one in which I was already implicated: did not these soldiers come precisely to avenge my supposed death? And was it not my responsibility that this Railway of mine, built for the greater good of common people, should now be the instrument of soldiers whose aim was entirely opposed to my grand aspirations? Or was it simply that the best of human endeavour was fated to be usurped by the grubby requirements of the powerful?

At length, I decided that my best course of action, as Historian, was to observe accurately the procession of events; and so I took up my position, with more than adequate concealment, behind head-stones at the summit of the grave-yard, from where I could make out the activity around the train; and also the activity in the town itself, which was now swarming with people, as the news of the arrival of the soldiers spread with the speed of fire. Many congregated in Mill-street, from where a good view of the train might be obtained; others walked or ran in the direction of the Caledonian Hotel, either to provide succour to those likely to be arrested, or in the hope of witnessing the final hour of the New Elders. Down on Shore-street, a score of boys had gathered, kicking at the horses and pulling their tails, anxious no doubt to be in the thick of the action. No such sense of excitement had gripped Ullapool since Jubilee Day!

Almost as soon as I had encompassed this scene, the soldiers were on the move. They broke into four detachments, all, I supposed, having as their goal the Caledonian Hotel. One group marched off down Shore-street, jeered at and pursued by the town's undisciplined youth; the remaining three came up Mill-street. Of these, one group wheeled off down Argyle-street; another remained at the junction with Pulteney-street; and the final group went, I deduced, to secure the road leading out of town to the north. Each was led by two officers on horse-back, and, apart from the tramping of their feet on the frozen mud of the roads, all the men were quite silent. A smaller detachment of soldiers remained beside the train, guarding both it and the road to the south. All in all, I judged, they seemed to have ample knowledge of how to take possession of our town.

Despite their careful preparations, the soldiers found it not so easy to capture those parts of town which were their strategic goals. Partly because of the unruly crowd of boys and the missiles being thrown at them from concealment, the group which had proudly marched off down Shore-street was not in command of the Pier until well after nine o'clock. This was the group which I decided to follow, *incognito* as it were, with my hat pulled down over my eyes. The soldiers found their way hampered by over-excited dogs, by a precipitation of rotten fish launched from the dark upper windows of the houses, and by the boys flinging themselves in and out of their ranks. When they finally reached the Pier, there was a crowd of fishermen, led by Mr. Donald Mackenzie – who I knew to be a fierce opponent of Rinck – standing their ground and refusing to let the soldiers past; they argued that the town was quite capable of dealing with its own problems: the soldiers should please leave. The officer in charge was at a loss to understand this cool welcome, and struggled to find a means of persuading the crowd to disperse. There was a bitter argument, which the officer knew he had already lost; in proportion as he floundered, so the jeering and cat-calls from the crowd increased. At length, and out of sheer desperation, the officer ordered his men to present their arms and to march upon the line of fishermen. The fishermen stood firm, with the points of the rifles pressed against their chests, staring down the soldiers. The entire situation began to take on the aspect of some musical comedy; until at last another officer, who was later named as the famous Major Byers himself, galloped up, firing shots into the air from his revolver. Small boys were greatly excited by this demonstration.

"Is there a problem, Captain Dalling?" he demanded to know.

The Captain talked to his superior officer in a low and urgent voice, no doubt admitting that the situation had "got out of hand".

There was a bit of a commotion as the Major took charge, shouting orders here and there, bullying and cajoling the men on to the Pier, slipping and sliding on the many nameless and stinking marine items now lying there.

His goal achieved, Major Byers galloped off whence he came; no sooner was his back turned than the greater portion of the assembled crowd followed him, leaving the soldiery to guard the Pier against not a single soul. Our main interest was at the Caledonian Hotel on Quay-street, which was the place where Rinck and his nearest associates were expected to be found. But it was of some satisfaction to most people in the crowd that the place did not fall to the Major's siege straight away. (Indeed, there were two distinct crowds gathered at the cross-roads: a larger one, comprising most of the able-bodied population of Ullapool; and a much smaller one, of perhaps three dozen individuals, at the centre of whom could be discerned the kirk ministers and – rather surprisingly – Mr. Hay Mackenzie of the Bank, who had returned to the town, alerted to the planned events of the day. All of the latter group were snugly wrapped up in warm overcoats, choosing to ignore the insults being hurled at them by the larger crowd. The two constables, Mr. Hutchison and Mr. Macdonald, one crimson-faced and one white, stood resolute between the two parties, occasionally threatening a member of the general citizenry when a stick or stone was launched into the air).

Major Beuzeville Byers and a fellow-officer spent some time negotiating with an unseen figure at a ground-floor window – we supposed this to be Mr. Mackenzie, the landlord – in an attempt to gain entrance to the Hotel. What the substance of their discussion was, I have no idea. Some *bel esprit* among those gathered suggested that they were discussing terms for a cooked breakfast, and continually shouted warnings to the Major concerning Mrs. Mackenzie's "Black Pudding", much to that lady's detriment. But I do not believe that a cooked breakfast was the subject: it is more reasonable to suppose that it had to do with the rendering up of the wanted men as prisoners, in return for leaving the Hotel undamaged. For Major Byers could see that any plan of his to storm the "Citadel" would result in his own men being attacked in the rear by the partisan crowd. At shortly after ten o'clock, some agreement was reached and the front door of the Hotel was set ajar, allowing entrance to Major Byers and a number of his soldiers.

But it was soon clear that the unseen defender of the Citadel had been playing for time, for, within a minute, the Major emerged with fury writ large upon his brow, and ordered his officers to muster the troops. Every crowd has its own source of news: and the news now spread that Rinck and the other wanted men had either never been in the Hotel at all, or had managed to escape from the back-door, during the period of negotiation. The person who had been behind the window turned out to be the bar-man of the Hotel; he was dragged out ignominiously and placed into the custody of Mr.

Hutchison, to vociferous protests from the crowd and the setting alight, for a diversion, of a stray cat, which fled across the road ablaze and howling piteously.

Although the official history of the Battle of Ullapool will make no mention of it, the mood of the people of the town was – as I have indicated – scarcely sympathetic to the soldiers; this may seem surprising, for the recent actions of Rinck and McManus had so greatly annoyed the citizens that the sympathy which had been gained in September had almost completely disappeared by February. Mr. Jarvie, who had joined me by then, was of the opinion that most people were waiting to see how Rinck's "forty-second day" would pass, before they either chased him from town or let him continue with his "tricks". Such a policy did not seem irrational, given the stakes: no man is likely to plan his future if there is a chance that God's Apocalypse will come down to-day or to-morrow. Mr. Jarvie did express a heart-felt wish that Mr. McBoyle could be seen off along with Rinck, before too long; but that he was not of the mind that soldiers should be let loose, "for to turn the saloon-bars upside down and ravish the women" – a prospect which he seemed to relish rather too much for my liking.

Because of these sympathies, the bar-man placed into the custody of the constabulary was delighted to find that his captivity was of no lengthy duration. No sooner was Major Byers' attention diverted than a section of the crowd brushed Hutchison aside and set the waiter free; he ran off down Argyle-street, shouting as he went that he would not stop until he was safe with his mother in his home town of Inverallochy. "Och, but ye'll come back for the black-pudding!" urged a voice from the back of the crowd, to no avail, as the man disappeared beyond the steaming train.

The next two hours were most exciting, as the soldiers methodically searched every shop, every church and every house up and down Red-row, Quay-street, and all the adjoining streets, in their search for the missing New Elders. Twenty-four Elders there had been, and in the course of the hunt all but seven of them were found, many concealed in the houses of friends, some even in their own houses – Mr. Ross and Mr. Macrae, for example, were discovered blithely serving customers in their shops on Shore-street, and were not discomfited to be arrested in so doing; those Elders who lived out of the town had made for the mountains, where they could; but where they had slept too late, they found themselves already in captivity before the train ever reached Ullapool. Rinck, Alexander Mackenzie and the Fraser brothers were hunted down in the yard belonging to Mr. Campbell, the bone-boiler, at the western-most end of Red-row. I did not witness this last event, being confined by a crowd which had its nose pressed against the shop-window of Mr. Aird, where the Reverend MacMillan was insisting that a repair to his handsome pocket-watch be completed before the watch-maker was led away.

As each was found and placed under arrest, he was brought back to the Caledonian Hotel; as each appeared under armed escort, there were jeers or cheers, depending on the mood of the crowd. Each was marched into the Hotel, where Major Byers had now set up his head-quarters, and the door was firmly closed behind him. By noon, under a grey sky, seventeen New Elders were under arrest. Significant among those who did not appear in this way were: James Finlay; Gilbert McBoyle; and Miss Keir, who, I was pleased to learn, seemed to have vanished into thin air.

When the excitement subsided once more, many in both crowds began to disperse back to their homes for their dinners or to go about their legitimate business. The Bank-agent and the ministers were permitted access to the prisoners, but the rest of their group faded away, no doubt well-pleased with the events of the day and anxious to re-gain their position in Wester-ross society. For my part, my head felt as a miserable shell which surrounded a throbbing, agonising pain, caused no doubt by my lack of breakfast, to which misfortune I am frequently a martyr. Not wishing to leave the town at this momentous time, I determined to visit Thomas Jarvie and see if he could offer me some soup and a slice or two of bread. And perhaps a cup of tea and a biscuit. Maybe even some eggs and a rasher of bacon.

Which, I am glad to say, he willingly did. I found him still in the crowd of on-lookers and cast in his way several easily-understood hints about my hunger; accepting which, he invited me back to his lodgings, which were not at McBoyle's workshop, as I had supposed

— and, in any case, that workshop was now guarded by a thin-faced soldier — but in a miserable house along Red-row, where many of the poorer sort lived. But his soup was wholesome, and the bread, though cold and un-adorned, filling.

At about two o'clock, as we sat at Jarvie's table drinking a mug of tea with a dash of whisky in it, to ward off the cold, a pleasant slumber fell upon me, despite the damp coldness of Jarvie's room. But then there was a commotion at the far end of the street and, our ears by now being finely attuned to such disturbances, we noticed men and women, and the usual crowd of hooting boys, who cannot have had so much relentless excitement in all their young lives, running towards the Hotel. Erupting from the house, we did likewise.

While the soldiers had been at their dinners, and Major Byers and his officers were toasting each other in Mr. Mackenzie's beer, a small group of men, led — it was popularly supposed — by the ever-resourceful Finlay, managed to break into the Caledonian Hotel and to spirit away Rinck and three other Elders, through a window at the back. No one noticed until the prisoners had fled from sight, and that was when a hue and cry was set up.

Within minutes, the entire town was once again in uproar, and we joined a crowd, perhaps even larger than before, which had instantly assembled at the cross-roads in expectation of some fine sport. Naturally, the presence of such a crowd seriously hampered the Army's plans to re-capture the escapees; but Major Byers' attempts to disperse the crowd only made the situation far worse: it would take more than a few dozen soldiers with rifles to prevent a man of Ullapool from enjoying a spectacle after his dinner.

However, the prospect of a lengthy drama was dashed by the news that the escapees had taken refuge in Thomas Telford's justly-famous "Parliamentary Church" in Red-row, barely a stone's throw from the Hotel. This news was brought post-haste by Mr. Macdonald, Minister of the Church of Scotland, into whose territory the chase had now come. Notwithstanding his hatred of Rinck and his fellows, the Reverend Macdonald was adamant that no one should force their way into his church to capture the men, for that would be a scandal and a blasphemy against God, which would rebound upon all men who allowed such a thing to happen. Mr. Macdonald's brother in the cloth, Mr. MacMillan, was seen to disagree violently with him on this matter, arguing that it was God's Will that the men should be arrested, and that it was a strange thing indeed that they had sought refuge in Mr. Macdonald's church, which might suggest to any man of decent morality that there was a whiff of Socialism about Mr. Macdonald. Mr. Macdonald, of course, chose to disagree and soon the two men were thrusting at each other with passages of the Psalms and Proverbs, as they had not done for many years, each with face enlivened, and made almost youthful, by the need to score points off his rival.

Meanwhile, from two o'clock until five o'clock, Major Byers could only surround the church with his men, to ensure that no further flight was possible. Every so often, some leading member of the community would be sent in to ask whether Rinck wished to give himself up, usually emerging within less than a minute with the announcement that Rinck would wait for "the Judgement of the Lord on this Day of Apocalypse", rather than hand himself over to the soldiers. The minutes ticked past, the crowd – mostly disappointed – wavered; people came and went. The sky darkened at four, snow began to fall in the fading light, and it was difficult to see with any clarity. A faint light came from one of the windows of Telford's church, where a candle or two had been lit.

At five o'clock, to my great astonishment, the unmistakable figure of GilbertMcBoyle came down the street. He seemed nervous. The crowd began to murmur, but no one encouraged him to turn back or to run. But there was apparently no need for him to do so, for Major Byers approached him, not as his captor, but as a man of business expecting to complete a transaction. There was a brief discussion, McBoyle approached the church door, knocked, entered. We waited outside for some illumination to be shed on this great mystery.

McBoyle's meeting in the church lasted considerably longer than those which had preceded it, and it was not until about twenty minutes after the hour that he emerged, opening the door cautiously, peering out. Then he stepped outside, with the four Elders at his back. No one else moved until the five men had reached the gate in the low wall which led into the street.

But no sooner were they in the street than a sharp order was given and all, save McBoyle, were surrounded and placed under arrest. I heard Charles Fraser, who was one of the four, shout, "Ye've betrayed us, McBoyle! Ye told us we could take refuge in Tabor! Ye told us it was safe to come through the Den of Lions!" before he fell silent. McBoyle stood back, with his head lowered, and soon melted into the darkness.

And with that, the prisoners were back in custody.

The Citadel at Ullapool had fallen.

The events of the day were by no means over: at about seven o'clock, the prisoners were brought out from the Hotel, under the careful guard of all the soldiers who had been deployed in the town since the morning, and were marched off to the further end of Shore-street, where the train still waited, with steam up. A crowd accompanied them every step of the way, but now was unusually silent. All that could be heard was the thump of the soldiers' boots on the road and the metallic clink of their rifles as they were shifted uneasily in their hands.

When we reached the train, the prisoners were loaded into one carriage, and most of the soldiers embarked into the others. A detachment of some twenty men was left in position, under the nervous command of Captain Dalling. At about half-past the hour, the engine released its brakes and reversed back up the line, as cautiously as it had arrived.

No sooner had the train disappeared up towards the Braes, than there was a shout from the back of the crowd. "The Caley is on fire! The Hotel's burning!" Sure enough, we could see a red glow in the sky above the houses on Shore-street. Naturally, we all ran back as fast as we could to behold this new spectacle, the boys as always to the fore, along with a pack of barking dogs.

There was nothing anyone could do to save the Hotel, for the fire had caught hold in every corner and on all floors. Smoke was billowing out through the roof, and flames licked up through the smoke; the roof itself soon collapsed inwards, and then the whole structure was slowly but surely consumed by the inferno. It was a sad sight, I said to Mr. Jarvie, as we shook our heads and had a nip of whisky, from his flask, to lament the falling of such a great place.

Speculation was rife: had the fire been started by Major Byers, as an act of revenge; or by James Finlay, for the same reason – the man was rumoured to be at liberty still; or by Rinck, as a lasting memento of his sojourn in Wester-ross? All were agreed: it could not have been an Act of God. The whole town, regardless of loyalty, came to watch, for it was by far the most dangerous fire the people had ever seen.

The blaze began to die down after about an hour, at which time there were shouts from the back of the crowd, indicating that even more spectacles awaited us: flames were now seen in Montague Fowler's coal-store at the Pier. Minutes later, another shout: a building in West-terrace had gone up. On the arrival of the crowd it proved – to no one's great concern – to be the shop of Mr. McBoyle that was in flames, coffins and all. So much exercise had the population of Ullapool never had, as it ran from one scene of flagrant devastation to the next!

Word spread around the town that James Finlay had been seen darting through the town, appearing now here, now there, with a blazing firebrand in his hand, an Avenging Angel of Cromarty. When McBoyle's shop had gone up, Finlay was to be seen pedalling his Visionary Bicycle, like a Fury, on the road to Ardmair; not one of the soldiers thought to stop him, transfixed as they were by the blazes in the town. With the number of burning buildings, it seemed almost as if the Day of the Apocalypse *had* come!

Now Captain Dalling was beset by panic. A young man barely out of school, one would judge, he had received no training which fitted him for the task of calming an excited crowd of people, or of controlling the razing of a town's buildings by arsonists. Losing his head utterly, he commanded his paltry force of soldiers to make random arrests, to push the crowd hither and thither with their rifles, to fire shots into the air and generally to pour oil – as it were – upon the bonfire of passion. The only sensible act he did perform was to send a swift rider after the train to fetch re-inforcements, as we discovered at about nine o'clock.

From that moment onwards, the town presented a confusing scene of milling citizenry, soldiers, fires burning (although no more buildings were set ablaze, the Reverend Macmillan's entire supply of winter fuel provided a merry light), of roads blocked by soldiers; and, among it all, all the overjoyed and utterly uncontrollable pupils of the school, who played havoc with citizen and soldier alike. At this moment, I realised just how important it is for children to be submitted to the guiding and controlling discipline of a good school-mistress; for the children would listen to sense from no man, heeded not even a skelp around the ear as they raced past their mothers.

A running battle ensued between various factions, which spilled into all the streets of the town. At some minutes after nine, I found myself at the edge of a crowd which had been forced on to the Pier by a troop of soldiers. This particular troop was led not by Captain Dalling, but by a sergeant who had a good idea of what he was about, as he herded us like sheep down Quay-street and on to the slippery boards of Mr. Macbrayne's Pier.

On turning when we reached the end of the Pier, I found myself facing a soldier who was bearing down on me like an Asian Thugee, swinging the butt of his rifle at me. My Readers will be horrified to learn that I was struck on the side of the head by this man, and that I tumbled immediately to the ground. Before losing my wits entirely, I glimpsed my watch which had fallen to the boards in front of my eyes: it was twenty-four minutes past nine.

Epilogue.

It is to-day, Sunday, the eleventh of February, 1900, two years on from the First Day of the Apocalypse. We have come beyond the End of Time.

I am now far from Strath-broom. Time has slipped in like a thief in the night and stolen two more years from me; but I have laid up enough Railway treasures that neither Moth nor Rust shall corrupt them nor Time steal them. The Railway from Garve to Ullapool is engraved on the land in wood, stone and steel: any man may go there and see it.

I have left behind Strath-broom, and the many kindnesses of Mrs. MacMahon, and have struck in with another enterprise. I would request my Readers' patient attention one more time in this History, as I set forth the final chapter, or Epilogue. Some passages in the preceding pages may seem fantastical, others tragical, and others still, unquestionably true. But I confess that my understanding of the events of the past two years is as firm as the grasp on sound engineering principles of the sadly expired Daniel McManus.

I now take up the tale as best I can from when you last saw me, lying unconscious on the fishy boards of the Pier at Ullapool.

When I awoke, it was evening; by the dim glow of a night-light, I found my watch which told me that it was twenty-four minutes past nine precisely (that fateful co-incidence of the long and the short hands!). I lay for a few moments, recovering from the dreams of a disturbed sleep; then, having determined where I was, I debated how I came to be there. I resolved to get out of bed, only to find, as my feet touched the floor, that I could not stand; indeed, I fell with a great clatter, as my legs simply folded up underneath me. Nor could I get to my feet having once fallen. I looked down in some astonishment, for my legs appeared gaunt and wasted.

While I was still puzzling over this unforeseen paralysis, I heard running foot-steps on the stairs and Johan burst into the room. At the sight of me, she shrieked "Mam!" and threw herself upon me, screaming and laughing at the same time. Rather astonished, I found that I burst into tears and allowed the good-hearted girl to hug me. Almost immediately, Mrs. MacMahon appeared in the doorway, helped Johan raise me and put me back in my bed. Then they both fussed about me, arranging my pillows and blankets.

When they had settled down somewhat, and my own tears had been dried, I asked what was the cause of the great commotion? I fear that the explanations which followed were confused, so I will paraphrase as follows:

That it was NOT the twelfth of February, 1898, a date which might appear reasonable to you or me; rather, Mrs. MacMahon suggested, it was the ninth of December 1899! Mortified at being, as I suspected, the butt of a practical joke, I agreed to differ with my friend, until Johan was despatched to the kitchen to bring up a recent copy of *The Ross-shire Journal.* Despite the stains of boot-polish, the starch from potato-peelings and sundry detritus of domesticity, the date on this trusted newspaper was unmistakable as Friday the first of December, 1899, and gave unassailable proof of Mrs. MacMahon's supposition.

Having abruptly opened up this chasm in my days, she pressed home her advantage with another astounding assertion: that I had been found in lamentable state on Ullapool Pier on the eighth of September, 1897, all evidence indicating that I had stepped too close to a fire and then fallen from a fast-moving conveyance. I had been carried back to Achindrean by some Ullapool men, principal among them being James Finlay. But, although I still breathed, and my eyelids twitched as do those of people in a deep sleep, I could not be woken up. I was laid in my bed, more dead than alive, and had slept there ever since.

Naturally, this second shock so discomposed me that I fell back into Oblivion; from which I emerged the following morning to find, to my horror, Johan immodestly washing my chest and arms.

Mrs. MacMahon enthusiastically nourished me with news of the outside world over the course of the next few days, between the exercises which she obliged me to undertake in order that I might re-gain the use of my poor withered legs. Principal among these items was the sad intelligence that Sir John Fowler had died just over one year previously, and had been succeeded in his estate by his son, Arthur. It came as a shock to me, as well as to much of the community – and doubtless to the younger Fowler himself – that Arthur then fell victim to a fever, and died suddenly on the twenty-fifth of March, 1899 (I note that this was exactly one year after the End of the Apocalypse), leaving behind wife, three daughters and two sons, the elder of whom, John Edward, had, at barely fourteen years of age, succeeded to the baronetcy, and was in expectation of a long and leisured life.

There were quiet rumours and scandal to the effect that James Finlay had departed for the hills, to take up a life of outlawry which would shock any decent body, accompanied by "that school-teacher", as his Maid Marian. As for Mr. McBoyle, he had extended his business interests in the town to include ownership of the Caledonian Hotel, and his head was said to gleam more than ever like polished mahogany.

In a futile attempt to convince Mrs. MacMahon of the error in her chronology, I spent many hours in closely-argued debate. I imparted to her – leaving out some minor details which I thought would offend, and especially any reference to Miss Keir, from my continued tenderness towards that lady – the history of the five months which elapsed between the night of the "Burning Angel" and the "Battle of Ullapool". To my despair, almost everything which I told her drew from the good woman gasps of surprise and exclamations of horror – but only in protest that I could have made up such "a yarn"!

I know Mrs. MacMahon to be of a charitable and inventive disposition: perhaps her denials were kindly meant to protect me from any feelings of guilt for my part in the downfall of the Citadel.

Here was a true dilemma: the course of events such as I have heretofore described has a strong logic in it, and I find that the more I read my own words, the more I know them to be the true recital of events: I have not written a Romance, after all, but a History! Swift arithmetical calculation, of which Miss Keir herself would have been proud, turned up this surprising fact: if I had been "asleep" since February, 1898, then I had awoken after 666 days!

The significance of this number gave me a cast-iron proof of my own memories. It seems clear to me that Mrs. MacMahon had nursed me after the Battle of Ullapool, had presented me to the outside world as some commercial traveller taken ill on the road; and had thereby preserved me from such acts of retribution as befell the citizens of Ullapool and the surrounding country after all the riots and the excitements.

But I was troubled that Mrs. MacMahon's alternative version of events seemed to be confirmed by the back-numbers of the newspapers kept "in case I awoke", which gave no hint of any past unrest. There was only one caustic reference by a correspondent to *The Ross-shire Journal* in the "Notes from Ullapool", dated the second of December, 1898, who compared a Lecturer on a Speaking Tour of the North-West to the "unlamented vagabond rabble-rouser R——". There was no report of any untoward events involving the New Elders; copies of *The Journal* for the first three months of 1898 were, alas, not available (Johan explained that it had been a wet summer and she had visited the archive of old newspapers on a hourly basis for to dry out boots and shoes); so neither could I prove that something had happened, nor could Mrs. MacMahon prove that something had not happened.

I comforted myself with this thought: the simple fact that an event was not reported in *The Ross-shire Journal* did not thereby mean that it had not occurred. I propose to investigate the National newspapers when I am next in Edinburgh. But it seems likely to be in the interests of Government not to report such events as I believe took place in Ullapool, for fear that similar sedition might be sown in other parts of the land, where Republicans and Socialists have a firm grip. There would be a sober expectation that, if Ullapool could fall into the hands of radical men, then Paisley or Coatbridge or Loanhead or Inverurie would desperately follow suit. This would not be the first time that historical events have been concealed from an en-thralled Nation!

As soon as I could walk once more, I made preparations to find profitable employment. There was little point in presenting myself at the offices of the Great North-West of Scotland Railway Company: Mrs. MacMahon advised me that the health of the Company had been far from robust since the expiration of the Fowlers, father and son, and that the Company's affairs will presently be settled.

Last month, therefore, I made my way south to the perpetually dismal Kingdom of Fife and installed myself once more in a gloomy room in a damp tenement in Dunfermline. I found employment in the maintenance gangs on the Bridge over the Forth. At first, I found some pleasant reward in working on such a magnificent construction; but hours spent in its dizzying heights, battling the gales, choking on the smoke from passing trains, suspended above a grey and unwelcoming sea, soon cured me of this romantic attachment. Fifty-seven working men had died and dozens were cruelly injured on this Bridge during its seven-year construction; its service continues to exact a toll of life. Day after day, my skills as an engineer scarcely stretched, I walk the length of the Bridge, from North Queensferry to Dalmeny and back, checking the girders and the stone-work, dodging into the shelters when the trains whistle to announce their approach, suffering the insults and threats of the supervisor — whose name, by a terrible twist of Fate, is MacAulay! At night, I return to the northern shore and take a seat in the third-class carriage of the train to Dunfermline. All that inspires me now are my detailed plans to pay back the debt to my sister and, by my work at this History, to re-pay some of Mrs. MacMahon's trouble in those lost days of my illness.

Despite these trials, I can proudly repeat: the Railway of Kininmonth connects Garve and Ullapool. The proof is there on the ground — any man may purchase a ticket to travel upon it.

And I live in the hope that this Twentieth Century will be the end of the Tunnel through which Man will drive his Engine of Progress, that he will come thundering at last through the wayside Stations of Iniquity and coast down the Gradients of Reform to a Common Brotherhood! A Hundred Years in which Man the Engineer, Man the Scientist, Man the Socialist will surely abolish war and build a New Jerusalem of physical comfort and social justice; a New Century in which his Railways and his Machines and his Electricity will bring untold treasures and equality to all of the Human Race; a New Age, in which even Glaswegians will walk in the Light of Cultivation!

DOBIE & McINTOSH PUBLISHERS

Catalogue of Popular Books

10, Newington Road, Edinburgh 9

THE POPULAR "SIXPENCE" SERIES.

6d. each.

Imperial 8vo. 100 pages. Many Illustrations.
Cover printed in five colours.

"Messrs. Dobie and McIntosh's Sixpence Series of Books is the cheapest and one of the best we know. How such books are produced is mysterious. About 100 pages of thick paper, admirable printing, a neat wrapper, and good, healthy, new literature—the thing is beyond me."

THE BRITISH WORKMAN

Unexplained Apparitions. By Angela Einhorn.

Four Years in a Cave. By Ethelreda Keir.

From Rags to Riches. By William Wallace Forbes.

Great Undertakings. By Gilbert McBoyle.

Alexander; or, The Power of Love. By Mrs. MacCallum.

The Immolation of the Hittite; or, A Strange Death Indeed. By Grant Prophet.

Maude's Love: The Story of a Faithful Little Heart. By Hattie Fatner.

Encounters in Subterranea. By James Clark.

And a Treasure Trove of Titles besides!

BOOKS FOR GIFTS AND PRIZES.

1s. each

Size 9 by 7 inches. Coloured and numerous other Illustrations.
Handsome Coloured Cover, Paper Boards with Cloth Back.

A Sack With Holes, and Other Addresses to Children.
By Mrs Mary-Ann Hogg.

The Jeweller; or, a Short Biography of Sir Thomas Urquhart.
By the Hon. A. Crichton.

Fanny from Forfar, Nancy from Nairn, and Other Jolly Stories.
By the Rev. M. Fowler.

The Magic Spectacles. By Dr. Alexander Kind (M.D., Madras).

366 Soups and Puddings, One for Each Day of the Year,
Including February 29th. By Mrs Macbeth.

Facts and Fancies About Flowers. By the Rev. H. MacInnes.

Five Children on a Boat - not to Mention Old Jack. By G. Isle.

Popularity: Chats About Chaps Who Have Won It.
By M. M. Macaulay.

A First Moral Reader for Girls. By Prof. Henry Calderwood
(Deceased).

True Tales of Derring-Do for Boys. By Captain Elsinore Dalling.

My Friends David Livingstone and Florence Nightingale. By
Miss Jessie Lennox.

Winking Willie of Wanlockhead. By William Cumstie
Williamson.

The Knights of Arthurville; or, a Dream Come True.
By Hugh MacPherson.

Tadpoles. By Mrs Muncaster.

And many others.

"TO THE LAST DROP" TEMPERANCE LIBRARY.

1s. 6d. each

Crown 8vo. Cloth Boards. Fully Illustrated

The Secretary of the Saturday Christian Missionaries
League writes:—
"Amongst all the many missionary works published we find
that those issued by your firm give us the most satisfaction,
both with regard to interesting matter and to binding and
general get up."

Some of our latest titles: -

John Yellowlees' Secret; or, The Gambler's Daughter.
By Charles Bicknell. *"A cautionary tale."*

Nearly Lost, but Dearly Won.
By Rev. T. P. Wilson, M.A.(Oxon), Author of *"Frank Ifield"* etc

Hoyle's Popular Ballads and Recitations. By William Hoyle.
"A capital book for Sunday School."

Come Home, Mother. By the Rev. Melchior Rinck.
"Illuminating"

How the Farthing Became a Shilling; or, Honesty Is the Best
Policy. By Miss Jemima Kilroy.

How the Shilling Became a Farthing. By the same author.

Among the Wild Navvies. By Neil Ferguson, M.B., C.M.,
Medical Missionary. With an Introduction by Lord Inverpolly.

Dick and His Donkey. By the Author of "Hugh and His
Husky."

The Oldest Trade in the World, and other Addresses to
Younger Folk. By the Rev. George H. Morrison, Dundee.

*A Full Catalogue of this Library, of over three hundred
volumes, may be had, on request to the Publishers.*

"THE WIDE WORLD AND ITS WONDERS" SERIES.

Each Work Complete in One Volume,

2s. each.

Of Thick Crown 8vo. 320 pages.
Many Illustrations, including Maps. Cloth Boards.

A Promise Kept; or, A Voyage to Van Diemen's Land.
By Captain George Harris.

Roaring Adventures in the China Seas. By the same author.

The Voyage of the "Polar Star". By William S. Bruce

The Whaling Wars Between Paraguay and Finland.
By Captain V. Sorensen.

The Hanging Gardens of Babylon; and Other Untutored
Misconceptions. By Professor Charles Clyde Cardew-Smith.

Among the Hedge-Rows of Iceland. By Mrs. G. Snorrison.

"Out for a Duck" in Peking. By Captain Simon Long, late of
the 3rd Kowloon Lancers.

A Thousand Miles in the 'Rob Roy' Canoe.
By John MacGregor.

Journeys by Rail on the Falkland Islands.
By William Fell, of Macallanes, Chili.

On Foot from Dieppe to Kamchatka; or,
The Essential Waistcoat. By Captain John Cochrane.

The Green Being of Aurora, Texas:
Of a Mysterious Airship and How It Crashed There.
By Icarus H. Himmelfahrt.

Schroter's Valley and Its Volcanic Eruptions.
By Rev. I. M. Hazelwood

Write to Dobie & McIntosh, enclosing 60 stamps,
to subscribe to this Educational Library.

FROM "THE PROFESSOR'S STUDY" SERIES.

2s. 6d. each.

Crown 8vo. Cloth Extra. Copiously Illustrated

TALES FROM THE FUTURE. By Andrew McKelvie.

THE ILLUSTRATED LONDON NEWS :—
"The book is a good book. The characters of Macaulay and Macadam are admirably constructed. The duel between these antagonists, which extends throughout the story, is exciting...The circumstances described are unusual... There is a very fair allowance of wrong-doing in the novel; but, on the other hand,—which is quite unusual nowadays—things all come right at last."

THE BOOKMAN:—
"There is really not a dull page in the book."

THE BAND OF HOPE REVIEW:—
"We can recommend '**Tales From the Future**' as thoroughly readable"

VOLAPÜK FOR THE PRACTICAL BUSINESS-MAN. By William Justice.

THE DALKEITH ADVERTISER:—
"This book cannot be too highly praised"

THE MIDLOTHIAN INSIDER:—
"A Most Interesting and Clever Book. I was startled at how little I understood."

THE FRIENDLY VISITOR:—
"An excellent introduction to an exceedingly difficult subject"

CHILIADES AND THEIR MANY SECRET SIGNIFICANCES. By Sven Tennyson.

THE LITTLE ARITHMETICIAN:—
"This is a masterly study. There is a sufficiency , and more, of numbers in this encyclopaedic book."

THE CHARTIST:—
"We await the next century with lively expectation."